A WICKED WIND

THE FOURTH EMPIRE
BOOK 3

KAT ROSS

ONE

The hunger was the worst part.

Felippa dreamt of summer peaches and fresh-churned butter, dripping honeycombs and crusty bread still steaming from the Duc's great ovens. Savory mince pies and apple tarts dusted with cinnamon. Sweet, creamy milk cold from the root cellar and thick wedges of blue-veined cheese.

When she woke, she kept her eyes closed for a bit, pretending it was all just a nightmare. But she lay on hard ground, not her straw pallet in the servants' quarters. Instead of Da's snores, she heard the distant thunder of surf.

The last time Felippa felt so hungry was when she was little and her family had been forced to flee to the village of Swanton across the Forkings River. One winter, they'd eaten bugs to survive — woodlice, to be exact. Teo said they tasted like pee, but Felippa thought they weren't that bad, more like the craw-fish she used to catch in the old horse pond. It was the same year Cas got arrested for stealing apples and was thrown in the margrave's jail.

Hunger could make you do stupid things.

Her third day on the isle, she'd come across a thicket of purple berries. They tasted bitter, but she ate them anyway, gobbling them by the handful. It wasn't long before her eyes blurred and her gut cramped like she was being stabbed with needles. She crawled under a bush, convinced she'd die, but the pain stopped and she felt better. After that, she noticed that the birds didn't touch the berries.

It taught her a lesson. She had to pay attention. Had to watch and hide and never let her guard down.

She didn't remember how she came to the isle. Only that she had banished the mortifex named Justinian before he could kill her brother, and then they were alone on a beach. How empty his eyes were, even as rage twisted the melted ruin of his face. Justinian had reached for her, but then he disappeared. Vanished into thin air and didn't return.

How long ago that happened, Felippa wasn't sure. A week? More? It was hard to judge time. The only sun and moon were engraved on the silver disk Cas had given her. She wore it on a cord around her neck. Her good luck charm.

But luck wouldn't get her home.

Felippa regarded the sad little pile of mussels she'd collected from a nearby tidal pool. Her foraging had been cut short by one of the flying bird-lizards, which were the second-worst thing about the island. It was always cloaked in mist, and they appeared without warning. Sometimes they carried riders. High Dead mortifexes like Justinian.

The reason they hadn't caught her yet was the cave she'd found in the cliffs above the beach. Its opening was too small for an adult. Felippa was thirteen, but she'd never grown right and looked more like a child of seven or eight. The cave kept her safe, but more important, it had fresh water. A little trickle down the wall. She'd found a rock with a shallow indentation to catch what she could.

Now she pried open the last mussel and slurped the briny contents. She'd need all her strength to carry out the plan. She had to do it before she got too weak to leave the cave. It was easy to hunker down and daydream about getting rescued. But if she didn't know where she was, how could Cas find her?

Felippa tried not to dwell on her family, but their fates nagged at her. Da had been taken to Blackwater Jail. The last she saw Teo, he was fighting with the rebels at the Duc's palace. What if they were both dead? What if Cas were dead, too? No one to remember she even existed. She'd slowly starve in this place, all alone—

"Stop that shite," she muttered, her voice a dry croak. "Just quit."

Felippa poked the stick ahead of her and wormed through the crevice, pausing at the end to check for lizards. Seeing none, she squeezed all the way out and tipped her face to the rain. Her body smelled sour, but she hadn't dared to wash in the sea for fear of being seen.

The mortifexes came and went in a big two-masted ship with black sails. They also had smaller boats that they rowed back and forth from the ship. Felippa had glimpsed their dwelling from the beach. A craggy fortress perched atop the isle's highest peak, which stuck up like a fang. The only way up there seemed to be on the backs of the flying lizards. Not that she wanted to visit.

She crept down to the shore, watching the sky. There weren't any trees on the isle, just scrubby bushes and rocky ledges. Seabirds nested there. Once, she'd found a clutch of eggs and tried to steal one, but the mama spotted her and made such a fuss that she ran away, terrified the ruckus would draw the flying lizards.

Through the billowing mists, Felippa spotted the mortifex ship bobbing at anchor. It looked deserted. And there, about fifty paces down the beach, one of the smaller boats sat pulled up on the rocks. She wondered how heavy it was.

Felippa didn't weigh much to start with. Now her dress hung on her bones like an empty grain sack. Cas used to say that her body might be a few sizes littler than normal, but her brain was ten sizes bigger. He meant it kindly, but she wished it was the other way around. Teo would have no trouble hauling that boat into the water.

She tried to avoid the mortifexes, naturally, but she knew their habits. They sailed off in the ship, and when they returned, they unloaded crates and hauled them back to the lair. Every time she observed this, they had stayed up there for a while.

Steeling her jangly nerves, she broke cover and hurried to the rowboat. There were other islands; she could see the dark humps on the horizon. Not all could be inhabited by mortifexes. She would row the boat to the nearest one. Then... Well, it couldn't be any worse, could it? Maybe there'd even be people to help her.

She set her stick on the wave-smoothed stones and pushed against the prow. The boat slid an inch, then stopped. It was heavier than she'd expected. Grunting, she bent her knees and pushed again. Another inch or so. The effort left her trembling with exhaustion. Felippa was about to try again when a harsh scream cut the air. She dove into the boat and flung herself under the rower's bench, drawing her knees in tight.

Moments later, a shadow passed over. Water seeped through her thin dress as she shivered beneath the wooden plank, which was scarcely wide enough to hide her. Felippa waited for another cry signaling that she'd been seen, but the only sound was the drumming of the rain. Still, she let several minutes go by before poking her head out. Nothing above.

Still, it might be close by.

Should she go back to her cave? Felippa felt ill and shaky. Just a quick rest, then she'd try again. She took three wobbly steps, leaning on the stick.

If you go in there, you won't come out again.

The voice was calm but forceful. It was the same voice that told her she had to take charge after they moved to Prydwen because Da drank and Cas was gone and Teo wasn't up to it. The voice that told her she might as well confess to Brother Brennos because he knew everything anyway.

Grownups lied, but not the voice. For an instant, she saw a small skeleton curled up in the watery gray-light of the cave. Clumps of golden hair stuck to the skull and a silver disk was clutched in the twigs of its fingers.

Tears blurred her vision. She bit her lip hard.

Stick with the plan.

Felippa trudged back and pushed the boat again, but it wouldn't budge. When she walked around to the back, she saw the problem. After a moment's consideration, she used her stick to lever the stern over a big stone. It moved a little easier after that. In a few minutes, she'd managed to push it halfway to the water. Felippa was starting to think she might make it when a hand gripped her shoulder.

She flinched, too surprised to scream. It was an old woman, older than she'd ever seen. She had stringy white hair that fluttered like cobwebs and piercing blue eyes with burning coals for pupils. Felippa tried to pull away, but the fingers dug deeper.

"Stealing, are you?" she hissed.

"Let go!"

The old woman cackled. "Not likely." She pinched Felippa's cheek hard. "Where did you come from?"

"I don't know. I'm sorry, please let me go!" Felippa went limp and choked out a sob. The withered claw loosened ever so slightly. She wrenched free and kicked the woman in the shin. Then she grabbed the stick and thumped her on the head.

When she'd done the same to Justinian, he fell down and didn't get up. But the stick was not Gui's special staff.

"You little wretch!" the old mortifex exclaimed. She licked her lips and gave a sharp whistle.

Felippa's heart clenched as the shadow fell across her again. All she could think of was reaching the cave. If she squeezed inside, they couldn't follow. But she didn't get ten paces before the lizard-thing landed in front of her. It had a crest of blue feathers and a wickedly curved beak. She spun around, but another swooped down behind. It carried a man with yellow braids, bone-white skin, and a face that might have been chiseled out of the isle's rocky crags. He was missing an eye; flames writhed in the empty socket.

"Grab her!" the ancient mortifex screeched.

Felippa dropped the stick and raised her shaking hands, eyes darting for an escape route.

"What's this, Gerda?" The man slid from the saddle with easy grace.

"She tried to steal the skiff." Gerda hobbled forward, mouth slanted like an angry toad. "We ought to throw her to the dukka."

The male mortifex peered down at Felippa with a quizzical expression, as if she were some odd bit of flotsam that had washed ashore. "But what *is* she?"

"A trespasser." Gerda sucked the gray stubs of her teeth. "And a thief!"

"That's not what I mean." He seized Felippa's jaw and

angled her face this way and that. The cold of his flesh made her teeth ache. "Is she a mortal child?"

"Who cares what she is? Blast you, Orm, she assaulted me!"

The man's white brows drew together. "But why is she *here*?"

"Give me that boat and I'll gladly leave," Felippa muttered.

Gerda snorted. Felippa's cheeks grew hot. All her life, she'd been the butt of jokes and sly laughter. Most people assumed she was dull-witted. The other scribes at the Duc's court used to talk about her as if she weren't even there.

"What's so funny?" she demanded sullenly.

"You wouldn't make it far," Gerda said.

Felippa raised her chin. "I'm stronger than I look."

"Which is not saying much." The old mortifex bared her teeth in a smile. "The dukka would make a quick meal of you."

"Dukka?"

"They lurk beneath the waves, waiting for little morsels like yourself." Gerda turned to Orm, a speculative gleam in her eye. "Shall we let her try?"

The way he regarded the ancient mortifex made Felippa think the two of them did not care for each other. "It isn't our place to decide her fate, Gerda Kafsnjór. We will bring her to King Magnus."

Which is how Felippa found herself clinging to Gerda's bony back as they soared up to the mortifexes' mountaintop lair. What if Justinian were there? The thought almost made her let go and put an end to her misery. But they were over the sea now, circling around, and the thought of being eaten by the dukka — whatever they were — stopped her.

The fortress had no outside walls, just open archways where more of the bird-lizards lay drowsing. She glimpsed guttering torches beyond, and cavernous stone halls. The whole gang must be inside. They would suck the life from her just like Justinian did when she was little, but this time Cas wouldn't be there to stop them. Felippa's mind went blank. Her fingers, already numb with cold, began to loosen.

Don't panic now. You were a spy in the Duc's court for a full year. If you'd been caught, they would have burned you alive. But they didn't because you were smart and careful. You stole the Grand Menotte right out from under their noses. You can manage a few mortifexes.

The voice sounded confident, but Felippa was not sure of the last part. Not at all.

Yet... If Magnus were anything like Duc Marcel, he held himself in high regard. If she could only make herself useful to him, worth keeping alive, it might buy a little time.

Her breath caught as the bird-lizard banked sharply, folding its wings at the last instant and swooping through one of the stone archways. Orm alit next to them.

"You'll speak when spoken to," he rasped, "and you'll kneel when we present you."

Felippa bobbed her head. "Aye, sir."

He seized her around the waist and set her down. They stood on a sort of open platform. There was no wall, no railing. Her heart tripped against her ribs. One quick shove and she'd go over the edge.

Gerda seemed to guess her thoughts. "The way down is much swifter than the way up," she said with a nasty smile.

Orm jerked his head toward a torchlit corridor. "Get moving, girl."

Her breath made a white cloud as they entered the lair. Of course, it was cold as a witch's tit inside. Felippa blinked frost from her lashes and followed her captors.

Two

Despite its promising name, Dreamhaven looked decidedly grubby up close. It consisted of two dozen dingy white structures that leaned slantwise like drunks holding each other up. A rickety wooden pier jutted into the water, empty of vessels. Beyond the town, hills rose up to barren peaks wreathed in gray clouds.

Cas lowered the spyglass as the *Wind-Witch* wallowed into the harbor mouth. Her mainmast was a broken stump, torn asunder when they passed through the portal. Thistle was the reason they'd made it this far. The demonic cat had summoned a westerly wind that nudged the boat toward land.

"Looks quiet," Cas said to Tijah, who stood beside him at the starboard rail.

"Huh." Kaethe's hunter squinted at the shore. Drops of rain beaded her multitude of dark plaits and battered leather coat, and a curved blade rode at her hip. "Dreamhaven might be a dump," she said wryly, "but it's still the nicest dump for fifty leagues around. Place is usually busy."

"Think there's been trouble?" Cas asked.

"Maybe." Tijah shrugged. "We'll find out soon."

A few minutes later, the *Wind-Witch* bumped against the pier and Lo dropped the storm jib. She'd expended a great deal of power taking the ship through the Veil, but the unnatural whiteness of her skin had faded and her cheeks were flushed, blue eyes fever-bright. Rain lashed the deck as she vaulted over the railing, mooring line in hand. Their captain was always footsure, even in rough conditions, but her boot heel caught something and the leap turned into a belly-flop onto the wharf.

Cas winced. "You okay?"

Lo raised a hand. "I'm good!" She rose stiffly and limped to the bollard. With deft movements, she secured the thick, salt-stiffened rope.

"We'll visit my friend's place first," Tijah said. "Anamaria knows everybody. There used to be a resident shipwright. She can make the introduction." Her voice went flat. "Where's the necromancer? The live one, I mean."

"In his cabin," Cas replied.

Tijah tossed Lo a second rope. "We're not leaving him aboard alone, that's for sure."

Cas had no love for Nathan Ouvrard, but Tijah's hatred was hard and uncompromising. Lo said she despised all necromancers. An old grudge — something Cas was familiar with.

"I'll get him," he offered. He climbed down the ladder to the passageway joining the cabins. Nathan's door sat ajar. Cas pushed it wide. Brassbound trunks and leather bags stamped with the left hand of Vendagni littered the cabin, but he saw no sign of their owner.

The galley was empty, too. Unease coiled in his gut as Cas continued downward into the hold, a low-ceilinged space crammed with dry goods and water barrels. Voices drew him forward, instinct warning him to tread quietly. He peered around the last stack of crates.

A tall silhouette stood in the shadows. *Nathan.* He wore a black coat with a high, stiff collar that made his pale, angular face appear to float like a sickle moon against the night sky. Nathan's gaze rested on a mirror in an ornate silver frame. A voice was speaking from its depths. Cas strained to hear, but the words were too soft.

What he wouldn't give to know what skullduggery they were up to. Nathan was bad enough, but his distant ancestor was far worse. Jaskin Cazal was insane, for one thing. Driven mad by the Grand Menotte. Hearing the voices of a hundred fexes in your head would push anyone over the edge, and the necromancer had killed himself after hiding the evil talisman he'd created.

Dead — but not gone. Like the unfortunate souls he'd bound to the menotte, Jaskin's essence was trapped in the black mirror.

The voice fell silent. Nathan turned in his direction, gaze narrow. Cas was about to pretend he'd just arrived when Jaskin spoke, loud and clear this time. "What ho! The reaper is here."

Cas walked over. "Plotting behind our backs?" he asked.

"Hardly," Nathan said. He had the slurred accent of the far east. "I asked Uncle Jaskin to explain in greater detail how he plans to beat Magnus. Is that unreasonable?"

"No, but it's something we should all discuss together. Any secrets you want to share?"

"Pay no heed to this churlish coxcomb," Jaskin sniffed. "Reapers have their uses, but they aren't the brightest." Onyx eyes glittered with malice. "Do you know what the life expectancy of a reaper was in my time?"

"Not a clue," Cas said mildly.

Jaskin's smile could have cut glass. "Twenty-six days."

Cas regarded the necromancer in the mirror. Like Nathan, he was thin and sharp-featured. Unlike Nathan, whose clothes were cut in the latest fashion, Jaskin sported a lace-trimmed frock coat with puffy sleeves that were at least nine centuries out of date.

"Ouch," Cas said. "Good thing I'm not a reaper."

Jaskin chortled. "Nathan says they call you a Quietus now. It does have a certain ring to it!"

"I'm not that, either." He turned to Nathan. "I came to tell you that we've arrived."

Nathan arched a brow. "So?"

"So you're coming into town."

Nathan looked unhappy, confirming Cas's suspicions that they were up to something.

"Why?" he demanded.

Because none of us trust you. "We might need your help," Cas said.

Nathan sighed. "I prefer to wait in my cabin. Is my presence truly required?"

"Aye." Cas shrugged. "Or I can send Tijah down to get you."

"No, no, I will come," Nathan said hastily. "Are we taking rooms?"

"I hope not. I have no desire to linger here."

Cas tried to keep the anger from his voice. The chain of events that led to his sister Felippa being pulled through the Veil started with Nathan Ouvrard. If he hadn't sent Lo to search for the Grand Menotte in Prydwen, none of it would have happened. In the end, they had failed, costing Lo another life for nothing. The menotte was lost, and so was Cas's sister.

He turned away and started up the ladder. After a moment, he heard Nathan following behind. Back on deck, Lo announced that Thistle would remain to guard the ship. Ironically, although he was an *ala*, a storm demon, the cat hated rain. He crouched in the pilot house, watching with eyes like yellow lamps.

The rest of them disembarked and ventured up a muddy lane. It was gouged with wheel tracks, yet none looked fresh. Cas could have sworn he'd seen lights as they sailed into the harbor, but it must have been a trick of the storm for the town looked abandoned.

His skin prickled as they passed darkened windows. Tijah said nothing, though he noticed that her hand did not stray far from her sword. Cas had brought Gui's staff, which served chiefly as a walking stick since his former mentor had failed to explain the runes along its shaft.

"Something happened here," Lo said, rubbing her left arm. "I don't sense any dead, though."

"The dead never come to Dreamhaven," Tijah replied, her dark brown eyes flicking to the alleys between buildings.

"So who does?" Cas asked.

"Creatures with the power to walk between worlds," Nathan put in. "Jaskin wrote about it in his journals. He traveled often to the Cold Sea."

"Living creatures?" Lo asked.

"For the most part," Nathan said, ducking his head against the wind. "It is a neutral gathering place for beings of myth and legend from many realms."

Tijah stopped walking. "Here we are." A fierce gust flapped her cloak. "Words of warning: If you drop something on the floor, I strongly suggest you leave it there."

Cas peered at the swaying board above his head. *The Laughing Gull.* The sign was warped and weathered, the paint faded to gray. But pungent smoke drifted from the chimney and lights shone within.

"If they have a mug of hot mead," he said, "I don't care how dirty it is."

"Well, I do." Nathan shook a lock of sodden hair from his brow. He regarded the inn's façade, which appeared to have been cobbled together from barnacles and bird shit. "I doubt that a decent vintage is to be found in this establishment. Why can't we seek out a better class of hostel?"

Tijah stared at him. "One, because I know the owner. Two, there is no better class."

Nathan opened his mouth, but Lo spoke first. "Your fancy coat will probably get our throats slit wherever we go," she said with a smile. "At least we can dry off before we're murdered."

Nathan frowned at his cuffs, which were thickly embroidered with silver thread. "This? It is hardly my finest—"

"Feel free to stay out here, necromancer," Tijah cut in. She glanced up at the angry sky. "Although it doesn't look like this storm is breaking anytime soon."

She pushed the door open without waiting for an answer, leathers creaking as she strode inside. With a small but audible huff, Nathan shouldered past and followed.

Cas braced for a dive like the Two-Fisted Wife, where he'd mopped floors while waiting for Lo to arrive in Tjanjin. His thoughts slipped back to the stuffy attic room where he had summoned Lucius for the first time. They'd been forced to flee when the owner glimpsed the mortifex's inhuman face. It seemed a lifetime ago, though only a few weeks had passed. Cas wondered where Lucius was now.

"Anamaria?" Tijah called.

Cas looked around. The tavern wasn't as seedy as she'd made out. Fresh sand covered the planks and a fire crackled in the hearth, dispelling the damp. Someone had even arranged plants in clay pots along a windowsill. They were the only sign of life.

"Anamaria?" Tijah called again, leaning over the bar. Glass

cabinets stretched along the back wall, filled with vials in a rainbow of colors. They glowed faintly from within.

Cas jerked his chin at a row of curtained alcoves. Tijah nodded, and the two of them walked the length of the room, checking each one. Each alcove held an armchair and small table with a lace doily and rolled length of black silk. None were occupied.

"What's this for?" he asked, unfurling one of the cloths.

"Blindfold," Tijah replied in a distracted tone. "They're dream chambers. Anamaria! Where the hells is everybody?"

"Body!"

"Maggot-ridden corpse!"

A pair of gulls with crisp black heads and reddish beaks alit on the bar. Nathan stepped back, one hand sliding into his coat pocket.

"Where's your mistress, Bilmek?" Tijah addressed the bird on the left.

It studied her with a beady eye. "Dead."

"Gone to the far shore," the second screeched, then burst into raucous laughter.

"Don't lie to me, Golgoth." Tijah scowled. "Where is she?"

Bilmek took off, flapping through a doorway at the end of the bar. The second bird watched them malevolently.

"I knew it was a mistake to come here," Nathan said. "I suggest we leave now before that vile creature returns."

"Vile," the remaining gull spat with a throaty guffaw. "Vile and reprehensible!"

"The place does look different," Tijah said with a frown. "Maybe we should—"

She cut off as the door behind the bar banged open. A tall man with pure white hair and a kind face strode through, Bilmek perched on his shoulder. A dark cloak covered his broad shoulders. Across his barrel chest, leather braces held vials of Kaethe's Tears. Cas stiffened. *It couldn't be.* Then a terrible thought occurred to him.

"Gui?" he muttered, as Lo exclaimed, "Javid!" Nathan looked astonished, his face slack.

Tijah was staring, too, with a somewhat softer expression. Then she smiled uncertainly. "Bergmann? Is that you?"

"Who else would it be?" He spread his arms. "So what do you think? I've been fixing the place up. Little changes at first, but then I got carried away. I said to myself, Tijah, I said, why can't it be nice? Why can't it be classy?" His gaze swept her companions. "Where's Achaemenes?"

Tijah blinked, then tore her gaze away. "On his way." She paused. "Is it true about your mother?"

Bergmann nodded, his jaw tight.

"I'm sorry." She reached across the bar and laid a hand on his thick wrist. "What happened?"

He drew four mugs of foamy black ale from a tap and slid them down the bar. "A lot. But you better tell your friends about me first. Get it over with."

"Right." Tijah took a draught of ale, grimaced, and wiped her mouth. "Bergmann is a two-toed humbug."

He winked. "Not to be confused with the four-toed variety. Those are venomous, not to mention crooked and double-dealing. Steer clear, my friends."

Lo stared at him. "Why do you look like my adopted father?"

"And my..." Cas trailed off. Gui was a mentor once, but those days were gone. "Old friend."

"It's an illusion." Bergmann tapped his temple. "Conjured by your own mind."

"Humbugs are psychically resonant," Tijah explained. "They look different depending on who's doing the looking. To me, he's Achaemenes." That was her bonded daēva. One hand wandered to the gold cuff around her other wrist, touching the metal as if for reassurance.

Cas eyed the humbug. At first, he'd feared Gui was dead and had somehow ended up in this tavern. The illusion was perfect except for the voice, which was deep and gravelly. He wasn't sure if that made it less weird or more weird.

"Can you read my thoughts?" he asked.

Bergmann laughed. "No. I don't even know who you're seeing right now."

"Fascinating," Nathan murmured, his gaze intent.

"Who do you see?" Cas asked him.

"My servant Vigo, of course," Nathan said smoothly. He turned back to Bergmann. "How is it determined? Whom you resemble, I mean?"

Bergmann spread his hands. They bore the same scars Gui had. The same that marked Cas's own palms. "Well, I'm the person you trust the most." He grinned. "Can't complain. It greases the wheels of commerce."

"Not that you aren't honest in all your business dealings," Tijah said dryly.

"Of course, of course." Bergmann cleared his throat. "So what brings you back to Dreamhaven?"

Tijah leaned forward. "What do you think?"

"Ah, yes." The humbug swallowed hard. "*Him.*"

"Magnus, you mean," Lo said. She sipped her ale, winced slightly, then tossed it back.

Bergmann made a small gesture. One gull flapped out the window, and the other perched on the sill. "Bilmek and Golgoth will keep away prying eyes," he said. "Just in case."

The humbug whisked a rag from under the bar and started wiping down the glowing glass vials, one by one. They looked spotless, but he seemed to need to keep his hands busy.

"You asked what happened to Anamaria," Bergmann said.

"Well, Magnus's crew has been shaking down all the taverns. He calls himself a king now. Claims we're his subjects and we owe him taxes." The humbug shook his head in disgust precisely the way Gui did. "We paid for a while, but then Anamaria got tired of it. She kicked his collector out. Next day, I found her dead on the beach. It looked like she drowned, but you know Anamaria. She couldn't swim. Never went near the water."

Tijah swore. "What did you do?"

"What do you think? I paid." Bergmann sighed at her expression. "You have to understand, it's gotten worse since the last time you came. A lot worse. Many of us have been driven out of business. I do what I have to."

She gave a grudging nod. "So that's why the town is empty."

"Oh, they didn't clear out on account of Magnus." Bergmann gave a peculiar half smile.

Cas broke down and tried the ale. It tasted like tar and seaweed, moonlight and clover, with a dram of day-old fish guts. All in all, better than the swill at the Two-Fisted Wife.

Bergmann downed his own mug in one long swallow. "You heard of Telasius?"

"Nope," Tijah said. "Do I want to?"

"Styles himself the patron of weddings." A deep, dry chuckle. "Problem is, his unions aren't so blissful. Anamaria claimed he introduced Bel and Kaethe."

Cas choked on his ale. Lo gave him a hearty smack on the back.

"The Sun God and Drowned Lady were actually *married*?" Nathan asked, brows climbing. He hadn't touched the ale.

"Oh, yes. Anamaria said they had many good years together. But then..." Bergmann shrugged. "When it didn't work out, Kaethe put a bounty on Telasius's head. He's been hiding out in the Cold Sea ever since. Moves from isle to isle, trying to keep a step ahead of the Lady of Shadows."

"I can believe *that*," Tijah muttered. "She's scary."

"Scary as shit!" shrieked Bilmek, or possibly Golgoth.

The gull dissolved into grating laughter.

"But what does he have to do with Magnus?" Lo asked.

"Nothing," Bergmann said. "Except that Telasius was here, and that's why everybody's gone. They all got married. Weddings for days." Bergmann clucked his tongue. "Then they sailed off to keep the party going."

"When was this?" Tijah asked.

"Yesterday."

Cas and Tijah shared an exasperated look. Jaskin Cazal had warned that their luck would sour.

"Well, we know where Magnus is hiding," Tijah said, "but our ship needs some work."

"How much work?"

"New mast for starters."

Bergmann hissed air between his teeth. "You're out of luck, then. That djinn who lived in a barrel behind Patsy's place – you know the one, Tijah – he would have done it for the right price, but like I said, they're all gone."

She eyed him incredulously. "So there's no one here at all?"

"No," Bergmann replied after a longish pause.

"You don't sound sure about that," Tijah said.

"What? I'm sure. Have a look if you don't believe me."

"So what are we supposed to do?" Cas asked.

Bergmann shrugged. "Someone will show up eventually."

"Eventually isn't good enough." He wanted to kick something. "It's a long story, but Magnus has my little sister."

The humbug looked solemn, and Cas felt the sudden, dizzying certainty that he'd been here before. Then he realized that Bergmann looked exactly the way Gui had when he bequeathed Cas the useless staff.

It's coming from my own head, he reminded himself. But feckin' hells, it feels real.

"I'm sorry about your sister," Bergmann said. "I'd help you if I could." He held up one of the glass vials. It glowed a soft lilac color. "Perhaps you'd like to pass the time with a dream?"

"Thank you, no," Cas muttered.

"I'll try one," Nathan drawled. "What's available?"

Bergmann gestured to the shelves behind him. "All manner of reveries, daydreams, and phantasms to whisk you away while you slumber."

He pointed to a vial filled with iridescent green liquid shot through with ribbons of bronze. "A gorgon's dream." He spread his arms. "Picture a vast garden where every plant, flower, and tree is carved from stone. The gorgon can stroll through its creations without fear of petrifying any living thing. Total peace and control over its curse."

"Hmmm." Nathan tapped his chin. "What else do you have?"

Bergmann chose a sky-blue vial flecked with glints of gold. "This one holds a dryad's dream of an ancient grove. Trees older than time, whispering forgotten tales of fallen empires and lost ages."

His finger skimmed past an indigo vial glimmering with silvery threads. "And here, a centaur's reverie. Galloping across an endless starlit plain, guided by celestial patterns to a mythic homeland."

"Intriguing," Nathan allowed, "but all rather...*nice*." He spoke the word with distaste. "Have you nothing more rousing?"

Bergmann frowned. "I don't deal in nightmares, if that's what you mean. They attract the wrong sort of clientele. And the Dream Collectors' Collective keeps tight control over *those*."

Nathan laughed. "Is your guild really called that?"

"D.C.C., if you prefer," Bergmann said, a bit stiffly. "But yes, every tavern and hostel that sells dreams must follow the guild's rules. The paperwork can be a headache, but it keeps things orderly."

"Are they all owned by, ah, creatures like yourself?"

"Humbugs, you mean? Yes. Our special talent allows us to harvest dreams and store them in vials. My wares are authentic, I can assure you. But like I said, I don't traffic in the darkest sort."

"Didn't there used to be that one place?" Tijah said. "You know, down the street?"

Bergmann nodded. "Talon's Roost. Run by a four-toed humbug of the same name."

"Yes!" she exclaimed. "I remember he had these shifty eyes. Looked like someone different every time I saw him, but those eyes never changed. They scurried around like beetles. Like he was always trying to find an angle."

"That's Talon," Bergmann agreed sourly. "He peddled the violent fantasies of mortifexes and loup garou, among others. Vicious, gory stuff. All under the table, but he finally got caught. The D.C.C. revoked his license. It's been closed for years now."

Nathan studied the vials, a wistful look on his face. "If we must remain here, I long to be something else. Preferably something nocturnal—"

"Hold on, hold on." Lo tugged his sleeve. "Why not just magic the broken mast into a new one? Like you did when you turned me into a rat?"

Cas frowned. "He turned you into a rat?"

"Briefly."

"When did this happen?"

"Back at the castle. Never mind that. Can you do it, Nathan?"

"A fine idea, demoiselle," he said, "but my spells are fleeting. Most last for minutes only."

Lo stared at him. "So your threat to trap me as a spider forever was a bald-faced lie?"

Nathan shrugged.

"That's low." Lo dropped his sleeve in disgust.

"Another mug of ale?" Bergmann asked.

She shook her head. "Okay, here's an idea. Back to basics. We're not totally incompetent, are we? We chop down a tree and use the trunk for a new mast. If you could lend me some tools..."

"There are no trees left anywhere on the isle," Bergmann said with regret. "They were cut down for firewood years ago."

"So what's burning in the hearth?" Cas asked. The fire gave off an earthy, moss-scented smoke.

"Peat. We have a nice little bog around the point. It's worth a visit, if you have the time."

"Damn." Lo sighed. "I suppose we do have the time."

A bleak silence fell.

"How much for a dream?" Nathan asked, producing a gold coin.

Bergmann eyed him speculatively. "Money's no good here. What can you trade?"

Nathan rubbed his hands together. "I love haggling! Let us begin. Now, it depends on what you can offer me. I miss the eternal darkness of my homeland. I am the Duc of Vendagni, in the Moon Courts. You have not heard of it?" He showed Bergmann the coin. "You see? That is my profile."

Nathan obligingly turned his face to the side as Bergmann studied the coin. "By the Five," he said with a note of wonder, "it is you. Never had a Duc in here before." He returned the coin. "But gold's no good. I deal in barter."

"*Bien sûr*! I am certain we can reach an agreement."

The negotiations began to heat up as Cas leaned to Lo. "Want to get out of here?" he whispered.

"Desperately," she whispered back. "I'd even go to that peat bog."

He turned to Tijah. "We'll see if we can spot any other ships."

She nodded and held out her mug to Bergmann for a refill. "I'll keep an eye on dream boy."

THREE

A tepid drizzle was falling as Cas and Lo stepped outside. Gusts of wind swept the empty street, rattling loose shutters. The damp seeped into Cas's bones and he pulled his coat tighter.

"We need to find another way off this island," he said. "Any ideas?"

Lo scanned the misty coastline. Her gaze settled on a switchback path in the distance. "Let's try higher ground."

They set off, boots splashing through deep puddles in the road. A few doors down, they passed the abandoned tavern that Bergmann had mentioned. Talon's Roost, whose owner had lost his license for selling nightmares. The sign was still there, dangling by one rusty chain. The hostel looked even more sinister and rundown than its neighbors.

At the edge of town, the land rose steeply to a bluff overlooking the sea. Several sections of the path had washed away, leaving narrow ledges. Cas hesitated, but Lo was already scrambling upward. He followed at a slower pace, grasping clumps of saw grass and using the staff to prod ahead.

"Bel's balls," he grumbled the third time she nearly fell to her death. "Watch your feet!"

Lo shot a defensive look over her shoulder. "I am. It keeps crumbling underneath me."

"Just wait, aye?" He made his way up to her, wrapping an arm around her waist. Far below, the surf dashed against jagged rocks. "This way, we go down together. I'll try to land on top of you."

She laughed. "You would, wouldn't you?"

He grinned. "You're the one with lives to spare."

They pushed on, finally crawling over the grassy rim. Lo stripped off her wet coat and rolled up her sleeves.

"See any ships?" Cas asked, catching his breath. She was half daēva, and her vision was sharper.

The Cold Sea stretched out before them, an endless expanse of white-tipped waves and distant islands. Lo squinted through the drizzle. Finally, she shook her head.

"I guess we'll have to rely on good old-fashioned luck," she said.

Cas snorted. "Your luck or mine? Because neither seems promising."

As soon as the words were out, he felt a stab of guilt. *Tell her. You should have done it already.*

"Jaskin said something to me in the ship's hold," Cas began, "just before we left Castle Cazal. He claimed that when a Shadow Soul nears their last life, fortune turns against them. He called it the Quickening."

"Huh." Lo looked thoughtful. "The Greeks tell stories of the Fates. Three women called the Moirai. They weave the threads of our lives... and cut them short."

Cas eyed the lightning scars on her arms, their fernlike patterns stark against her white skin. Each, he noticed, had exactly nine branches. *Kaethe's number.*

"Do you believe in the Moirai?" he asked.

"I don't know." Lo's expression darkened. "But if it's true, let them try to interfere with us." She shook a fist at the sky. "I'm here, Bitches! Send your worst. I dare you!"

Cas stared at her. Then he took a long step back. "Do you have to taunt the gods?" he asked. "Do you really?"

"The Fates are not gods."

"What are they?"

She shrugged. "Some say they're above the gods."

"Is that supposed to make me feel better?"

She glanced at the tattoo on his hand. "You still have the blessing of Kaethe. That counts for something."

"I'm not so sure. I did quit her service."

"You quit Orlaith's service," Lo said. "It's the not the same thing."

Just hearing her name was like a breath on banked coals. Anger flared to life. "I wish I'd never met her," he muttered. "All those years I spent doing her bidding without question."

"Only to be betrayed in the worst way," Lo finished. She was quiet for a minute. "When Bergmann came through that door, I didn't see either of my parents. I suppose that means I don't trust them, either." Her mouth set in a line. "They lied to me, Cas. About who they were, where they went. Everything. I spent the last eight years looking in all the wrong places. A complete waste of time, all because they never confided in me — or anyone else."

"I didn't see my own Da," Cas reminded her. "I stopped trusting him years ago. But that's the thing with family. We keep loving them even when nobody else does."

"Even when they don't deserve it?"

"Especially when they don't deserve it. And I'm talking about myself."

"Well, you're lucky to have your brother and sister." Lo

stared at the horizon. "Here's a thought. I can try summoning one of the dead ships. We give the passengers the boot," she illustrated this with a heave-ho gesture, "take their vessel, and sail off."

Cas stiffened. "What? No, no. Bad plan."

"How's it bad?"

"Because you can't meddle with souls journeying to the afterlife." He rubbed his scarred palm, feeling the old wounds burn. "Even if we're not in Kaethe's realm, it's crossing a line."

"But we need to find Magnus. Let the dead people get another boat. Or swim, I don't care. Do you think they can swim?"

"I have wondered that," he admitted. "My theory is that if they knew how to swim in life, they can swim in death." He shook his head. "But that's not the point. It's just wrong."

"I promised you we'd get Felippa back. At any cost." A new darkness flickered in her gaze. It stirred something deep within him, something he'd tried to bury.

"Lo—" he began, but before he could protest further, a new sound reached them—distant laughter, followed by splashing. They exchanged a glance and sidled closer to the edge.

"Down there." Lo pointed to a notch in the coastline that had been invisible from the path. A dozen figures swam among the wave-battered rocks. They had long green hair and skin the light blue of a starling's egg.

"Who are they?" Cas wondered.

Lo lifted a brow. "I think the question is *what* are they?"

"Tijah said we shouldn't talk to anyone," he reminded her.

"That was before we found out we were stuck here."

"Wait," he hissed, but she was already slipping and sliding down the muddy bluff.

By some miracle, they both reached the bottom in one

piece. Not far down the beach, an odd creature was sitting in a white chair, one knobby knee hooked over the armrest, watching the women frolic. It had a wedge-shaped head and mottled gray skin. A cloak woven from seaweed was draped over its shoulders.

"Listen," Cas said softly. "I don't have a good feeling about—"

The creature's head turned their way. It waved merrily and beckoned them closer. "Hail, strangers!"

The tone was friendly enough. A man, Cas judged from the low timbre of his voice.

"Hail, yourself," Lo said, walking up. "I like your chair. It's so shiny!"

The chair was made of some material that gleamed like lacquered bone. It looked all of a piece, with no joint or seam.

"Why, thank you. I made it myself." The creature's grin widened. He smelled like the bottom of a pond. "Baba-hor, at your service."

"I am Delilah," she said, returning the smile. "And this is Castelio."

Baba-hor winked. "I will not ask what brought you to Dreamhaven. Your business is your own."

"We're staying at the Laughing Gull." She tilted her head. "But the owner said everyone had gone."

"Ah, we just arrived, though not in a manner I would wish. We sailed too close to the wind and the storm drove our vessel onto the reef. It broke into pieces and sank." Baba-hor heaved a sigh. "The sea is unforgiving of mistakes."

"We're sorry to hear that," Lo said. "Is everyone safe?"

"Oh yes." He eyed the women. "My crew are as content in water as they are on land. But I'm afraid we are marooned here."

"Then we share your predicament," Cas put in. "Our mast snapped."

Baba-hor had no nose to speak of, but the slits of his nostrils flared. "That is your only damage? Perhaps I can be of aid."

They swapped a cautiously hopeful look.

"How?" Lo asked.

"I am bestowed with certain powers." He waved a hand. "For example, to change one thing into another thing."

Cas thought of Nathan and his empty promises. "Then why don't you just turn a shell into a ship and sail away?"

Baba-hor chuckled. "A ship is too large and complicated. A mast is simple." His eyes glinted. "But nothing is given freely in the Cold Sea."

"What do you want in return?" Lo asked.

"Ah, straightforward," Baba-hor said. "I deal in riddles. Solve mine, and I'll repair your ship. Fail, and you must each give up your dearest possession."

Cas gripped the staff tighter. It was the only thing he had left of any value.

"A simple game, but one with high stakes." Baba-hor winked. "Are you prepared to play?"

"Can we talk it over first?" Lo asked.

Baba-hor yawned, revealing a pink cave lined with small, pointy teeth. "I'm in no hurry."

They moved a short way down the beach.

"Are you any good at riddles?" Lo whispered.

"Gui knew some. We used to trade them when there was naught to do but sit around a lichyard and wait for fresh dead to wake up. How about you?"

"I'm decent." Her eyes flicked to Baba-hor, who gazed out to sea with a gentle smile. "What do you think?"

Cas shook his head. "It's another shite idea."

"When did that ever stop us?"

"True. But still..."

Her jaw set. "It's this, or I summon the dead."

Cas knew when he was beaten. "Very well," he said. "But I want him to prove his powers first."

They returned to Baba-hor. "Show us what you can do," Lo said.

"A demonstration? Certainly!" He rose from the chair and it shrank down to a white pebble. Baba-hor bent to pick it up. Not a pebble, Cas saw, but a tooth. Baba-hor closed his webbed fingers around it, then opened them with a flourish. The tooth vanished, and two gleaming white bowls floated in the air. A globe of water rose up from the sea and filled the first bowl.

"The water will pour from one to the next," Baba-hor said. "When the first bowl is empty, the time to answer is up. Do we have a deal?"

Lo reached out and touched the nearest bowl. "Feels solid!" she said.

It was at this point, Cas would reflect later, that they might have shown a glimmer of common sense and walked away.

Instead, he said, "We're in. But we get to ask riddles, too."

Baba-hor clapped his hands together, long nails clicking. "Excellent! Who goes first?"

"Me," Cas said.

Baba-hor paced along the shoreline, seaweed cloak trailing behind him. "I'll start with an easy one. *You saw me where I never was and where I could not be. And yet within that very place, my face you often see. What am I?*"

Cas froze, the words tumbling in his mind. He glanced at Lo, who was frowning deeply.

"He's trying to trick us with something simple," Cas muttered. "Something we see often but... isn't really there?"

The water trickled from one bowl to the next. Sweat erupted on his palms.

"My face... where I never was..."

A memory drifted up from the depths. The well at his family's old homestead in the Boundary. Dark, still water and a wavering image, shattered by the fall of stone.

"Is it a reflection?" he guessed.

Baba-hor's face fell for a moment before he recovered, forcing a smile. "Well done! Your turn."

Cas leaned on the staff. He had his riddles ready. "A box without hinges, lock or key, yet golden treasure lies within. What is it?"

Baba-hor began to pace, wet sand crunching beneath his flippers. The green-haired crew had swum closer to watch. Their eyes were solid white like boiled eggs.

Ironically enough.

"Golden treasure," Baba-hor murmured, stroking his chin. "An egg," he exclaimed, triumph in his voice. He stopped pacing and faced them.

"Aye," Cas admitted.

"My turn again," Baba-hor said, his grin turning predatory. "It is mightier than the Five Gods and more greedy than Magnus the Merciless. The poor have it, the rich need it, and if you eat it you'll die. What is it?"

Cas's mind raced. The wind riffled his collar, slipping chill fingers down his nape. "Not gold," he muttered. "Not power. Mightier than gods. Time?"

"Is that your official answer?" Baba-hor asked.

The creature's expression was a studied blank, yet Cas knew it didn't quite work. The poor worked far harder than the rich, who had plenty of leisure time to hunt and hawk and scheme against each other. He shook his head, chewing on a nail. Lo sidled closer. He could tell from her eyes that *she* knew.

"What's worse than Magnus?" she whispered.

"No consulting!" Baba-hor admonished. "No hints! He must solve it alone."

Orlaith came immediately to mind, but she obviously wasn't the answer. "You'll die if you eat it... What the feck? Not poison."

He glanced up. Baba-hor was watching him, smugness curling his slimy lips as the last drops of water spilled from one bowl to the next.

"Death?" Cas guessed, though he knew it was wrong.

"I'm afraid not," Baba-hor said with false sympathy. "The answer is... nothing."

Cas swore. It felt unfair somehow, but it did make sense. Baba-hor extended a taloned hand.

"Your most prized possession, young stranger."

Cas handed over the staff. He seemed destined to keep losing Gui's gifts. Baba-hor examined it closely. "A fine treasure, indeed." He looked at Lo. "Shall we continue? Or have you had enough?"

She gave a tight smile. "Why would I quit now?"

"Excellent! Here is your first riddle." Baba-hor did an odd little sideways shuffle. "What is in seasons, seconds, centuries and minutes but not in decades, years or days?"

Lo bit her lip. "Seasons change, seconds tick away, centuries... History? No, that doesn't fit."

"Time's a'running out!" Baba-hor sang, dancing a jig.

"Seasons, seconds..." Lo repeated, desperation creeping into her voice. "Centuries, minutes..."

"Time's up," Baba-hor declared. "Stumped, I see."

Her lips moved for a moment more, gaze distant. "No." She bowed, flourishing an imaginary cloak, then spread her arms like an actor soaking up wild applause. "It's the letter N."

Baba-hor grunted. Cas flashed her a fierce smile.

"My turn," Lo said. "What always runs but never walks, often murmurs, never talks, has a bed but never sleeps, has a mouth but never eats?"

Baba-hor laughed. "Every child knows that one. A river."

Lo made a face.

Baba-hor paced in a tight circle around her. "The more you have of it, the less you see. Oh, what could it possibly be?"

Lo's blue eyes narrowed. "Darkness," she said after a moment. "Here's yours. Feed me and I live, give me a drink and I die. What am I?"

The contest had begun somewhat lightheartedly, but there was a thickness to the air now. The rain had stopped and everything went quiet. Cas watched the water trickle from one bowl to the next. He thought about how she'd insulted the Fates.

Baba-hor tapped his fingers on his cloak, thinking hard. "Fire," he said at last. "My turn. This one will be your undoing."

Lo smiled. "We'll see."

Baba-hor gripped invisible reins and galloped down to the waves, where his crew hooted and cheered. "An iron horse with a flaxen tail," he called out. "The faster the horse runs, the shorter his tail becomes. What is it?"

"Iron horse," she muttered. "Not a real horse, though."

Cas knew this one. His Ma used to tell a variation of it. He tried to catch Lo's eye, casually tapping a frayed patch on his coat.

"Horse's tail..." Lo mumbled, face screwed up in concentration. "Not the mane, the tail..."

Cas picked at his sleeve, trying to hide the action from Baba-hor. *Come on, Lo. Look at me.*

"Time's up!"

"Shit," she grumbled. "I don't know. A kite?"

"The answer," Baba-hor twirled his new staff, "is a needle and thread."

Cas sighed.

"I haven't lost yet," Lo said stubbornly. "I get one more chance to stump you."

He clacked his teeth together. "You have played well and fairly. I give you one chance. Best me and I'll repair the ship. Fail, and the vessel is mine."

Her dearest possession. Well, of course it was the *Wind-Witch*. Which Baba-hor already seemed to know.

"Alright," she said. "Your final riddle: The one who makes it doesn't need it. The one who buys it doesn't buy it for himself. And the one who gets it doesn't know he has it."

Baba-hor's grin faltered. He stared at her, fingers tapping against his leathery chin. Water trickled from one bowl to the next. *Just a few more seconds and we'll beat him.*

Finally, as the last drops slipped from the rim, Baba-hor stopped pacing. He slapped his head. It was a theatrical gesture, and Cas realized with a sinking heart that he'd known all along.

"Now that," he said, "was a fine riddle. But I'm afraid I have the answer. A coffin."

Cas worked it through. *The one who makes it doesn't need it. The one who buys it doesn't buy it for himself. And the one who gets it doesn't know he has it...* He turned to Lo, dread in his gut.

Her face twisted, as if she were fighting some invisible force. Her mouth opened and closed, but no words came out. Then she gave an angry toss of her head. "The riddle has two possible answers. I meant to say it was a poisoned cup if you said coffin, or coffin if you said cup."

A poisoned cup... Cas frowned. It could work.

Baba-hor's jovial demeanor vanished, replaced by a cold, calculating gaze. "So you meant to cheat?"

"Yes," Lo blurted. Her gaze darted around, frantic. "But I can't... *I can't lie.*" She pointed a finger at Baba-hor. "You did this to me!"

He snorted. "I did nothing of the sort. But I have won this contest."

Cas kicked himself. He might have warned her. It was the nature of a Shadow Soul to be divided; Jaskin Cazal had said that whatever qualities Lo had in the living world, she would have the opposite behind the Veil. And, well... The old Lo did have a penchant for deceit.

Lo stared at Baba-hor, blue eyes suddenly intent like a fox eyeing a plump chicken. "You won't take my ship."

Baha-hor snapped his fingers and the bowls vanished. The tooth fell into his palm. He stuck it back into his jaw. "A deal is a deal."

His crew emerged from the surf, forming a ring around them. They wore rustic white dresses and garlands of soggy flowers, like diabolical milkmaids. Each had a coral dagger strapped to her wrist. Cas's hand went to his side, where his staff should have been.

"Take me to your ship and you will not be harmed," Baba-hor said. "In fact, I will allow you to fetch your personal effects. Nothing of great value, mind."

It had all happened so fast. Cas couldn't quite believe what they'd done.

"Fair enough," he managed.

The green-haired women surrounded them, and they all set off for the pier.

"I knew this was a bad idea," Cas whispered, half to himself.

"The worst," Lo agreed.

"Why do you look happy then?"

Lo wiped the smile from her face. "Is it that obvious?"

One of their guards shot them a suspicious glance. Cas waited until her attention moved elsewhere.

"What?" he whispered.

"Don't worry, Sleepy Eyes. I've got this." A moment later, Lo tripped on a rock and would have tumbled into the sea if he hadn't grabbed her arm.

Cas said, "That's what worries me."

Four

Felippa hurried to keep up with the old mortifex, who hobbled along at a surprisingly swift pace. Gerda carried a burning brand in one claw-like hand that cast just enough light to see by. Icy mist swirled around their ankles.

The one-eyed giant called Orm had left them, but Felippa didn't seriously consider running, and Gerda appeared untroubled by the prospect. Where would she run to? There was no escape except on the back of one of the lizard-birds. She was just glad to be indoors, even if the corridor was as cold as Kaethe's kiss.

The route from the ledge where they'd landed had wound through one part of the citadel and then across an arching bridge linking two towers. Rain slicked the stone span, the wind buffeting Felippa this way and that. She'd nearly dropped to her knees and crawled like a baby. The only thing that stopped her was stubborn pride. She wouldn't give the old fex the satisfaction of laughing at her again.

"How much farther?" Felippa panted. She'd hardly left her cave for a week and was feeling the strain of so much walking.

"Nearly there." Gerda paused to scowl back at her. "You look a fright. Like a scruffy little scarecrow."

"I haven't eaten or bathed in days. What's your excuse?"

A gnarled finger poked her chest. "Guard your tongue, girl."

Gerda turned away and Felippa grasped her sleeve. "Wait! Is Justinian here?"

A flash of surprise crossed Gerda's face before she managed to control herself. "How do you know that name, pip-squeak?"

"I'll tell Magnus, not you. Is he here?"

Felippa held her breath. At last, the old fex shook her head. "He has been gone for years."

Relief almost buckled her knees. If Justinian had come back, they'd know everything. Now she had a slim chance.

"One more," Gerda announced as they rounded a corner and daylight filled the tunnel again.

Felippa groaned when she saw the bridge. This one was even longer and narrower than the last, plunging above a deep, shadowed ravine.

If Justinian *had* been there, she might have stepped over the edge rather than face him again. At least it would be a quick death. But even weak and half-starved, Felippa possessed a fighting spirit and was not ready to give up. She kept her gaze fixed on Gerda's snowy hair, not looking down until they were almost across. Waves flashed below. She recognized the dip in the shoreline. They were above the cove where she scavenged for mussels.

Then they were stepping from the bridge to another open ledge flanked by black marble columns as thick as century-old oaks, and Felippa forgot all about mussels or anything else. Her jaw slowly gaped. An enormous hall stretched beyond, ten times bigger than the Duc's audience chamber in Prydwen. Felippa had thought it very grand, but it was nothing compared to this.

The side she stood on was wide open to the sky, the view stretching for a hundred leagues across the sea. The wall opposite held archways and niches with blank-eyed marble statues gripping stone swords. Treasure was heaped everywhere — chests overflowing with gold coins, stacks of embroidered silks and velvets, mounds of jewelry. There were tapestries and paintings, silver goblets and gold plates, delicate glass vases and jeweled daggers. A hoard of riches beyond anything she had ever imagined, piled haphazardly like a magpie's nest.

About twenty mortifexes occupied the hall, both men and women. They wore rich attire, though it looked mismatched, a jester's motley of clashing colors and textures. At the far end stood a raised dais with a throne. Gerda gave Felippa's arm a hard pinch.

"Follow me," she hissed.

The hall fell silent as they made their way down the blood-red carpet. As she neared the throne, Felippa saw that it was made from hundreds of small figurines fused together. She recognized several of Bel, holding a lyre. The rest were unfamiliar. Some had six arms, or the heads of animals. Were they all gods? That he'd made a chair of them said much about the man who sat there.

Magnus wore a long robe sewn with tiny diamonds that glittered like frost. A crown of gold rippling with flames rested on his head, his white beard falling to his waist. His nose was large and red, giving him an absurd appearance, but there was nothing funny about the empty pits of his eyes.

"Your Majesty," Gerda said, bowing. "I bring you a thief and trespasser."

Felippa spread her filthy skirts and gave a deep curtsy,

hoping her knees weren't visibly knocking. "Forgive me, I meant no offense," she whispered.

"Thief?" Magnus boomed.

"This little chit tried to steal one of the skiffs at Imp's Claw Point," Gerda clarified.

Felippa lifted her gaze to the bejeweled figure. "I beg your pardon, sire," she said, her voice small and contrite. "I was frightened and acted rashly in my desperation."

Magnus harrumphed, staring at Gerda. "Why is she here?"

"Orm thought you'd want to question her." Gerda's shrewd eyes fixed on Felippa. "If not..." A nasty smile twisted her wrinkled mouth. "Well, the sea is always hungry."

Felippa suppressed a shudder. She curtsied again, so low her hem brushed the marble floor, and did her best to mimic the flowery language of Duc Marcel's courtiers. "Please, sire, I am at your mercy. Command me as you will. I am but your humble servant."

Magnus regarded her. Finally, he sniffed. "You have nothing I want." He waved a hand, the gems on his fingers catching the firelight. "Take her away."

Gerda smacked her lips and gave a satisfied smile. "The quick way down it is!"

"Wait!" Felippa cried, before the old fex could grab her. "Master Justinian sent me with an urgent message for you, sire!"

"Justinian?" Magnus's wispy brows shot up. "He sent you?"

"The girl is lying," Gerda spat. "She just asked me if he was here. And she never mentioned any message."

"I thought he might have returned," Felippa said, hating the old mortifex more than ever. "And the message wasn't for you." *You nosy old bat*, she added silently.

The mortifex king sat back, torchlight illuminating the

hollows of his waxy face. "What is this message you bear from Justinian?"

This is your chance. Don't feck it up. Felippa cleared her throat. "He bade me tell you, sire, that he has found the Grand Menotte at last. And that he will be bringing it to you directly."

Silence fell over the hall. Felippa's heart thumped so hard she was sure they could hear it.

Magnus went very still. "The Grand Menotte?"

"I saw it myself, sire. I mean, the box that holds it."

Magnus's gaze sharpened. The room grew even chillier, the smoke cast by the torches stretching towards her like groping hands.

"Describe it," he commanded.

Felippa swallowed hard. She raised her hands, holding them half a pace apart. "It's this big and made of iron, sire. And it has an insignia. A left hand with flames above the fingertips. One must hold a candle above the lid to see it."

She'd witnessed as much herself when she followed Cas and Justinian to the Duc's bedchamber.

Magnus's expression didn't alter, but a muscle feathered in his jaw. "If you are lying to me, I will throw you over the edge myself."

"I swear, sire," Felippa said quickly. "On my life, I would never dare to deceive you." She sniveled. "I am no one, and you are a king of noble blood!"

There was a taut pause. Felippa feared she'd laid it on too thick. Then Magnus leaned back in his throne, stroking his beard. "Where did he find it?"

She flashed back to the terrible chill as she huddled up the chimney, the box dangling in a sling from her skirts. Justinian's fury as he tore apart the room looking for it. "The captain of the Duc's guard had it hidden in his chambers," she said.

"And how did Justinian send you here?"

Felippa felt the weight of their eyes. This was the weakest part of her story, but she hadn't time to come up with a better lie. "Some dark magic beyond my understanding, sire. He didn't explain it."

Gerda sneered. "The tale makes no sense. If Justinian had the Grand Menotte, why didn't he simply come himself?"

"He... he said he couldn't," Felippa stammered.

"Couldn't," Magnus repeated flatly.

"Y-yes, sire. That is indeed what he said." *Think!* "Iron... Well, no disrespect, but it burns ... your kind." She plunged ahead. "My brother is carrying the box for him. He's Justinian's manservant. He bade me tell you to expect him within a fortnight."

Murmurs swept through the mortifexes. Magnus tilted his head, considering. The seconds crawled by, each one an eternity.

"You bring glad tidings," he said at last.

Felippa managed a stiff nod and another curtsey.

"But now that the message has been delivered, what use are you?" He gestured to Gerda. "Take her to the Cliffs of Howl."

"And throw her over?" Gerda asked hopefully.

"As you see fit," he replied in a jaded tone that suggested he didn't care either way.

Felippa's guts turned to water. She played her last card. "You *could* do that, sire," she said, "and then you'd be rid of me forever."

He eyed her impatiently. "Yes, that is the point."

"But what good are all your valiant deeds, my liege, if no one knows about them?"

Magnus went still. "What do you mean?"

"The wealth in this room alone speaks to your power, but what bard sings of your feats? What tome recounts your many victories?" She took a step forward, hands clasped. "Let me commit your legend to the page, so that generations to come will know of King Magnus the Merciless!"

He stared at her, unblinking. The flames in his eyes flickered. "You would ... write down my story?"

Felippa nodded earnestly. "Yes, sire." She gestured to the heaps of treasure surrounding them. "Someday even this vast hoard will fade to dust. But the written word, that is a legacy that endures! I was trained as a court scribe—"

Gerda laughed, a crow's harsh caw. "You? A scribe?"

"I'm thirteen years old." Felippa lifted her chin. "I am just ... a bit small for my age."

"A bit?"

She ignored Gerda's mocking snort, holding up her ink-stained fingers. "You see, sire? I speak the truth. I can document your heroic deeds, your battles, your victories. For posterity."

"Posterity?" he echoed slowly, as if tasting the word. "You speak of those yet to come, who would look back and marvel at my accomplishments?"

"Precisely, sire." Felippa held his glowing gaze. "The great rulers of history live on because their stories are told and retold. Let me ensure that your name is remembered forever."

She held her breath, not daring to move. Magnus studied her for a long, tense moment.

"You're not seriously considering keeping her?" Gerda sniffed. "The child has already proven herself untrustworthy. I say we throw her out the window and be done with her."

Magnus's brow furrowed beneath the flaming golden crown. He opened his mouth to reply, but before he could speak, the echo of footsteps announced a newcomer. Everyone turned to a man with shaggy dark hair and a sword at his hip.

He moved with easy grace and confidence. Gerda's scowl deepened.

The man's gaze swept over Felippa, assessing her with cool curiosity. "Orm told me of the child you found," he said. "Give her to me. I will take charge of her."

Gerda's nostrils flared. "Mark my words, she will be more trouble than she's worth."

The undead king sat motionless, his expression inscrutable beneath his bushy white beard. If Magnus refused, what would become of her? Would she be thrown to the dukka, as Gerda clearly longed to do? Or would they find some even more horrific fate for her?

Felippa silently willed him to persuade Magnus. The man's eyes met hers, and she thought she saw a flicker of pity.

"Come, sire. She is just a child." He studied the sheer drop beyond the open archways. "Unless you believe she will steal an abbadax," he said dryly, "she's not going anywhere."

The mortifex king hunched on his throne, staring at Felippa. "Very well," Magnus grumbled at last. "But I hold you responsible for her."

The man inclined his head in acknowledgement. Magnus leaned back against the throne. His mood had shifted, and he eyed Felippa with a mix of amusement and anticipation. "Very well, little scribe. You shall write the tale of Magnus the Merciless. But first, you'll need proper tools. Parchment, quills, ink." He turned to Gerda. "Do we have such things on hand?"

Gerda's lips pursed as if she'd eaten a live snail. "I suppose I could scrounge some up, if His Majesty insists on indulging this mortal street rat."

"Good." Magnus fixed his attention on the man. "Make her look presentable. My official scribe mustn't be dressed in rags like some filthy urchin."

The man bowed. "I'll see it done."

Felippa felt a rush of exhausted relief. She was safe, at least for now. But she couldn't shake the feeling that she had just exchanged one danger for another.

As she followed her savior from the chamber, Felippa glanced back over her shoulder. The vast throne room seemed to waver and twist like a dust devil over a barren field. The piles of gold and jewels blurred, their sharp edges softening. Even Magnus himself looked misty and insubstantial on his throne, as if he might dissolve into smoke at any moment.

Felippa blinked, shaking her head. Hunger clawed at her belly, making her dizzy. When she opened her eyes again, the throne room had snapped back into focus, solid and unchanging.

Magnus was staring at her, one eyebrow raised. "Is something wrong?"

"No, Your Majesty. I thought... It's nothing."

"Then be gone." He waved a dismissive hand.

The man led her through a maze of twisting corridors, his strides long and purposeful. She quickened her pace to draw alongside him. She knew her reprieve dangled by a hair. She needed an ally — especially since Gerda would be plotting her downfall at the first opportunity.

Felippa gathered her courage and tugged at the man's sleeve. Unlike the others, he wore a plain woolen coat, with brown trousers and hard-used boots. The only adornment was a pink shell on a cord around his neck.

"Thank you for saving me," she said.

He gave a brusque nod, not slowing.

"My name is Felippa. What's yours?"

The man was silent for so long she thought he wouldn't answer. But then he halted and peered down at her. "I am called Darius."

His tone was not unkind. And he was nearly as handsome

as Brother Brennos, though in a brooding way. Yet that wasn't what made her heart beat swiftly.

Darius's eyes were a clear blue, with no trace of the eerie flames that marked the undead.

FIVE

Thick tentacles flexed, propelling him like an arrow through the inky depths. The speed! The power! It was more intoxicating than any drug. He exploded into a school of silvery fish, scattering them into the gloom, then roamed onward until the outline of a vessel appeared.

Now we're talking...

With savage glee, Nathan's leviathan form burst from the water and wrapped suckered limbs around the hull. His single great eye rolled in its socket, affording him a panoramic view of the chaos. Half the sailors sank to their knees, gabbling for mercy. The rest screamed themselves hoarse.

"Kraken!"

A harpoon glanced off his thick hide as Nathan lifted the ship thirty paces above the water. He shook it like a dicing cup. Bodies splashed down into the maelstrom. He performed a lazy barrel roll, snapping his beak.

In the waking world, he was stuck at a fourth-rate tavern in some gods-forsaken village with companions who despised him. But here...

Here he was a god. A glorious deity of wanton destruction.

Another tentacle caressed the hull like a monstrous lover. Wood splintered. One more squeeze and the ship would burst like an overripe melon—

Then the sailors' shrieks morphed into raucous cackling. The kraken's exertions paused.

Fichu. Something was amiss.

Years of practice had honed Nathan's control over altered states. He willed himself to wake, eyes opening to a curtained booth at the Laughing Gull tavern.

He'd traded his coat for the dream, and Nathan was irritated to cut it short. Technically, it wasn't a nightmare. Bergmann had persuaded the guild to categorize it as a Class Two phantasm since no one was actually eaten.

Nathan tugged off his silken blindfold and peered through the curtain. The pair of rowdy gulls had just alit on the bar, where Tijah sat with Bergmann. Nathan still found it disconcerting to see a tall, whip-slim young man clad in black from head to foot. The humbug took on the appearance of whomever the viewer most trusted. This was not his servant Vigo, as he had claimed. No, to Nathan, that was apparently himself. Well, he did look rather dashing.

The larger gull, Bilmek, tilted its head. "Lost the ship, they did! In a contest with Baba-hor himself. Watched it all from a hidden perch on the bluff." The creature burst into grating laughter.

"Riddle me this, riddle me that!" chortled the second bird. Its name, Nathan recalled, was Golguth.

Tijah set her mug down. "Say again?"

"Yes, yes! To Baba-hor. Shadow girl tried to cheat, but he wasn't having it!"

"Cheat and lie," Golguth echoed with spiteful glee. "But

she couldn't." The gull ducked its head and gulped. "Quickening!"

"Ill luck and trouble," Bilmek agreed enthusiastically.

The gulls erupted into gales of monotonous laughter.

"Oh." Bergmann scratched his lean jaw. "This is bad, Tijah."

"Would you shut up for a second?" she snapped at the gulls. She turned back to Bergmann. "I have no idea what they just said."

"It's Baba-hor." Bergmann watched her face for a reaction. A gasp of horror, perhaps. When none was forthcoming, he clarified. "Khaf-hor's youngest son."

Tijah seemed bewildered. "Who's Khaf-hor?"

Bergmann glanced around. He cleared his throat and declared loudly, "Khaf-hor is a mighty and terrible being for whom I have the greatest respect." He lowered his voice. "He's a giant eel."

Tijah shot the humbug a look of disbelief. "So?"

"Baba-hor, the son, is a demon," Bergmann whispered. "And now he has your ship."

She stood abruptly. "You knew he was here, didn't you? When I asked if anyone else was in town, you hesitated."

Bergmann held his hands up in a placating gesture. "He just arrived."

"Why would he want a damaged vessel anyway? The *Wind-Witch* isn't going anywhere."

"That's the thing. He has the power to fix it."

Tijah gave a weary nod. "Except that he's an asshole who'd swindle his own grandmother."

"I didn't say that." Bergmann swept a rag down the bar. "But no one's ever bested him in a riddle contest, and that's the only currency he deals in."

"Of course," she said calmly. "A fucking riddle contest."

Tijah shook her head. "Where are they now?" she asked, directing the question at Bilmek.

The gull jutted his beak out. Bergmann reached under the bar and tossed a fish head, which the gull snatched from the air.

"Baba-hor's gone to claim his prize!" Bilmek squawked.

Tijah's fists clenched. "This is ridiculous. I won't hand over our ship because those kids lost a wager!"

"Cheat Baba-hor and you will not make it far," Bergmann warned. He folded his arms, leaning back against the wooden counter. The movement was catlike and elegant. "He's the son of a god, and not just any god. One of the Five whose domain you happen to be in."

"Shit." Tijah rubbed her temples. "The giant eel is a god? I mean, I've heard of the Five, but I can't keep them all straight."

"You'd best rouse your friend," Bergmann said.

Nathan jerked back from the curtain as they both turned toward his alcove.

"He's not my friend," Tijah said, her voice tight. "But he's the only one of us whose power extends behind the Veil."

"Another demon?" Bergmann asked.

"Worse. A necromancer."

She makes it sound so dirty. Nathan sank into the plush chair and slid the blindfold back on. Then he propped his long legs on the footrest, adopting the relaxed posture of a man lost in slumber as Tijah's footsteps approached.

"Wake up." A strong hand gripped his shoulder.

Nathan let her shake him twice before groggily lifting the blindfold from one eye.

"Must you? I paid double for this dream, and it's just getting good."

"Sod your dream," Tijah said. "We have a new problem."

Nathan feigned surprise as she repeated Bilmek's tale.

"How unfortunate," he said. "What do you expect me to do about it?"

"Help me get our ship back."

He stood with a yawn. "How? All my tools are aboard the *Wind-Witch*."

Tijah's piercing gaze swept him up and down. "I know you're carrying something."

"I might have a bit of spell dust," he admitted. "What's your plan?"

"First, let's see what we're dealing with."

He peered out the window. "Has the rain stopped?"

"Does it matter?"

"Well, I did just give up my coat," Nathan said.

Tijah's head slowly turned. The look in her eye reminded him of a sixth-circle drak'thros he'd once summoned on a dare. "Are you asking to borrow mine?"

"I would never presume, demoiselle." He smiled. "But if you're offering...?"

"Call me that again and I'll strangle you with your own blindfold."

They walked to the door. Nathan made a courtly gesture. "After you."

Tijah snarled something at Bergmann and marched into the downpour. Nathan followed, his shirt instantly soaking through.

"So we're dealing with a demon," he said.

"Looks that way." Tijah shot him a warning glance. "But we can't hurt him. The last thing we need is daddy looking for us."

"Yes, that does make it harder. Still, if it's only one adversary, I'm sure we can find a solution."

They moved quickly, avoiding the road and taking the deserted lanes behind the hostels. Within a few minutes, they were crouching among wind-bent bushes that afforded a clear view of the pier.

"Oh dear," he whispered, nudging the *mercenaire*'s leather-clad arm.

"Don't touch me," Tijah whispered back, her gaze fixed on the ship.

A creature with mottled gray skin and a wedge-shaped head paced the deck. It looked like something dredged up from the lightless seabed. Castelio and Delilah stood nearby, flanked by twenty green-skinned women with long, flowing hair and blank white eyes.

"Rusalki," he and Tijah said at the same time, then eyed each other with distrust.

"I have never met one," Nathan admitted, "but there are several colonies in the Nightwood. They're surprisingly sociable for water spirits. Of course, their idea of *fun* is to seduce mortal men and then drown them in ponds."

"Great," Tijah said. "Of course they work for this riddling eel spawn." Her eyes narrowed as she noticed something else. "Is that—"

"Castelio's staff," Nathan finished.

Baba-hor was leaning on it. A grin played at the edges of his frog-like mouth.

"So they lost that, too," Tijah muttered. "Okay, listen. I'll swim under the pier and climb aboard when they're not looking. When I give the signal, you create a distraction."

"What's the signal?"

She stared at him. "I'll wave at you, okay?"

"*Bien sur.*" Nathan smiled. "What could go wrong?"

"Just be ready," she said curtly.

Tijah belly-crawled under the pier and slipped into the water. Nathan shifted, fingers grazing the pouch of spell dust in his boot. He was only here because Lady Chaos had asked him to come, and Nathan, who'd loved her since they were children, could not refuse.

But that was before he found out about the Quickening. Jaskin had admitted that Castelio already knew. Nathan assumed Delilah and Tijah did, as well. None had bothered to share this relevant bit of information. Now they expected him to pull their fat from the fire.

So what if Baba-hor did take the ship? They would be stranded here, but Nathan could buy more dreams to pass the time. The journey was cursed from the start.

Of course, if they remained in Dreamhaven, Justinian might catch up with them. The mortifex had killed Nathan's parents. He was six at the time. If Vigo had not returned to the castle, Nathan would have been dead, too. The murders were twenty years ago, but the memory of his parents' screams was as fresh as yesterday.

He gazed at the *Wind-Witch*, long fingers drumming against the pouch. Baba-hor had gone below with his captives. Tijah had not yet reappeared.

When she did... Well, Nathan still wasn't sure what he planned to do.

SIX

Baba-hor paced the deck of the *Wind-Witch*, seaweed cloak flapping in the damp breeze. He inspected the ship with a critical eye, running webbed fingers along the rigging and poking his narrow head into every nook and cranny.

"She's a little battered," he declared at last, "but she looks seaworthy. What do you think, Elka?"

His emerald-haired companion hissed a reply. Baba-hor nodded, a smile spreading across his face. "Yes, I quite agree." He circled the broken mast, black fingernails clicking against the wood. "Where shall we go next, lovelies? The Devil's Back-water? The Isle of Wraiths? Or perhaps a sojourn among the water horses?"

Lo crossed her arms. She wasn't surprised she'd lost the riddle contest. That was to be expected, considering she was cursed.

But losing the ability to lie... Well, shit, it was very incon-venient!

"There's too many to fight," Cas said in a low voice. "If we plan to do something — anything at all, really — now is the time."

"Baba-hor!" Lo called abruptly, causing him to whip around. "I have another proposal."

The creature blinked at her. His eyes were pale blue with vertical pupils like a goat. "I am willing to listen."

She tried to sound valiant and noble, like her parents. "We came from the living world with a single purpose. To find the mortifexes who have been terrorizing the Cold Sea."

"You seek Magnus?" Baba-hor asked in surprise.

Lo nodded. "You already know I can't lie. We aim to send them all to the far shore."

"Hmmm. I am no friend of those ruffians."

"Then let us borrow the *Wind-Witch* and I swear we'll return the vessel after we're done."

Baba-hor tapped his slash of a mouth. "A fair offer."

Here it comes.

"But you already tried to cheat me once." He shook his head. "No, I'm afraid I must refuse. The *Wind-Witch* is mine." He regarded her with pity. "Count yourselves fortunate. I think it far more likely that Magnus would have sent both of *you* to the far shore. In which case, I would never see my pretty ship again."

He rubbed his hands together. "Speaking of which, it is time to make the *Wind-Witch* whole."

Baba-hor plucked one of the baby-shark teeth from his upper jaw and set it on the stump of mast. He whispered under his breath. The tooth stretched and thickened, spiraling upward like Jengu's fabled beanstalk.

In a matter of moments, a forty-foot pole stood on the deck, its surface gleaming like polished ivory. The pointed tip made it look more like a horn than a mast, but it seemed sturdy enough. His crew sprang into action, bare feet slapping the deck as they began taking down the tattered remnants of the sails.

"Make haste, my watery temptresses!" Baba-hor cried. "This old mariner is eager to be underway."

"Wait," Cas said, his voice edged with desperation. "What if we agreed on another wager—"

Baba-hor cut him off with a sharp gesture. "I've made my decision. The ship is mine, and that's the end of it." He smiled. "But don't lose heart! I'm sure another vessel will come along eventually."

Lo gazed at the empty horizon. Well, she'd tried to take the high road. Baba-hor could only blame himself.

Although she had never studied Tongues, the language of the dead, she knew it fluently. Her lips moved in silence.

Nener yarierer sinarun. *I summon thee.* Nener din geruteh sinarun. *I bind thee.*

"You make a grave mistake."

Lo turned as Thistle stalked out from the pilot house. She assumed he was speaking to her, but the cat fixed Baba-hor with a baleful yellow eye.

"I am Shelithoth, son of Anuketmatma, Mother of Storms," he snarled. "By interfering with our quest, you risk her wrath."

Baba-hor threw back his head and laughed. "Anuketmatma? She hasn't set paw in this realm for centuries. Last I heard, she was off gallivanting with the Selk Marakai in the living world."

He crouched down, bringing his face level with the cat's whiskers. "And even if she did take an interest, what of it? I won this ship fairly." Baba-hor pointed a webbed finger at Lo. "If anything, she was the one who tried to cheat *me*." He jerked his narrow chin dismissively. "Now skedaddle, cousin."

Lo half-expected Thistle to launch himself at Baba-hor's throat, but after a long, tense moment, the cat hissed and backed away. Lo didn't blame him. The green women had stopped working to watch the encounter with their creepy blank eyes.

"Very well," Lo said, careful to speak only the literal truth. "But you promised that we could each take a single bag of personal belongings."

Baba-hor waved a hand. "Yes, yes. Gather your things and go."

Lo glanced down at Thistle, who stood at her side, tail lashing. "Wait on shore," she said softly.

The cat stared at her as if he knew what she was thinking and did not approve. Lightning forked on the horizon. Then he bounded away, belly swinging as he leapt to the pier.

Lo and Cas headed for the ladder leading belowdecks. Baba-hor and two of the green women fell into step behind, coral daggers glinting at their wrists. They escorted Cas toward their shared cabin, while Lo led Baba-hor in the opposite direction.

"I'll show you where the sailcloth is stored," she said.

"That would be most appreciated," he replied in a jovial tone. "I promise, I shall take good care of the *Wind-Witch*."

They reached the hold. As Baba-hor rummaged through the various chests, humming happily to himself, Lo sauntered over to Jaskin's mirror.

"Let me out." His voice slithered from beneath the black cloth. "I'll show that jumped-up eel boy the door."

"How?" she whispered back. "I'm pretty sure he's alive."

Jaskin gave a condescending laugh. "You know nothing, child. But I can instruct you in all the subtle aspects of your gift. Verily, there exist means to pluck a spirit forth from its mortal vessel."

It took a moment to translate that in her head. "You mean, rip a soul directly from a living body?"

Baba-hor glanced over, the mottled, leathery skin of his brow furrowing. "Did you say something?"

"Oh, I'm talking to a ghost," Lo replied. "An ancient, unspeakably evil one who lives in the hold. He just offered to kill you."

Baba-hor gave her a searching look. Then he shook his head and laughed. "If you are trying to scare me off, you'll have to do better than that."

He turned back to the chest of folded sailcloth. Lo shrugged.

"Last chance," Jaskin wheedled. "Break my mirror or you could be marooned here for weeks. Magnus will slip through your fingers. But with our powers united, we shall be nigh invincible."

Lo twitched the black cloth away. Darkness rippled across the mirror's surface. Jaskin appeared, half his foxlike face lit by Baba-hor's candle, the other half in shadow. It gave him a theatrically sinister appearance.

Cas would say it was a shite plan, but it's all she had. She couldn't let Baba-hor take her ship. Lo was about to give the glass a solid kick when her left arm went numb.

She paused, staring into space. Then she leaned down and smiled. The necromancer in the mirror recoiled.

"Thanks for the offer," Lo said with a wink, "but I won't need you after all."

SEVEN

Nathan crouched in the bushes, watching the rusalki swarm through the rigging. The spirits were beautiful in a terrifying way. He could see how they managed to lure lonely travelers, although he himself was partial to short, plump women with silver canes and a talent for communing with the recently deceased.

A rusalka wearing a lotus crown emerged from the hold carrying an armload of canvas. Her sisters set about rigging it to the new mast, hissing to each other in their sibilant tongue. Nathan felt grudging admiration as he remembered how Babahor had conjured the spar from a single tooth. The demon wielded potent magic.

Ah, well. I've faced worse.

Even as the thought crossed his mind, Nathan wondered if it were true. Yes, he was a prodigy who, by the age of eleven, had bound incubi from the Shattered Realms and forced them to reveal secret knowledge. By fifteen, he had swum the black marshes and climbed the twisted steps of the Obsidian Spire of Zhexh'rix.

But that was all shadow-casting. In the real world, Nathan had spent his entire life sequestered in his ancestral castle, pulling strings from afar.

Now, crouched in the rain worlds away from home, he felt unsettlingly exposed.

The sky was too wide, the light too bright, even with the clouds. He was accustomed to communing with his ash servants — and his mortifex Vigo, of course — but none of them spoke often. Not like the living, who never shut up. What he wouldn't give for an hour's solitude, with no one nagging him—

Movement at the stern caught his eye. Tijah's head popped up, dark braids streaming. She waved, the signal to cause some chaos. Nathan weighed his options, acutely aware of each passing second. He owed the woman no favors. And they were outnumbered five to one.

Tijah gestured again, impatient now. *Putain.* Nathan was about to stand when a needling pain raked his leg. He looked down to find Delilah's demonic cat sinking its claws into his thigh.

"Do you mind?" he whispered with a scowl.

Thistle's ears flattened. "We're in trouble, necromancer."

Nathan glanced at the busy rusalki, then back to Tijah's angry face. "That much is evident."

"Let me clarify," the cat growled. "*More trouble.*"

An icy wind ruffled the creature's fur, slicing through Nathan's wet shirt like a cutlass. He turned to the harbor mouth. Nine ships with square black sails glided silently toward the piers. An eerie stillness shrouded them, as if they sailed through a void. Nathan dipped a finger into his ash pouch and traced a complex symbol in the air. It shimmered, then rearranged into another rune — the answer to his question.

"There are low dead aboard those ships, but they are far off their usual course." He gave the cat a grim smile. "I see only one explanation. Your mistress draws them like blood flies to offal."

Yellow eyes narrowed to slits. "Watch your tongue."

A hissing rose among the rusalki, like steam escaping from a giant cauldron. They had spotted the ships. Baba-hor stormed out to the deck, his ragged black cloak flapping.

"Raise the sails!" he shouted, a cracked edge to his voice.

So he fears the dead. That is one difference between us.

Nathan whispered an incantation, the words harsh and guttural. The air around him thickened. With a flick of his wrist, ash burst forth, swirling into a dark cloud. Binding threads coalesced around his fingertips. Nathan directed them towards the ships.

He felt the souls inside quiver and recoil at his touch. A cacophony of wailing voices erupted in his head. Nathan pulled the threads tight and they fell silent. He sensed fear and confusion.

"Me tudetor pe sisise tasem nularis!" His voice vibrated with power.

By the master's will, begone!

The ships slowed... But then the spectral energy of his spell dissipated like mist in sunlight. Nathan's brow furrowed. He was not accustomed to failure. He tried again, all too aware that his store of ash was dwindling.

"It's not working," he muttered.

"Delilah's power may supersede your own," the cat suggested.

Nathan turned sharply. "You mean she summoned them on purpose?"

Thistle blinked. The ships drifted closer, their black sails stark against the roiling clouds. When Nathan looked back at the *Wind-Witch*, Delilah was standing at the bow. He was glad to see her. So, apparently, were the dead. They drifted from the hatches, voices raised in a joyful chorus. "Sarg eresh'kigal!"

Shadow Soul.

These were not the shambling risen one found in lichyards, nor the docile walkers from the Dominion, Kaethe's realm, which sat between the living world and the Cold Sea. These dead had faded to pure spirit. Their bodies were translucent, with a spark of light within, so bright he could not look at them directly.

"What do they want?" Nathan wondered.

"I don't know," Thistle replied, his tail lashing furiously now. "But I fear they will overwhelm the *Wind-Witch*."

Lo gazed at the approaching ships as if in a trance, her pale face bathed in spirit-light.

Baba-hor rounded on her. "This is your doing! Twice you've tried to cheat me!"

"I offered you a compromise." Her voice sounded distant. "You refused."

The rusalki formed a circle around her, drawing coral knives. Three more dragged a struggling Castelio up from the hold. Where was Tijah? Nathan saw no sign of Kaethe's cranky mercenaire.

He sighed. Very well. *Time for a little mayhem.*

"Sha'etemmu!" He flung his last handful of sparkling ash into the air. Tentacles of darkness erupted, lashing the deck like a ghostly kraken. The rusalki hissed in alarm, stumbling back from the shadowy whips.

At least something still works. Nathan's discomfort faded as the familiar thrill of control surged through him.

"My father Khaf-hor will make you pay!" Baba-hor snarled. "There is nowhere in the Cold Sea you can hide from him!"

He turned to dive overboard, but Cas lunged forward,

grabbing the staff. They struggled over it, staggering across the deck. Baba-hor was a head taller and on the verge of winning when Tijah vaulted over the stern rail. She swept a kick at Baba-hor's legs and he stumbled, losing his grip on the staff.

With a curse, he leapt into the water. His rusalki followed, green hair trailing as they vanished into the depths.

Tijah's scimitar slashed the mooring line. The ship began to drift away from the pier just as the boats of the dead pressed close, their spectral hands grazing the hull.

"Don't let them touch you," Castelio warned.

"Get the sails up!" Tijah shouted.

Castelio ran to finish rigging the canvas. The *Wind-Witch* caught a gust and surged forward.

"You're not leaving me behind," Nathan muttered.

He broke from the bushes, sprinting down the pier with Thistle bounding alongside. Nathan threw himself across the widening gap, landing hard on the deck. Thistle leapt after him.

"Hsssss-PHAW!" The demon cat spat a curse. Icy wind luffed the sails, but whatever magic cloaked the ships of the dead, it seemed to be interfering with the ala's power. The *Wind-Witch* spun in lazy circles.

Cas grabbed Lo's arm. "You feckin' called them. Now get rid of them!"

"I already tried to open a portal," she snapped. "It didn't work."

Nathan checked his pouch. *Empty.*

"I think I know the problem," he said grimly. "These souls are near the end of their journey. The Cold Sea will not allow us to send them back. Only forward — to the far shore."

Lo closed her eyes. Her lips moved silently, though Nathan could make out the words.

Rosori solemar. Rosori pe rehiera.

I bid thee farewell. I bid thee go in peace.

The nine ships surrounded them now, bumping against the hull. The spirit-light they gave off blinded Nathan's sensitive eyes and he backed away, a chill burrowing into his gut. If Delilah couldn't manage a few boatloads of low dead, what hope did they have against Magnus and his army of mortifexes?

Somewhere off to his right, Tijah uttered a terse prayer to a goddess called Innunu. Nathan rubbed the ash residue clinging to his fingertips along each eyelid. Blessed shadows dampened the glow enough for him to see Tijah unhook an iron chain from her belt and start swinging. The spirits shrank back. Those it touched broke into wispy fragments.

But seconds later, they began to re-form.

"There's no choice," Nathan said. "We need Jaskin."

"Not yet." Cas stepped into his path, eyes wild. "I can hold them off."

Nathan frowned at his staff. "I thought you hadn't a clue how to use that."

"Behind you!" Tijah cried.

A specter was drifting towards them. Castelio spun and sketched a nine-pointed star in the air. It glowed weakly for an instant, then sputtered and faded away. This was not Kaethe's realm; she had no authority here. The specter advanced. Castelio jabbed at it with the staff. Lo stood at his side, chanting feverishly in Tongues. Her words had no discernible effect, and the runes on the staff remained dark.

By Urthrok's fiery whip, we're a sad bunch. Nathan caught Tijah's gaze. Judging by her expression, she was thinking the same thing.

"I have charms of iron and silver in my cabin," he called. "They might work."

She swept the chain in a broad arc, dispersing a wave of spirits. "You're not freeing that crazy old bastard?"

"No, I swear it."

Tijah hesitated, then gave a curt nod. Nathan spun towards the hatch.

A child-sized glow drifted from the shadows of the pilot-house. Its form was faded, but he caught a glimpse of pretty black curls and bloodless lips, with dark patches beneath the jaw. The Blue Death.

Tiny hands stretched toward Lo. Castelio screamed her name, but Nathan could see it was too late. Without proper warding, the touch of a raw spirit was always fatal—

Crimson light exploded, searing Nathan's vision. The force hurled him backwards mid-step. His head struck something hard, and darkness claimed him.

EIGHT

Darius led Felippa down a corridor with ceilings so high they were lost in shadow, the ever-present mist hovering above the floor. The air grew colder as they descended deeper into the keep, and she wrapped her arms around herself, teeth clacking together.

Presently, they reached a large door. With a grunt, Darius pushed it open, revealing an octagonal chamber beyond. Felippa stepped inside and gaped.

It was filled with a haphazard mountain of clothing — silks in vivid jewel tones, roughspun wool in earthy hues, delicate lace and stiff brocades. Plush velvet tangled with coarse russet, linens and wools.

Some styles were familiar, like the camicias and breeches from her homeland, while others were completely foreign, adorned with feathers and intricate beadwork.

"Where did all this come from?" she asked, an uneasy feeling stirring in the pit of her stomach.

Darius leaned against the wall. "Just find some things that fit."

Felippa hesitated, then approached the pile and picked up a delicate gown with gold and green thread fit for a noble. She eyed him accusingly. "These clothes are stolen, aren't they?"

"Yes," he admitted. "But the owners did not need them anymore."

Her bad feeling gathered into a knot of dread. "Did you kill the people they belonged to?"

"I can promise you we did not," Darius said. "They were already dead."

"Already ... dead?"

"Of course." He eyed her quizzically.

"Where are we?" Felippa whispered.

"Don't you know? This is an isle in the Cold Sea."

Felippa's legs gave out, and she sat down hard on the pile. She thought of Cas and the prayer he used to say every night when they were little.

Bless us, Kaethe
Guide us through the thickets of night
Let our feet not lose the path
And at the last hour
When your cold hand beckons
Lend us courage to cross the stormless sea.

But that wasn't the only name. It was also called the Cold Sea.

Deep down, Felippa had suspected that she wasn't in the living world anymore. She'd banished a mortifex, after all.

"So I'm dead," she said, her voice oddly calm. "It must have happened when I passed through the portal."

Darius shook his head. "I do not think so. You are warm. And your heart beats, does it not?"

Felippa placed a hand on her chest. "I can't feel anything."

Darius placed two fingers at the hollow of his jaw. "Press there."

Felippa copied the movement and felt the swift beat of her pulse. Instead of relief, she was filled with sudden anger.

"I don't want to wear any of this!" she exclaimed, scrambling to her feet.

Darius regarded her for a long moment. "You have not seen Magnus truly angry," he said at last. "Please, just choose something."

Felippa wanted to run out the door and keep going as far as she could. The thought of wearing dead people's clothes made her skin crawl.

I won't do it. I won't!

But she already felt feverish. She looked down at herself — the thin gown and sandals were no match for the frigid air. Prydwen had been scorching hot, a city where the sun never set. But the mortifex citadel was like a tomb carved from ice.

You have to survive long enough to find a way out of this nightmare, the voice advised her. *And the dead people... Well, they don't care anymore, do they?*

Jaw clenched, she dug through the pile — each piece telling a story she would rather not hear. She ignored the fancy garments and focused on finding something sensible. Something she could escape in, when the time came.

Finally, she found a woolen gown, child-sized, the weave thick and warm. Her eyes caught on a small bloodstain on the sleeve and she hesitated, imagining what might have befallen the previous owner. But survival trumped revulsion and she pulled it over her head.

"Good," Darius said. "Now I will show you to your chamber."

"May I find some shoes, as well?" she asked. *In for a copper pyre, in for a gold coronet,* as Da used to say.

Darius nodded with a touch of impatience.

Felippa rooted deeper into the mound, hands fumbling through layers of fabric. Her fingers closed around a small pair of boots —sturdy leather, scuffed but serviceable. She slipped them on, relieved to find they fit with only a bit of extra room at the toe.

Last, she pulled out a cloak, sky blue with a crow embroidered on the breast. Bel favored crows; Felippa hoped it would bring her luck to have an icon of the sun god in this dark place. The cloak was too big and trailed on the floor when she wrapped it around herself, but it made her instantly warm.

"Ready?" Darius asked, pushing away from the wall.

"Yes," Felippa said firmly.

He led her down another corridor. The stone walls seemed to close in on her, the air making her breath fog, but her new cloak kept out the chill.

Finally, they reached a small chamber. Save for a slender balustrade, the far side was open, revealing the vast expanse of the Cold Sea. To the east, the sky blushed with hues of rose and coral. To the west, touches of gold added a warm glow that softened the edges of departing daylight. Darius gestured for her to step inside.

An oval standing mirror stood in one corner, surrounded by mismatched furnishings — a battered wooden chair, an intricately carved table inset with turquoise, and a faded tapestry of a white stag.

Felippa walked to the balustrade and looked out over the islands dotting the horizon like stepping stones to the unknown. It made her think of Ma. Had she sailed this way? Felippa barely remembered her. She'd been four when Ma died. It was the thing she envied Cas and Teo for most. They'd had a chance to know her. They had memories.

"What lies on the far shore, Darius?" she asked.

"I don't know. No one does."

Felippa glanced at the mirror. The girl staring back looked big-eyed and frail, wrapped in clothes that didn't belong to her. Her gaze landed on a chipped basin. "May I have water for washing?"

"Of course." Darius left without another word.

Felippa hugged the oversized cloak tighter, peering once more at the distant islands. Her hopes that Cas would find her dimmed with the knowledge of how far she had come. Could there be any way back to the living world? Perhaps Darius knew the answer. But she had to be careful. He was kind, but he was also loyal to Magnus.

In a few minutes, Darius returned with a steaming bucket. He set it down, gave her a brief smile, and pulled the door closed behind him again.

Felippa dipped a cloth into the hot water, the warmth seeping into her numbed fingers. She scrubbed at the blood-stain on the sleeve of the woolen gown. The crimson mark stubbornly resisted. As she scrubbed harder, she couldn't help but wonder about the original owner. What happened to her—

"Stop it," she whispered.

Satisfied that the stain had faded, she turned again to the mirror, the glass fogging from the steam still rising from the bucket. Dark smudges ringed her eyes, and her bones jutted sharply. The image wavered, and dizziness washed over her.

Before she could hit the floor, a hand steadied her. She blinked up at a pair of bright blue eyes filled with concern.

"Are you ill?" Darius asked.

"Just hungry." She managed a smile. "Starved, really. How far is the feast hall?"

His brows knit. "I can carry you on my back," he offered

after a moment's hesitation. "I think... I think I might have done that for a child once before."

He crouched down, just like Cas used to do. Felippa's heart twinged at the familiar sight.

"Come on," he urged, glancing over his shoulder. "Hop up."

She gathered the cloak and threw her arms around his neck.

"Hold tight," he said, standing up.

Felippa pressed her cheek to his back, legs wrapping around his waist. The cold air bit at every inch of exposed skin, but she felt a powerful drowsiness come over her. The smell of ancient stone and damp wool filled her nose, mingling with the scent of salt carried on the wind as they crossed one of the bridges.

"Almost there," Darius said.

Felippa nodded against his warm shoulder, too weak to speak. Her thoughts drifted incoherently.

"You're not like the others," she mumbled. "How did you come here?"

He stiffened. "You are mistaken," he said softly. "I have always been here."

It was a strange reply, and her mind was too muddled to make sense of it.

They finally emerged into the feasting hall. Darius set her down on one of the benches. Felippa's stomach gave a mighty rumble, her mouth watering at the repast before her.

Five tables stretched the length of the room, each laden with elaborate dishes. Fresh bread and herbed pottage, alongside small dishes of fruit preserves, pickled vegetables, and glistening olives. There were savory pies and stews seasoned with cinnamon, cloves, and pepper. Platters of buttered carrots and roasted parsnips, honey cakes and fruit tarts, thick custards and... Oh! Her favorite dessert, marchpane, with white icing and little stars of gingerbread.

The mingled smells almost made her faint. They were intoxicating — rich and heady.

Candles floated above the tables, suspended by some unseen magic. They cast a warm glow on golden goblets brimming with wine, polished silverware and crystal decanters. The soft strains of a harp came from one corner of the hall, which was draped with gay bunting.

"Eat," Darius urged, filling her plate with a bit of everything.

Felippa's hand trembled as she reached for a piece of bread. It was halfway to her mouth when her gaze shifted to the young woman on Darius's other side, who was in the midst of telling a story about some battle. She had light brown hair and amber eyes. Felippa's spirits lifted. Another live person!

"—and so *she* said to Victor, 'My advice is to protect your balls. The gods know I won't.'"

The mortifexes at the table erupted in laughter, stamping their feet. Some were dark-complected, their bodies adorned with intricate tattoos that peeked out from beneath short vests and wide, billowing trousers. Others had silver hair and fur-lined white leathers. A few looked like Darius, clad in hues of green and brown that would blend into a woodland forest.

"Drink, little scribe," Magnus called out, his voice booming across the hall. He caught her eye and raised his goblet in a toast.

Felippa set down the bread and reached for her cup, but before she could lift it to her lips, Darius leaned over and whispered into the ear of the young woman beside him. She looked over, her eyes locking onto Felippa with an intensity that made her skin prickle.

She was short and stocky, though not as small as Felippa. There was something fierce about her. She reminded Felippa of

Duc Marcel's consort, though there was a warmth in her face that Lady Morgen lacked.

"This is my wife," Darius said. "Nazafareen."

Felippa managed a nod. "Pleased to meet you," she murmured.

Nazafareen tossed back the contents of a jeweled goblet. As she did so, the sleeves of her coat rode up, revealing a gold cuff identical to the one Darius wore. One arm ended at the wrist. She'd lost her right hand.

"Welcome, scribe," Nazafareen said.

Felippa nodded, feeling the weight of a hundred flaming eyes upon her. She glanced once more at Darius, hoping for reassurance, but his face remained impassive. Nazafareen tilted her chair back, dropping her boots on the table with a thud. The plate of the mortifex beside her slid to the floor with a clatter. Its owner, huge and sporting a forked black beard, muttered under his breath. Before Felippa could blink, Nazafareen drew her sword and laid the blade against his throat.

"Did you say something, Skegg?" she asked softly.

Skegg swallowed, the edge pressing into his skin. "Ah," he stammered. "Don't believe I did."

"I thought not." She released him and turned to the revelers. "Our king has a new scribe. She isn't to be touched. Understand, you daft bunch of scapegraces?"

Murmurs and frowns greeted this statement. Some exchanged uneasy glances, while others eyed Felippa with naked hunger. Nazafareen jumped up onto the table, kicking more plates aside.

"Understood?" she bellowed, eyes gleaming with a mad light.

The mortifexes nodded vigorously this time. Magnus, sitting at the head of one of the tables, watched with a smile playing on his lips. In contrast, Gerda's face twisted into a scowl.

"Then let's eat!" Nazafareen declared, sliding her sword back into its sheath. The tension in the room eased slightly.

As the mortifexes returned to their meals, Felippa caught Darius's eye. He gave her a small nod, as if to say, *You're safe for now.*

For the last week, hiding in the dank cave, her mind had been filled with visions of succulent roasts and sweet pastries while she gnawed on tough roots and slimy mollusks. Now those fantasies were reality, spread out on gleaming silver platters within arm's reach.

There was roasted goose, its skin golden and crackling, stuffed with tart apples and fragrant herbs. Bowls of mashed potatoes swirled with butter sat beside plump sausages sizzling in their own juices. Freshly baked bread rolls steamed invitingly, their crusts shining with a glaze of honey.

Sweet treats beckoned from another table; pastries dusted with powdered sugar, pies bursting with ripe berries, and cream cakes topped with delicate swirls of frosting.

Surveying the banquet before her, Felippa's spirits lifted. At least she wouldn't perish of hunger in this place. But as she brought the first forkful to her lips, the silver disk Cas had given her grew hot against her skin and the illusion shattered.

The mortifexes were eating ... nothing at all.

Felippa watched them pass empty platters up and down, spooning imaginary fare into their mouths. It was like the parties she used to make with her straw dolls.

The only real food was on the three plates before her, Darius, and Nazafareen. Fish and chunks of some pale yellow tuber. She took a tentative bite. Bland but filling. She peered into her goblet. Water, not wine.

She took a cautious sip. It was clear and cold, with a

metallic taste that made her think it came from a source deep in the mountain. Her mind raced. What kind of place was this?

After sating their appetites on air, the mortifexes broke into song, their deep, raucous voices echoing off the stone walls. Felippa hunched her shoulders and slid down on the bench, trying to make herself as small as possible. Maybe if she stayed quiet, they would forget about her.

Then Nazafareen's voice cut through the din. "Sing to us, scribe!"

The room fell silent for a heartbeat, then the chanting began. "Sing! Sing! Sing!"

Felippa stared down at her plate, willing herself to disappear. The chanting grew louder, more insistent. At last, she stood on unsteady legs. Before she could try to object, Darius lifted her by the waist and set her on the table. As she gazed out at the sea of High Dead, Felippa's mind went blank for a terrible moment.

Darius gave her an encouraging smile. "Anything you like," he said.

She cleared her dry throat and launched into the first song that popped into her head. It was one that Cas had taught her, and she sang it as he did, with a gruffer voice for the ferryman's part.

Ferry me across the water, do, boatman, do!
If you've silver in your purse, I'll ferry you.
I have silver in my purse, and my eyes are blue;
So ferry me across the water, do, boatman, do!

Step into my ferry-boat, be they gray or blue,
And for the silver in your purse, I'll ferry you.

The mortifexes laughed and stamped their feet. Felippa's sweet soprano gained strength.

> Ferry me across the water, do, boatman, do!
> I have silver in my purse, and my eyes are brown.
> So ferry me across the water, o'er to yonder town!
>
> Step into my ferry-boat, be they dark of hue,
> And for the silver in your purse, I'll ferry you.
>
> Ferry me across the water, do, boatman, do!
> I have silver in my purse, and my eyes are red.
> Ferry me across the water, so I might mourn my
>   dead.

Felippa jabbed her finger in mock outrage, just like Cas did.

> Get thee from my ferry-boat, I'll not carry you
> Not for all the silver in your purse, nor bitter
>   tears you've shed...

Her voice faltered. The whole room was staring at her, the mortifexes' eyes glowing like banked embers. They were no longer clapping along. Suddenly, the meaning of the song became clear. She had always thought it was about someone crying for a loved one, but it was about *them*. How fexes hated running water and used tricks to get across.

She felt like she might throw up the little she'd eaten. Then Nazafareen slammed a palm on the table, making the silver rattle.

"Well, that was bloody depressing," she declared. "Can we have something that doesn't make me want to stab Orm over there?"

It was the one-eyed giant who had helped Gerda catch her on the beach. Orm laughed nervously.

"Of course," Felippa said, forcing a smile. Her mind raced, searching for another song, *anything else.*

Once there was a cat so fat,
That he could scarcely chase a rat.
But one fine day, he gave it a try,
And my oh my, did he fly, fly, fly!

Nazafareen gave a bark of laughter and the tension eased.

That rat was quick, that rat was spry,
He darted left, then right, oh my!
But that fat old cat, he rolled and stumbled,
Till both of them were mighty humbled...

The hall erupted, stomping feet keeping time with the tune.

Now they sit, side by side,
A friendship forged, no need to hide.
For who might guess, in all this spat,
That a rat could love a big fat cat?

It was a silly nursery song, but the mortifexes liked it better than the last one. Felippa dipped a quick curtsy and climbed down before they tried to make her sing more.

"An adept recovery," Darius said, his voice amused.

Felippa ducked her head, letting her long hair curtain her face. Others took up their own ballads as she finished her meal, most of them about fighting. It wasn't the feast she had first imagined, but it filled her stomach.

Why was she the only one who saw through the illusion? It must be the necklace. It *was* magic. She drew the disk from the neck of her dress. When she glanced up, Darius was staring at it.

"What is that?" he asked, his eyes narrowing.

Felippa closed it in her fist. "Nothing."

"Nothing?"

"My brother gave it to me."

Darius leaned closer. "May I see it?"

She reluctantly loosened her grip.

"It is unusual," he murmured.

Felippa quickly tucked it into her dress again. "It's mine."

"I do not mean to take it from you," Darius said. He rubbed his temples, a look of confusion crossing his face. "It is just... the symbol seems familiar. A moon on one side, a sun on the other—"

"Scribe!" Magnus's voice boomed across the hall.

Felippa stiffened, then turned to face him. She glanced at Darius, who nodded gravely. With tentative steps, she made her way to Magnus's table.

"Sit," he commanded, gesturing to a chair opposite him.

As she took her seat, Gerda approached with a sneer, thrusting a quill and a sheaf of parchment at Felippa.

"Leave us," Magnus ordered, his eyes never leaving Felippa.

The room fell instantly silent. The mortifexes filed out of the hall until only Felippa and their king remained. Once the last was gone, the wreckage of the "feast" vanished. Dirty platters, spilled wine, and crumbs of food disappeared as if they had never been — which, Felippa reflected, they actually *hadn't*.

Once the tables were spotless, Magnus waved a hand and flames erupted in the great hearth. They cast flickering shadows but gave off no warmth — just another illusion.

Felippa dipped the quill into the ink. She tested the nib on a scrap of parchment, writing Magnus's name. The ink flowed smoothly, the quill sharp and precise. Satisfied, she selected a clean leaf of parchment.

"Ready?" he demanded.

Felippa nodded. The mortifex king leaned back, gazing into the illusory flames.

"Listen well, scribe," he began. "I was not born to wealth and power. On the contrary, I had to seize it for myself..."

NINE

A dull ache throbbed behind Cas's eyes as he sat up in
the captain's cabin of the *Wind-Witch*. The motion
of the ship was smooth, no rolling or pitching.

He swung his legs over the side of the bed and staggered to
the porthole. The rose-streaked sky stretched in either direction. Far below, cobalt waves raced past.

Relief washed over him. They'd not only made it out of the
harbor, but the ship was flying again.

Gui's staff sat propped against the wall by the bed. He
picked it up, running his thumb over the carved runes. An
image flashed through his mind — a small, dead hand reaching
for Lo.

Just like the lich. He couldn't watch her die again.

He remembered crimson light bursting from the staff's tip,
the runes glowing blood-red. He must have finally mastered its
power and driven back the horde long enough for them to
escape Dreamhaven — not that he could recall anything that
happened after.

The hatch swung open. Lo stepped in, her raven hair in a

loose braid. He perked up at the sight of a tray with bread, soup, and two steaming mugs.

"Ah, you're awake," she said cheerfully, setting the tray down on the bed. Cas reached for a mug, inhaling the bitter aroma of strong black tea.

"How's the new mast holding?" he asked.

"It hasn't turned back into a tooth, so we're good there."

She glanced at the staff, then back at him. This new Lo was an open book, and it wasn't hard to tell something was amiss.

"What exactly happened?" he asked.

"Well, you did clear out the dead." She patted his hand. "Well done. But the blast of power also knocked Tijah and Nathan out cold." She shook her head. "You, too. Luckily, I only caught the edge of it. Thistle managed to get us aloft."

Cas stared into his mug, triumph curdling. "Perhaps the staff knows I'm not a Quietus anymore. It won't serve me."

Lo took a bite of bread. "It's a piece of wood. Tell me about..." She paused, hand flying to her throat. Her mouth opened and closed, but not even a wheeze of breath emerged.

Cas leapt off the bed, hot tea spilling on the carpet. He pounded her back until the morsel of bread popped out. Lo coughed, eyes watering.

"That was a ... cheap try," she muttered hoarsely. Her voice rose. "Better luck next time, Bitches!"

A small, clawed animal skittered along his spine. He prayed the Moirai weren't listening.

"Are you alright?" Cas eyed her closely.

Lo composed herself, tucking a strand of hair behind her ear. "Where was I? Oh yes, the man who gave you the staff. Tell me about him."

He owed Lo the truth. All of it, this time. "His name is Gui Harcourt. He came to our farm the night Justinian killed my ma and nearly killed Felippa too." The old pain rose in his chest. "Gui bought time for me and my brother and sister to escape on the ferry. He used this same staff to hold Justinian off on the banks of the Forkings River."

Cas stared at the grain of the wood. "After that night, we couldn't go back to our farm in the Boundary. Ended up in a village called Swanton. Da took to drink. Things got hard. One winter, I banished a ghost plaguing the miller's house. Afterwards, he gave me a sack of flour as thanks."

Cas grimaced. "Then the margrave accused me of summoning the dead myself, so I could banish them for coin. I thought I'd swing from the gallows for sure."

He glanced up at Lo. "Gui came to Swanton, got me out of jail, and took me back to Aquitan with him. He trained me as a Quietus."

Lo cocked an eyebrow. "Seems Gui keeps saving your neck."

"Aye, he does. That night at the farm, Gui had given me a vial of Kaethe's Tears. Like a fool, I broke it. If I'd had it when Justinian came... "

"You might've saved your mother," Lo finished. "And your sister."

Cas didn't mind her brutal honesty. It was a relief to hear someone else say it.

"But maybe it all worked out as it should," Lo continued.

"How do you figure?"

"Well, because of all that, you became a Quietus. Haven't you helped people?"

He thought of the infant he'd saved in Swanton. "Aye."

"So perhaps this is the path you were meant to walk."

Cas lowered his voice to a joking whisper. "I thought you didn't hold with the Fates."

"I don't." She grimaced. "But they fuck with us whether

we believe in them or not. Don't be so quick to throw away the gifts you're given, Castelio zah Nerides."

"Fair enough. But what if I lose control again?"

Lo sipped her tea, a thoughtful look on her face. Then she set down the cup and began to slowly unlace her cami. "That sounds terrible. Whatever would we do?"

Her beauty made his chest ache. Cas dropped the staff and reached for her. She came into his arms, her laughing mouth finding his. They stumbled back onto the bed, hands roaming, tugging at clothes. Her skin was hot silk against his. He lost himself in her scent, her taste.

Afterwards, they lay entwined, Lo nestled into the crook of his arm. "Jaskin tried to talk me into breaking the mirror," she admitted, "just before the dead ships came."

The old weasel. "What did he say?"

"That he could fix my fiasco with Baba-hor."

"Our fiasco."

"Ah, I knew I loved you, Sleepy-Eyes. *Our* fiasco. So I said to Jaskin, no you can't, because Baba-hor might be a demon, but he's alive. And Jaskin says he knows how to rip souls straight out of living bodies." She laid her palm on Cas's chest and made a sucking noise.

He propped his head on one arm. "Shite, really?"

"I'll admit I was tempted, but it's too evil, even for my withered little half soul. Then Jaskin reminds me that we'll need his power to send Magnus and his mortifexes to the far shore." She sighed. "The worst part is that he's right. I couldn't do it on my own, Cas. I tried. I mean, I really tried."

"And when Jaskin turns on us?"

Lo traced the blue star tattoo between his thumb and forefinger. "I'll have to fight him. But I believe he will uphold his end of the bargain first. Jaskin fears the mortifexes. He enslaved them, but he no longer controls them."

Cas gave a slow nod. "If they ever caught him…"

"Exactly. His remorse might be fake, but he has a powerful interest in getting rid of them for good. But we'll deal with all that when the time comes. For now, you must try to understand that staff."

Cas knew she was right. "It can't be too hard. I've seen Gui use it. I'm just missing something."

The look she gave him was apologetic. "I know you don't care for Nathan, but … go see him. He did offer to help."

Cas reluctantly dressed and knocked on the necromancer's cabin door. A curt voice bade him enter. Nathan reclined on his bunk, nursing a split lip. When he saw Cas, he held out a hand, beckoning impatiently.

"Bring it here."

Cas handed the staff over. Nathan studied the runes etched into the dark wood, turning them in a slow spiral.

"Just tell me what it says," Cas said.

"The literal translation?" Nathan traced the jagged script. "*Blood, frost, bile, and rot. Know the four humours of the dead. Master is servant, and servant is master.*" He looked up. "What do you make of it?"

Cas felt a surge of irritation. "Aren't you going to tell me the meaning?"

Nathan returned the staff. "The four humours are anger, sorrow, regret, and envy. The last one can also be translated as greed. They are the reasons souls linger."

Cas nodded slowly. "Aye, that part I get, though I never heard them called humours. What about the other part? Blood, frost, bile, and rot."

A shrug. "Your guess is as good as mine."

"Master is servant, servant is master?"

"It sounds like one of those banal platitudes that get tacked on at the end. To master the staff's power, you must be humble, blah, blah." Nathan made a dismissive gesture. "It is fluff, Quietus."

Cas's temper began to fray. "How many times must I repeat myself? I'm not a Quietus anymore."

Nathan quirked a dark brow. "Then throw the staff overboard. Perhaps we're all safer that way."

His words echoed Cas's own doubts, stoking his anger. "I find it hard to believe that you don't know what the runes mean. Not the translation, but what they *mean*. How to make them *work*."

Nathan rolled his eyes. "What could I possibly gain by lying to you?"

"I don't know. But I heard you whispering with Jaskin in the hold. Don't pretend it was innocent!"

"He merely warned me about our cursed luck." Nathan's lips thinned. "Since none of you bothered to do it. In light of recent events, it's clear he was telling the truth. I am not the one who sabotaged this mission."

Cas hated that he was right. Hated his own helplessness and ignorance. "I still don't trust you," he said. "Maybe you don't want the staff to work."

Nathan muttered under his breath.

"You nobles are all the same." Cas felt a rant coming on but couldn't stop himself. It was like purging an infected wound. "You care only for yourselves. Using people as pawns in your vicious games."

"What games?" Nathan erupted, throwing his arms up.

"Oh, let's see." Cas scratched his ear. "Didn't you conspire with Orlaith to start a war?"

Nathan sat up. "I was trying to *stop* a war, you dimwit. I despise Orlaith. I intended to reveal the truth, that she arranged for her own son to be kidnapped by wraiths so she could blame

Ladies Chaos and Caul. The woman is obsessed with avenging her dead husband."

"It doesn't change the fact that you put the boy's life at risk." Cas leaned forward. "Speaking of Duc Robert, did you know she keeps him chained up in her manor house? He's a ghoul now. Preserved by the dark arts for the last twelve years." Cas thought of the revenant he'd been trapped with. "*Preserved* might be too kind a word. Robert is … rather the worse for his condition."

For once, Nathan Ouvrard was rendered speechless. His sharp features slackened in amazement. Then he started to laugh, wincing as he touched his split lip.

"You think it's funny?" Cas asked. "I was stuck in the feckin' wine cellar with him for hours while he tried to break free—"

"*Merde.*" Nathan held up a hand. "I am not laughing at your expense. Rather at Orlaith...she is always so prim and proper, that hypocrite—"

Cas wasn't sure whether he wanted to punch him or join him. Before he could decide, the cabin door banged open. Tijah stood there, looking grim. She had a nasty lump on her forehead, he noticed with a twinge of guilt.

"Up on deck, both of you," she said. "Magnus's lair is in sight."

TEN

Baba-hor hunched over the bar at the Laughing Gull, black nails tapping the rim of his mug. His third ale... Or was it the fourth?

"Did you know that woman was a sorceress?" he asked sourly.

Bergmann shook his head. "I only knew Tijah. Never met the others."

To Baba-hor, the humbug looked like his mother, a sea nymph wearing a gown of sheer green silk with combs of black pearls in her hair. Even though Baba-hor knew better, it evoked warm feelings every time he glanced at the tavern owner. Well, the illusion wasn't Bergmann's doing. None of it was. They had been friends for years and always treated each other squarely.

"I don't blame you," Baba-hor said. "But the strangers stole my tooth, and that I will not abide."

Behind them, the rusalki had taken over a corner of the room, flipping clam shells with their coral daggers. One arced

87

through the air, landing neatly in a mug. A chorus of cheers erupted from the table. The rusalki never held a grudge for long.

Unlike their captain.

"Nor should you," Bergmann said stoutly. "But if they're going after Magnus," he ventured after a brief pause, "it *would* be nice to be rid of him—"

"Bah!" Baba-hor slammed webbed fingers on the bar. The ale sloshed but did not spill. "They're cheaters. And I won't let it be known that someone can cheat me and get away with it. I'll find them, never fear." He stared morosely into the dregs of his ale. "No one keeps their word anymore. It didn't used to be like this, Bergmann."

"No, it didn't." The humbug sighed. "When my mother was a girl, Dreamhaven was twice as big. We had some illustrious visitors then. Vorthyx, the Abyssal Judge. Nymara the Tidekeeper. That was the golden age, my friend."

"Wasn't there a famous lord of shipwrecks?" a rusalka hissed.

"Tzarneth the Reclaimer," Baba-hor said. He hooked his hands into claws. "His fingers long and sharp like the hooks of an anchor, and carrying a massive trident—"

Baba-hor cut off as a gull careened through the open window. "Ship of souls! Ship of souls!" Bilmek announced with a bout of shrill laughter.

Baba-hor and Bergmann exchanged a worried glance. Could the dead have returned? They bolted out the door, nearly knocking over a rusalka named Sveta, who hissed in annoyance. The salt wind slapped their faces as they gained the top of the lane and peered down at the wharf. A solitary vessel glided through the harbor, black sails limp. It was indeed one of the soul ships that made the final crossing.

The vessel slid alongside the pier and a solidly built man

with cropped dark hair leapt from the deck. Baba-hor sagged with relief. Like most denizens of the Cold Sea, he avoided the specters at all costs. This man was clearly not one of them. Although there was something wrong with his face…

"Oh no," Bergmann muttered.

"Who is it?" Baba-hor asked.

"Magnus's right hand," Bergmann replied tightly. "Worst of them all."

Baba-hor frowned. "Here to collect taxes?"

Bergmann gave a disconsolate nod. "I'll give him what he wants, and then he'll go away."

"Did he always look like that?" Baba-hor wondered.

Distaste curled Bergmann's pretty sea-nymph lips. "No. Come on before he sees us."

They scurried back into the tavern, watching through the window as the mortifex strode up the lane, his smile like a scar. He pushed open the door to the Laughing Gull and scanned the room with red eyes.

"I've got your tithe, Master Janus," Bergmann said quickly, waving an empty sack. "Just a moment."

"I'm not here for that." The gentle tone was at odds with his ghastly countenance. "I seek a friend."

Up close, the mortifex looked like someone had carved the skin from his face with a dull oyster knife. Bergmann shot a warning look at Baba-hor. "There's no one else in town. Have a look around if you like."

Janus's gaze lingered on each of them in turn. The rusalki stared back with blank white eyes, their game forgotten. Baba-hor's hand drifted toward his mouth, ready but not eager. He had already lost one tooth today and they took decades to grow back.

"I don't mean the dregs of the Cold Sea that frequent this

piss-stained hovel," Janus said. "I'm looking for a man with a tattoo of Kaethe's star on his hand. He carries a staff."

Baba-hor had no loyalty to the strangers — in fact, he fully intended to avenge their betrayal — but he disliked bullies.

"Haven't seen him," Baba-hor said regretfully.

"Nor I," Bergmann said. "But we'll keep an eye out, won't we?"

They all nodded. Baba-hor wished Janus would leave. He smelled of madness ... and something worse. Something Baba-hor could not name but that made the fins on his spine quiver with apprehension.

Janus turned for the door. Then he spun, quick as a sea serpent, and seized Elka by the throat. She kicked and writhed as he lifted her from the ground as easily as one would lift a child. "Tell me the truth," he said, "or I'll snap her neck."

The threat held no menace. There was nothing at all in his voice, just a disturbing emptiness. The rusalki shoved their chairs back, daggers glinting. Baba-hor raised a hand. He would not lose Elka to this monster. Not to protect the strangers who had stolen his rightful prize.

"Now that you mention it," he said, "the man you describe was just here. In fact, he cheated me out of a ship. It is called the *Wind-Witch*. You can probably catch him if you leave quickly."

The mortifex stared at him, unblinking. Baba-hor wondered if they were all about to die. Then Janus let Elka go. She collapsed into a chair, rubbing her throat and glaring. Her sisters formed a protective circle around her, hissing softly.

"Was he carrying an iron box?" Janus asked.

Now there *was* something — an odd hunger.

"Not that I saw," Baba-hor replied, "but it might have been aboard the ship."

Bergmann watched the exchange with folded arms, his large violet eyes hooded.

"Where was he going?" Janus asked. "Quick, or I'll burn this place to the ground."

"The man was with three others," Baba-hor admitted. "They are hunting your king. That is all I know."

Janus let out a low growl. "You say they cheated you? Well, here is a fair deal. I will give you my own ship if you banish me."

Baba-hor covered his surprise. "Doesn't that require telling me your true name?"

"I will not be trapped in this purgatory much longer," Janus said with an edge of weariness. "But if you try to summon me with it, I will cut your tongue out."

"Cut it right out!" Bilmek echoed with a guffaw.

"Nasty, slimy Baba-tongue," Golguth added, bobbing his black-feathered head.

Janus swiped at them, and the pair of gulls flew out the window, their laughter fading into the distance. Baba-hor thought hard. The offer struck him as decidedly fishy, and he'd already been swindled once today.

"I'm afraid I don't make that sort of bargain, Master Janus," he said, choosing his words with care. "Simple trades are not my style. But if you would care to engage in a contest of riddles—"

"*Riddles?*" The web of shiny scar tissue tightened, causing his lips and nose to twist in unfortunate ways. "I don't give a rat's fuck about riddles. Yes or no?"

Baba-hor glanced at Bergmann, who looked on helplessly as Janus walked behind the bar and began hurling dream vials to the floor, one by one. Colored vapors rose up as the glass shattered. Baba-hor caught the scent of fresh grass, followed by a whiff of chalky stone.

"Did I mention..." *Smash.* "That if you refuse me..." *Smash.* "Everyone in here burns?" *Smash, smash.*

Baba-hor wished he had never washed up in Dreamhaven. He turned to Elka, who gave a slight nod. She was right, Baba-hor decided. Fishy deal or not, banishing this creature seemed like an excellent idea.

"Where," he asked, "shall I draw the nine-pointed star?"

ELEVEN

A bitter wind swept Magnus's audience chamber, guttering the torches along the walls. Felippa drew her blue crow cloak tighter, sealing the gaps where it poked cold fingers. At her elbow sat a sheaf of parchment filled with neat, precise script — a testament to the hours she had spent listening to the mortifex king drone on about sieges and battles, conquests and glory.

"...and then," he boomed, his voice echoing off the high ceiling, "the armies of the east fell before my might. The siege lasted nine days and nine nights, but their will crumbled on the dawn of the tenth." He leaned forward, white hair spilling over his shoulders like a cascade of winter snow. "It was I who turned the tide. A hundred men fell to my blade—"

"You fought alone, sire?" Felippa interjected, her expression innocent.

"Of course not," he said, waving a dismissive hand. "But it was my cunning that led us to victory. I shall have you write that down!"

Felippa's fingers cramped as she dutifully transcribed his

words. The tales were fanciful and laced with impossible feats, but she didn't dare question their truth aloud. They were the only thing keeping her alive.

"What else do you remember about the siege of Ravenmoor?" she asked.

"Er... It was so long ago..."

Magnus seemed to be running out of steam. Felippa felt a twinge of worry. Perhaps he needed help.

"Did the beautiful ladies of the court throw flower garlands at your feet afterwards? I mean, you freed them from the yoke of the eastern tyrants."

Magnus blinked. "Indeed they did," he said, puffing out his diamond-encrusted chest. "The celebrations lasted for a full week. We had games and feasting. All the most famous singers wrote ballads about me." He stared into space for a long moment. Then the corners of his mouth drew down. "But here... I am not shown the proper respect. The deference that is my right."

"Sire?" she asked, quill hovering above the parchment.

As she gazed at Magnus, his form blurred at the edges, distorting the air like a piece of thick glass. Felippa rubbed her eyes. She had been staring at her own spidery handwriting for too long. When she looked up, the effect was gone.

Magnus leaned forward. His voice was cold, his gaze sharp. "Do you know of the Dream Collectors' Collective?"

Felippa mutely shook her head.

"A guild of humbugs." He uttered the word with disdain. "They think they have the right to set the rules for the rest of us. But I will make them bow to me." He gripped the arms of his throne. "No, crawl on their worthless bellies. I have been amassing dreams, you see. Already, I have thousands stored in this keep. One day, I will own them all, every single dream in the Cold Sea. Then they will be begging my forgiveness!"

Felippa had no clue what he was talking about. It seemed a bizarre digression, but his stories were often rambling. "Should I..." She bit down on a yawn, "be writing this down, sire?"

"No," he grunted after a moment. "Where was I? Ah, yes. Now I shall relate the treaty I brokered with the centaurs." His voice cracked on the last word. Magnus cleared his throat. "Spring came late to the Ringfell Mountains. The centaurs' emissary, Kadaeon, was trapped by heavy snows in Wolfwood Pass with his whole entourage..."

She scribbled furiously. The sheaf at her elbow grew thicker. At last, Magnus finished his tale and gestured for her to gather the parchment.

"My memoirs shall remain private until the work is complete," he said sternly. "You will tell no one of what is said in this room." His gaze drifted to the slender bridge that connected Glash's Tusk with the next tower. "Unless you wish to fly like the abbadax."

It was their fifth session together, and he said the same thing each time.

"I have no one to tell, sire," Felippa said. "But I swear on my life that I will reveal nothing until you say so."

A gruff nod. "You will attend me tomorrow at the same time."

Felippa curtsied. All she wanted was to soak her stiff fingers in hot water. Not even at the Duc's court had she been forced to scribe for so many hours straight without reprieve.

Magnus took the sheaf of papers and dismissed her. As she walked to the pointed archway at the far end of the long chamber, she risked a glance back. Magnus was crouched behind his throne, thrusting the parchment into some hidden niche. Felippa turned away before he saw her.

Darius waited in the corridor beyond, his smile lifting her spirits. "How goes it?" he asked.

"Oh ... er, fascinating," she said. "We have made good progress." She was tempted to share her suspicions that Magnus was weaving his memoirs from thin air, but the mortifex's warning stopped her.

Darius always escorted her from the throne room to the feasting hall. She pestered him with questions, hoping to discover how a living man came to serve Magnus the Merciless, but he was very good at twisting the conversation to meaningless things. It was almost as if he didn't know the answer himself.

Still, Darius was the only person she trusted in this place. And time was running out. Magnus would eventually tire of her; or worse, Justinian would return. She had to get away before that happened.

Felippa was just about to beg shamelessly for his aid when a tall shadow slipped from between two columns. It was the one-eyed mortifex, Orm.

"Is the ship ready to sail?" he asked.

"Nearly," Darius said. "We'll leave after the feast."

Felippa's pulse beat faster. If she could somehow slip aboard...

"There's been a change of target," Orm said.

"Where?"

Orm glanced at Felippa. "Fall back, girl. This is none of your concern."

Felippa bit her lip and let them walk ahead. As usual, they weren't worried she would slip away. There was something terribly odd about this place — beyond the obvious. Even though Darius took the same route from the throne room to the great hall every day, little details changed. The position of a tapestry, the color and pattern of the floor tiles, things like that. One day, a window would be round; the next it would be square. She knew it was the same window because the view beyond matched exactly. When she remarked on the change, Darius acted like he had no idea what she was talking about. If anything, he gave her a worried look, as if *she* were losing her grip.

But Felippa knew she wasn't. More illusions, that's all it was. But where did they come from? Who or what was the source?

Orm and Darius turned a corner, moving out of sight. Felippa considered running, but she knew they would catch her. Magnus would be furious and Darius would be blamed. No, better she find a way to speak with him alone later, at the "feast."

Her too-big shoes scuffed the stone as she trudged behind them. Time was slippery as a buttered eel in this place. She would sleep, then go to Magnus and *scribble scribble scribble*. After that, she and Darius would join the others in the great hall, where they ate the same fake food and drank the same fake wine. When Nazafareen shouted for the scribe to sing, as she invariably did, Felippa would launch into the stupid ditty about the cat and the rat. The mortifexes would laugh and stomp as if they'd never heard it before.

The only person who ever seemed different was Darius. She often caught him looking at her with a furrowed brow, as if he wasn't quite sure what to make of her. He stared at the silver coin around her neck, too, but he never tried to take it. There was good in him, Felippa felt sure.

She followed Darius and Orm into the feasting hall. Trestles stretched before her, laden with an extravagant banquet that flickered in and out of existence — crispy haunches of meat, perfectly ripe strawberries, and goblets overflowing with dark wine. Bright banners adorned the walls, musicians played a dulcimer and harp in the far corner, and a juggler wound through the tables, a ring of six burning brands blurring through his hands.

But when Felippa squinted her eyes, she saw the hall as it really was: draped in cobwebs, the tables thick with dust, and the only morsels of actual food set before her, Darius, and his mad wife.

Nazafareen held court in her usual place, her cheeks flushed and amber eyes fever-bright. Sometimes she picked a fight with Skegg. Sometimes it was with a woman named Ingvild, who had short auburn hair and scarred knuckles.

The same brawls. The same songs. The same revelry. It would never change.

As they settled into their usual seats, Felippa leaned closer to Darius. If she told him the truth, it might dispel the illusion. What did she have to lose?

"None of it's real," she whispered.

He eyed her warily. "What?"

"Look." She poked a platter of sugared plums, her finger going straight through it. "Nothing but air."

Uncertainty flickered across his face. Then he shook his head. "You are mistaken." He forked a chunk of half-cooked tuber into his mouth and chewed with a sigh of ecstasy. "That is the most succulent crab I have ever tasted."

Felippa's frustration boiled over. She seized Darius's sleeve. "Don't you realize that every day is the same day?"

It came out louder than she intended. At that exact moment, someone reached the end of a bawdy ballad. Felippa's words dropped like stones into the sudden silence. Magnus stared at her, his eyes holding a dangerous glint. A hundred heads turned. Felippa shriveled, wishing she could crawl under the table.

"That is," she stammered. "I meant to say..."

Nazafareen grimaced and stood abruptly; Felippa suspected

Darius had just stepped hard on his wife's foot. She swirled her goblet, then took a long draught and tossed the cup away. It clattered against the stone floor as if it were real and not a will o'the wisp.

"The scribe claims that every day is the same day," Nazafareen said loudly. "I fear she is right."

Magnus's gaze went even flatter, like two beetles sunk deep in the sockets.

"So I ask you," Nazafareen continued, "which day *is* that, my sweet hell-goats?"

The assembled company exchanged confused looks, fiery eyes dimming with uncertainty.

Nazafareen's sword rasped from the scabbard. Felippa flinched.

"A glorious day to be a fucking pirate!" she shouted, stabbing the blade down between Orm's spread legs. "All hail Magnus, greatest of the Cold Sea kings!"

Tables shook as the mortifexes roared approval and echoed the chant. "All hail, all hail!" Magnus basked in the adulation, his ire forgotten. Felippa felt a bubble of hysterical laughter rise in her throat. Nazafareen — moonlark she might be — had saved her once again.

Darius leaned over and whispered something in his wife's ear. She nodded, then turned to Magnus, who watched them with a bemused smile.

"Sire," Nazafareen said, "it's time we set sail and increase your riches. Do we have permission to go carousing in the Shadow Passage?"

Magnus stroked his bushy beard. He gave her an indulgent smile. "You do, my daughter."

He waved a hand glittering with rings. The feast dissolved as his court departed to prepare for their next raid. Across the room, Gerda gave Felippa a thin smile. The ancient fex had not forgotten her.

Felippa stared at the goblet Nazafareen had thrown away. It lay under the table. The plates and cups were real, she decided, borrowed from Magnus's treasure hoard. Which meant that the cutlery was likely real, too. She glanced around. No one was looking at her. Felippa slipped a knife up the sleeve of her shawl, gripping the hilt. It was better than nothing.

"Are you ready to retire?" Darius asked. "I will escort you to your chamber."

Felippa looked up. "Oh, er, yes."

They walked together through the winding corridors of the fortress, Felippa hurrying to keep pace. He seemed distracted. In another minute, they would reach her bedchamber. Felippa gathered her courage.

"Please, take me with you," she whispered, grasping his coat. "Let me hide in the hold. I'll do anything! Just don't leave me here alone."

He frowned. "Is it Magnus you fear?"

"No." Felippa thought quickly. She couldn't tell him about Justinian. "It's Gerda. She hates me."

Darius's eyes softened. "Gerda can be ill-tempered, but she would not dare defy Magnus's orders. You have nothing to fear from her."

"Please! I can't stay here. I can't!"

"Magnus would not permit you to leave," Darius said firmly. "But Orm and Skegg are remaining behind. They'll protect you. And when I return, we will seek the king's permission to allow you to..." He trailed off, eyes going foggy. She'd seen it before.

"Go home?" she prompted.

Darius blinked. "Yes. Just be patient."

Felippa wanted to believe him, but she knew his oaths were

meaningless. He often said the same things, over and over, having forgotten that he'd told her before. Within hours, Darius would not remember his promise.

He stopped outside her chamber door and laid a reassuring hand on her shoulder. "We shall return soon," he said.

She nodded, swallowing the knot in her throat as he disappeared into the maze of passages. She stepped into her cold, dim room and closed the door. How she wished it had a bolt on the inside! Then she moved to the window and watched as the flying lizards — abbadaxes — carried their riders down to the ship.

When the last was gone, she curled up beneath her blue cloak. After a moment's thought, she hid the stolen knife under the bed. Felippa wasn't sure what good it would do, but she felt better having it.

TWELVE

The bracing sea air whisked away the last of Cas's headache as he joined Tijah and Nathan on deck. Lo waited at the rail, dark hair flying. Thistle butted Cas's knee, and he leaned down to give the storm demon a scratch behind the ears.

"Any luck with the staff?" Lo asked, darting a glance at Nathan.

"None whatsoever." Cas peered down at a chain of rugged islands below. "Are we truly near Magnus's hideout? I thought it was still days away."

Lo started to reply, but an imperious voice cut her off.

"Do you see that spit of land, reaper?"

The black mirror was lashed to Baba-hor's former tooth. Jaskin Cazal's eye rolled around, magnified behind the glass. "It is called Imp's Claw Point. The mountain beyond is Glash's Tusk. That is where Magnus built his lair."

Cas squinted but couldn't make out many details. It was all a dark, misty blur. Yet his nerves thrummed. Felippa was down there; he knew in his heart that she was still alive.

"The defenses are formidable," Jaskin continued, "but we have the advantage of surprise." His laugh was a rusted crypt grating open. "Magnus does not expect a flying ship!"

"Plus their elemental power doesn't work behind the Veil," Cas said. "I traveled with a mortifex through the Dominion. He was nearly torn apart by Kaethe's hounds when the bridge we meant to cross turned out to be washed away."

Lo arched a brow. "Lucius?"

"Aye, on the journey to Prydwen. The gate was across a river. I had to carry him. If he could have used his power, believe me, he would have."

Tijah nodded. "It is true for living daēvas, too. They cannot touch the Nexus here."

"I can attest to that," Lo said. "And it's the only reason this mission isn't hopeless. At least they can't just toss us around like rag dolls."

"Or set us on fire," Nathan added helpfully.

"But those you call High Dead are still stronger and faster." Tijah eyed them each in turn. "So here's the plan. We fly over the keep, drop down on ropes, and sneak inside. Nathan will cloak our passage in shadows. Once we find all three hostages, we break the mirror and free Lord Bag o' Bones so he can send those fuckers to the far shore."

"I told you not to call me that, woman," the necromancer growled.

Cas regarded the parchment-skinned face floating in the black mirror. "Tell us how that works again. Sending them to the far shore, I mean."

"The spell requires the blood of both a reaper and a Shadow Soul," Jaskin said.

Tijah's gaze narrowed. "How much blood?"

"Yeah, better not be all of it," Lo said.

"A few drops will serve." Jaskin smiled thinly. Simian

fingers adjusted his lace-trimmed frock coat. "I shall tell you the rest when the appointed hour doth arrive."

"Not good enough," Tijah said. "You'll doth tell us now, Archmage Spookypants."

Cas snickered. Jaskin scowled, his dark eyes flashing in the mirror's depths. "By much laughter may you distinguish a fool," he muttered. "I will reveal the incantation at the necessary moment, but never fear, it is so simple even Nathan could manage it."

No one found this amusing. Jaskin's shoulders slumped. "I jest, but of course this quest is no laughing matter. I am eager to rectify the error I made in forging the Grand Menotte." Long, sharpened nails scratched at the inside of the mirror, making a rather horrendous sound. Then he pressed a hand to his breast. "By my troth, I will endeavor with all my might to thwart their malicious designs."

Cas didn't trust the old necromancer as far as he could fling him — how tempting that was! — but there was no going back now.

Nathan rifled through a leather satchel. "Hold this, would you?" he said absently.

Cas accepted the brown, withered thing with reluctance. It looked like a slice of dried apple. He sniffed it. It smelled of dry, peppery spices. "What is this?"

"Mummified ear of my third cousin, Belladonna Ouvrard," Nathan murmured, still digging through the voluminous bag. "Do not drop it, it is très valuable."

"Feck me." Cas made a face, holding the ear with two fingers.

"Ah, here it is! My pouch of spell dust." Nathan returned the ear to his satchel and sprinkled a pinch of ash over the mirror's surface. It shrank to an oval small enough to slip into a pocket. He tucked it away, then headed to his cabin to gather an arsenal of silver charms.

Cas decided to leave the staff behind. Too risky. His iron daggers would have to suffice — weapons he knew as well as the scars on his palms.

Lo took nothing at all. "If it's pointy," she said, "I'll probably impale myself before we reach the fortress. Fists and feet will do." She leapt up and performed a high kick, followed by a muffled grunt of pain.

"Did you just…" Cas trailed off.

"Kick myself in the face?" She gingerly touched her nose. "Yes. Yes, I did."

She sat down next to her cat, who rolled to one side and allowed her to rub his prodigious belly.

"I'm a lost cause," Lo said glumly. "You should just leave me behind."

"The stars may guide your voyage," Thistle growled, "but they do not decide the port. Navigate your own course through the storm."

She tweaked his tail. "Well, aren't you full of wise, pithy sayings today?"

"Here's another. *You cannot change the wind, but you can adjust your sails.*"

Lo snorted. "But you do change the wind! That is your essence."

"Me. Not you." His yellow eyes slid halfway shut. "Love or hate the hand that fate deals you — but play it as your own."

"You must stop," she said with mock severity. "The Moirai will send a lightning bolt for us both."

His paws curled; little white fangs winked. "We are not prisoners of fortune, but captains of our souls—"

"Oh, you horrid thing!" She turned to Cas. "Make him stop!"

Cas laughed. "I'm afraid he is not mine to command." He gave them both a bow. "But I wish you ... luck."

"Now we're doomed," she said. "Wait, I thought of one. *The road less traveled is made by those bold enough to walk it.*"

Thistle rolled to his feet and scraped one paw along the deck in the universal feline sign language for *shite*.

Lo gasped. "You didn't..."

Cas's laughter faded as he spotted Tijah. She was alone at the bow, gazing back the way they'd come. Cas joined her and they stood in companionable silence for a while.

"I wish Achaemenes were fighting at my side," she said at last. "His sword would have given us a great advantage."

Cas touched her shoulder. "He will find us."

"I know." She smiled. "I look forward to meeting your sister. And seeing Darius and Nazafareen again will lift my heart."

They both turned to Lo. She'd fallen silent, one hand resting on Thistle's fur, her gaze distant. Cas could only imagine what she was thinking. Eight years of searching, and the moment of truth was finally at hand.

Nathan returned to the deck. He wore a severely cut, long black coat that flared out at the waist, its pockets bulging. Rings of bone circled each finger. His gaze fixed on Glash's Tusk. "I will bring all my power to bear against them," he said quietly. "For my parents."

Cas's pulse picked up. Faint lights twinkled through the fog. Nathan sketched a sigil in the air, muttering an incantation. Wings of shadow folded around the ship, cloaking it in darkness.

Lo and Thistle took their place in the pilot house. The breeze shifted and they began to descend. Cas gripped the rail so tightly his hand ached. The other rested on his iron blades.

"Kavi watch over us," Tijah whispered.

The *Wind-Witch* plunged into the dense mist.

FELIPPA LAY IN HER BED, turning restlessly beneath the cloak. Would she ever escape this wretched place? Or would the days blur together until she forgot who she was, like poor Darius? Time had little meaning. Did the living grow old here, or were they doomed to some eternal half-life like the mortifexes? She imagined herself as ancient and wrinkled as Gerda, the two of them still at war, and allowed herself a small, bitter smile. At least she would have some entertainment.

That made her think of the feast. Where did the real food come from? The fish and tubers she ate each night, someone must gather and cook them. And the dreams Magnus spoke of collecting... Is that where Darius had gone? How did one collect a dream, anyway?

In the living world, *her* world, fexes couldn't stand running water, yet here they sailed about with no trouble. Obviously, it had something to do with the Cold Sea. Maybe it didn't make them sick because they belonged here. Yet they didn't really belong, did they? They were stuck, unable to go any further and reach the far shore.

That was the greatest mystery of all — what happened once you did. Was it a paradise, like some claimed, or did you get punished for all you did wrong? Would Ma be waiting for her when Felippa's time came?

Questions, always more questions — they swarmed through her head like moths around a lantern. Picking them apart gave Felippa comfort, an escape from the despair that threatened to overwhelm her. Magnus, in particular, vexed her. The way his form sometimes grew insubstantial, as if he were fading away into nothingness. Perhaps that would happen to them all, one day. Surely not even a talisman could anchor a soul forever.

But then, why weren't the others fading, too? Gerda was as solid as an old stump. Felippa knew this because Gerda often pinched and prodded her ribs, like that old witch who fattened children for—

Soft footsteps sounded in the corridor, startling her from her reverie. Felippa tensed, half-sitting up. Not Gerda. Her leather skirts always announced her approach with a telltale swish and creak. For one wild, hopeful moment, she imagined Darius returning for her...

The footsteps paused. The door swung wide.

Justinian stood in the doorway, a ravaged mess of scars and burned flesh. Felippa's heart stopped as he strode toward her. She cast about wildly, but there was nowhere to hide this time. Panic rising in her throat, she snatched up the knife from under her bed.

"Get away from me!" she cried.

He gave a mocking laugh. "Brave little mouse. What do you plan to do with that?"

"Come c-closer and you'll see," she stammered.

He was at her bedside in three strides. With a wild yell, she plunged it to the hilt into his thigh. Justinian plucked the blade out as if it were a splinter. Then he clamped an icy hand over her mouth.

"Hush," he said. "I won't harm you."

Felippa wrenched her head to the side and sank her teeth into his fingers. He grunted and released her. She scrambled away, chest heaving.

"Why don't you just die?" she spat.

His ruined mouth twisted. "I wish I could. If not for you, little one, I would be quit of this place. But your brother has the Grand Menotte."

Felippa edged back. "What would you do with it anyway?"

His eyes flared. "I would destroy it."

Despite her terror, Felippa's innate curiosity got the better of her. "How?"

"There is a very special woman here. A breaker of talismans. She has one hand."

He meant Nazafareen.

"I've met her," Felippa said. *Keep him distracted.* "And her husband, Darius. Did you bring them here?"

He slowly advanced. "I didn't need to. They were foolish enough to come hunting us. But they fell victim to their own trap, just as Magnus said they would."

The pieces clicked into place. Darius and Nazafareen were not Magnus's followers — not willingly, at least. They were his captives, just like her.

"You stole their memories!" Felippa exclaimed.

"Not I," he growled. "'Tis the magic of this place. Why does it not affect you?"

It had to be her silver necklace, but Felippa wasn't about to tell him that. "I don't know," she said. "Maybe because I'm still a child."

For a moment, Justinian looked confused. "Mayhaps," he conceded.

"I understand now why you want the Grand Menotte," she said, retreating as he pressed forward. "I didn't realize—"

"No, you didn't," he interrupted coldly. "You have no idea what it's like. I want to move on, but a piece of my soul is trapped. Until it is broken, I cannot rest."

Felippa met his furious gaze. "I didn't do this to you. Haven't you taken enough from me?"

Something shifted in Justinian's expression. "Do you think I like what I've become? The murders I've committed, the blood on my hands..." He shook his head. "I came to your farm that night fresh from the gate, hungry and needing to cross the river." His jaw worked. "I am sorry for what I did to you. But I had no choice."

The stone balustrade dug into her back. She could sense the void beyond, a drop of at least a hundred paces.

"If you're sorry, then let me go!" she begged. "I don't have the menotte. I can't help you."

A flicker of anguish crossed his face. For a moment, he looked almost human. Then it faded and his eyes were empty again. "But you can. If I drain you, it would improve my looks at least."

Felippa's fear heated to scalding anger. After all she'd been through, to end as nothing more than a quick meal. Why had Kaethe allowed her to live in the first place? No one would know what had become of her. Darius might ask when he came back, but in time he would forget, too.

Tears stung her eyes. There was one person who would never stop looking. Never forget her.

"My brother is coming for me," she hissed.

"I'm counting on it," Justinian said, his eyes blazing with a fevered light. "But he will come whether you are alive or not."

THIRTEEN

The *Wind-Witch* glided silently through the mist like a night-ghast. Cas settled into a relaxed but watchful pose Lo had seen before; cross-legged, back against a coil of rope, eyelids drooping at half-mast.

"Don't fall asleep on us," Tijah said.

Lo snorted. "Trust me, he's more alert than he looks."

Tijah drew a whetstone along her scimitar. "I sincerely hope so."

"There's something ahead," Nathan hissed.

Through the dense fog, a hulking shape emerged. A stone tower, ancient and foreboding. They were close now, too close.

"Aloft," Lo hissed.

The ship lurched upward and the tower slid past a handspan below. Thistle steered them into a silent circle above the roof.

Lo turned to Tijah, who was clearly far more experienced at this sort of thing. "Now?"

"Or never," she replied with a tight grin. "Everyone, clip into your harnesses. Cas, lower us down, then follow."

They buckled in and he turned the winch, lowering them one by one to a bridge below. Nathan fumbled the release and nearly plummeted into the mist, but Tijah's hand shot out and caught him. He flashed her a look of thanks. She scowled back, releasing him as soon as his feet touched stone.

Once Cas had joined them, slithering down a rope, Tijah led them at a swift crouch across the bridge into a deserted courtyard. She jerked her head at an open archway and they slipped through into a torchlit corridor. Once inside, Lo vented a breath. They huddled together.

"No guards?" Lo whispered. "Don't you think that's strange?"

"It's like Bag o' Bones said," Tijah whispered back. "They're cocky. They think no one can get to them." She held up a hand, head tilting. "Listen."

They all fell silent. From somewhere deeper within the citadel, the faint sound of music reached them. Someone was singing, poorly, to a lute. Tijah shrugged and took the lead again, which no one objected to.

Lo leaned toward Nathan. "You go next," she said. "It's thanks to you we stand a ghost of a chance. Ah, no pun intended."

He looked surprised, then pleased. "Thank you," he said, and stalked off behind Tijah, with Cas and Lo taking up the rear.

The corridor went on for a while, then dog-legged around a bend. The singing grew louder. Tijah slowed and held up a hand, beckoning them forward.

The hall opened into a rather tacky room that reeked of patchouli. Red velvet cushions littered the floor, nestled among water pipes trailing thin ribbons of fragrant smoke. Anatomically correct tapestries of frolicking nymphs and satyrs adorned the walls.

A dozen figures lounged on the thick carpet, some locked in passionate embraces, others arguing in low voices. None looked dead, but they weren't human either. A few were covered in fur, while the rest had fins and scales.

"What. The. Fuck?" Tijah said softly.

In the center of the room, perched on a stool, sat the singer. Her fingers plucked at the lute strings as she warbled an off-key rendition of *Lewyn's Lament*. Lo stared at the long brown hair, the stubborn chin. The dagged sleeve concealing her lack of a right hand...

Cas squinted and shook his head. "No, no, she doesn't play the lute." He turned to Lo, jaw tight. "Who do you see?"

"Shite," Lo muttered in disgust. "Not again. It's my mother."

Nathan frowned. "That's Lady Chaos."

"I see Lip," Cas said.

They exchanged aggravated glances. Something was very wrong here. Then a familiar figure strode across the room, stepping carefully over the garish cushions. Achaemenes, looking just as he had when they last saw him in Prydwen. A flop of sandy hair, white tunic, sword at his belt, gold cuff circling his wrist. The only difference Lo could see was that he'd lost his limp, and he looked decidedly rumpled.

Achaemenes halted, staring at Tijah. "Is it really you?"

Tijah's hand tightened on her scimitar hilt. "I could ask you the same thing."

"Well, I'm me." A trace of amusement curled one corner of his mouth. "But are you *you*?"

"You're making my head hurt." She reached out and poked his shoulder. Then she turned to the others. "You see Achaemenes, too?"

They all nodded. Tijah's gaze warmed and she pulled him

into a quick hug. "You smell right," she said with a laugh. "That part's tough to fake."

Achaemenes grinned back. "I've been seeing you everywhere. The singer looks like you, too."

"Same," she said. "I mean he looks like you. By Kavi, this is confusing." She leaned in. "Where are the mortifexes?"

"There are none here." He eyed her quizzically. "We're in Losthaven, on the Shadow Passage."

"Losthaven?" Tijah absorbed this news, her expression turning murderous.

Lo seized Achaemenes by his tunic. "So what you're telling us," she said slowly, "is that this is *not* Glash's Tusk."

He shook his head. "We're in a hostel owned by two-toed humbugs. Shapeshifters who appear as the person you most desire to see." He cleared his throat. "They run a brothel on the side. For, ah, obvious reasons. I arrived not long after this bunch. They took every damned room. I had to sleep on a balcony."

Lo's gaze swept the room, taking in the bickering couples. "The newlyweds from Dreamhaven. Bergmann said they left the day before we arrived at the Laughing Gull, remember?"

Cas gave a hollow laugh. "Feck me, it's the wedding party."

At that moment, the humbug singer approached, her form rippling with each step. "Welcome to the Velvet Embrace," she said with a smile. "We have no accommodations left, I'm afraid, but would you care for supper?"

No one replied for a long moment. Nathan stepped smoothly into the breach. "Thank you, mistress, we'll take a private dining room. Your best wine to start, and then a sampling of the local cuisine. Generous portions, please."

The humbug — who had now morphed into Lo's Papa, with his curly chestnut hair and twinkling blue eyes — gave a bow.

Cas turned to Nathan. "We're not eating here," he hissed.

"Why not? I'm starved." Nathan slid a corner of the mirror from his pocket. "Don't you want to find out what went wrong? We might as well do it in comfort."

Tijah shrugged. "I could eat. I mean, I'm pretty tired of those pickled tentacles, and that's all we have left."

"Fine," Lo growled. She smiled at the humbug. "Lead on!"

They followed the creature to an airy chamber overlooking the sea. It had a table with a snowy linen cloth and six place settings. A parade of humbugs brought in bottles of wine and trays of food. Crispy fish and a savory seaweed broth, with garlicky mussels and thin little pancakes.

"You roll up for dipping, like this," one demonstrated.

Lo wished they didn't all look like her parents. It was salt in the wound of her utter incompetence.

"Take Jaskin out," she said grimly after the humbugs had retreated and closed the door.

Nathan pulled the mirror from his pocket and propped it against a candelabra. The surface remained a dull black.

"He's hiding," Cas said.

"Get your scrawny ass out here," Tijah snapped, giving the mirror a shake and then tapping the glass.

"Stop that, woman! It sounds like a mallet breaking rocks!" Jaskin's face slowly materialized. He looked defensive. "It's not my fault. Verily, I was assured this was the rightful locale." He hesitated. "It *has* been a thousand years since I last set eyes upon Magnus's lair..."

Lo leaned across the table. "So we brought you along only because you said you could find him, but in fact you have no idea where we're going?"

"Er..." Jaskin squirmed under her glare. "Pray, allow me to behold the map once more—"

"By Innunu's rusty scythe, you're useless," Tijah growled,

rolling up a pancake with great force and thrusting it into her broth.

"Someone must know where to find Magnus," Cas ventured.

"I've already asked around," Achaemenes replied, "trying to find you. Everyone's heard of it, but no one knows where Glash's Tusk actually is. I've had a dozen different answers."

"What about Telasius?" Nathan swirled his wine, then took a sip. "Not terrible," he murmured.

"Who's Telasius?" Cas asked.

Glass shattered in the hostel's common room, followed by raised voices.

"The charlatan who blessed all those happy unions," Nathan said.

Tijah's spoon lowered. "Didn't Bergmann say he was a god?"

"Something like that." Nathan chuckled. "Remember, he introduced the Sun God and the Drowned Lady?"

"Now he's running from the latter, who wants his head on a platter!" Jaskin sang.

"Shut up." Tijah turned to the others. "That's perfect. We'll say we're hunters for Kaethe, which is partly true. That'll get him talking."

One of the humbugs — it was impossible to say which — bustled in again with a plate of sweets and asked if they were ready for the bill.

"Ah, yes," Cas said. "Just give us a moment."

When the creature was gone, he looked around the table. "How exactly are we paying for this meal?"

"It's barter," Tijah said. She glanced at the bill. "Highway fucking robbery. Do you know how much the mussels cost?"

Achaemenes downed the dregs of his wine. "I'm not giving up my sword. I suppose I could sacrifice my boots."

"Yours smell," Lo said, as Cas started working on his laces.

"They do not!"

"There is no need," Nathan interjected hastily. He sprinkled a pinch of ash over one of the dirty plates. In an eyeblink, a poniard dagger with a magnificent hilt of pearls and rubies sat in its place. He drove it into the table, point-down. "A fair trade, I'd say."

"I thought your transformations don't last," Lo said.

"They don't. But by the time the humbugs realize it, we'll be gone." Nathan grinned. "Give them a taste of their own medicine."

"Normally, I don't approve of thieves," Tijah said, "but I don't feel like walking out of here barefoot either." She cast Nathan a guarded look that seemed, Lo reflected, more tolerate-hate than hate-hate.

They returned to the common room, weaving between the cushions. Lo approached a pair of rusalki, their bluish-white skin and flowing green hair unmistakable.

"We're looking for Telasius. Have you seen him?" she asked.

The rusalka's solid white eyes were unreadable. "He wasss here, yesss. But now he isss gone."

Her head turned to a pair of male selkies whose argument was rapidly escalating.

"You sound like a grinding mill when you eat," snarled the first.

"And you snore like a hull grating on rocks," his husband retorted, turning his back.

"You can't just swim away from me every time we have a disagreement!"

"Well, I'm tired of you prioritizing the tides over our marriage. We agreed on a balance between land and sea, but lately, it's all sea! Every time you dive under the waves, I wonder if you're coming back."

Lo moved away from the squabbling couple, who were now throwing salted nuts at each other. The humbug servers mingled with the crowd, all of them wearing her mother's face. It made her want to throw nuts, too, but she couldn't get distracted now.

Lo grabbed a passing Nazafareen by the apron. "Where's Telasius?"

The humbug tried to pull away, eyes darting nervously. "I don't know anything about—"

Lo's grip tightened. "Tell me."

"He left," the humbug squeaked. "Just a few minutes ago."

"For where?"

"The harbor!"

Lo let go and the humbug scurried off.

"Let's move," Tijah said. "How the hell do we get out of here?"

Achaemenes led them to the door, which was on the opposite side of the hall where they'd come in. As it turned out, the hostel wasn't very big at all. When they stepped outside, the mist had cleared. Lo saw that it was not a fortress but a simple manor, and it sat atop a gentle hill, not the steep crag they'd imagined.

Had Tijah not arrested Nathan's fall, he would have walked away with no worse than a bruise or two.

Oh, you Bitches.

Lo cupped her hands and shouted up to the *Wind-Witch* circling above. Thistle's pointed ears poked over the rail. Lo gestured emphatically toward the harbor. Thistle steered the ship in a wide circle down to the water.

Achaemenes pointed at the shore. "There!"

A figure was scrambling into one of the flower-bedecked

wedding boats. They sprinted to the water's edge. Tijah waded to her knees, seized the boat's trailing bowline, and hauled it back.

Telasius let out a nervous laugh. "Did that lot up at the hostel send you? I never promised anyone eternal bliss, you know."

The deity of weddings was attractive, naturally, with warm brown skin, a hawkish nose, and wavy dark hair. He wore a simple belted robe and sandals. His teeth were perfect, his accent pleasant and musical. Yet there was something distinctly oily about him, too.

Lo decided that she wouldn't mind watching him squirm. She turned to Cas, their eyes met ... and she forgot what she was about to say. Love walloped her like a cudgel; she saw the same intense adoration reflected back.

Tijah and Achaemenes stared off in opposite directions, their backs stiff.

"Well, it was a pleasure meeting you all," Telasius said with a smirk, tugging the line free of Tijah's slack hand. "But adventure awaits—"

"Not so fast," Nathan said. "We have some questions for you."

"Ow!" Lo rubbed her arm, staring at Nathan reproachfully. "You didn't have to pinch so hard."

"Yes, I did."

Whatever spell Telasius exerted seemed to fade. Tijah spun back to him, clearly annoyed. "We come at Kaethe's bidding," she said, her voice low and menacing.

Cas blinked and shook his head. He held up his hand, revealing the nine-pointed star tattooed between thumb and forefinger. "She demands your return to the Dominion," he intoned. "At once."

Telasius shuddered. "Mercy, I beg you!"

"We *might* let you go on your merry way," Tijah said gruffly, "if you tell us where to find Magnus. He's wanted by Kaethe, too."

"Magnus?" Telasius wilted. He pressed a hand over his heart. "I swear on the Five, I know nothing. Only whispers of a remote and inaccessible fortress. But I've never laid eyes on it myself. When I see their ship appear, I do the sensible thing: run."

"Aren't you a god?" Lo wondered.

"Patron deity," Telasius corrected. "Of weddings. That's my entire domain. But why don't you ask one of the Five? They are true gods. Surely one must know where Magnus is to be found."

The Five. Lo turned as Thistle waddled up, his gray fur ruffled by the wind. She knelt down. "Can you call your mother, Anuketmatma? Ask for her aid?"

Telasius looked startled. Then he gave Thistle a deferential bow, which the cat ignored.

His chorus of demonic voices were all somber. "Baba-hor spoke true. Mother is too far away, sailing the living world with the Marakai daēvas. She would not hear me."

"Can you try anyway?"

"If you wish."

Thistle rolled to his back. His belly looked even larger and rounder than usual.

"Are you well?" she asked.

His ears flattened. "I grew peckish waiting for you. I may have eaten all the tentacles in the food barrels."

Despite everything, Lo huffed a laugh. She stroked his fur. "Oh, you poor dear."

Nathan cleared his throat. "What about the other Cold Sea gods?"

Telasius tapped his chin. "Hammu the great carp swims in

the vast northern waters, but finding him could take you months. The Isles of the Nehresi Water Horses are two weeks away, but they are notoriously hostile to strangers." He flashed a white smile. "Trample first, questions later."

Thistle hissed softly.

"Then there is faceless Sat-Bu," Telasius continued, "but I fear her whirlpool would turn your vessel to kindling. That leaves Khaf-hor. Your safest bet, without a doubt."

"The one whose son you robbed," Nathan muttered.

Lo lifted her chin. "Our need was greater than his."

Achaemenes's hazel eyes were grave. "Khaf-hor might not see it that way."

"How do we find him?" Cas asked.

"Khaf-hor's trench lies two days north of here," Telasius said. "When you spy the white cliffs of the Isle of Wraiths, you'll be above it."

Lo's brow knitted. "And how do we call him?"

Telasius picked up the bowline. "The trench plunges six hundred fathoms deep. You'll need to shout. Loudly." He sketched another bow, casting an anxious look at the hostel up the hill. "Now, if you'll excuse me."

He clambered into the flower-draped dinghy, fitted the oars to the locks, and rowed out past the *Wind-Witch*, which bobbed next to a rickety dock. Soon he was a pale smudge in the mist, whistling a jaunty tune.

"You are fools to go there." Jaskin's voice wafted from Nathan's pocket. "Khaf-hor has no kindness in him, nor mercy. Just permit me to examine the map again. I will guide you to the right place this time. By my troth!"

Tijah laughed long and hard. "Right. I'd rather take my chances at the trench. Who's with me?"

They all raised their hands.

"I can't see!" Jaskin's voice quavered. "What's happening?"

"You'll have to sail by water," Thistle rasped. "I'm in no state to summon wind for flight." He crawled over to Nathan and hacked a pinkish lump onto his obviously expensive suede shoes.

Nathan let out a stream of curses and tried to scrub them clean with sand.

"That's right, get it all up," Lo said, giving Thistle a sympathetic pat. She gazed at the horizon, where the Cold Sea vanished into a pearly haze. Toward Khaf-hor's trench and then... A reckoning long overdue.

Shouts rang out from behind them. Lo looked over one shoulder to see her father pelting down the road, waving a piece of paper.

"Run!" Cas yelled.

FOURTEEN

The stone balustrade dug into Felippa's back, her scalp tingling at the sheer drop behind. Gusts of wind tugged at her braid as she gazed up at Justinian. His eyes were black holes with pricks of flame at the center. Whatever small part of the man he'd been was gone again.

So this was it. Well, she was already halfway across the Cold Sea. At least she wouldn't have far to go.

Lacking any other options, she kicked him in the shin. He snarled and grabbed her by the throat. Her air cut off, his terrible face blurring. Then he hissed, yanking his hand back as if burned.

The silver necklace. Once again, it had saved her. Felippa dodged around him and bolted for the hallway. Her heart banged against her ribs, the guttering torchlight making the shadows seem to grasp for her.

She careened around a corner and slammed into someone, nearly falling on her rump. Icy fingers snagged Felippa's arm. Panting, she looked up into Gerda's sour face.

"Where are you running off to in a such a hurry, girl?" the old fex demanded.

"Let go of me!" Felippa twisted and writhed. "Let go!"

The sound of pounding footsteps made her pulse spike even higher. Justinian stalked towards them, his gait slowing now that his prey was in sight.

An animal moan tore from somewhere deep inside her. She tried again to break free, but Gerda's grip was unyielding.

"Give her to me," Justinian growled.

Gerda gaped at him in surprise for a moment. Then she drew herself up and sniffed disdainfully. "The brat might have carried your message, but she does not belong to you. She is Magnus's scribe and under our king's protection."

Felippa's struggles ceased. Of everyone in the keep, Gerda was the very last person she expected to stand up for her.

"Listen, old woman," Justinian said, "I don't care what she told—"

He blinked as Gerda stepped up, wagging a gnarled finger under his nose.

"Don't take that tone with me, you insolent pup," she scolded. "You'll mind your tongue when addressing an elder widow of the Kafsnjór clan. Did no one ever teach you manners? Why, in my day..."

Her rant went on for several minutes. Justinian stared at her, momentarily robbed of speech. But under Gerda's withering barrage, the monster seemed to slowly seep out of him, replaced by chagrin.

Finally, he held up his hands in surrender. "Peace, Widow Kafsnjór. I yield. We shall bring the girl to Magnus together — unharmed."

A minor reprieve, yet cold dread trickled up Felippa's spine. Her lies would soon be laid bare. And there could be no escape from that.

Hunching her shoulders, she let them lead her across the long, narrow bridge to the audience chamber. Gerda released her, and Felippa rubbed her arm, watching Magnus warily.

As always, the King of the Cold Sea was sitting on his throne of stolen icons. His eyes crinkled into a welcoming smile. "Justinian! You have returned at last." Magnus took in the state of his face. "A rough journey, I see. But you bring me the Grand Menotte, I trust?"

Justinian's jaw clenched. "No, sire. I briefly had it in my grasp, but it was taken from me. By a Quietus."

Magnus's jovial expression darkened. "What?"

"The man had a vial of Kaethe's Tears. He blinded me and banished both the girl and myself through a nine-pointed star."

Justinian did not meet Felippa's eye. They both knew that she had been the one to push him into the star and speak the words of banishing. But he could not bear to admit a mere slip of a girl had bested him.

"I am late because the Quietus summoned me back to the Duc's bedchamber and left me trapped there," Justinian continued tersely. "I finally escaped but was forced to travel through a gate."

"This is a disaster!" Magnus's face purpled with fury, his jowls wobbling.

"Sire, I am certain this Quietus has the Grand Menotte. I stopped in Dreamhaven and they told me he is on his way here—"

Felippa's heart leapt. Cas was coming for her! She fought to keep the elation from her face.

"Dreamhaven?" Magnus cut in sharply. "Who did you speak to?"

"The humbug Bergmann at the Laughing Gull. And some creature called Baba-hor." Justinian shifted uneasily under

Magnus's piercing glare. "They did not actually see the Grand Menotte, but it must be aboard the Quietus's ship."

"So all he must do is put it on, and we will be his slaves," Magnus ground out.

"He has not done so yet, sire. I think he plans to trade it for his sister." Justinian's burning gaze fell on Felippa.

"So we are worse off than before you left!" Magnus roared.

"I had no idea he was a Quietus. He seemed a simple country boy." Justinian's fists clenched. "But no matter; he either has it, or he knows where it is. He will come for the girl. We need only wait."

Magnus slammed his fist on the arm of his throne. "You'd better be right," he snapped. He whirled on Gerda and jabbed a finger at her. "You will take charge of her. See she causes no more trouble."

Gerda's cloudy eyes widened in disbelief. "Me? I do not want the knock-kneed little imp!"

"And I don't care what you want!" Magnus roared, his braids quivering with rage. "You will take her to your chamber and watch her like she's your own suckling babe. If she escapes, it will be worth your hide!"

Felippa's heart sank. Being trapped with the spiteful old crone sounded almost as bad as being given to Justinian.

Almost.

Magnus turned back to Justinian, dismissing the women with a flick of his hand. "Tell me every detail of what happened."

Felippa studied the pair, her gaze arrested by something odd — something she couldn't quite put her finger on. There was a subtle difference between them... Subtle but important.

She nearly had it when Gerda's claw clamped around her arm in exactly the same sore place she'd gripped it before. Then her new jailer was hauling her toward the narrow bridge.

"You'd best behave yourself," Gerda muttered. "Not a word, you hear? Or I'll feed you to the dukka!"

Felippa bit back a tart reply. Provoking the old bat would only make things worse. Yet as Gerda dragged her through the cold, twisting corridors, a flicker of hope sparked.

Cas was coming.

She just had to survive long enough for him to get here.

FIFTEEN

Enrigo Redvayne and the Damiata Aldonza Beatriu do Santillan strolled beneath a long colonnade in the secluded grounds of the Alcazar. Fluted marble columns rose to either side, shielding the pair from the unrelenting drizzle. Vellio was up in the mountains, where nine days of ten were overcast and cool.

Lucius flanked them at a distance. The damp soaked his copper hair, but he relished the chance to walk beneath the sky without hiding his face under a hood. These days, he clung to such small gifts.

High brick walls enclosed the orchard, boughs heavy with golden fruit. Lucius could no longer remember the crisp sweetness of a pear on his tongue, but he could still appreciate their beauty against the dreary gray sky.

Two nuns of Kaethe followed on an adjacent path, keeping watch over the young Damiata. The elder sister gazed straight ahead, her stern face impassive. But the younger, a girl barely out of maidenhood, blushed crimson each time her gaze flitted to Lucius.

He cut an imposing figure in a long cloak of blue woad over a crimson doublet and snug trousers tucked into black boots. A gold clasp fashioned in the phoenix of House Redvayne gleamed at his throat, and a bonewood sword hung at his hip. Playing the part of Orlaith's fearsome mortifex came naturally after so many centuries. Lucius smiled and the young nun quickly averted her eyes.

Enrigo and Beatriu's words would be inaudible to the nuns, but Lucius heard every syllable as if the children walked beside him. He listened with half an ear to their awkward conversation.

"You look beautiful today, my lady," Enrigo told her stiffly.

The boy was trying his best to play the gallant. His dark blond hair was neatly combed, and he had a stocky build that might one day be impressive. But at twelve years old, the young Duc-in-waiting was still firmly tied to his mother's apron-strings.

"You are too gracious, my lord," Beatriu replied in her high, piping voice.

The Damiata's skirts dragged several paces behind her, the ruffed neck of her embroidered gown crusted with seed pearls and violet gems. The whole ensemble looked so heavy it was a wonder she managed to walk at all.

"Does the sun never shine here?" Enrigo gave a half-hearted laugh.

"Rarely, my lord," she replied. "That is why the court always passes the summer at the Alcazar. Conbelin is frightfully hot and humid this time of year."

"The Galatian capital!" Enrigo seized this new topic with desperate enthusiasm. "My tutor taught me all about it. Your primary exports are tin, figs, and cod oil."

This failed to elicit a smile, or any reaction at all. Her doll-like features seemed painted on porcelain. "You are learned indeed, my lord."

Lucius couldn't tell if Beatriu's remark was sarcastic; apparently, Enrigo couldn't either. A painful silence stretched between the pair, filled only by the patter of rain on leaves. Beatriu gazed into the middle distance, a bored expression on her face. Well, the Damiata was only eleven. No doubt she would rather be off playing with her dolls.

They were nearing the end of the colonnade. Enrigo cleared his throat, shoulders squaring.

Here it comes.

"I had hoped to speak with you about a matter of grave importance to both our duchies, my lady." The words left him in a nervous rush.

Beatriu arched a brow. "You make it sound like we are going to war."

"That is not my intention." Enrigo's face reddened. He drew a deep breath. "I only hoped to ask if you have had adequate time to consider the terms of my—"

"Proposal," Beatriu cut in. She gave him a beseeching look that seemed a bit too practiced for her tender age. "We will speak of that later, I promise." Her stormy eyes slid to Lucius. "But first, tell me about your mortifex."

Lucius kept his face impassive, as though he hadn't heard, but he strained to catch every word.

"Lucius Bittencourt is a loyal retainer." Enrigo glanced over. "He saved my life only a few weeks past."

"I heard rumors of some outrage committed against your house." Beatriu's voice sank to a whisper. "What exactly happened?"

Enrigo shifted, looking uncomfortable. "It is not a tale for a lady."

She laid a hand on the sleeve of his doublet, her white

fingers bunching the fabric. A flicker of impatience crossed her face before it smoothed back to innocence. "You know my own history. I have seen things that would turn your hair from gold to white in an instant. You can confide in me, my lord."

Enrigo's shoulders relaxed. The flowery speech Orlaith had forced him to practice before the mirror was chucked out the window. Lucius covered a grin. The boy seemed thrilled at a reprieve from alliances and politics.

"I was kidnapped from my bed by wraiths," he whispered back, clearly relishing the tale now that it was all over. "They carried me across the Boundary to the Courtenays' seat at Mystral."

Beatriu's eyes widened, sparking with genuine interest for the first time. "They held you for ransom?"

"No, they released me with no bounty paid. I am certain the Courtenays had nothing to do with it."

"Then who was the scoundrel behind this vile crime?" Beatriu asked.

"Nathan Ouvrard."

"The Duc of Vendagni! I have heard many tales about him, all of them dastardly. You must have been terrified."

"Not for a moment, my lady." A swagger entered Enrigo's walk as he warmed to the story. "I knew I would manage to escape my captors. I had faith in my own abilities."

Lucius suppressed a snort. He vividly remembered Enrigo squirming in the sack, red-faced and teary-eyed.

"You are very brave," Beatriu said. "To have bested them on your own."

"Well, I did have help," he admitted. "Lucius came after me, and it was he who brought me home again."

And there, Lucius thought, is the difference between you and your deceitful, cold-blooded mother.

"It must be nice to have such a devoted protector," Beatriu remarked, a wistful note in her voice.

Enrigo patted her hand where it rested on his arm. "I will always watch over you, my lady."

The pair reached the end of the covered colonnade. Lucius stopped walking, as did the nuns. He pretended to survey the orchard, but he could feel Beatriu's cool gray eyes boring into him.

"Why do you not claim the menotte, my lord?" she asked.

Lucius's head turned sharply.

Enrigo looked befuddled by the sudden change of topic. "Today?"

She nodded, ringlets bouncing. "I would be much inclined to wed a man who already commands such a formidable servant."

Enrigo flushed. The words "man" and "wed" were a heady combination.

"I will inherit the menotte when I come of age—" he began.

Beatriu cut him off with an impatient wave. "But you are nearly thirteen now. Surely your mother would not begrudge you an early gift."

Enrigo opened his mouth, then closed it again. Lucius could practically see the gears turning in the boy's head as he grappled with this new possibility.

Clever girl. Clever and dangerous. Still, Lucius would much prefer Enrigo to command him. Orlaith was increasingly unhinged, and Lucius feared what she might make him do.

"It is tradition in Clovis—" Enrigo stammered, but Beatriu interrupted him again.

"We must make new traditions, my lord Redvayne." Her gaze sliced to the nuns, who watched from a distance. "I am weary of being told what to do. And forgive my candor, but what if your mother changes her mind once we are wed? What if she refuses to relinquish the menotte?"

Enrigo looked scandalized. "She would never do such a thing. It would violate every law and custom!"

Beatriu's tone cooled a few degrees. "Nonetheless, promises can be broken. We must be certain." She twined her arm in his again. "Once you are bound to Lucius, I will gladly join our duchies."

Enrigo bit his lip. Lucius could see the war playing out on his face — the desire to please Beatriu battling with his ingrained obedience to Orlaith. Finally, he squared his shoulders.

"I will speak to Mother," he promised.

The pair turned back, retracing their steps along the colonnade. As they passed Lucius, he bowed deeply to the Damiata. She smiled at him, pearly teeth flashing. It was the first genuine smile he had seen her give anyone.

When they reached the Alcazar, a castle of warm sandstone with many pointed turrets, Beatriu was whisked away by the nuns. Lucius fell into step with Enrigo, escorting him back to their chambers. The suite occupied a corridor of the north wing, with sweeping views of the distant Sturmborg Mountains.

As they entered the sitting room, a black and white blur came barreling across the rug. Jak, Enrigo's terrier. The dog danced around his master's legs, barking madly, until Enrigo picked him up and accepted a sloppy lick on the nose. The boy laughed, looking relieved to be himself again.

The room held ancient, dark furniture, faded tapestries lining the walls. One depicted the battle of Hellgate, where east and west had clashed at the northern edge of the Boundary. Robert Redvayne, Enrigo's father, had taken a mortal wound that day, alongside scores of soldiers from both Clovis and

Galatia. Lucius wondered if the choice of chambers was a deliberate provocation, or a reminder that the Do Santillans and Redvaynes had fought and died as allies.

Robert's widow sat at a writing desk in the corner, her head bent over a sheaf of parchment. Orlaith wore her customary black bombazine gown, laced tight to the throat, with a deep plum lace mantilla covering her golden hair in deference to Galatian fashion. At the sound of their entrance, she looked up, a bright smile already in place.

"And how fares your bride-to-be?" she asked, setting down her quill.

Enrigo dropped into a chair by the hearth, scratching Jak behind the ears. "We are not betrothed yet, Mother."

Orlaith's smile was fixed, but her blue eyes cooled a fraction. "Why not? We discussed exactly what you were to tell her."

"I did," Enrigo replied, not meeting his mother's eyes. "But it is a ... delicate negotiation."

Orlaith came around the desk, skirts swishing. "What could be so delicate about it? Her only other suitor is dead."

"We don't know that for a fact," Lucius pointed out. "Vazsoly Marcel might still be alive and in hiding."

Orlaith eyed him sourly. She was still upset about his numerous failures in Prydwen. "Deposed, then. Either way, his margraves have failed to restore order." Another pointed glare at Lucius, as if this were *his* fault. "It's more important than ever that Galatia be a bulwark against the rebellion in the far west. We must not allow the chaos to spread..."

Lucius let the familiar rant wash over him, his attention drifting to the desk. Stacks of cream-colored envelopes were neatly arranged, addressed in Orlaith's looping script to various cousins and lesser houses of the Clovis nobility. So she was already preparing to send out wedding invitations.

"...let this chance slip through our fingers." Orlaith fixed Enrigo with a stern look. "I'm not suggesting you pressure her, but nor can we wait forever on a child's whims. You must take a firm hand with her, Enrigo."

The boy glanced at Lucius, a mute plea in his eyes, then back at his mother. "May we speak privately?"

Her brows arched. After a long moment, she turned to Lucius. "You may carry out the errand we discussed."

Lucius bowed, hand to his chest. "I will comb the silk market for the finest fabrics, Your Grace."

"Bring back samples for the seamstress. Our house colors, of course, red and gold," Orlaith said. "I will foreswear the dark hues of mourning for the occasion. I must have a dress adequate for your nuptials, Enrigo. It will be a great affair of state."

Enrigo nodded distractedly. He looked like he might throw up at any moment. So he meant to keep his word to Beatriu and ask for the cuff now. Lucius wished him luck.

He bowed and took his leave of them both, striding through the humid corridors of the Alcazar. His thoughts turned to the conversation he'd had with Orlaith just that morning.

Now that Enrigo was on the cusp of inheriting the menotte, her self-assurance was slipping. For the first time, Lucius had detected a hint of uncertainty beneath her imperious facade.

"I only want Enrigo to be happy. He is everything to me. You must know it was for the good of the duchy. To avenge Robert's death. Nathan swore he wouldn't be harmed." A hint of panic entered her blue eyes. "Enrigo must never know the truth. Promise me! Swear it, Lucius!"

He had vowed to keep her secret. What choice did he have?

He knew her remorse was genuine because he could sense her emotions.

Now he stepped out into the rain-washed courtyard, breathing in petrichor and damp stone. The sky hung low and gray, mirroring his mood. Fat droplets pattered against the leaves of the holm oaks, their reddish-brown acorns the only spot of color.

Beyond the gates of the Alcazar, Vellio's narrow lanes twisted up the mountainside, barely wide enough for a single horse and cart. A dog resting on a baker's windowsill roused itself as he passed, baring yellowed teeth. Some animals instinctively feared him. Others, like Jak, didn't seem to mind his presence.

The people took little notice of him at all, too preoccupied with their own business. Farmers in rough homespun guided laden carts through the steep streets, wheels clacking on cobblestones. Women swathed in black haggled energetically over late summer produce. The scents of baking bread, rotting garbage, and wet stone permeated the air.

Lucius wove through the streets with preternatural grace, his dark cloak billowing. He couldn't help but appreciate the town's rustic charm, a world away from the teeming port city of Conbelin far to the south. Flower boxes beneath mullioned windows overflowed with red geraniums. Vines of wisteria and clematis clung to the stone walls, their purple and white blooms sodden with rain.

Traffic picked up as he neared the Convent of Kaethe. Nuns moved along in their plain white robes, their heads shaved and nine-pointed stars swinging from their rope belts. The sisters took no vow of silence, chattering amongst themselves.

The domed shrine to Kaethe loomed ahead, its white marble walls covered in climbing roses of deepest maroon.

They were a cultivar exclusive to the region, with petals soft as velvet and dark as blood. Kaethe had many names, but in Galatia, she was most often called the Black Rose.

Vendors hawked their wares on the temple steps, crying out in Galatian: "Charms against the evil eye! Wards to protect against wraiths and night-gaunts! Talismans blessed by the Sisters of Kaethe!"

There were no holy figurines or icons to be seen. The Galatians considered it blasphemy to depict the death-goddess in human form. Only variations of her nine-pointed star sigil were carved above doorways and into lintels. Lucius passed the steps to Kaethe's shrine. The interior was open to all petitioners, but the cloistered buildings beyond housed only women. No man could pass those gates, not even a servant of death.

Lucius left the temple behind, striding through the bustling silk market. Merchants called out aggressively from all sides, holding up bolts of shimmering fabric in the deep blues and purples popular with the wealthy.

"Finest silk from Tjanjin, my lord!" one cried. "Feel the quality! Smoother than a maiden's..." He paused to give a lecherous wink. "...cheek!"

Lucius ignored their entreaties. Gradually, the market stalls grew shabbier, the streets narrower and strewn with filth. This was the seamy underbelly of Vellio, where cutpurses and ruffians plied their trade. Beggars huddled in doorways, hands outstretched. From shadowed alleys came the stench of piss and worse.

Lucius pressed on. In his centuries of carrying out dirty work for various masters, he'd learned to sniff out the shadow brokers, the ones who traded in secrets. Several hours and a dozen carefully coded conversations later, Lucius found himself sitting across from a woman in the parlor of a once-grand townhouse. The walls were peeling and moths had feasted on the velvet curtains, but the furniture was well-made, relics of a more prosperous past.

The lady's maid — *former* lady's maid, she'd stressed — of House Do Santillan perched on the edge of her seat, hands twisting anxiously in her lap.

Lucius smiled, careful not to show too many teeth. "You have nothing to fear from me," he reassured her. "I only want the truth about your former mistress."

For this was the true errand Orlaith had sent him on. An answer to a simple question: Was Enrigo's intended a victim or a monster?

Sixteen

The room was stuffy and dim, drapes drawn against the drumming rain. Lucius's informant had taken care to place her own chair in the deepest shadows, leaving the candles unlit. She didn't realize that his catlike gaze discerned every detail of her fine-boned face, the dark smudges beneath her eyes and threads of white in her hair.

Her cultured accent suggested she had been a lady's maid, as she claimed, but he would need more proof than that.

"Milord, I cannot give you my name." The woman glanced past his shoulder, fidgeting with her worn shawl. "I fear what might befall me if it were known I spoke to you."

"What if I double the sum we agreed on?" he asked.

She swallowed hard, then shook her head. "My lord, I cannot take the risk."

Was she bluffing? If so, the woman was a fine actress.

"Triple," Lucius said.

Her hands knotted in her skirts. "Please, do not press me on this," she replied coldly. "Go, then. You needn't pay me anything. I am sorry I wasted your time."

Her fear was genuine, at least. Lucius leaned forward. "I understand your trepidation. But I must ask you to describe the Damiata's audience chamber. It would prove you have been there."

She answered at once, with no hesitation. "Her throne is crafted from the skulls of her Do Santillan ancestors, a dedication to Kaethe. I suppose everyone knows that. There are tapestries. I never looked at them closely, but I do remember one of men in helms carrying long spears. They've hunted a lion, spilled its blood. I never liked it."

So she spoke true. Lucius nodded. "How is it you left the Damiata's service?"

"I feigned illness, milord. In truth, I could no longer bear to work there. The fear of that child, it haunted my every step." She pulled the shawl tighter, as if it could shield her.

Lucius cut straight to the heart of the matter. "Tell me, how did the Damiata's brothers and sisters die?"

There were five. None had lasted two years past their parents' demise.

The woman's fingers twisted the frayed edge of her shawl. "The eldest, Lucon, was the first. Barely a month after taking the throne, he fell from the balcony of the east tower." Her voice dropped to a whisper. "The guards below heard raised voices. A heated argument. But that was common for the family. By the time they found Lucon's body, whoever else was there had gone."

Lucius absorbed this in silence. The maid continued, her tone bleak. "Two months later, Onorato, the next eldest, was discovered in the river. Drowned, they said, after a night of carousing in the taverns."

"And so the title passed to Tristan, the third son?"

She nodded. "Yes, milord. He lasted half a year before he was stabbed while walking in the palace orchard."

Lucius leaned forward. "Where in the orchard, exactly?"

"The covered colonnade, milord."

The same place where Beatriu had strolled with Enrigo mere hours ago.

"Someone overpowered him?" Lucius asked.

"I heard from a guardsman that the body reeked of wine. Drugged, perhaps. Tristan would not have put up much of a fight in that state."

"How did the killer escape? Surely Tristan had guards after the earlier deaths."

A bitter laugh escaped her. "Oh, the guards swore they saw nothing. But their silence must have been bought." She hesitated, then added, "Tristan was fond of Beatriu, milord. He called her Scarpetta. It means 'little slipper.'"

Lucius stared at her, his eyes narrowing. "You are saying a ten-year-old girl crept up on a healthy young man and stabbed him to death?"

The maid's jaw set. "I am not saying that." A pause. "But it would not be impossible."

"Hmm." Lucius tapped a finger against his chin. A clever child, raised in this nest of vipers, learning to strike first or be struck down. Perhaps it wasn't so far-fetched. "What about the sisters, Gentil and Ursola?"

"Gentil burned to death the following year. The nuns said a tipped candle set the room ablaze. She was overcome by smoke before she could escape, they claimed."

"Do you believe that?"

The maid met his gaze squarely. "Do you, milord?" Her voice hardened. "I think Gentil was poisoned in her bed. And then her body was burned to conceal the evidence."

Lucius leaned back. If the woman's accusations were true... He couldn't decide if he should be impressed or appalled. Perhaps both.

"That leaves Ursola," Lucius prompted.

The former maid shuddered. "The most ghastly one of all," she whispered. "She was only two years older than Beatriu."

She paused to take a sip of water, her hand trembling. "They were both sequestered in the convent together. For their own protection, you understand."

She set the cup down. "I heard whispers that Beatriu..." A hard swallow. "That she summoned a demon. They say Ursola was torn to pieces. Ripped apart by something ... not of this world."

Lucius couldn't keep the skepticism from his voice. "Now you claim Beatriu is a necromancer?"

The maid shook her head. "I do not know, milord. But I never saw Her Grace shed a single tear for any of them. It wasn't natural." She looked at him meaningfully. "And once she ascended the throne, it all stopped. She is the last of the line."

"That is your evidence?" Lucius asked flatly. "That she survived?"

The woman lifted her chin. "It is what I know. I never promised you more." She leaned forward, her voice an urgent hiss. "But I left the palace service as soon as I heard she would be raised up. Mark my words, milord. You will see." Her eyes glittered in the dimness. "There is something wrong with that girl."

Lucius sat back, his mind awhirl. A string of mysterious deaths, a child ascending to the throne, whispers of demons and unnatural powers. And at the center of it all, Beatriu.

He counted out the promised coins and stacked them on the table. The woman scooped them up quickly, as if afraid he might change his mind, and retreated up a flight of stairs.

Lucius stepped out into the rain-slick streets, raising his hood against the downpour. As he made his way back to the

Alcazar, he mulled over the maid's tale. Lies? Exaggerations? Or ugly truths long buried?

Lost in thought, he almost didn't notice the small procession entering the convent of Kaethe as he passed. A tall sister with a shaved head, accompanied by two girls with light hair roughly cut in the style of novitiates. They all looked thin and travel-weary, carrying small bundles. Lucius wasn't good at guessing mortal ages, but one girl was in her teens, the other around Beatriu's size.

Something about the nun's proud, almost arrogant bearing made Lucius look closer. With a jolt, he realized she closely resembled Morgen, Duc Marcel's necromancer.

He slowed his steps, staring, but the sister and her young charges disappeared into the convent. Men were not permitted inside on pain of exile. There would be no pursuing them.

Unease prickled the back of his neck. First, whispers of demons and a murderous young queen. Then a nun who was the spitting image of the most dangerous necromancer he'd ever met.

Of course, he might be mistaken. What could have drawn Morgen to Galatia? Perhaps the maid's grim tale had him jumping at shadows.

He continued on, the towers of the palace just ahead. He had no proof of anything yet. Only the word of a frightened servant and a glimpse of a mysterious nun. He resolved to keep the latter to himself for now. See what other secrets he could uncover before riling Orlaith with his suspicions.

Guards in silver and black livery made way as Lucius jogged up the steps of the Alcazar, the maid's words ringing in his ears. *You will see. There is something wrong with that girl.*

"NOT A WORD," Morgen hissed at the girls as they passed through the gates of the convent. "Keep your eyes down and your lips sealed."

Dravka looked surly, as usual. Her sister Jaelle gave a meek nod.

"What if they ask us questions?" Dravka hissed back.

"I will answer them," Morgen said firmly. "You are mute. Do not forget it." She stopped walking. "Or I will turn your tongues to jelly."

Dravka fell silent, but her blue eyes smoldered. Unlike Jaelle, who was quiet and obedient, Dravka had the Marcel temper. She'd struggled to play a convincing novice on the road from Prydwen; her manner was impudent, her gaze far too direct. Morgen was starting to understand why the nuns there had thrown the Marcel girls to an angry mob. *Nothing but trouble*, the abbess had said — clearly meaning Dravka.

The thick, heady scent of black roses filled Morgen's nose as they crossed a cloister and entered the domed temple to Kaethe. She sketched a nine-pointed star, elbowing the girls to do the same. Vellio had one of the oldest shrines to the Lady in all of Aveline. Stone walls twelve paces thick, ventilated only by small barred embrasures, a testament to the centuries of conflict with the Sons of Bel.

Candles flickered in niches carved into the walls, casting a warm light on the enormous nine-pointed star that occupied the center of the circular temple. It was not inlaid with tile or bone, but carved into the marble floor, leaving grooves three inches deep. Even Morgen felt a slight chill looking at them. In the old days, the nuns had carried out blood rituals here that made her own spells seem tame by comparison.

She cast a quick warning glance at the girls as a moon-faced sister in white approached. "You are newcomers," she said with a smile.

"From Cavet," Morgen said, softening the harsh accent that marked her as a native of the Western Isles. "Refugees."

"Ah." The nun looked sympathetic. "We've heard about the troubles in the west, of course. Come, we will find a place for you."

They left the temple and entered a connected building with dormitories and administrative offices. Morgen paused as they passed the convent's library; she was eager to begin her research into the Grand Menotte. But the nun continued, leading them to a comfortably furnished study with a view of the Alcazar.

The abbess, a tiny, wizened woman with a face like a dried mushroom, rose from her chair. Her brown eyes were sharp and assessing. "Welcome, sisters, I am Mother Pedrosa," she said briskly. "Your names?"

"I am Sister Mara," Morgen said. "These are my charges, Daveen and Jora. Orphans. The poor things haven't spoken a word since the attack."

Dravka and Jaelle kept their eyes downcast, though a muscle ticked in Dravka's jaw.

"Attack?" The abbess's brow furrowed. "On the road?"

Morgen shook her head, injecting a quaver into her voice. "You have not heard, then? It was terrible. A mob came looking for Duc Marcel. When the abbess said he wasn't there, they sacked the convent. We barely escaped with our lives."

It was partly true, at least. Morgen left out the part where she'd sent a dozen of them straight to Kaethe.

The abbess looked troubled. "I knew it was bad there, but I did not realize... Well, you are safe now."

She clasped Morgen's hands, her own roughened by the harsh quicksilver decoction the nuns used to wash the dead. Morgen forced herself not to recoil at the touch.

"Thank you, Mother Pedrosa," she murmured. "We are grateful for your kindness."

As the abbess turned to lead them to their new quarters, Morgen caught Dravka's eye. A mutinous flicker, quickly masked. The girl did not want to be here, a fact she had made quite clear. When Vazsoly took the throne, he'd exiled his sisters to the nearby convent, where they lived for a year. Jaelle was more pliable, but Dravka despised the nuns of Kaethe almost as much as she hated her brother. Morgen regretted bringing the girls along, but they had that much in common at least.

The abbess led them up several flights of worn stone steps to the top floor of the dormitory. "I'm afraid we're rather full at present," she said over her shoulder, stopping before a heavy wooden door. "You can share a single room for now. I'll send a novice with food and fresh robes."

Morgen inclined her head. "You are most kind, Mother Pedrosa."

"Yes, well." The abbess cleared her throat. "I'll leave you to settle in. We'll speak more on the morrow about your duties." She paused. "But I am glad to have extra hands. There's been a rash of risen in the city. If you have experience preparing corpses for safe burial, as I imagine you must, it would be a great help."

"Of course," Morgen said, "thank you, Mother."

The instant the door closed, Dravka rounded on her. "I hate it here already!" Her voice was low but fierce. "Why must we stay?"

"Because you have nowhere else to go." Morgen dropped her travel bag on one of the cots. "Be grateful that the nuns will keep you safe."

Dravka stared at her. "*Grateful?* To those stuffy old bitches? We'll run away!"

"You will *not* run away," Morgen replied. "That might raise questions I do not care to answer."

The girl's brow lowered. "I *won't* be a nun of Kaethe," she snarled. "I would rather kill myself!"

Was I so melodramatic at seventeen? Morgen wondered. Her own mother had died that year, of the black bile that began with a lump in her armpit. Morgen was not sure she had wept, although she felt the loss.

"It is only temporary," she lied. "Until I conclude my business in Vellio."

"What business?"

Morgen silenced her with a look. "It's not your concern."

Dravka paced to the narrow window, glanced through it without interest, then threw herself on a cot. "That's what you keep saying. Why did you bring us with you, anyway?"

"Would you prefer I had left you in Prydwen?"

Dravka's jaw worked. "No," she said at last.

Jaelle sat on the narrow cot, her eyes watchful. She rarely spoke, but Morgen suspected she missed nothing.

"Just tell me," Dravka pleaded, pressing her palms together in a theatrical plea. "How long must we anoint corpses for these miserable women?"

"Until Vazsoly comes." Morgen sat beside Jaelle, smoothing her silky hair. For some reason, she did not mind touching Jaelle. "We must wait for him."

Dravka snorted. "How can you be sure he'll come?"

"Because he has nowhere else to turn."

She propped her chin on one hand. It had a winsome cleft, just like her brother, though her bones were more delicate. "What if he's with his nobles? Or dead?"

A worm of doubt stirred. Morgen crushed it.

"He cannot be dead," she said evenly, "because I am meant to kill him."

Half her life she had waited to exact vengeance on the Marcels. She had suffered Vazsoly's caresses, his slaps and kicks, all to make his suffering greater when she finally claimed his soul. No, he had to be alive. And her original plan of killing him at his own wedding, before all the nobles of the land... Somehow, she knew it was still possible.

Dravka watched her warily. "Then what?"

Morgen reached into her oilskin travel bag and took out the iron box. It was wrapped in cloth, but the cold seeped through, chilling her fingers.

"Do you remember," she said, "what I did to the men who came after you in Prydwen?"

Jaelle paled, but Dravka met her gaze. "You killed them with magic."

"That's right. If either of you so much as think about touching this box, you will wish for such a clean death."

Dravka's curious eyes flicked to the box. "We won't. What's inside?"

"Something very dangerous." Morgen stood and scanned the room, searching for a suitable hiding place.

The chamber was sparsely furnished, with only three hard plank cots and a washstand. She pushed the empty cot against the far wall and clambered up to peer out the window. It faced a cloister at the rear of the convent.

Morgen groped along the lintel, her fingers encountering ancient dust. A pigeon roosting there fluttered away with an indignant coo. But the space behind the bird's nest was just wide enough to accommodate the iron box.

She wedged it into place, making sure it was secure. The box was heavy enough not to be disturbed by the wind, and its dark color would blend with the weathered stone of the convent walls. Anyone glancing up from the cloister would see only shadows.

Satisfied, Morgen climbed down and shoved the cot back into place. Dravka and Jaelle watched in silence.

"I must leave you for a while," Morgen said, brushing pigeon droppings from her hands. "There is a library at this convent, small but distinguished. It might hold some answers."

Dravka arched an eyebrow. "To what?"

Morgen scowled and Dravka held up her hands in mock surrender. "Never mind. I will not ask any more questions!"

Morgen turned to go, but Dravka caught her sleeve. "Wait! Tell me one thing." Her blue eyes gleamed with a fierce intensity. "Someday, if I obey all your commands, will you teach me your witchcraft? I will be a devoted student, I swear it."

Morgen studied Dravka's face. The girl had the same hungry look Morgen had once seen in her own reflection. The Marcels always did crave power.

"Why do you want to learn?" Morgen asked.

Dravka's jaw tightened. "So I am never at a man's mercy again."

Morgen understood that sentiment all too well. It was the same fire that had driven her to master the dark arts, to become a weapon unto herself. But she neither needed nor wanted an apprentice. Especially not a Marcel.

But it was better the girl didn't know that. She would be more agreeable if she hoped to earn Morgen's favor.

"I will consider it," she said. "Admit no one until I return."

Jaelle spoke up, her voice soft. "What if the sisters come and ask where you went?"

Dravka grinned. "I will pretend to vomit." She clutched her stomach and made a terrible retching noise. "They will think we caught ill humors on the road."

Despite herself, a smile tugged at the corner of Morgen's mouth. Outside, the bell tolled for evening rites. Vellio's dead would be coming in on barrows, to be shrouded and stilled with silver charms. It was another reason she had chosen to stay at the convent; her power fed on death itself, though she wouldn't tell the girls that.

With a final nod, she slipped out the door into the quiet dormitory, her mind already turning to the secrets that might lie hidden in the library's ancient scrolls. Thus far, she'd been unable to open the box that held the Grand Menotte. But Morgen had yet to face a warding spell she couldn't defeat eventually.

Let Vazsoly come. She would be ready for him.

SEVENTEEN

L ucius's boots rang against the polished marble halls of the Alcazar, servants and courtiers alike hastily clearing a path the moment his grim face came into view.

He had trained himself to ignore it, but today the iron menotte burned around his wrist. Orlaith's stew of emotions bubbled in a corner of his mind — pride, fear, anticipation. He couldn't read her thoughts, but he didn't have to. They all centered on her son and the match she'd become obsessed with.

Lucius was supposed to report what he had learned in the city concerning Beatriu. The former maid's tale had been a mix of rumor and innuendo, none of it definitive. Either the Damiata was a homicidal prodigy or a tragic victim. In the end, it mattered little. He was still trapped.

On impulse, he decided to put off meeting with Orlaith. He already knew what she would say. *Of course Beatriu is ruthless. She's a Do Santillan. It runs in their blood. But that is no reason to discard her. Galatia is too valuable a prize. We must simply watch her very carefully.*

Instead of returning to the Redvaynes' suite, Lucius made

his way out to the walled orchard where he had trailed Enrigo and Beatriu earlier that day. Rain dripped from the roof of the colonnade. He paced the covered walkway; somewhere along here was the spot where the elder brother Tristan had been stabbed. He'd called Beatriu by the affectionate nickname Scarpetta. *Little Slipper.* Did those tiny feet creep up behind him and commit murder? Of course, any evidence would have been scrubbed away long ago. No angry spirits lingered to whisper the truth, either.

A deep weariness settled over him. If only he could end it, drive a blade into his own chest and be done. But to take his life, he'd need a beating heart to still.

Lucius clenched his fist, the iron biting into his wrist. A thousand years he had been shackled to this bloodline. His fate tethered to their schemes and ambitions. All so the House of Redvayne could play at power while decaying from within.

He was pacing along the colonnade, lost in dark musings, when a needle of pain lanced through his chest. It quickly spread, icy knives scoring his marrow — a sensation he knew all too well. The insistent tug of a summoning.

Claudius Quintus.

The sound of his true name was like a silent gong, reverberating through his essence. He sank to one knee, teeth gritted, resigning himself to Orlaith's usual tactless demands. The woman had all the subtlety of a battering ram. Could she not simply follow their bond and find him like a normal person?

But as the magic took hold, whiting out his vision, Lucius realized something was different. The lips that spoke his name were not hers at all—

Reality warped and twisted. With a jarring wrench, Lucius found himself kneeling inside a large tent. Thin shafts of sunlight crept under the edges of the heavy canvas, but the entryway flaps were secured, allowing no direct illumination into the interior.

"Bel's flaming eye, it worked!" said a deep, delighted voice.

Lucius blinked, adjusting to the gloom. He hardly dared trust the evidence of his own senses. "Brennos?"

The rebel priest once known as the Red Rogue wore the traditional raiment of a Son of Bel — a pleated wool skirt and hooded cloak clasped at the shoulder with a copper sunburst denoting his rank as general. The uniform left his muscular, bronzed torso bare.

His sable hair was shaggier than the last time they had met, and he needed a shave, but the scars on his face had faded to white lines against his olive skin. Shadows bruised his eyes as if he had not slept much of late, but they warmed as he regarded Lucius.

"I hope you weren't in the midst of something important," he said with a crooked smile. "Or taking a piss. Though I don't suppose you need to do that."

Lucius shook his head, fighting a swell of emotion. Just like that, despair vanished, replaced by something bright and fragile kindling in his chest.

"Nothing that can't wait. It is good to see you again, Strategos," he said, then inwardly winced. Why did he sound so stiff and formal?

Brennos glanced down at the nine-pointed star in which Lucius had materialized. He'd drawn it with his own blood, as evidenced by the linen bandage wound around his left hand. He quickly seized one of the candles and dripped wax along the line.

Lucius stepped out of the broken star, taking in his surroundings. The tent was spartan but well-organized. A neatly made bedroll occupied one corner, a sturdy chest at its foot. In the center stood a table strewn with detailed maps of the region, along with quills, ink, parchment, and sealing wax. A plate held crumbs of cheese.

"I am sorry to take advantage of your offer so soon," Brennos said, "but I would be grateful for your counsel."

"Then I am happy to oblige. Where are we?"

"Four leagues from the Galatian border." Brennos gestured for Lucius to sit on a stool, then joined him on another. Books on military tactics were piled next to the bedroll, some bristling with scraps of paper to mark specific pages. A sword and shield leaned against the corner, along with a boiled leather jerkin. Candlelight flickered over the maps, softening the burn scars on Bren's face.

"Recruiting from the shrines in the countryside has gone well," Brennos said, his enthusiasm returning. He jumped to his feet again, full of restless energy. "Would you like to tour the camp?"

Lucius hesitated. Brennos looked embarrassed. "How stupid of me. The sun burns you." He glanced around the tent. "I did remember that. It's why I secured the flaps. I am just... glad you are here."

Lucius smiled, aiming for nonchalance rather than unbridled joy. "I spent my life in army camps. It was a long time ago, but I have not forgotten." He closed his eyes, recalling all the mundane details. How vividly they returned, undimmed by the ocean of time in between.

"I see smoke rising from the cook fires," he murmured. "Smell freshly turned earth and trampled grass. There are horses tethered on picket lines. Half the men asleep, the other half oiling weapons or drilling under a commander's eye."

"You're partly right," Bren said ruefully. "They eat far too much, but they lack training and weapons. We don't have any horses, either. They haven't faced a real battle yet." He met Lucius's gaze. "I fear what will happen when they are tested."

Lucius leaned forward, resting his elbows on his knees. "What resources do you have?"

Brennos lowered his voice. "Gold. A lot of it."

Lucius's eyebrows rose. With enough coin, Bren could hire mercenaries to leaven his eager but inexperienced ranks. Equip them with decent weapons and armor. Maybe even secure a few horses for his officers.

"That will be useful," Lucius said. "What news from Prydwen?"

Brennos scrubbed a hand over his jaw. "It's chaos. Many have fled the city. The nobility have sellswords and remnants of the Ducal guard at their command. They mount sneak attacks, sabotage any attempts at repair or rebuilding. I plan to march there and put a stop to it once I can be sure my followers won't be slaughtered."

"How many soldiers do you have?"

He cleared his throat. "About two hundred."

It made no sense. Lucius knew what a persuasive leader Brennos could be. As the Red Rogue, he'd united the people of the Shambles and helped launch a revolution. The man had raw charisma to spare. Besides which, the Sons of Bel had been a paramilitary order for centuries; had they grown soft so quickly?

"There must be thousands of brothers across Cavet," Lucius said. "Aren't they up in arms about the massacre at Bel Mara?"

"That's the other problem," Brennos admitted. "There's been a schism in the order. Another faction has risen — a substantial one — that blames the Sisters of Kaethe for the Duc's treachery. They claim the nuns manipulated Marcel into murdering the archpriest."

"That's ridiculous," Lucius scoffed. "It's an excuse to revive old grudges against the nuns. They're just a convenient scapegoat."

"I know." Brennos looked as tired as Lucius had ever seen him. "Yet a lie repeated often enough becomes the truth in the minds of many."

It sounded like an unholy mess. Lucius wondered how long it would take for the fighting to spill over the border into Galatia. Not long, he suspected.

If only he could stay at Brennos's side, but he was bound to a different fate. Yet here, in this moment, he could offer the support and counsel of a friend.

"Have you heard anything of Vazsoly Marcel's whereabouts?" Brennos asked.

Lucius shook his head. "You summoned me from the Damiata's court at Vellio. I can assure you he is not there."

"I heard a rumor that he fled north to rally the pagan tribes to his cause." Bren looked thoughtful. "Though I doubt the truth of it. His father persecuted them for decades when they refused to give up their gods and worship Bel. Why would they aid him now?"

"I agree, it is unlikely."

Brennos sighed. "Well, Marcel is the least of my problems. There is a brother called Arnulf who has declared himself the *true* Strategos. His army is twice the size of mine, and he is camped twelve leagues to the west." He tapped a spot on one of the maps. "Apparently, it was he who started the rumor that the Duc was hiding inside Kaethe's convent."

Lucius studied the map, surveying the terrain. There was a scattering of low hills, but the border between Cavet and Galatia was a fertile river valley with wide, grassy plains.

"Does Arnulf have horses?" he asked.

"Sadly, yes." Bren shook his head in disgust. "Instead of restoring order to the city, he means to go about burning innocent women. I must do something about him before he gains more followers."

"When the shit gets stirred, the biggest turds float to the surface," Lucius observed.

Brennos barked a laugh. "I have missed your razor wit, Lord Bittencourt."

"Well, your life is far more exciting than mine," Lucius said drily.

"I will not ask what you are doing in Galatia," Brennos replied. "I did not summon you here to serve as a spy."

Lucius waved a hand. "There is nothing to hide. Orlaith is foisting her naive young son upon Beatriu do Santillan. The Damiata is the most interesting thing about the whole affair. I cannot seem to get a handle on her..."

He trailed off at the sudden heat in Brennos's gaze. They'd slept together once, before Lucius had any idea who he actually was. It was a tryst that replayed often in his mind during the long evenings when the Alcazar slept and he had nothing to do but dwell on his own regrets.

"I meant what I said. It is good to see you again, Lucius. I have missed your company."

Brennos reached for him, but Lucius flinched back.

"Don't." The word came out harsher than he intended.

Bren's brow furrowed. "Why not?"

Because you are alive and free and far too handsome for the likes of me.

What he said was, "I am cold."

A saucy grin. "I do not remember you so."

"Because I had just fed at the time," Lucius said bluntly. He would not pretend to be something he was not. "But this is my natural state."

Bren sobered. "I know that." He exhaled a long breath.

"Never mind. Well, you know my full plight now. I would still hear your advice, if you are willing to give it."

Here, at least, was something untainted. Something true. "That I can share freely," he said.

They bent their heads over the maps spread across the makeshift table, Brennos pointing out potential sites for a defensive camp as Lucius offered suggestions, drawing upon his own experience as a field officer in the days of King Gaius's war.

"Put the river at your back," Lucius said, tapping a blue line snaking across the parchment. "And have the men dig a trench around the perimeter."

Brennos nodded. "We'll need to stay near a main road for supplies and fresh recruits."

"Send your most silver-tongued men to the nearest towns," Lucius advised. "Persuade the young and idealistic to join up."

"We could use some seasoned fighters as well," Bren mused, tracing a ridge of mountains with his finger.

"Hire mercenaries from the north to train your green troops." Lucius's lips quirked. "Time to spend some of that gold."

Bren laughed. "With pleasure. Half of it came from the Marcel treasury. He owed the brothers so much money, just the interest came to an exorbitant sum."

"And the rest?" Lucius asked.

"Earned on our backs," Brennos replied with a wink.

Lucius couldn't help laughing. The Strategos was a confounding man. His physical beauty had placed him among the ranks of Bel's sacred courtesans, but he didn't seem to mind that he was exploited for coin in such a way. In fact, he took it all very seriously. Last time they met, when Lucius had shared his true name, Brennos claimed that lying together under Bel's roof allowed him to see inside Lucius's heart.

You are broken in places, poisoned with regret and cynicism, but your spirit remains pure.

It was the nicest thing anyone had ever said to him, and Lucius had not forgotten a word of it.

They spoke at length as the candles burnt to stubs, debating strategy and logistics. Despite himself, Lucius felt the old thrill of purpose stirring in his chest. He had missed this — the easy camaraderie of men united in a cause. Time slipped away unnoticed.

"I cannot thank you enough," Brennos said at last, clasping Lucius's forearm.

He showed no sign of revulsion, and Lucius did not pull away this time. He had a brief fantasy of finding Brother Arnulf, draining him dry, and returning to the camp with a beating heart and hot blood coursing through his veins.

Lucius was grasping for some way to express his own gratitude for this reprieve from Orlaith's scheming when a sudden storm of alien emotions battered at his mind. He stiffened, eyes wide and unseeing.

"What is wrong?" Brennos asked.

"I don't—" Pain flared, threatening to split his skull in two. This summoning was raw, uncontrolled. It grasped his power, then released it, over and over, like a babe with a new toy.

Understanding crashed over him. It couldn't be.... So soon?

"Farewell," he gasped, gripping Bren's shoulder.

The last thing he saw before the fiery darkness swallowed him was his friend's stricken face.

THE CLOYING SCENT of rosewater filled Lucius's nostrils, jarring him to his senses. Orlaith's perfume.

The Ducissa's chamber swam into view, followed by

another nine-pointed star, the lines of blood still wet and glistening.

Enrigo stood just beyond the edge, his face chalk-white, pupils blown wide with shock. The iron menotte encircled his left wrist, its phoenix glowing a sullen red. Lucius felt their connection like a burrowing animal under his skin.

Orlaith's gaze bored into him, blue eyes flinty. "Where have you been?" Her voice was tight. "I sent a servant to fetch you from your rooms. You weren't there."

Lucius pulled himself upright, ignoring the way the room spun. "I went for a walk in the orchard, Your Grace."

"You might have told me first."

"My apologies. It was unplanned." He met her glare with studied indifference. Inside, his mind raced with something akin to glee.

"Well, it is done now." Orlaith turned away, skirts swishing. "You must swear fealty to my son."

Lucius stared at her, marveling at how she discarded him as easily as a worn glove. Enrigo shuffled his feet, drawing his gaze. The boy looked lost, hunched in on himself like he was trying to disappear. Neither showed any sign of a wound. Kaethe knew where they'd gotten the blood.

"You must release me, my lord," Lucius said quietly. "So that I may swear my oath."

Enrigo blinked at him. "What?"

He gestured to the star. "The circle. It binds me."

"Oh." Enrigo flushed scarlet, clearly embarrassed at having to be told. He scuffed a gap in the line with his boot.

Lucius stepped free. He gracefully sank to one knee and bowed his head. Which Redvayne was this one? Two hundred? Three hundred? He'd lost count ages ago.

"By the menotte that sustains me, I vow to serve you with unwavering loyalty. I shall protect you against all enemies, obey your every command, and stand guard at your side until the day death claims you. And when that time comes, as it must, I shall bow to your heir, continuing this bond of eternal service until the end of all things. Your will is my purpose, your bloodline my eternal duty."

From the corner of his eye, he saw Orlaith's lips curve in a minute smile. He was still a slave. Only the hands that held his chain were different.

But that didn't mean he couldn't allow himself a measure of revenge.

Lucius smiled back at her, relishing his next words. How many times had he imagined the look on her face when her fraud was exposed at last?

He turned to Enrigo, who had made an effort to master himself. The boy affected a casual air, shoulders back and hands loosely clasped, but he still looked like he wanted to rabbit out the door.

"My lord," Lucius said crisply. "As your sworn servant, I owe you the full truth, no matter how unpleasant it may be."

Enrigo looked befuddled. "The truth about what?"

"About your abduction, my lord."

Orlaith drew an audible breath, hands clenching her black skirts.

"We conspired with Nathan Ouvrard to arrange your kidnapping," Lucius continued. "He sent three of his wraiths to possess the guards and spirit you away."

Enrigo blinked. "We?"

"Your mother and I." He glanced at Orlaith. "Mostly your mother."

The boy went very still. "Is this a jest?"

"Not at all, my lord. One of the wraiths planted a dagger bearing the sigil of House Courtenay. To cast suspicion on them." The words came faster now, a poison purged. "I was to give chase and retrieve you before they crossed the Boundary. Unharmed, but suitably distressed."

"I don't understand." Enrigo looked at Orlaith. "Mother, what is this?"

She gave a brittle laugh, the sound sharp as shattered glass. "Of course it is a jest. And one in poor taste, I might add."

Lucius saw the flicker of doubt in the boy's eyes. The worm of suspicion, burrowing deep. Good. Let it fester.

"It was all a ruse," he continued relentlessly. "A ploy to justify invading Nyons. Your mother couldn't march her troops through Duc Scalici's lands. Not without cause. But the Duc is quite fond of you. If you were abducted by Nyons's agents, well..." He spread his hands. "Alessia would have no choice but to let her pass."

"You snake!" Orlaith hissed. "How dare you fill my son's head with these vile accusations!"

Lucius ignored her. He met Enrigo's eyes, which were clouded with distress and confusion. "As soon as we return to Aquitan, I will take you to the smith, my lord. The one who forged the false dagger. He was an unwilling participant. Coerced, as he will testify. He should not be punished for your mother's schemes."

Orlaith surged forward, eyes wild, hands hooked into claws. "You idiot! He's already—" She choked off, face draining of color.

"Dead?" Lucius cocked his head, lip curling in disgust. "Why am I not surprised."

"I didn't mean— How dare you twist my words!" she sputtered, trying to recover.

A soft rap on the door interrupted the drama. "Go away," she snapped, her eyes never leaving Lucius. "I am occupied at the moment."

"Your Grace." The measured voice of her steward Albion

filtered through the oak door. "I believe you will want to hear this news. It is rather urgent."

"Oh, come in then!"

The door swung open, admitting Orlaith's unflappable servant. He sketched a bow, signet ring glinting on his pinky finger. "Your Grace. My lord." Dark eyes flicked to Lucius, assessing. "I apologize for the interruption. But Duc Vazsoly Marcel has just arrived at the Alcazar. He is currently in audience with the Damiata Beatriu."

Lucius felt a rush of satisfaction at the stricken expression on Orlaith's face. *Let the games begin.*

EIGHTEEN

Enrigo froze, eyes turning to his mother. Orlaith recovered quickly, slipping on her usual mask of icy calm.

"How long ago did Duc Marcel arrive?" she asked the steward.

"I am not sure, my lady," Albion replied. "Not long, I think."

Lucius relegated Enrigo's churning emotions to a dusty corner of his mind and laid a hand on the boy's shoulder. "I will accompany you to the audience chamber, my lord," he said.

Enrigo nodded, his face grim. Orlaith smoothed her skirts and drew as deep a breath as her bodice permitted. She started to follow them to the door, but he whirled on her. "I'll handle it alone, Mother."

She looked aghast. "*Alone?* In that den of vipers? You'll need my advice—"

"I command you to stay here!" His fair skin flushed pink.

She recoiled as if he'd slapped her. As Lucius guided the

boy from the room, he glanced back. Orlaith's blue eyes burned with venom. The game had changed, and she could fault no one but herself.

"You must release my power, Your Grace," Lucius told Enrigo as they followed Albion down the corridor.

"What?" The boy gazed up at him, uncomprehending. He looked like a prisoner being led to the gallows, pasty and sweating.

"You've severed my elemental power," Lucius repeated patiently. "I cannot touch it. If Marcel attacks, I must be ready. Loosen your grip."

Enrigo gave an uncertain nod. He squeezed and released the connection several times before opening the channel fully. It was, Lucius reflected, like being clumsily groped by a virgin.

"Did I do it?" Enrigo asked.

"You did, my lord."

Lucius tried not to sound patronizing, but Enrigo flushed an even deeper shade of red. "I'm not a child," he muttered. "You needn't coddle me."

"That wasn't my intention, Your Grace. I apologize."

Enrigo gave a stiff nod. They rounded a corner.

"Marcel will try to bait you," Lucius cautioned. "Make you lose your temper. Don't let him."

"I won't." Enrigo chewed his lip. "Do you think he's here to woo Bea?"

No, he just happened to be passing by.

"I expect so," Lucius said. "But you have already won her heart. There is nothing to fear, my lord."

Lies, but the boy needed to be confident if he stood half a chance. Two guards admitted them to the audience chamber, where Beatriu sat on her throne of skulls, gray eyes fixed on the tall, striking man before her.

Enrigo faltered at the threshold, but Lucius urged him

forward with a gentle push, nodding to Albion. The steward bowed and backed away.

Duc Marcel turned. He seemed leaner, harder, *hungrier*. The look of a wolf in midwinter. Enrigo studiously ignored him, bowing to the Damiata.

"My lady," he said.

Vazsoly glanced around in mock confusion. "Did somebody call for a stableboy?" He flipped a coin at Enrigo's feet. "Bring my stallion around and you'll earn another."

Enrigo scowled but seemed at a loss for a riposte. The moment stretched out. In an alcove behind the throne, Lucius recognized the pair of nuns — one young, one much older — who had watched over Beatriu during her walk with Enrigo in the orchard, along with several other sisters, all in white with shaven heads. Two dozen Galatian nobles were also in attendance, dark eyes watching the exchange closely — and with evident amusement.

"Ah, look what the wind blew in," Lucius remarked, sauntering forward. "It's the Fugitive Duc."

Vazsoly's icy blue eyes narrowed.

"I think it's time to amend the Marcel motto, don't you?" Lucius continued. "*We yield to none* doesn't quite fit anymore. How about..." He stroked his chin. "*We squeal and run?*"

There were a few titters. Vazsoly brushed off the jibe. His stare remained on Enrigo, full of contempt. Then his eyes widened, catching on the petit menotte around the boy's wrist. Surprise and calculation warred on his face.

"Leash your dog, Redvayne," Vazsoly said in a bored tone, "before I make mincemeat of him."

Enrigo raised his chin, cheeks flaming. "You can't tell me what to do!"

Vazsoly smirked. "My apologies, Your Grace. Only your mother does that."

Beatriu coughed into a dainty scrap of black lace, but it was obvious to all that she was trying not to laugh. If only Orlaith hadn't treated her son like a child, if she had let him attend her councils and hone his wit, he might be more nimble on his feet. But the boy was chum in the water for a barracuda like Marcel.

Lucius, on the other hand, had dealt with such men for what felt like eternity.

"How fares the revolution?" he asked. "Last I saw your palace, the Red Rogue's banner was flying from the highest tower." He lowered his voice to a stage whisper, turning to address the courtiers. "It appears even the Duc's throne found him insufferable and decided to stand up against him."

Muffled laughter rippled through the crowd. Vazsoly's nostrils flared, but his arrogant smile never wavered. "I have no intention of bandying insults with filth like you, Bittencourt."

Lucius's lip curled. "No, you've come here to beg for scraps from Her Grace's table, haven't you?"

Vazsoly waited for Beatriu to do something about Lucius's impertinence. When she did not, he gathered himself and launched into a litany of bald-faced lies.

"The peasants staged a minor revolt, my lady, but I have nearly crushed it. I will be back in residence at my palace by autumn." Vazsoly waved a hand. "The traitors will be hung from the walls by their own entrails, to set an example to the rest."

Lucius rolled his eyes. Did he truly expect anyone to believe this nonsense? Judging by some of the courtiers' uncertain faces, perhaps so.

He stepped forward. "Since the Duc seems incapable of uttering a single word of truth, allow me to provide it." He met Beatriu's gaze. "I witnessed the so-called parley between him and the Red Rogue at Bel Mara."

Vazsoly scoffed. "You would take the word of a mortifex over—"

"It was a trap. Marcel's soldiers massacred nearly two hundred priests and their servants," Lucius continued. "Capturing the rebel leader was merely a pretext. His real reason was far more base. The Duc owed the priests a great deal of money and butchering them was more economical than paying his debts."

Murmurs rippled through the audience chamber. Vazsoly's jaw tightened, but he remained outwardly unruffled.

"This is ridiculous," he said. "That creature will say anything to discredit me so Robert's little whelp can lay claim to your throne, my lady."

Beatriu eyed them both without expression. Unlike Enrigo, she had obviously been trained to conceal her thoughts.

"So we have two conflicting accounts," she said. "Can either of you provide proof?"

Lucius and Vazsoly stared at each other. Then the Duc smiled. He didn't seem worried at all. No, he looked triumphant.

What was he up to?

"If you are asking me to prove a negative, I cannot, my lady," he said. "But I swear on my honor that my men had no hand in the tragic massacre. Nor do I seek your aid in restoring order to my duchy. I ask nothing. But I have brought you a treasure beyond compare."

Beatriu leaned forward on her throne, interest piqued at last. "A gift? What is it?"

Vazsoly's gaze slid to Lucius. "A device that commands a hundred of his kind."

Excited whispers hissed through the crowd. Some shook their heads in open disbelief, but Lucius felt a nasty shock.

Vazsoly had to be lying again. He couldn't possibly have the Grand Menotte... Could he?

"Imagine it," Vazsoly said, striding to the foot of the throne. "An army that never tires. Never sleeps. That can march a thousand leagues without food. Soldiers who cannot refuse an order. Who cannot die because they are already dead."

His ice blue eyes glittered with ambition. "With such a force at our command, we will rule this continent from the Western Isles to the Eastern Icemarch."

"Where is this fantastical weapon?" Lucius called out.

Vazsoly smile's was sharp as a blade. "Do you think I carry it with me? The talisman is in a safe place."

A bluff. It had to be. The alternative was unthinkable.

After standing like a waxen mannequin for the last ten minutes, Enrigo finally stirred. He swallowed hard, Adam's apple bobbing, then stepped forward. "You, sir, are a deceitful knave!"

Vazsoly rounded on him. "Go hide in your mother's skirts, you cunt-bitten pup!"

Enrigo flushed to the roots of his blond hair. "I am the Duc of Clovis! I will not be spoken to in this manner!"

"Then act like a man instead of a mewling kitten," Vazsoly sneered. "Did Robert leave you nothing between your legs when he rode off to die?"

"You dare insult my father's memory?" Enrigo looked ready to lunge, hands clenching into fists. He had taken a single stride forward when Beatriu's patience snapped.

"SILENCE!" the Damiata shrieked. She stamped her slippered foot. "We will not tolerate such uncouth behavior in our court. Get out, all of you!"

The nobles fled, followed by various retainers and guards.

Lucius escorted a visibly shaking Enrigo toward the double doors.

"Not you, Lucius Bittencourt." Beatriu's gaze pinned him in place.

Vazsoly whirled, amazement on his face. "You cannot mean to be alone with that creature?"

She eyed him coldly. "This is the Alcazar. I do as I please here. Or are you my nursemaid now?"

For a moment, Vazsoly looked as if he might argue. Then he bowed, mouth twisting with barely concealed fury, spun on his heel, and stalked out. Beatriu beckoned Lucius closer with a crook of her finger. He approached the dais warily, watching her toy with a garnet ring on her small hand.

"Tell me," she said, "is this relic real?"

Lucius hesitated. If he denied it outright, it might seem like Vazsoly was right — that Lucius only wanted to secure Enrigo's betrothal.

He chose his words carefully. "It's difficult to say, Your Grace. The Grand Menotte is more legend than fact. Rumors of its existence have circulated for centuries, but it was reportedly lost ages ago."

She tapped her nails against the armrest, considering. "And if Vazsoly did possess it?"

Lucius sighed, well aware he was treading on potentially dangerous ground. "With all due respect, my lady, then why would he come *here*? Why not march on Prydwen with his immortal army and reclaim his palace? I just came from there, and I can promise you that the uprising has not remotely been put down, as Vazsoly claims. The whole city is aflame and for good reason. He was bleeding his people dry."

Beatriu's brow furrowed. Lucius pressed on, sensing an opening. "Your Grace, if I may be so bold, Enrigo is the better choice. He is kind and decent, with a gentle heart. And he is much closer to your age. Besides which, Clovis is flourishing, while Cavet descends into chaos and ruin."

She leaned forward. "From what I hear, many of your villages have been overrun by the dead, and Lady Redvayne is not overly concerned with whether her subjects have bread on their tables."

Lucius studied her ruefully. "That is true, my lady. I exaggerated. But this talisman is all Vazsoly can dangle before you. It is a mirage, meant to distract from the fact that he has nothing of substance to offer."

Beatriu stared off into the distance, looking young and vulnerable. "In truth, I do not wish to marry either of them," she confided. "But if I do not choose one, my throne is at risk. I fear the nobles will kill me, just as they did my brothers and sisters. The Do Santillan dynasty will come to an end." Her gray eyes met his. "If you were my advisor, what would you tell me to do?"

Lucius felt a pang of sympathy. "Play the suitors against each other," he suggested. "Keep them busy vying for your favor. It will buy you time." He held her gaze. "But I must warn you, Vazsoly would make a very poor consort. I know you think I say this only out of loyalty, but I can assure you that Enrigo would treat you with respect. Vazsoly sees only your crown."

Beatriu tilted her head. "You were in Prydwen. Is it true his people despise him?"

Lucius nodded grimly. "The masses starve while he lines his coffers. And he has taken to burning the bodies of the poor. For many, it is a sacrilege and an offense to Kaethe."

The Damiata leaned back on her throne, looking troubled. After a long moment, she inclined her head. "Thank you for your honest counsel. Enrigo is fortunate to have you." Her eyes drifted past him, scanning the gloomy audience chamber. "May we ask for a demonstration of your abilities?"

Lucius bowed. "Whatever my lady desires." A reckless urge seized him. "Shall we set something on fire?"

Beatriu clapped her small hands together. "Yes. I want..." She paused, considering. Her gaze settled on the ancient tapestries lining the walls, their colors muted and faded with age. "Burn those," she declared.

"All of them?" he asked.

The Damiata gave him one of her rare smiles. "All of them!"

Lucius extended his hand, reaching for the wellspring of power coiled inside him — which Enrigo had forgotten to take hold of again. Flames kindled along his fingertips, growing into a writhing ball of fire hovering over his open palm.

With a flick of his wrist, he sent a stream of flame arcing across the room. It struck the tapestry of the lion-killers, the one the former maid had so disliked, consuming it in seconds. The fire spread rapidly, leaping from one wall-hanging to the next.

Acrid smoke filled the air as the last of the tapestries dissolved into ash. Through the haze, he heard Beatriu's laughter, bright and clear as a bell.

NINETEEN

Enrigo slammed his fist against the wooden door, causing Jak's ears to twitch. On the other side, his mother's muffled sobs continued unabated.

"Leave me alone," he shouted. "Just be quiet!"

Her weeping only intensified. Barring the connecting door between their chambers, he stalked over to the fireplace and threw another log on the dying embers. Sparks swirled up the flue.

Jak trotted over, his nails clicking on the polished wood floor. The terrier huffed and plopped down at Enrigo's feet.

"At least you still love me, eh, boy?" Enrigo scratched the dog behind the ears. "What a mess this all is. I was meant to be a proper Duc, like Father. Noble and brave."

Father. A hazy figure he'd never known. All those daydreams of following in the man's footsteps, of being respected and admired, seemed like childish folly now.

Enrigo sank into an armchair, staring listlessly at the tapestries on the wall. Another cruel mockery — the Battle of Hellgate, where his father had been cut down by the Courtenays' mortifex Mace. Robert had died a hero, though Enrigo never quite understood why since he'd lost the fight.

He'd asked Lucius once, when he was much younger. The mortifex had dropped to one knee so they were eye to eye, smiled, and said, "Nothing polishes a man's reputation like a good premature death."

Enrigo hadn't understood at the time, but now he did. Everything was just for show. A stupid farce, and he was the biggest fool of all.

His humiliation at court played over and over in his mind. But worse than that was Lucius's accusation. It couldn't be true. Mother would never...

Doubt gnawed at him. The missing iron pickets around the manor house that allowed the wraiths to gain entry. The furtive glances between Mother and Lucius upon his return from Nyons. A host of damning facts that couldn't be ignored.

"I don't know what to think anymore, Jak." The dog cocked his head. "I suppose I ought to confront her. Demand the truth. But..."

He trailed off, swallowing hard. He was only a boy still, playing at being a man. Thrust into a bond with a bitter undead creature he barely knew.

Enrigo wished he could go back — before the wraiths, before Lucius, before any of it, when his future had been bright and uncomplicated. Now it loomed as twisted as a moonlit path through a haunted wood.

A knock sounded at the door. He opened it to find a black-clad maidservant holding out a folded note. "From the Damiata, Your Grace."

Enrigo scanned the message, penned in Beatriu's hasty scrawl. She wanted to meet him at the colonnade where they had walked before. His heart quickened. At last, a chance to speak to her alone. It might be his last.

The maid led him through hushed corridors, down a back staircase, and out into the orchard. The pear trees dripped with rain. Low clouds pressed close, making the air thick as jelly.

"Wait there, my lord." The girl gestured to the end of the long colonnade. Then she retreated, leaving him standing alone between the pillars.

He paced, wondering how to convince Beatriu that he was the better choice after the debacle in the audience chamber. All his mother's carefully crafted arguments flew from his head; all he could think of was how dashing the Duc of Cavet had looked in his gold and silver armor.

If only he had armor like that instead of the stupid ruffed doublet his mother made him wear. Well, he had the menotte now. That made him a Duc, too. He could wear whatever he liked.

But where was Beatriu? Enrigo peered into the gray drizzle. Not a flicker of movement anywhere. Even the birds were silent.

Then a branch snapped in the orchard. He whirled around. The colonnade was deserted, the flagstones beyond puddled with water.

"My lady?" he called softly.

No answer came, but a soft sound reached his ears. It sounded like the whisk of a slipper on stone. Columns lined the gallery, stretching into shadow. Could Beatriu be toying with him?

Unease prickled Enrigo's skin. What if the note wasn't from Beatriu at all? What if it was a trap, some scheme of Vazsoly Marcel's? He cursed under his breath. Running off alone, without telling a soul where he'd gone, was foolish. *Childish.* He should return to his chambers at once...

The hair on his nape stood up. He felt a presence behind him. Heart in his throat, Enrigo turned.

Beatriu stood there, gray eyes luminous in the gloom. He sagged with relief, a startled breath escaping him. "How did you sneak up on me like that?"

She glided closer, the long, pointed sleeves obscuring her hands. "You look troubled, my lord."

"I'm well." Enrigo forced a smile. His palms were damp, but he didn't pull away when Beatriu laced her fingers with his. Her skin was cool and dry.

"I do not love Vazsoly Marcel," she declared, lifting her chin. "I hate him!"

"I am relieved to hear you say so, my lady." Enrigo struggled to contain himself. *Be dignified.* "I must admit, I wasn't certain of your feelings on the matter."

Beatriu pushed up his sleeve, exposing the iron cuff. She studied it, head tilted. "What is it like to wear such a device?"

Enrigo wanted to appear confident and in control, as Vazsoly undoubtedly would in this situation. "I'm still growing accustomed to it. But I can sense Lucius's presence lurking in my mind."

"Does it work in both directions?" Beatriu's gaze was sharp. "Can he feel *you*?"

"I believe so, yes. Mother said I'll need to guard my thoughts, but..." His mouth twisted. "She neglected to explain how, of course."

Beatriu traced a finger over the cuff. Then she dropped his hands and turned away. "At least you do not live in constant fear for your life."

"I've sworn to protect you, my lady." Enrigo reached for her, but she stepped out of reach.

"I want to trust you. If you would only..." She shook her head, curls bouncing. "Never mind. You would never agree."

"Agree to what?" Enrigo's brow furrowed. "Tell me, Bea."

She looked up at him through lowered lashes. There was a

new intensity in her gray eyes, a hunger. "What if we were to share the burden of the menotte? Take turns wearing it?"

Enrigo blinked. The thought had never occurred to him that he might be free of the cuff before his death. In truth, he loathed it. The constant intrusion of Lucius's presence was not at all what he had anticipated. Enrigo was certain the mortifex could read every fearful, doubting thought and was secretly laughing at him.

After the devastating revelation about his mother's treachery, Enrigo was desperate to wed and begin a new life. Galatia would not be so terrible, if he and Beatriu were to marry. They could establish their own court here, far from his mother's reach.

But he resisted, schooling his features into a slight frown. He didn't want Beatriu to glimpse how much he wanted to be rid of the cuff, lest she think him weak. "That has never been done before, my lady."

"The menotte is yours now," she pressed, stepping closer. "You may do as you wish with it." Her voice dropped to a coaxing whisper. "If you share the power with me, it will be proof that your love is true. That you're not simply using me for your own gain, as Vazsoly would. We can then announce our formal betrothal and force him to leave." She placed a soft, pale hand on his chest. "It is you I love, Enrigo."

The words rang hollow. As he gazed into her impassive eyes, he knew she did not truly love him. But perhaps, given time, her affections could grow.

And the thought of how his mother would react if he relinquished the cuff gave him a grim satisfaction. For Enrigo to cast his legacy aside would be the ultimate act of defiance, a severing of the strings she used to control him.

"Well, my lord?" Beatriu inched closer, her heart-shaped face tilted up at him. "Will you consider my proposal?"

LUCIUS HUNCHED over his desk in the cramped bedchamber, quill scratching against parchment as he penned a letter to Brennos. The room, devoid of windows, was lit only by a single candle. He wrote feverishly of Vazsoly Marcel's appearance at court and his claims about the Grand Menotte, the nib digging into the paper with each stroke.

In his secret heart, he imagined Brennos laying siege to the Alcazar, his untrained but valiant soldiers storming the gates and overpowering the Galatian defenders. The dashing warrior-priest would cut his way to this very chamber, bare chest heaving, and then... A pleasant fantasy, but reality quickly intruded. If it came to a siege, Orlaith would order Lucius to burn the attackers. When he refused, she would instruct Enrigo to use the menotte to discipline him.

Not a happy ending after all.

Lucius stared at the letter, the wet ink glistening. With a muttered curse, flames sparked from his fingertips and devoured the parchment, reducing it to a pile of feathery ash.

His thoughts turned back to Brennos, not in carnal longing this time (well, not entirely) but in admiration for what a complicated man he was. The priest reminded Lucius of his younger self: driven, principled, willing to hurl himself beneath the thundering wheels of a chariot for a greater cause. An honorable idiot, in other words—

Lucius stiffened as the psychic connection tethering him to Enrigo winked out like a snuffed candle. He had sensed the young Redvayne leave his chambers earlier, but assumed the boy merely needed to clear his head after the day's events. Now he felt nothing on the other end of the bond. A perfect void, as if Enrigo had vanished from this earth.

More disturbing, the new hand gripping his leash showed no hesitation or uncertainty.

A single thought crystalized: Enrigo was dead. Vazsoly had killed him and taken the menotte by force.

Lucius shot to his feet, toppling the chair. He raced from the chamber, following the bond like a glowing thread through the palace's labyrinthine corridors. It led him to the covered walkway in the orchard, where he drew to an abrupt halt.

Beatriu stood waiting, one slender wrist encircled by the iron cuff. He could not sense even a hint of her emotional state. In all his centuries of servitude, no mortal had ever erected such an impenetrable mental wall against the menotte.

"What have you done?" he breathed. "Where is Lord Redvayne?"

"I have not harmed a hair on his pretty flaxen head," Beatriu said. "I merely sent him back to bed. Let us walk."

"My lady," Lucius stammered, thoroughly off-balance. He fell into step beside her as they strolled down the moonlit colonnade. The air was heavy with the scent of pear blossoms.

"Do not presume to interfere in my affairs, Lucius," she warned. "Should the need arise, I will not hesitate to use my authority."

His mind raced, trying to fathom how this child had so easily outwitted him. "Your mind is closed to me," he said. "How do you manage it?"

An amused smile played at the corners of her mouth. "I used to spy on my brothers during their swordplay lessons. The Galatian blade masters teach tricks to discipline one's mind. I mastered their techniques."

In that moment, the truth crashed over Lucius like a gout of icy water. The maid had been right all along. Beatriu was more dangerous than Orlaith could ever hope to be. And he had no one to blame but himself. His decision to reveal the truth to Enrigo had placed them all at her mercy.

"I intend to wed Duc Vazsoly Marcel," Beatriu announced. "His cunning and ambition are better suited to my own."

"That is a grave error," Lucius said, heart sinking.

"I do not believe so. He will try to command you, but do not forgot that you are mine. You may go now."

She dismissed him with a wave. Lucius watched her retreating skirts.

I must know.

"Your Grace?" he called out.

She turned back.

"Are the rumors true?" he asked.

A twinge of surprise shot through the menotte before she blocked it. So there were chinks in her armor, after all.

"Rumors?" she hedged.

"I think you know what I refer to, my lady."

Beatriu regarded him for a long moment, gray eyes wintry.

"That is an outrageous accusation," she said at last. "We should punish your insolence."

Lucius sensed that showing fear could prove fatal. "I am yours now," he said. "If you have secrets to protect, it's best I am aware of them. So I will ask again, plainly this time. Did you kill them?"

Another tense beat passed. He braced himself. Then Beatriu shook her head in bemusement. "Frankness is not a quality my father valued, but practice deception too often and one may be caught in one's own snare. You are forward, my dear mortifex, but we shall forgive you this time."

My dear mortifex. Lucius felt quite certain he had never been called that before.

"I am grateful," he said dryly, "but it is still not an answer, my lady."

"Very well, Lucius." Her pale lips twitched. "Only one. You may guess which."

MORGEN SHIFTED on the hard bench, her back twinging in protest as she hunched over the stack of leather-bound tomes and brittle scrolls. The smell of ancient parchment filled her nose. Days of searching the convent library and she'd found nothing that would help her to open the iron box — but perhaps that was for the best. What she *had* learned was disturbing. The only person who had ever worn the Grand Menotte was Jaskin Cazal, the talisman's creator, and it had driven him mad.

Morgen was not afraid of dark power, but she was starting to realize that the Grand Menotte was in a class by itself. Too evil to be touched.

I will bring it home with me to Juniper Isle, she decided. There was a place, a few nautical miles to the west, where the seafloor dropped away and the clear, turquoise water turned darkest blue. She would take a boat out past the line and throw the box overboard. It was the only way to be certain it never fell into the hands of a man like Vazsoly Marcel.

She rubbed her eyes. Motes of dust drifted in the shafts of wan daylight slanting down through the high oval windows. The quiet was broken only by the occasional scratch of a nun's quill at the distant writing stands.

Morgen ran a hand over her stubbled head. Her hair had been nearly waist-length before she was forced to cut it off. The itch of rough-spun robes was another irritation, a reminder of the role she played. For how much longer? The Marcel girls were getting antsy, Dravka in particular. She loved to complain and swore like a Bashuan sailor. Every day,

Morgen asked herself why she had brought them along. They served no purpose in her plans. If anything, they were a liability.

And yet. She had no other family. No brothers or sisters, aunts or uncles. As a child growing up, she'd never had friends. Her mother said it was too risky to allow strangers into their life. It was always the two of them. After her mother died, she had lived alone at the cottage.

Morgen missed the solitude, the rattling *kek-kek-kek* of the kingfishers and rhythm of the tides her steady companions. But sometimes, when Dravka said something outrageous that made her laugh, or when Jaelle crept into her cot at night and curled against her back, it was pleasant to have sisters.

The scuff of plaited reed sandals approached. Morgen tensed, then relaxed as Dravka slid onto the bench beside her. The younger woman leaned in close, her short silver-blonde hair brushing Morgen's ear.

"My brother has come, as you said he would," she whispered.

Morgen prided herself on remaining in control. *Ice for blood and salt for heart.* Her mother had taught her that. Yet she could not help a small thrill of satisfaction.

"I managed to get inside the Alcazar," Dravka whispered. "I sweet-talked one of the nuns into bringing me along to court. I saw the big shit myself!"

Morgen kept her gaze on the book in front of her, hiding her irritation lest the librarians notice. "That was exceedingly foolish," she hissed. "You are supposed to be mute. Too traumatized from your ordeal to speak! And if you saw him, he could have seen *you.*"

"I'm sure he didn't," Dravka replied softly. "He'd never in a thousand years expect me to be here. Besides, all nuns look the same to him."

Morgen knew that much was true. They all looked the same to her, too.

"Still," she whispered, "you will do nothing else without my permission, is that clear?"

Dravka gave a reluctant nod. "Very well. But I have another piece of gossip that ought to make you happy. The Damiata has rejected Enrigo Redvayne's suit. She will marry Vazsoly."

The last threads of Morgen's plan wove together. "The child is stupider than I thought," she said. "I suppose she believed his claim about this magical gift that commands an undead army."

Dravka's light blue eyes gleamed. "You mean, the thing that *you* have?"

Morgen turned slowly to face her, caught off balance at last. "What?"

"Isn't that what you hid in our rooms?" Dravka continued. "The Grand Menotte? Don't worry, I will tell no one. I'd much rather you have it than my bastard brother."

Morgen stared at her for a long moment. Dravka looked nervous, but then her jaw hardened and she lifted her chin. The Marcel arrogance.

"I have killed people for far less," Morgen said stonily.

"Well, you won't kill me," Dravka replied, reverting to her usual cockiness.

"How can you be so sure?"

"Because you saved our lives. It'd be a waste to murder me now." Her gaze searched Morgen's face. "Jaelle doesn't know," she added quickly.

"Good. Keep your mouth shut." Morgen turned back to the book, idly turning the pages. "What else have you learned?"

"They've set a wedding date. Four days from now."

A thrill raced through Morgen's blood. Finally. After all these years, vengeance was within reach.

Dravka shifted beside her. "What now?"

Morgen gathered up the books and scrolls, her movements brisk. "We return to our duties."

"Ugh," Dravka muttered. "I hate the dead!"

A few of the nuns glanced up from their tables. Morgen shot the girl a dire look, and they quickly made their escape.

"The dead do not care if you hate them," Morgen said once they'd passed through the library doors.

"Obviously," Dravka muttered.

"It is a service to the living that you perform. To keep their loved ones from returning and doing harm."

Dravka snorted. "Kaethe's watery twat, you sound like one of *them*."

She jerked her chin at a group of nuns crossing the cloister, but Morgen's gaze snagged on a figure lurking near the end of the path. A man, big and unkempt with a thatch of blond hair. He stared at them for a moment too long.

Her hand drifted to the pouch of spell ash concealed beneath her robes. She scanned the rainy lawns but saw no one else. When she looked back, the man was gone.

"Keep your face down," she murmured to Dravka.

For once, the girl obeyed without question, staring meekly at the ground. They took the curving pathway, pebbles crunching beneath their feet.

"Who was that?" Dravka asked after a minute. "Do you know him?"

Buried beneath that surly exterior was a clever mind, Morgen thought. The girl paid attention even when it seemed she didn't.

"He looked familiar," Morgen admitted, "but I'm not sure from where. Most likely a tradesman making a delivery to the kitchens."

Still, she kept a close eye out as they walked back to the dormitory. The man did not appear again, and she saw no one besides other sisters. When they entered their small, spare chamber, Jaelle leapt to her feet. Her face was red, her eyes puffy.

"Please." The girl's voice trembled, fresh tears welling. "When can we leave? If Vaz finds us..."

"He won't." Dravka set her hands on Jaelle's shoulders. "I won't let him hurt you again, I promise."

Morgen frowned. "Hurt you? I thought he exiled you to the convent in Prydwen."

"Well, he did that," Dravka said. "But I quarreled with him often, before. He would beat me, but then he realized I didn't care, so he would beat Jaelle instead if he was angry with me."

"I see." Morgen studied them. No wonder the little one was so quiet and fearful.

"Vaz said we were worthless, except for our names and the sons we'd bear," Dravka continued in a dispassionate tone. "He wanted me to wed one of his margraves. A disgusting old goat with gray hairs sprouting from his ears. When I told him to fuck off, he sent us both to the convent."

Jaelle was staring out the window. She looked like a fox who just heard the baying of the hounds. "I can't stay here."

"Well, you must." Morgen knew she sounded uncaring, but she couldn't help it. *Ice for blood, salt for heart.* "You have nowhere else to go. And there is no reason to think he will find you. Just don't do anything stupid."

Jaelle stared at her, big blue eyes shining with betrayal. "You're leaving us, aren't you? When you're done with him?"

When Morgen did not reply, her face crumpled. She flung herself onto her pallet and burrowed beneath the thin blanket. The lump quivered but didn't make a sound.

The room felt too small, suffocating. Morgen ignored Dravka's hot glare boring into her back as she strode out the door and slammed it behind her.

TWENTY

L o leaned forward, her newly chin-length hair tucked behind her ears as she watched Cas and Achaemenes spar on the quarterdeck. The dull thwack of wood on wood echoed across the ship. Tijah stood beside her with a bemused expression.

Cas wielded his staff with more enthusiasm than skill, lunging at Achaemenes. The daēva sidestepped the clumsy attack, twirling his broom handle to rap Cas on the back of the knees. Cas stumbled forward but managed to smack his opponent's shoulder – more by accident than design.

"Keep your stance wide," Lo called down. "And hold the staff more in the middle."

Cas adjusted his grip and jabbed at his opponent. The broom handle cracked against his staff, deflecting the blow.

Lo itched to demonstrate the proper forms herself, but she'd probably knock them both overboard. In the last two days, she'd tripped and fallen six times, nearly put her own eye out with a toothbrush, accidentally started several fires, and somehow got her braid stuck in the bilge pump. After collective efforts to free it had failed, Cas had sawed the hair off with his iron knife. He'd insisted on keeping the braid, which she thought was weird but sweet.

"Achaemenes fights well enough with a blade," Tijah remarked, "but I fear he has not yet mastered the broom."

Well enough? Back in Prydwen, Lo had seen him take on half a dozen soldiers at once. The daēva's sword was a lethal blur.

"You could give them some pointers too, you know," she said.

Tijah crossed her arms. "I prefer to let fools learn from their own mistakes."

Lo couldn't really blame her. Tijah still had a lump on her head from the last time Cas had accidentally ignited the staff's runes.

"Better he just thumps people with it," Lo said. "Look, the thing is quiet as a frozen pond. No magic whatsoever—"

She trailed off as a beam of ghostly light pierced the sky. After a moment, she realized it was not, in fact, coming from the staff, but from the top of a stone watchtower rising from the sea ahead.

"The Last Beacon," Nathan said quietly.

It was the first time he had emerged from his cabin since Losthaven. Now he stood behind them, face upturned in something approaching awe. "I've heard of it, but never thought I'd see it with my own eyes."

As they drew closer, Lo saw the intricate carvings of vines and stars that etched the surface. Where the stone had cracked, wildflowers burst forth. At its pinnacle, the lighthouse emitted a pearlescent radiance that rolled across the waves in a slow, pulsing rhythm like the heartbeat of a sleeping animal.

"A resting place for souls on their final journey," Nathan explained. "There are twelve in the Cold Sea — or there used to be. Jaskin's journals claimed that most have fallen to the waves, their lights extinguished. But the Last Beacon still stands. Its name is Dandariel."

"Who built them?" Tijah asked.

"No one knows," Nathan replied. "Perhaps the Five. Perhaps something even older."

As the *Wind-Witch* drew closer, Lo smelled oakmoss and blue juniper, wild strawberries and green plums, melted snow and freshly turned spring earth.

Memories flooded her.

Of laughing as her pet goat Minerva nibbled grain from Lo's fingers, her soft lips tickling.

Of holding Papa's strong, calloused hand as they walked through the bazaar in Susa, the taste of cardamom cake on her tongue.

Of Mama singing lullabies in the musical, throaty language of the Four-Legs Clan.

Moments of pure, simple happiness, strung like beads along the thread of her life — until the day eight years ago when it snapped.

Yet there was joy to be found in the later time, too. The kindness of her foster parents, Javid and Katsu. Her pleasure at learning to fly wind ships. The countless people who had gone out of their way to aid her search, like Culach Kafsnjór and his wife, Mina.

And most of all, the plump cat at her feet, her oldest and stoutest friend — in both senses of the word.

Her ability to feel things had been blunted since she came to the Cold Sea, but Lo was forced to sneakily wipe one eye. She saw Tijah doing the same.

The lighthouse sat upon a verdant isle. Silver-winged birds flitted through the trees, and spiders spun their webs in the secret places. An urge to stop there tugged at Lo's heart. Just an hour to feel the grass beneath her feet.

"It's so beautiful," she murmured.

"Aye," Cas said from the quarterdeck. "And not meant for us." His voice was a bit thick. "I always hoped... I promised so many people that what came after would be better, but I wasn't sure. But if the ones who built this are waiting on the far shore... They must be good."

Achaemenes stood at his side, leaning on the mop. "There is evil in the world, but that is our work," he said shortly.

The *Wind-Witch* sailed on. They watched in silence as Dandariel's pulsing light faded beyond the horizon. Lo's memories faded with it, leaving an emptiness inside. She turned to Tijah.

"What sort of bargain did my parents make with Kaethe?" she asked.

"They agreed to hunt restless dead for half the year. That's all I know." Tijah's expression softened. "They loved you more than anything—"

"But that's not true, is it?" Lo cut in. "Or they wouldn't have left me behind."

"It's not that simple—"

"Seems simple enough to me. They made their choice, and I'm the one who had to live with it."

Tijah winced. "I can't blame you for being mad, but they do love you. You mustn't ever doubt it."

"Why not?" Lo muttered, not especially liking herself but unable to stop.

"Because it doesn't have anything to do with you," Tijah said patiently. "Nazafareen is the type to kick a burrow of red scorpions when she gets bored. Not one for the quiet life. And Darius isn't much better." She shook her head in wonder.

"Girl, you've barely scratched the surface of the dumb shit those two have done."

Lo couldn't help but smile. "You'll have to tell me sometime."

"Glad to. They fucking deserve it." Yet Tijah's own smile was fond.

"When Nathan showed them to me in a shard of mirror, they seemed happy." Lo chewed her lip. "What if they don't want to go home?"

Tijah shot her a look. "Are you joking? Magnus is messing with their minds. They're not happy. They're enchanted! But hey, at least they're not hanging upside-down in a dungeon."

A thump drew their attention to the quarterdeck, where the sparring had resumed. Cas hooked Achaemenes's ankle with his staff, sending him sprawling. Achaemenes let out a surprised laugh as Cas pulled him to his feet. With a grin and a clap on Cas's shoulder, Achaemenes ambled over to join Tijah, and they fell into conversation.

"That was ... less than terrible," Lo said to Cas.

"From you, I'll take it as high praise." He wiped his brow.

"Want some tepid water that's been sitting in a barrel?"

He nodded and they headed astern. As Lo passed the boom, a line snapped with a twang. The heavy wooden spar swung straight for her head. Without breaking stride, her hand shot out. The boom smacked into her palm.

"Nice try, Bitches!" She turned to Cas, voice lowering to normal again. "Now tell me again what the runes say."

He cleared his throat, glancing around a bit nervously. "Blood, frost, bile, and rot. Know the four humours of the dead. Master is servant, and servant is master."

"The four humours," Lo repeated. "What are they?"

"Anger, sorrow, regret and envy."

"When you lost control in Dreamhaven, the runes flared red," she said. "Like blood."

They dipped two mugs of water from the barrel and sat shoulder to shoulder, legs dangling over the side.

Cas's brow furrowed. "I was scared witless. I thought you were going to die again."

"So did I." She studied him. "But knowing you, Sleepy-Eyes, the fear masked something else. Something deeper. I'm willing to bet it was anger."

He stared at her for a moment. "I can't remember. It all happened so quickly. But...you could be right."

"Indeed I could. You told me once that red is the color you see when banishing an angry ghost. Blood must mean anger."

Cas absently thumbed the scars on his palm. "I think you're onto something."

"So if anger, represented as blood, makes the staff attack, what about the other humours?"

"Frost... That's white. It's the color I see when someone has endured extreme pain. Agony."

"Sometimes frost looks blue," Lo pointed out.

"I've seen that color, too, when I banish the dead. It means sorrow." He threw his head back and laughed. "Kaethe, it's fecking simple. Bile is yellow — that's regret. And rot must be green. Envy or greed."

They clinked tin mugs.

"I need to rein in my emotions," Cas said. "Gui was always telling me how important it is for a Quietus to set their own feelings aside. To be an empty vessel."

"But doesn't the power come from your emotions in the first place?"

He stared at her. "Not mine. *Theirs*."

"Ah. That's been your mistake. Why it went haywire and knocked out Tijah and Nathan."

"Master is servant." Cas was silent for a moment. "The four humours must awaken different powers in the staff. But we can't test it until we encounter something dead."

"Shouldn't take long around here." Lo peered up at the rigging. For two days, the *Wind-Witch* had made good speed, but now the sails hung limp.

"The wind no longer answers me," Thistle growled, padding over to them. "Something is wrong."

The ship drifted, its wake a bare ripple. Sweat slid down Lo's back. The air had grown suffocatingly hot and still.

"We'd make a faster pace swimming," Cas grumbled.

"I don't recommend it." Tijah pointed at six sleek, dark heads off the starboard bow. They looked like seals, with whiskers and large, liquid eyes. "Those are dukka. They can strip your bones of flesh in less than a minute."

One yawned, flashing needle teeth, then dove beneath the surface. The rest retreated, following the *Wind-Witch* at a distance like vultures after a dying horse.

Gradually, the water darkened to indigo, then midnight blue. They had reached the edge of the Thalassic Deep. Lo imagined the seabed plunging down to seven hundred fathoms.

"Sail ho!"

She turned. Achaemenes leaned out from the crow's nest. He pointed to a black speck on the horizon behind.

"There's little chance that whoever is pursuing us will be friendly," Nathan drawled, emerging from the hatch with his usual grimace. A silky black cloth was wrapped low across his forehead to shield his eyes.

"Did you filch that blindfold from the Laughing Gull?" Tijah asked with a frown.

"I paid for an entire dream," Nathan replied, "which was cut short. The humbug cannot begrudge me a souvenir."

"Oh, Bergmann can and he will," Tijah said.

The dukka had vanished, but the ship behind them was gaining. At first Lo assumed the black sails meant the dead had found her again. As it drew closer, she saw the vessel was being towed by a pair of massive eels. A tall figure in a ragged cloak stood at the bow.

"Shite!" she said. "That looks like Baba-hor. Can't you make us go faster?"

The last remark was directed at Thistle, who paced the deck, fur crackling with electricity.

"I am doing my best," he snarled. "It is like trying to roll a boulder uphill with one's breath." His tail vibrated like a tuning fork. "There is greater magic at work here."

"How the hell did he find us?" Cas wondered.

"Does it matter?" Nathan replied caustically. "One point for the Quickening."

He sat cross-legged on the deck in a meditative pose. Despite his hauteur, the Duc of Vendagni was no longer the polished noble Lo had met at his keep. A beard stubbled his sharp jaw, and his hair was in want of combing. The elegant black wool coat had a generous helping of cat hair on the left sleeve (Lo heard him complaining to Thistle earlier about napping on other people's things) and his shoes still bore traces of the unfortunate incident with the regurgitated tentacles.

"Travel suits you, Nathan," she said.

His eyes narrowed. "That must be ... true?"

"Yes. I think I have never seen you so happy." Lo chuckled at his consternation. "You even have a bit of color in your cheeks!"

"It's called heatstroke," he said dourly.

Time seemed to halt as they wallowed in the doldrums. It affected Baba-hor's ship as well, for he remained a league or so behind, though the gap steadily narrowed. At last, the white cliffs of the Isle of Wraiths came into view, towering against the sunless sky.

"We must be over the eel god's trench," Nathan said, peering over the side. "Who wants to knock first?"

No one spoke.

"Feck it, I'll go." Cas cupped his hands around his mouth. "Mighty Khaf-hor! We humbly beg your aid!" His voice echoed across the glassy surface.

"Yeah," Lo shouted, "we're sorry we robbed your son! But we come on a matter of great importance to all who dwell in your domain!"

They took turns pleading and gesticulating at the sea, even Nathan, though he complied with ill humor.

"I feel stupid," Tijah said after a while. "He's not coming."

Baba-hor's ship was near enough now to see the bedraggled flower crowns adorning his crew. The rusalki's expressions were tough to gauge, but Lo figured they were pissed.

"Perhaps Khaf-hor cannot hear us," Nathan said. "I hate to say it but..." His gaze slid to Lo.

"Someone has to go down there," she finished. "And it has to be me. Don't argue, Sleepy-Eyes."

Cas looked furious. "Why?"

"You know why."

"I'm not letting you drown!"

She sat down and tugged her boots off. "I'm the only one of us who can come back."

"And what if you don't?"

She rolled up her sleeves, exposing the feathery lightning scars. Once, she'd been ashamed of them, hidden them under coats with high collars. But she no longer cared what other people thought. The ones who loved her didn't mind, and the rest didn't matter.

"Pshaw," she said. "I must have one life left."

"You keep saying that," he snapped. "But one day you won't."

"For Felippa, then."

"Oh, that's dirty." His fists balled. Then he nodded once, a sharp jerk of his chin.

Tijah walked over, eyes tight. "Dumb shit must run in the family." She gave Lo a fierce hug, then kissed each cheek. "They'd be proud."

"A moment, demoiselle," Nathan said. "I have a gift for you."

He hurried to his cabin and returned with a charm of finger bones strung on a silver chain. "Lady Chaos made this. It will preserve your awareness for a short time after death." He pressed it into her hand. "Then you can remember the encounter when you return to us."

Lo nodded slowly. "But I am not like most people."

"It will work even for you, I think. Lady Chaos is unrivaled in her mastery of bone charms."

Lo recalled the beast the young necromancer had summoned from a single bone in her hair.

"I believe you," she said with a faint smile. "And now I must be gone before we are boarded by rusalki."

She started to secure Tijah's iron chain around her waist, but Cas caught her wrist.

"I'll do it," he said, fixing the links. "This is a highwayman's hitch. One tug, right here, and you're out."

She nodded gravely. "I understand."

The others turned away as Cas pulled her close. He said nothing, just kissed her as if it might be the last time ever. Lo thought of the last eight years, how lonely they had been. She cupped his face.

"You're one of the good things," she said. "The best thing."

His brows rose. "So are you," he said hoarsely.

Before she could doubt herself, Lo climbed up to the railing, eyed the black water below, and jumped.

TWENTY-ONE

The iron chain dragged Lo down, down into the twilight realm of the Thalassic Deep. In less than a minute, a band of pressure circled her chest, forcing a stream of bubbles from her lips. She tipped her head up and watched them rise to the surface, where the shrinking silhouette of the *Wind-Witch* floated against the light.

Don't look. It only makes it worse.

A sharp ache throbbed in her ears. Lo pinched her nose and blew. They popped hard, and she forced more bubbles out, her lungs emptying.

The water grew colder and faded to blue-black. The silence felt crushing.

She saw no dukka nor anything at all. Just an endless expanse, as though she sank into a bottomless void. The urge to loosen the chain and swim back up before it was too late was hard to resist. What if she was throwing away another life for nothing? Khaf-hor might not know where Magnus was. Or he might decide to simply eat her up. Eels were carnivorous, weren't they?

Numb fingers gripped the chain, but she forced them open.

Not for Felippa. Not even for her parents.

Because her gut told her it was imperative that she find Khaf-hor. Meddling Fates be damned, this was something she was meant to do. Calm descended and she closed her eyes, relaxing into the frigid embrace of the sea.

Falling, falling, falling... It was almost peaceful.

At thirty fathoms, light was a distant memory and the need for air grew unbearable. Sudden terror made her heart trip into an erratic rhythm. Then the inevitable gasp, and the sea rushed in. Death came swiftly, if not painlessly, a silent knife in the depths.

Lo felt her spirit begin to slip its mooring, but Nathan's charm dragged it back, and both mind and senses remained intact as she sank deeper into the black. It was the first time this had ever happened. She observed the process with curious detachment, as though it were happening to a stranger.

At last, her feet touched bottom, stirring up a cloud of silt that she sensed more than saw. Time passed as she drifted blind along the abyssal plain, tugged by the currents. How much time, she could not begin to say.

Her blue lips formed a fragment of riddle.

Seasons, seconds and centuries... Decades, years and days...

Slowly, memory and thought coalesced. Dead, yes, but a spark within her was stirring. She had come for answers, but would she find them before she woke again?

Drifting, drifting.

The spark inside her grew warmer, brighter. Tingling returned to fingers and toes.

I will not drown twice, she thought, reaching for the chain with clumsy hands.

Then something approached in the blackness. Something

so massive, its movement sent her spinning like a leaf in an eddy. Her mind reeled, trying to grasp the size of the behemoth that bore down on her.

Out of the inky blackness came a great shining circle. Iridescent silver-blue with a vertical stripe. An eye? It looked bigger than the *Wind-Witch*... She felt herself being sucked toward the fanged cave beneath the eye and kicked wildly, but it was useless. There was nothing to grab hold of, nowhere to hide, and help lay seven hundred fathoms above her head.

Lo was fumbling to release the chain when a voice exploded in her mind, vibrating her teeth, the marrow of her bones. It was ancient and displeased.

"Why have you disturbed my peace, sarg eresh'kigal?"

CAS PACED THE DECK, watching Baba-hor's black-sailed ship draw steadily closer. Hours had passed since Lo jumped into the sea. It had been a mistake to let her go. A terrible, terrible mistake.

"She should have been back by now," he muttered, stripping off his boots.

"Have faith," Nathan said. "I am certain the charm worked."

"But if it didn't, then she's dying down there." He gazed at the dark water, panic building. "Again and again."

"I hope you don't mean to follow her?" Nathan looked worried now.

"As far as I can, aye." Cas tugged his cami off.

Tijah gave him a hard nod. "Go." Her gaze shifted to the rusalki lining the deck of Baba-hor's boat.

"We'll deal with them," Achaemenes added.

Cas strode to the stern and dove into the glassy water. He swam down, lungs burning, eyes straining in the gloom.

Nothing.

He surfaced, sucked in a breath, and dove down again, deeper this time.

Come back. Come back. Come back.

He stopped at about three fathoms to tread water, fighting the natural buoyancy that tried to haul him back up again like a cork. That's when it struck him — the flaw in Lo's plan.

He knew death intimately, had seen it in every guise. A drowned body was waterlogged and wouldn't float for a few days, not until it bloated. The chain might carry her down, but she'd have to swim back up, fighting the weight of the water that filled her lungs.

Spots danced in his vision. Cas kicked to the surface.

"Anything?" Tijah leaned over the rail. Her self-command was rarely dented, but he could see the anxiety below the surface.

He shook hair from his eyes. "No, but—"

A head popped up thirty paces past the starboard bow. His heart lifted... Then two more appeared.

"Dukka!" Tijah shouted. "Get your ass aboard!"

"I see them," he said tightly.

One more try. Just one more.

He submerged and kicked deeper, so deep the light faded and a vise tightened around his chest.

There. A pale form drifted in the gloom. Cas reached her in seconds and hooked an arm around her waist. The chain was gone, which meant she'd taken it off. Tried to save herself. Kaethe, she must have swum as far as she could before...

Her flesh was icy, her eyes closed and lips parted. Cas clawed for the surface with one arm, trying not to pass out.

The ship bobbed above in a halo of light that grew brighter with each stroke. Lungs afire, he broke the surface with a gasp.

"Rope!" he spluttered.

Tijah quickly tossed a line. Cas looped it under Lo's arms and tied a noose. Her head hung forward, limp, hair obscuring her face. The dukka were closer now, many of them.

So was Baba-hor's vessel. As Achaemenes hauled Lo aboard, Cas saw a rusalka's arm go back, her coral knife flashing through the air. It whizzed past Tijah's shoulder and struck a dukka, sending the creature fleeing in a cloud of blood.

Cas stroked hard for the *Wind-Witch*. He was acutely aware that anything could be swimming up from below, unseen. The words *strip your bones of flesh in less than a minute* played in a loop through his head.

"Hurry!" Tijah urged — unnecessarily.

He didn't waste breath answering her, just kept swimming, long steady strokes like he'd taught Teo at the old horse pond. He was nearly there when a melody came to his ears, sweet and piercing. It sang of the dark, quiet depths, of everlasting peace. An end to pain and suffering. His sluggish thoughts turned to Dandariel, the Last Beacon. It waited for him, serene and welcoming, if he would just cease his pointless struggles...

Then hands were dragging him over the rail. He collapsed on the deck, panting. The song faded like a half-remembered dream. Lo lay next to him, her skin waxy. Thistle padded over and licked her hand.

A shadow fell across the deck. Cas looked up to see the prow of Baba-hor's black-sailed boat, its tethered eels writhing in the still water.

Rusalki lined the deck, eerily motionless like dressmakers' mannequins. Tijah and Achaemenes drew their swords. Thistle arched his back with a hiss. Nathan stepped forward, one hand in his pocket and a just-try-me look on his face.

Baba-hor raised a webbed hand. "I did not come to fight," he called over.

Cas's lungs were still aflame. He cradled Lo in his arms, stroking the sodden hair from her face.

"Then why are you here?" Tijah asked, sliding her blade halfway back into the sheath.

"To warn you." Baba-hor pointed to Cas. "The mortifex called Janus seeks that one."

Tijah swore softly. "You saw him?"

"In Dreamhaven. He came to the Laughing Gull not long after you left." Baba-hor's wide, frog-like mouth turned down. "I banished him."

"What?" She shook her head. "How?"

"At his own request. He told me his real name — Justinian. He gave me this boat in exchange."

Hatred boiled up. If Cas had been holding the staff, he might have blown them all to the four corners of the Cold Sea. "The banishing would take him straight to Magnus's lair," he said. "Which means Justinian is already there."

He shook his head bitterly. "If we had stayed at the inn, we might have captured him. Forced him to tell us where to find Glash's Tusk."

"That is ill luck," Baba-hor conceded.

"You have no idea," Nathan said.

"I came because I despise Magnus and his ruffians," Baba-hor said evenly. "But also because you still owe me a ship."

"For goddess's sake," Tijah growled, "you already have a ship! Why must you take this one? And how did you find us anyway?"

Baba-hor eyed the mast. "You stole my tooth," he said stiffly. "I can follow it anywhere."

"Then we'll return your damned tooth when we're done with it," she retorted.

He drew himself up to his full, towering height, flourishing his seaweed cloak. "Unacceptable."

"Then you *are* here to fight!" Tijah's sword rasped from its scabbard again.

"If we must." Baba-hor scowled. "You have no honor."

This remark seemed to crawl straight under Tijah's skin. Her jaw tightened. "You've put us in a very difficult position," she ground out.

"It is not so difficult. I was promised the *Wind-Witch*, and that is what I shall have. But I will not abandon you with nothing, as you did to me." Baba-hor looked around, to nods of agreement from the rusalki. "You may have this ship."

Tijah's brows climbed. "The dead people boat?"

"Yes, the dead people boat. It's seaworthy."

The vessel was barely a third the size of the *Wind-Witch*. The rusalki were crowded together like tadpoles, with more up in the rigging.

"What amenities does it have?" Nathan asked. "Bunks? A galley? I very much doubt—"

"Oh, be quiet," Tijah snapped. "Dead people don't sleep or eat."

Nathan rolled his eyes. "That is precisely the point I was trying to make. It is hardly an even trade."

"It's not supposed to be an even trade!" Baba-hor exclaimed with obvious frustration. "Do you grasp the meaning of a contest? There is a winner and a loser. I was the winner. You were the losers. I'm doing you a favor even offering you this boat as a consolation prize!"

Tijah folded her arms. "Unbelievable," she muttered. "Trust me, that thing is no prize."

The ship drifted closer and Baba-hor noticed the bloodless, unmoving figure on the deck for the first time. His large eyes blinked several times. "The sorceress. Is she...?"

Lo convulsed, coughing violently. Seawater spewed out. Cas rubbed her back and whispered a silent prayer of thanks to Kaethe.

"Dead?" she croaked. "Not anymore."

Baba-hor stared at her for a long moment. "You have seen my father," he said.

"Yes." She coughed some more. "He told me where to find Magnus the Merciless."

Baba-hor's nostrils flared. "What did you trade for this knowledge?"

"I promised to return the favor." She shivered. "When the time comes and He wills it."

Tijah pulled her leather coat off and slung it over Lo's shoulders.

"Unspecified bargain with a god?" she whispered. "Not the smartest idea, but I've been there."

Lo gave her a weak smile. She climbed wearily to her feet, Thistle twining around her bare ankles. "As captain of this ship, and duly authorized agent of Falcon Couriers, I accept your generous offer, Baba-hor. The *Wind-Witch* is yours, as it should have been in Dreamhaven."

Cas couldn't quite believe his ears. "You're giving him the ship?" he hissed. "Just like that?"

Her gaze was distant. "I must."

Baba-hor grinned. "Then we have a deal!" He rubbed his webbed hands together. "Let us board, my lovelies."

"Do we get to keep the eels?" Achaemenes wondered.

"They are my cousins twice-removed," Baba-hor replied. "No, you may not keep them."

Tijah grumbled under her breath, saw Nathan doing the same, and stopped immediately. Working with the rusalki, they tied the two ships together and made the exchange, including most of Nathan's trunks and the heavily swathed black mirror containing Jaskin Cazal. The spirit had gone ominously quiet. Either he was sulking that they no longer trusted him as their navigator, or he was plotting something. Most likely the latter, Cas thought.

For provisions, Baba-hor left them with two water barrels and a bit of hardtack.

"Good luck in your quest," he said, leaning against the mast.

"Don't even say that," Nathan groaned. He glanced at the dark hatch leading below. "I will make sure Uncle Jaskin is secure."

"Let us know if you find any dead people!" Tijah called after him. "I mean, besides Lord Bag o'Bones!"

As the *Wind-Witch* sailed off into the distance, Cas pulled Lo aside. "What did you do?" he demanded. The words came out harsher than he intended.

Lo met his gaze. "What I had to. Javid will murder me for losing his property, but—"

"I don't mean the feckin' ship!"

"I know." She sighed. "You mean the bargain I made with Khaf-hor. But that's not important. This is what's important." She leaned forward and kissed him, her lips deliriously warm. "Thank you, Sleepy Eyes, for saving me."

His anger fizzled. "I won't do it again," he warned.

"Yes, you would."

He blew out a long sigh. "Aye, I would."

"I know where they are now." Her blue eyes glittered. "Are you ready to finish this?"

Ragged nails dug into the scars on his palm. "Aye, I am."

A fresh gust of wind swelled the canvas. Thistle's bristling fur settled, his magic unbound once more, and Lo strode away to set a course for Glash's Tusk.

TWENTY-TWO

S*queak. Squeak. Creakedy-creak.*

Gerda rocked to and fro, sipping from a jeweled goblet. Her white hair stuck up in tufts like an aged vulture.

"Why are you so puny, girl?" She gave a disdainful sniff. "Did your mother deny you her teat?"

Felippa perched on a wooden stool facing the old mortifex, arms hugging her knees. The walls of Gerda's chamber glinted with frost, but she refused to shiver.

"Why are you so bitter, crone?" she asked. "Did someone piss in your wine?"

Gerda's harrumphed. Blue flames hissed in the hearth, yet the air remained as dank as an underground tomb. Firelight cast writhing shadows across her face as she took another sip.

"Bold words for a runt."

"Bold slurping for a puckered prune."

"At least I can reach the top shelf, tiny."

"At least my face doesn't look like a drowned troll's backside, you old bat."

Gerda smiled, revealing brown stumps of teeth. "I'd rather be old than stunted."

"I'd rather be small than a sour old hag."

The mortifex leaned forward, goblet clenched in gnarled fingers. "Careful, girl. I eat mice like you for breakfast."

Felippa lifted her chin. "Try it and I'll give you such a belly-ache, you'll be spewing out both ends for a week."

Gerda threw back her head and laughed. It was a rusty, uneven thing, like a door opening into a room that hadn't seen light in centuries.

"You've got spirit, brat. I'll give you that." She eyed Felippa with something like approval. "Now stop yammering before I use you for a footstool."

Felippa glowered but held her tongue. She had nothing left to lose. Magnus and Justinian were only keeping her alive as bait for Cas. At least the old witch seemed to be warming to her, if glacially. She'd take her victories where she could.

Gerda took another swig of wine, squinting over the rim of her goblet. "Is your brother a scrawny thing too?"

Felippa shook her head. "No, he's regular size."

"Then what's wrong with you?"

It was a tale she rarely told, certainly not to strangers. And there was little chance Gerda would find any sympathy in her withered heart. But she was the woman's prisoner now. What else did they have to do but talk?

"Justinian attacked me when I was very young," Felippa admitted. "After that, I never grew like other children."

Gerda grunted. The coals in her eyes flared. "Yet you lived."

"Barely."

"Still, you must be strong."

To Felippa's horror, her throat tightened. She looked away, blinking hard. She wouldn't cry, not in front of Gerda.

"I got lucky," she muttered.

"Luck is for weaklings. You're a fighter, girl." Gerda drained her cup and smacked her thin lips. "Enough talk of that whoreson. I'm parched. Fetch me another bottle."

Felippa sighed and trudged to the dusty shelves at the far end of the chamber. "Which one?"

"That blue bottle on the left!" Gerda called, rubbing her hands together. "It's muscadine. A special vintage."

As the fex poured herself another large helping, Felippa studied her. Other than the jeweled goblet, she didn't seem to care much for treasure. It was a stark chamber, with only the rocking chair, stool, and collection of colored glass bottles.

"How did you come to live here?" Felippa asked.

Gerda shrugged a bony shoulder. "I was crossing the Cold Sea when Magnus's reavers boarded my ship." She buried her face in the goblet. "They stripped us of what we carried. In my case, it wasn't much. I begged them to take me along when they left and they agreed."

"How long ago was that?"

"Don't know. Time's meaningless in this forsaken place."

Felippa tried to make sense of it. Most of the fexes had been here practically forever. But Gerda... it sounded like she had come more recently. She wasn't one of the pirates. She was one of their *victims*.

"So you're not stuck in purgatory like the rest?" Felippa asked.

"You're quick, brat." Gerda lifted her cup in a mock toast. "No, I am not."

"Then why didn't you cross to the far shore when you had the chance?"

Gerda's gaze dimmed. For a long moment, Felippa thought she wouldn't answer. Then she shook her head. "My family was brought to ruin, our holdfast taken by enemies. I had nothing left." She looked around the bare chamber, the chill flames dancing in the hearth. "But here at least I belong."

Felippa nodded slowly. She could understand that. To have lost everything, to be set adrift... Finding a place to call home, even one as strange as this, was no small thing.

Gerda snorted at her expression. "Save your pity, brat. I've no use for it." She tossed back more wine and thumped her chest. "I am a Kafsnjór. Once we were one of the oldest, most illustrious Valkirin families in the land of Nocturne. In fact..." She leaned forward, her eyes gleaming. "I am a direct descendant of Magnus himself, though he lived long before my time."

Felippa's eyes widened. "Truly? He never mentioned that."

"Did he not?" Gerda cocked her head. "And what has our king been telling you, *scribe*?"

As usual, she imbued the word with mockery, but it seemed more like force of habit. Felippa hesitated. She'd sworn not to tell anyone, but what harm could it do now?

"He said he was a great warrior, feared by all who knew his name," Felippa said. "That he led armies into battle and conquered vast lands."

Gerda's eyes narrowed. "Which battles?"

Felippa had an excellent memory. "The Battle of Bloodied Shields. The Siege of Solthiem. The Sundering of the Eastern Fjords."

Gerda let out a rasping laugh. "There is no place called Solthiem in all of Nocturne."

"I am not surprised," Felippa confided. "I think he made half of it up."

"What else?"

"He spoke of a brother named Valnor the Valiant who fought by his side."

"Magnus had no brothers," Gerda cut in. "He was an only

child." She drained her goblet and reached for the flagon to refill it.

An uneasy feeling crept over Felippa. She'd assumed Magnus had exaggerated his exploits, but surely there must be some kernel of truth.

"He also told me he had a castle called Stormholt in the Cloudpeak Mountains."

Gerda scoffed. "I know the names of every holdfast in Nocturne. There is no Stormholt, nor mountains of that name. Magnus was never a great warrior or conquerer. He was a schemer, always plotting and planning." She took another swig of wine, then peered at Felippa. "Do you want some, brat?"

Felippa blinked in surprise. Was Gerda actually offering to share? She didn't really want any wine, but she wouldn't refuse. "Yes, please."

Gerda tilted the flagon over a second goblet and handed it to Felippa. "A rare find, this. Stolen from Grindal's Tomb!"

Felippa sniffed the goblet, then tipped it to her lips. It wasn't even water. Just air. The bottles were empty. But Gerda was watching her expectantly, so she pretended to swallow.

"It's even better than the Duc's private reserve," Felippa said with a smile.

Gerda looked pleased. "Of course it is." She settled back in her chair, leather gown creaking. "Now, where was I? Ah yes, Fridlaug."

"Who's Fridlaug?" Felippa asked.

"Magnus's wife. Did he not mention her either?" Gerda snorted.

Wife? Felippa had always imagined Magnus as a lone warrior, unburdened by familial ties. "No, he never spoke of her."

"Fridlaug of Val Tourmaline. A fierce shield-maiden in her own right." Nostalgia tinged Gerda's voice. "She captured Magnus during a border skirmish. Kept him chained in her own hall for months."

Felippa's eyes widened. The idea of the mighty Magnus as a helpless captive was hard to fathom.

"Oh, he was furious at first," Gerda went on with relish. "Vowed vengeance and death. But Fridlaug was shrewd. She saw his potential."

"What happened?" Felippa breathed, drawn into the tale in spite of herself.

"She struck a deal. Magnus would be freed and they would wed, uniting their holdfasts." Gerda chuckled. "He got the better end of that bargain, if you ask me."

Felippa tried to picture it — Magnus and this mystery woman, ruling side by side. A political union, but still...

"Did they love each other?"

Gerda fixed her with a sharp look. "Love?" She tapped a gnarled finger against her goblet. "They were well-matched, I'll say that. Both ambitious. Cunning. Proud."

She took another drink, her eyes distant. "When Magnus became overlord, he wanted everyone to call him Magnus the Merciless. But Fridlaug just laughed."

A slow grin spread across Gerda's withered features. "Called him Magnus the Rather Unpleasant instead. To his face and in front of the entire court."

"And he let her?"

"Oh, he blustered and raged. But he never did tame her." Gerda shook her head, lost in memory. "They ruled together for centuries, and their names were feared across all of Nocturne."

Felippa's brow furrowed. "Centuries?"

Gerda waved a dismissive hand. "My race is long-lived, girl. Far beyond your reckoning."

"How old are you, then?" The question burst out before Felippa could think better of it.

Gerda squinted, her lips pursing. "I cannot remember precisely. Time loses meaning after a while." She shrugged. "I am certain I was quite old when I died, though. Five hundred years at least."

Five hundred years. The number staggered Felippa. To have seen and done so much.

Gerda was frowning now, her gaze turned inward. "I find it passing strange that Magnus did not mention Fridlaug to you. She was his queen, after all." Her eyes sharpened. "Did he never mention Val Moraine either?"

"Is that a person?"

"A place, foolish girl. The seat of his power." Gerda leaned forward, the first real interest sparking in her rheumy eyes. "Are you telling me that Magnus has not spoken the name of his own holdfast? His mighty fortress from which he ruled for centuries?"

Felippa shifted beneath that penetrating stare. "No. And I have an excellent memory."

They eyed each other, suspicion creeping in like a chill mist.

"I can see Magnus embellishing his exploits," Gerda said slowly, "making himself more of a hero than he was. But to omit Fridlaug and Val Moraine entirely..." She trailed off, her expression hardening. "Something is amiss here, and I mean to find out what."

Gerda's rocking grew more agitated. *Creakedy-creak.* Felippa watched the chair's shadow tip forward and back against the far wall. The edges were clear and sharp. It looked unoccupied, as though it moved on its own. Suddenly, the odd thing that had been nagging at her rose to the surface.

"Did you ever notice..." She stifled a yawn. "None of you cast a shadow, but Magnus does."

"What are you talking about, brat?"

"The torches in the audience chamber," Felippa continued. "It's hard to see because his throne is so big, but Magnus casts a funny-looking shadow." Her jaw cracked in an even wider yawn. "It doesn't match the shape of him. It's like..." She cocked her head, considering. "*Smaller.*"

"I hadn't noticed," Gerda said gruffly. "But I'll have a look for myself next time I see him."

She lapsed into silence, the goblet resting in her lap, gaze thoughtful. Despite Felippa's curiosity, exhaustion tugged at her eyelids. There was no bed in the spartan chamber, so she curled up on the rug before the hearth, seeking what meager warmth she could.

Something struck her back, making her flinch. Gerda had tossed a musty blanket at her.

"Cover yourself, scrawny," the old mortifex grunted. "Lest you freeze solid in the night."

Felippa pulled a face. "How thoughtful. I'm surprised you can even lift such a heavy thing, granny."

"Heavy? Ha! 'Tis light as a cobweb, much like the space between your ears."

"Better a cobweb than an airless crypt like yours."

Gerda's mouth twitched. She took a swig of fake wine. "Bold words for a pipsqueak."

"Bold claims for a feeble crone."

They traded barbs a moment longer, but there was no real rancor in it. Felippa burrowed into the blanket, trying not to imagine where it might have come from.

Gerda turned back to the hearth, refilling her cup with

exaggerated dignity. In the flickering light, the lines of her face seemed briefly smoothed away, and Felippa thought she glimpsed something in her eyes. A deep, ancient grief.

Then it was gone, and Gerda was just a cranky old fex, hunched in her rocking chair beside the fire.

TWENTY-THREE

Destiny seemed to smile on them at last, for Khafhor's trench was only a day's sail from the mortifex lair. It appeared through a gauze of mist, clinging to the island's highest peak like a crouching gargoyle. The citadel featured several towers, which were connected by narrow bridges. Looking at them, Lo felt sure she would slip and fall if she so much as placed a toe on one.

They dropped anchor just inside Imp's Claw Point — the real one, this time — a desolate promontory with waves on the windward side and a calm bay on the other. The land beyond lay hidden behind undulating tendrils of vapor. It obscured any paths that might lead up to the fortress, although Jaskin assured them there were none.

Lo and Cas lowered the black sails; Achaemenes and Tijah jumped into the shallows and dragged the vessel into a cove, hidden by brambles from prying eyes. Then they all gathered on deck, tilting their heads back to gaze up at Magnus's stronghold. It appeared to be carved into the mountain itself. No discernible route presented itself.

"If we had the *Wind-Witch*, we could sail right up there," Lo said wistfully.

Tijah grimaced and rubbed her lower back. "Too bad we have Baba-hor's crappy dead people boat." She eyed the hatch leading belowdecks. "Whatever happens, I'm not sleeping down there again. It smells weird."

Achaemenes stood at the bow, his sharp eyes scanning the skies around the citadel. "Abbadax," he muttered. "Circling. I see six."

"It won't be long before they spot us," Cas said. "We need a way up there."

Lo smiled. "I'm two steps ahead."

"How do I know I'm going to hate this plan?" Tijah asked of no one in particular.

"Because her plans are always shite," Cas said.

"Easy, now." Lo held up her palms. "Just hear me out."

Tijah grunted.

"Go on, then," Cas said, profound misgivings etched in every line of his face.

"Thank you. Here's the gist: Since whatever we do falls apart, we should set out to deliberately fail. Then the opposite might happen."

Cas cocked an eyebrow. "Come again?"

"If we fail at failing," Lo said slowly, as if speaking to the village idiot, "then what did we just do?"

There was a confused silence.

"Succeed?" Achaemenes ventured.

Lo beamed. "Correct! Now if this were a story, we'd scale the cliffs and fight our way through that citadel to rescue our loved ones. But we're not the heroes in this tale, we're the villains."

Nathan threw his hands up. "*Fichu*, she's gone mad."

"Not the villains, either," Cas said, brow wrinkling. "More

like minor characters who'll probably get killed in stupid ways."

Lo snapped her fingers. "Yes! Our only hope is to make no plan at all. Because whatever we do will go wrong anyway."

Cas nodded. "That *is* insane," he said with reluctant admiration.

Lo tapped her forehead. "I thought of it all by myself."

Tijah and Achaemenes exchanged one of those wordless looks that conveyed volumes.

"Yeah, we're not doing that," Tijah said. She held up a hand before Lo could argue. "I get what you're saying, and you might even be right. But Achaemenes and I will go our own way from here. If we're not with you, maybe we won't get caught in whatever maelstrom of misfortune the Furies have in store."

"Fates," Lo corrected.

"Same difference."

"I was going to say, shitstorm of woe," Achaemenes put in. "But maelstrom of misfortune does have a ring to it."

Lo nodded. "Don't tell us what you're planning then. In case we're tortured."

"Thanks for that," Cas said.

"I'm just being realistic."

They gathered in a tight circle, the mist curling around their ankles. Nathan cleared his throat. "I'll stay with Jaskin." He glanced at Thistle. "Keep an eye on us both if you don't trust me."

The cat blinked slowly, eyes narrowed to yellow slits. Apparently, that meant agreement.

"Give us an hour to get inside," Lo said. "We'll look for my parents and Felippa first. If they're hidden somewhere, we can't risk sending the fexes onward until we know where."

Nathan took a fragment of yellowed bone from his pocket.

He closed his fist around it and muttered a string of harsh syllables. When he opened his hand, the pebble had transformed into a small hourglass filled with black sand.

"That's a neat trick," Tijah said grudgingly.

"It is not a *trick*. You make me sound like a roadside conjurer."

"Oh, pardon me." Tijah widened her eyes in mock awe. "I've witnessed a miracle! The Five have nothing on you, O Mighty Magus of the Black Arts—"

"One hour exactly," Nathan said irritably. "When the last grain falls, if you're not back, I'll break the mirror."

Lo gazed up at the citadel. One way or another, this would all be over soon. It didn't feel quite real, but her heart knew they were in the right place. She'd paid dearly for the information — and the bill was still coming due.

When I call, you must obey. Do you swear it on your last life, sarg eresh-kigal?

Teeth had glinted in the black, each longer than a ship's mast. Khaf-hor's voice hummed in her skull.

DO YOU SWEAR IT?

"Demoiselle?"

Lo shook her head. "Sorry, what?"

"If you see Justinian, feel free to cut his head off." Nathan flipped the hourglass and set it on the deck. "Well, good lu—" He cut off at their looks of horror. "Just wreak some havoc. And try to stay alive."

"The first part shouldn't be hard," Cas said. "It's the second that worries me."

"I believe in you, reaper!" Jaskin's faint voice drifted up from the hatch, followed by gales of nasty cackling.

"Don't listen to him," Nathan said.

"Listen to who?" Tijah said with a grin. "See you around, magus."

She and Achaemenes slipped over the gunwale and disappeared into the scrubby brush that grew along the base of the cliffs. Thistle leapt down from his perch in the bow, prowling over to examine the hourglass. A paw lifted, slowly reaching—

"Don't knock that over!" Nathan chided. "*Putain*, what is wrong with you?"

They fell to arguing, and Cas and Lo took the opportunity to slink away.

"It's liberating to actually *try* to fuck up," Lo remarked. "I feel like I've finally found something I'm good at."

They picked their way up the beach, hopping over driftwood and boulders.

"So." Cas gripped the staff, which he felt certain was integral to Tijah's maelstrom. "I guess we're going in the front?"

"Oh yeah," Lo said with an unhinged smile. "Definitely the front."

"COME DOWN AND FACE US, you undead cowards!" The taunt echoed against the cliff face. Cas cupped a hand around his mouth. "Or do you only feel brave behind stone walls?"

Lo shook a fist at the fortress far above. "We heard this place was guarded by mortifexes, not little bunny rabbits! Are the real pirates on holiday?"

"Good one." Cas pointed his staff and declared with mock authority, "If your swords are as dull as your wits, we'll be through your gates by sunset!"

"You call yourselves defenders?" Lo scoffed. "We've seen better protection on a chicken coop!"

Cas chewed his lip. "I've run out. No, wait." He leaned back and sniffed. "Is this a fortress or a barn? I smell livestock and cowards!"

Lo wrinkled her nose. "That doesn't work. Plus you already used cowards... Oh, here we go."

The sky darkened as a pair of mortifexes appeared, mounted on their abbadaxes. The creatures' wings stirred up loose dust as they landed.

"What's this, Orm?" said the first, who sported a bushy black beard that he'd braided into a fork.

"Well, Skegg," said Orm, who had only one eye and was even taller than Baba-hor. "I'd say it's dinner."

Cas tried to spin the staff one-handed, dropped it, picked it up, and slashed it through the air with a blood-curdling war cry. Lo rolled her eyes to the whites and started chanting in a low, ominous tone.

"Looks like the ones His Majesty has been waiting for," Orm said.

"You mean the King of the Cowardly Sea?" Cas scoffed.

The mortifexes dismounted with lethal grace, drawing long white blades.

"What's she doing?" Orm asked.

With her unevenly chopped hair, scarred arms, and corpse-like complexion, Lo looked like something designed to scare children into obedience.

"Don't you wish you knew," Cas said.

The two fexes looked at each other. "Just come along," Orm said. "King Magnus wishes to speak to you."

Cas grinned and smacked the ground with his staff. "Ready to dance, bonemen?"

"Do we have to?" Skegg asked in a bored tone.

"It would be much easier to just skip the part where we break your arms and legs," Orm said reasonably. "So get on your knees, give my boots a kiss, and swear allegiance to your new masters."

"Never!" Cas spat. He turned to Lo. "It *would* be easier," he said in a low voice. "We want to get up there anyway."

She stopped chanting. "I know. But we're doing the opposite of whatever is smart, or even the slightest bit clever, remember?"

He stared at her. "Like, the whole time?"

"Yes," she hissed. Lo dropped into a fighting crouch. "Stay behind me and try not to get stabbed."

Skegg's sword sliced through the air, a pale blur. Cas threw up his staff to parry. The bonewood blade met ancient rune-marked ash in a shower of blue sparks. The mortifex snarled, eyes flaring. Cas retreated a step, then two. Skegg advanced, teeth bared in an amused grin.

Cas strained to open himself to the staff's magic, to use his opponent's emotions against him. But the fex moved like a snake, driving him steadily back. All he could feel was his own mounting desperation.

To his left, Lo spun away from a blurring downward slash. She pivoted behind the yellow-haired giant and kicked him hard in the back of the knee. Orm stumbled with an angry bellow.

Cas got the staff up again just as Skegg rained down a flurry of vicious overhead blows. Cas barely deflected them, the staff absorbing impacts that would have shattered an ordinary weapon.

Skegg pressed his attack, white sword flashing. Cas backpedaled, parrying clumsily. He knocked aside a cut at his ribs, then a slash at his neck. The mortifex's eyes widened in surprise as he swept his staff up, catching the crossbar. Shock jolted down his arms. Cas strained to push back against Skegg's unearthly strength. More sparks showered the beach as he finally twisted the blade aside.

He risked another glance at Lo. She ducked under a stab,

pivoted, and drove her fist into Orm's gut. The one-eyed mortifex grunted in anger. His weight shifted, taking him off-balance for an instant. Lo hooked his ankle and heaved. Three hundred pounds of undead flesh slammed to the ground.

We're actually holding our own, Cas thought in amazement.

Time seemed to slow. He let instinct guide him, flowing around Skegg's next strike and the next. The hours of drilling had taught him something after all. His movements became more fluid, anticipating Skegg's attacks.

Again, Cas sought the talisman's power. He could see faint colors swirling around his opponent. Red, mostly, but also flickers of blue and yellow. But the onslaught was relentless, and Cas could spare no attention for anything except staying alive.

Sweat stung his eyes as he saw an opening and jabbed the staff at Skegg's throat. It connected with a satisfying crunch. When the fex made a high-pitched whistle, Cas figured it was the result of a crushed windpipe.

"Who's the puny mortal now, eh?" he asked with a grin.

Screeches rent the air. Cas spun to see the pair of abbadaxes thundering toward them, talons digging furrows in the beach. Then the flat of Skegg's sword slammed into his ribs. He was flung backwards. Cas hit the ground so hard he rolled, the staff flying from his grip.

"Feck," he groaned, spitting a mouthful of bloody sand.

Through blurred eyes, he saw Lo crumple under the sweep of a wing. Cas struggled to reach her, but a boot pressed him back down. Someone seized a fistful of hair, wrenching his head back. Icy breath brushed his cheek.

"I've been waiting for you," a voice whispered.

It was one he knew well. Cas tried to jerk free, but Justinian tightened his grip. More fexes swarmed forward, pinning Cas flat. He thrashed until the edge of a blade pressed into his throat. From the corner of his eye, he saw Lo similarly subdued, blood trickling from a cut on her temple.

Their hands were bound with rope. Then they were dragged upright and thrown like sacks of grain over the backs of the abbadaxes. The creatures' carrion reek filled Cas's nose. With a spring of their powerful back legs, they launched skyward.

Your hero has arrived, Felippa, he thought, the ground falling away so fast he would have lost his breakfast had there been anything left to eat.

Tijah scrambled over the rocks, scanning the cliff face for any sign of a path leading up to Magnus's fortress. The sheer stone offered no handholds or crevices.

She paused beside a tidal pool, studying the clear water. A glint caught her eye. She reached in and plucked out a mussel shell, turning it over. A heap of them lay scattered nearby. All pried open and emptied.

"Achaemenes," she called softly. "Look at this."

He crouched at her side, examining the shell. His gaze lifted to the cliff, picking out a shadowed cleft nearly concealed behind a boulder. "There."

They approached cautiously. Achaemenes ran his hands over the limestone surrounding the opening. He unsheathed his knife and chipped at the soft rock, breaking off crumbling chunks.

Tijah helped widen the hole until it yawned just wide enough for them to enter. Cool air wafted out, carrying the faint scent of minerals.

Tijah drew her scimitar. "I'll go first."

She squeezed into the narrow crevice, finding it a tight fit even for her lean frame. The rock pressed close on all sides as she crept forward. After a short distance, the tunnel opened into a small cavern. Tijah rose to a crouch, scimitar at the ready. Achaemenes moved past her, the gold cuff around his wrist gleaming in the dim light.

"Someone's been living here," he murmured, indicating a hollow rock set beneath a trickle of water. More mussel shells were piled in a corner, near a nest of leaves and grass.

Tijah frowned. Who would choose this remote sea cave as a shelter? "Mortifexes don't eat," she said. "But that entrance was just about the right size for a kid. Cas's little sister?"

Achaemenes nodded slowly, his face grave. "Then where is she now?"

Tijah didn't want to think about the possibilities. "Let's see where this leads." She gestured to a narrow opening in the back of the cavern.

They proceeded cautiously along the upward-sloping tunnel, following the stale current of air. It wound on and on, narrowing and widening at intervals. The drip of water echoed off the stone and bats chittered overhead, their leathery wings fluttering past Tijah's face.

"As long as there's no fucking snakes in here, we're good," she muttered.

"I like snakes," Achaemenes remarked behind her.

"Because you're weird as shit."

Her braids were damp with sweat by the time the passage opened into a spacious chamber. Tijah straightened, rolling her stiff shoulders. Weak light filtered through a crevice overgrown with vines, affording a glimpse of the bay far below.

"We made it halfway up the cliff face, at least," Achaemenes said.

She nodded, savoring the salt breeze that wafted through the opening. "The citadel can't be much farther. If we—"

"Over here!" he called.

Achaemenes stood at the back of the cavern, staring into a shadowed alcove. She crossed to his side and sucked in a breath.

An iron cage squatted in the darkness, and within it, a naked man lay curled in on himself. His skin had the waxy pallor of a corpse, and a white beard covered him like a shroud. He did not appear to be breathing.

"What in the name of Innunu?" Tijah prodded the still form with the flat of her blade. The flesh was cold and unyielding but showed no sign of decay. She met Achaemenes's baffled gaze.

"Who is he? Why would Magnus imprison one of his own?"

"I don't know." Achaemenes knelt to examine the heavy iron lock on the cage door.

Tijah moved closer, studying the man's face. Harsh lines cut across his brow and around his downturned mouth. His eyes stared sightlessly from sunken sockets.

"He's perfectly preserved," she murmured. "As if frozen in time."

Achaemenes tugged on the lock. It held fast. "His beard is so long. Was it already like this when they locked him up? Or has it kept growing all this time?"

Tijah shook her head. The whole scene defied reason. Her eyes narrowed as a thought occurred to her.

"You don't think... Could there be a connection to whoever was hiding in that cave down below?"

Achaemenes straightened. "Who knows? This place is full of mysteries."

They spent a few minutes searching the chamber for any

other exits or clues, but found only damp stone walls. They'd reached a dead end.

"No grand staircase to the top. How inconsiderate," Tijah said dryly. An idea sparked in her mind. She moved to the vine-shrouded opening and angled her head out, peering upward.

"The cliff looks climbable from here. If we can squeeze through this gap, we might be able to—"

The words died on her tongue. Around the curve of the rocky headland, a large brigantine with black sails glided into view.

"Is that more of them?" Achaemenes muttered.

"Yeah." Tijah swore softly at the figures swarming across the deck. "A *lot* more."

TWENTY-FOUR

The abbadax touched down on a narrow platform. Gloved hands yanked Cas and Lo from the saddle and dragged them into an immense audience chamber. Cas craned his neck at the opulent space — ceilings so high they vanished in gloom, tiers of stone galleries with ornate archways, marble pillars it would take ten men to link arms around.

Through an open wall — the side they had landed on — the turquoise expanse of the Cold Sea stretched to the horizon, perhaps all the way to Khaf-hor's Trench. A narrow bridge led to another tower, seemingly suspended in midair and offering a gut-churning view of the drop below.

All impressive but not the strangest part. Here and there, in scattered mounds like the frenzied digging of a giant mole, were coins and plates, bits of armor, golden chalices, swords and orbs and raw jewels, all glittering in the torchlight. Statues in niches stood guard over the treasure hoard, their empty eyes unblinking.

Cas and Lo shared a look. *Holy shite.*

A crimson carpet led down the center of the hall to a single figure seated on a throne. They were shoved to their knees before the dais.

Magnus the Merciless looked much the way Cas had imagined he would — long white braids, a flowing beard, and a crown wreathed in blue flame. Rings glinted on every finger, diamonds encrusted his robe. His throne seemed to be made from partly melted figurines.

The icons, Cas guessed, that people had clutched for comfort as they exhaled their last breaths, only to have them stolen as they crossed the Cold Sea. *What a sanglant bastard.*

"So," Lo said, raising a brow. "We meet at last."

Magnus ignored her, his red stare boring into Cas from the dais. "Where is the Grand Menotte, you mangy little cur?"

Justinian knelt briefly before the throne. "He doesn't have it on his person, sire. But it must be somewhere close by."

Cas realized they had no idea he'd lost the box. But why would they? Justinian had been trapped inside a nine-pointed star at the time.

"It's somewhere safe," he said, lifting his chin defiantly, which seemed like a stupid and pointless thing to do.

Justinian strode forward and gripped his face, cold fingers digging in. "I won't ask again. Where is it?"

"Where's my sister?" Cas countered, though the words came out mushy. *Wersh my shushter?*

"You're in no position to bargain for anything." Justinian's scarred face twisted as he let go.

"Bring me Felippa. I need to know she's alive first."

Justinian's jaw clenched, a muscle ticking. "I would have had the talisman already if not for you." He leaned in. "No, I will hear it from your lips right now. Where is it?"

Cas laughed, since taunting one's violent captor seemed to fit their plan, or lack thereof.

"You have no power in this place!" he scoffed.

"That is true." Justinian smiled, scar tissue pulling taut. He drew a long knife from his boot. "I learned a few things in my service to Vazsoly Marcel. For example, how to flay a man in inches so that his dying takes days."

He traced the keen edge down Cas's cheek, not quite breaking skin. "Tell me where to find the Grand Menotte, or you will have a first-hand demonstration."

Next to him, Lo stirred. "Told you," she muttered. Her gaze moved to Justinian. "Ho there!"

Justinian turned slowly to regard her.

"You *could* torture him first," she said, "but he's obstinate as an old stump. He'll probably hold out for a good while, inconveniencing everyone. But we're madly in love, so it will hurt him far worse if you start with me."

Cas's gut wrenched. "She's lying."

Justinian scanned her face, then flicked a considering look at Cas. "Is that so?"

Orm stepped forward. Cas struggled against the mortifex's hold. "She's nothing to me. Just a means to an end. I don't give a rat's arse what you do to her."

"We'll see." Justinian nodded at Skegg. Meaty hands clamped down on Lo's shoulders. She didn't flinch as Justinian took one of her arms, examining the lightning scars. Then the knife slid lower, to her wrist. "Perhaps I should start with a hand. Like your mother."

Lo went very still, a new wariness on her face. When Justinian had figured it out, Cas didn't know. Panic clawed up his throat.

"Stop!" The word burst out of him.

Justinian paused. His gaze slid to Cas and he gave a hollow laugh. "She spoke true."

Lo sagged in Skegg's grip, relief and dread warring in her eyes.

"I cannot lie," she said. "Please, just tell us. Is Felippa here?"

Justinian jerked his chin at Skegg. "Hold her still."

"Her hands are tied," Skegg pointed out.

"She is the daughter of Darius and Nazafareen."

"I see your point." Skegg grabbed her by the hair, his other arm circling her chest.

"I've smelled fresher meat in a midden heap," Lo said. "When's the last time you had a bath? Was it before or after you died?"

"Shut up," Skegg growled.

Justinian's grip tightened on his knife.

"Wait!" Cas burst out. "The Grand Menotte — it's on our ship. I'll take you there right now! Just don't hurt her."

Justinian seized Lo by her coat, lifting her from the ground so that her feet dangled. "Is he telling the truth?"

Ah, feck.

"No," she admitted through clenched teeth. "We lost it. A necromancer took it."

"What necromancer?"

"Morgen. The Duc's consort."

Justinian scoffed. "She's dead. I killed her myself."

Lo stared at him coldly. "She came back. She has a habit of doing that."

Justinian snarled and threw her to the marble floor just as a man and woman strode through one of the archways. The way Lo's face went wooden confirmed they were her parents, but Cas would have known anyway. She had her father's intensely blue eyes and her mother's bold nose. The resemblance to both was obvious; Cas could see how Justinian guessed her identity.

He stared at the couple he'd heard so much about. Darius strode down the center of the hall with the same powerful feline grace as Achaemenes. Nazafareen, despite the fact that she was the shortest person there, had a cheeky, belligerent swagger that could be a bluff, but, judging by the haste with which Orm and Skegg moved out of her way, probably wasn't. Darius wore a sword at his hip; Nazafareen's was slung across her back. They both looked very young, barely out of their teens, but Lo had explained that the bond kept them from aging.

Lo's parents walked right past her without a glance. They were trailed by four mortifexes carrying heavy chests, which were dropped with a thud before the throne.

Magnus leaned forward, braids swinging. "What have you brought me?" he asked, a greedy glint in his eyes.

Nazafareen propped a boot on one of the chests. "We cleared out the dream stores from the Velvet Embrace, as you commanded, sire."

"Oh, you capital-B *Bitches*," Lo said with feeling as Skegg hauled her to her feet.

Velvet Embrace? Then Cas remembered. It seemed the Fates had a twisted sense of humor. That was the hostel they had stumbled over in Losthaven, believing it to be Magnus's lair. The one with Telasius and the squabbling wedding party. If they had lingered just a bit longer, her parents would have walked straight into her arms.

Magnus heaved his bulk from the throne and unlatched a chest. The hinges creaked as he threw back the lid. Mist curled out, shimmering with hints of color. He plucked out a crystal flask, held it to the torchlight, and uncorked it. Closing his eyes, he inhaled deeply.

"Ah, yes. The daydream of a lovesick rusalka pining for a lost sailor." He set it aside and selected another. "And here, a raging typhoon ridden by storm jinn." He chuckled. "What angry fellows they are."

Cas watched him sort through the dreams, listing each with covetous glee. In one vial swirled the violent fantasies of a siren; another held the night visions of a dryad as she slumbered in her oaken bower.

Nazafareen shifted her stance impatiently. "Is it time for the feast?"

Magnus waved a languid hand. "Soon, soon. Leave the bounty here so I can do a complete inventory. Then you can take it to an empty storeroom and we shall gather in the great hall and make merry."

The mortifexes hefted the chests, grunting at the weight, and dragged them off to the side, near one of the other glittering heaps. Cas wondered how many "storerooms" there were in the citadel. If the treasure in the audience chamber was a mere fraction of the total...

"Mama!" Lo shouted, as they passed her again. "Papa!"

Orm clamped a hand over her mouth, but Darius paused to glance at her. The hope in Lo's eyes faded as his gaze slid away without recognition.

"Who are these prisoners?" Darius asked, rubbing his forehead as if in pain.

Magnus flicked a dismissive hand. "Mortal trespassers. We will deal with them."

"Felippa is my sister!" Cas shouted. "Please. Have you seen her?"

Skegg gave him a hard cuff on the ear. "Be quiet," he growled.

Darius blinked. "Felippa? She is well. I—"

"The girl is not your concern," Magnus cut in gruffly. "You are dismissed."

Darius bowed. "Sire."

Cas sagged with relief. She *was* here. And she still lived.

"Wait, don't go!" Lo cried, struggling against Orm's grip. "I'm your daughter! My name is Delilah!"

Nazafareen and Darius strode from the chamber without looking back. The great doors at the far end boomed shut behind them with a sound like a death knell.

"What have you done to them?" Lo demanded. "What have you done?"

The King of the Cold Sea laughed in her face. "Resume the interrogation," he said to Justinian. "We must find the Grand Menotte."

Cas cursed and tried to free his hands from the rope, which bit into his wrists with no give at all.

It all rested on Jaskin Cazal now.

IN THE DIM HOLD, as Thistle stood watch on deck, the last inch of black sand trickled through the narrow waist of the hourglass. It reflected Nathan's long, pale face, his eyes hooded and dark like all the Cazal-Ouvrards. A line of necromancers stretching back more than a thousand years to the man who first ventured into Kaethe's realm to unearth its secrets.

Nathan turned to the mirror propped against the bulkhead.

"It is nearly time for you to do your part," he said. "As you promised."

There was a slight emphasis on the last word.

Jaskin regarded him. "The mortifexes are not easily commanded, boy. It took blood and will to bind them. The Grand Menotte was my greatest creation ... and my deepest regret."

Nathan's eyes narrowed. "So you've said. But thanks to

your *great creation*, my parents are dead. Justinian murdered them in a most brutal fashion when he came to Castle Cazal hunting it!"

"I've already apologized to them more than once," Jaskin's replied in a sulky tone, "though they're still holding a grudge."

"You destroyed my family," Nathan bit out. "That can never be undone."

Jaskin stared off to the side of the mirror, his gaze distant. "I had hoped the menotte would stay forgotten. The Sons of Bel kept it hidden for so long. They held the faith. But when Justinian came..." He shook his head. "I knew it was safe no longer."

"I should have brought it home myself," Nathan muttered. "But I was a coward. I feared the sun too much to travel to Prydwen."

"Which only makes you a proper Cazal-Ouvrard," Jaskin declared.

Nathan's eyes narrowed. "You never compliment me. What are you up to?"

"Nothing, boy." He winked. "You must admit that I did much good with the mortifexes before the end. When the sun ceased moving after the War of Sundering, the darklands became a lifeless waste. I turned them green again. Life, restored by the hands of the dead! Is that not a feat for the ages?"

Nathan grimaced but could not deny it. He loved the deep forests and misty vales where creatures of the night roamed. It was a place of wild magic, brimming with secrets.

"The daēvas you enslaved deserve their freedom," Nathan said. "Can they truly be sent to the far shore?"

Jaskin stilled, his gaze fixing on the hourglass. Only a minute or so of sand remained.

"I have waited a dozen lifetimes for the chance to atone for my sin." His voice dropped, full of remorse. "I should never have bound their souls without their consent. It was the most wicked thing I ever did, in a lifetime of infamy."

He looked up, meeting Nathan's eyes directly for the first time. In their depths, Nathan saw no madness, only a steely resolve.

"They will be dealt with, Nathan, I swear to you."

Nathan searched for signs of deceit. He found none, but the unease in his gut refused to abate. "I still don't trust you."

Jaskin shrugged. "I would not trust me, either. But your friends have not returned. I doubt they met with much success."

The final grain of sand slid through the neck of the hourglass. The two men watched it fall. An instant later, the device reverted to a yellow bone again.

"Very well." Nathan picked up a small silver hammer. Decades of dangerous spell-casting kept his hands steady, though his heart beat faster. Of all his preserved ancestors, Jaskin was the one who'd scared him the most as a child.

I am no longer an unfledged boy. Let him try.

Nathan struck the precise center of the mirror. Cracks spiderwebbed outward, spreading across the glass. The dull surface turned silver, then white with frost. An icy gust struck his face as smoke poured from the crevices, billowing and twisting until it coalesced into the shape of a man.

Jaskin stood before him, clothed in his antiquated finery — a velvet frock coat, silken hose, a neck ruff white as bone. The brocade of his sleeve shimmered as he lifted a hand to touch his own face wonderingly.

"I am here," Jaskin whispered. "On the other side!"

The mirror was clear again. Nathan stared, transfixed by the sight of Jaskin's hawkish profile in the polished surface. It wasn't possible. Spirits cast neither reflection nor shadow. Their earthly remains had long ago turned to dust.

"In fact, you look very much alive," Nathan muttered, shoving the bone in his pocket.

A smile played on Jaskin's thin lips. "That is because I am."

Nathan's head jerked up. "What?"

Jaskin's fingers traced the line of his jaw as if confirming the solidity of his own flesh. "I still have one life left. When my madness grew too great to bear, I begged my youngest daughter to end my misery. But Theophania could not bring herself to strike the coup de grâce. Instead, she found a way to imprison me, body and soul, within the mirror."

"She trapped you?" Nathan asked in amazement. "While you were still *living*?"

"My wife and other children had already fled the castle, but Theophania... She remained with me until the end. Of all my offspring, she was the most brilliant. The most loyal." Jaskin's mouth twisted. "And in her loyalty, she condemned me to an eternity of tedium."

Nathan listened to Jaskin's tale with growing impatience. "If you are a living man and not a spirit, how then do you propose to reach the citadel?"

Jaskin stepped back a pace. "By my troth, I *am* sorry, but there is no way to send a soul to the far shore unless they go willingly. Certainly not if they are bound to a talisman."

It took Nathan a moment to grasp the words. "No way?"

"None at all," Jaskin confirmed.

"Then why did you bring us here?"

"The Grand Menotte has a tracking spell," he muttered, plucking at his sleeves. "Once I find it, I will summon the mortifexes and bind them again to my will. It is the best we can hope for. The only solution."

Fury ignited. "You could have just told me that in the first place! I would have hunted it with you—"

Jaskin cut him off with a sharp laugh. "You would never have let me out of the mirror." His eyes darted about, paranoid. "You just want the Grand Menotte for yourself!"

Nathan shook his head vehemently. "No! Uncle, wait—"

But it was too late. Jaskin turned and stepped through a shimmering portal that had opened behind him. In an instant, he vanished.

Nathan kicked a trunk, sending it skidding across the hold.

He was pacing back and forth, trying to figure out his next move, when sharp claws sank into his calf. He swore and glared down at the culprit. "By the Infernal Abyss, must you keep doing that?"

Thistle's eyes slitted as he looked around. "Where is the necromancer?"

"Gone. He abandoned us."

The cat hissed. "More trouble approaches."

Nathan crossed to the porthole and peered out. A longboat full of mortifexes was rowing towards the ship, the flames in their eyes burning bright with anticipation.

TWENTY-FIVE

Felippa was dozing on the floor of Gerda's chamber when the door opened. She sat up, rubbing her eyes. Darius stood in the doorway.

"Have you no manners, boy?" Gerda snapped, half-rising from her rocking chair. "Barging in without so much as a knock."

Darius ignored her. "Your brother is here," he told Felippa. The words spilled out in a rush, as if he'd repeated them over and over so as not to forget. Darius rubbed his head, wincing in pain.

Felippa leapt to her feet. "Truly? Cas is *here*?"

Darius nodded. "In the audience chamber."

"I must go to him at once!" Felippa exclaimed.

"He is Magnus's prisoner," Darius said uneasily. "But he asked about you. I told him you were well."

Gerda rose stiffly from her chair, white hair crackling in a cloud around her head. Felippa tensed. Would the old mortifex try to stop her?

Darius dropped a hand to his sword hilt. "Do you have a quarrel with me, grandmother?" he asked mildly.

Gerda's eyes narrowed to slits. "You are too like your father," she said. "He…" She trailed off with a grimace and waved a gnarled hand. "Never mind. I will accompany you both to the audience chamber. Let us get to the bottom of this."

Nazafareen waited in the corridor, leaning against the wall with one knee bent. She grinned when they appeared. "Are we going to the feast now?"

Darius touched her shoulder, his voice tender. "Soon, my love."

Nazafareen turned to Felippa. "Scribe! You'll sing for us, won't you?"

Darius shot her a warning look. *Play along*, he mouthed.

Felippa smiled. "Of course, I'd love to."

Nazafareen patted her belly and spoke in an exaggeratedly deep voice. "Me want eats." Then she burst into rowdy laughter.

They started down the corridor, taking the now familiar route to the grand audience chamber. "I think I'll sit next to Gilli tonight," Nazafareen said. "He didn't pull his weight on the ship. Always slacking off." Her amber eyes glinted with mischief. "Time he was taught a lesson."

"Gilli's a lazy lout," Gerda agreed, hobbling along at Naza-fareen's side. "In my day, he would have been stripped naked, hung from the stirrup of an abbadax, and taken for a nice long flight over Mýrdalsjökull glacier."

Felippa barely heard their chatter. Her mind was consumed with thoughts of her brother. Cas had ruined Justinian's face when they fought over the Grand Menotte. The mortifex had every reason to hate him. How was she going to save them both?

She looked up to find Darius staring intently at the coin hanging around her neck. He leaned down to her ear, his voice tight with frustration. "I know that necklace. I'm certain I've seen it before."

"Maybe you have," Felippa whispered. "My brother gave it to me, but he got it from somewhere."

Darius was quiet for a minute. "You asked me once how I came here."

"And you said you were always here," Felippa replied warily.

"I did say that, but... I feel now that I was wrong." Another grimace. "My head..." He gripped his hair, tugging at it. "It's the bloody mist that cloaks this place, devouring everything." His gaze turned distant. "But I'm certain now that there was a ... before."

Hope fluttered in Felippa's chest. She reached out and squeezed Darius's hand. "I'm certain there was, too. Justinian told me so." She checked to make sure Gerda wasn't eavesdropping. "He said you came here hunting him, but then you got enchanted and forgot all about it!"

Darius stared at her. "He said that?"

"He admitted everything." Felippa shot a glance at Nazafareen. "He said she can break magic, and that's why he wants her. To break the talisman that binds them all here."

Darius drew a sharp breath. He seemed about to say something more, but they had reached the tall double doors of Magnus's audience chamber. Gerda flung them open.

Felippa's eyes locked on a struggling figure at the far end of the hall. She burst into a run. "Cas!"

"Felippa!" he shouted.

Hearing his voice made her feet take flight. Skegg and Orm scowled at her, but Felippa didn't give a fig for any of them. Cas had come, just as she knew he would—

A tall shape cut into her path. Justinian seized her arm in a bruising grip. "Not so fast, little scribe," he said mockingly. He turned to Gerda. "Aren't you supposed to be in charge of her?"

Gerda shrugged. She had brought her goblet of fake wine and took a noisy slurp. "The brat got away from me."

"Get her out of here!" Magnus thundered.

Felippa looked for Darius and Nazafareen. Her heart sank as she realized they'd left her. Well, she'd do it alone then. No more cowering. She forced herself to meet Justinian's annoyed gaze.

"Kill me if you wish," she said, amazed at the calm in her own voice, "but there is something you should know first. And if I'm dead you'll never find out what it is."

For a long, taut moment, he studied her face. Then something flickered in his expression and he released her. "Speak."

Felippa rubbed her arm, taking a moment to gather her thoughts. "How old are you?"

"Old enough," Justinian snapped.

"I mean, when did you live? It must have been a very long time ago because you were bound by Jaskin Cazal, and he came to Aveline just after the Sundering."

Mortifexes were drifting into the chamber in twos and threes, some gathering on the tiered galleries that lined the great hall.

From behind her, Gerda spoke up. "I know you're from the Vatra clan." She stepped to Felippa's side, fixing Justinian with a keen stare. "Did you live in the time of Gaius Augustus?"

"I was an officer in the third cavalry division of his army," he admitted. "What does that matter now?"

"Because the so-called King of the Cold Sea lived at that time as well." Gerda's lips peeled back from her few remaining teeth in a nasty smile. She turned to Magnus. "I hope your memory improves, sire."

Magnus scowled. "You dare—"

Felippa shared a look with Gerda, who gave a curt nod. The old woman hobbled forward and planted herself before the throne. "What was the incident that sparked the war between the Vatras and the Danai clan?" she demanded.

Magnus stared down at her, bushy white brows drawn together. "Have you lost your wits?"

"Ah." Gerda's eyes glittered. "You do not know, do you?" She clasped her gnarled hands at her waist. "Here's another. Under what circumstances did the Valkirins enter the war? Surely you must know the answer to that one." Her voice sharpened. "It was you who made the final decision!"

Magnus surged to his feet, fists clenched, face mottled with fury. "This is outrageous! I will not be questioned in my own hall!" He stabbed a finger at Gerda. "Get out! Get out now, before I have you thrown from the Cliffs of Howl!"

Felippa glanced at Justinian. He was staring at Magnus, lips pressed into a thin line.

Gerda drew herself up, fixing Magnus with a steely glare. "Here is an easy one. He was infamous even then." She enunciated each word. "What was the name of Gaius's closest advisor?"

Magnus opened and closed his mouth. A vein throbbed at his temple. At last, he spluttered, "I—you—this is—"

From the shadows, Darius stepped forward, his face grim. "His name was Farrumohr. I remember now." Darius nodded at Gerda. She must have sent him to assemble the others.

Voices echoed from the vast ceiling as the mortifexes muttered to each other. Felippa saw suspicion kindling in their flame-bright eyes, but they needed more. Hard evidence.

She stepped forward. "The memoirs." Her voice rang out.

"The ones he dictated to me. They're in a hidden compartment behind the throne."

"Those are private!" Magnus roared, casting her a look of pure hatred.

Justinian stalked over to the dais. As he fumbled around searching for the compartment, Felippa saw that Cas was not the only prisoner. A young woman had been tied to one of the statues that stood in the niches. She'd been gagged, too, but her bright blue eyes caught Felippa's and she gave an encouraging nod.

"Here." Felippa scurried to the dais and pointed to a lighter patch of stone. "This is where you open it."

Justinian pressed the stone. Gears clicked. A panel slid open with a grating rasp. He thrust his hand inside and drew out a sheaf of parchment, eyes flicking back and forth as he leafed through the pages. His face was an unreadable mask, betraying no hint of his thoughts.

Felippa's gaze darted to Cas. He was still being held by Orm, the hulking mortifex's hands clamped around his arms. She sidled closer, pulse fluttering in her throat. "Please, might I speak to my brother?"

Orm glanced down at her. His lips twisted. "Very well, scribe." He released Cas with a rough shove.

Cas couldn't hug her back because his hands were tied, but he whispered her name. She breathed in his familiar scent, tears pricking her eyes.

"Thank Kaethe you came," he said. "I badly need rescuing."

She pulled back, studying his face. A fresh bruise mottled his jaw, but the corners of his mouth lifted.

"Who are you with?" she asked.

"The beau I told you about." His gaze fell to the silver disk around Felippa's neck. "She gave me that."

Pieces fell into place. "Is she...?"

He glanced at Nazafareen and Darius. "Their daughter, aye."

A vile oath made her turn. Justinian hurled the stack of parchment to the ground and tossed a torch on top. Flames licked at the pages, reducing the memoirs to ash in a matter of moments.

He stalked forward, the firelight casting his angular features in harsh relief. Magnus shrank back against the throne. His eyes bulged, beard quivering.

"W-wait," he stammered, lifting a hand. "Surely we can discuss this like reasonable men—"

"Reasonable?" Justinian snarled. His sword rasped from the sheath; the edge pressed to Magnus's fleshy throat. The king made a thin, terrified sound. "You've played us for fools."

Felippa had never seen Justinian so angry. This was the monster from her nightmares made flesh.

"What are you?" A trickle of blood welled beneath his sword, staining Magnus's white beard crimson. "Show yourself!"

Magnus's form rippled like a pond disturbed by a thrown stone. The illusion fell away. In place of the imposing king sat a sad, bitter-looking man with a weak chin and patchy tufts of orange hair above his bat-like ears. He wore Magnus's robes, but they engulfed his slight frame like a child playing dress-up.

Justinian hoisted the creature from the throne by his collar. Bare feet twitched below the diamond-spangled hem. Felippa squinted. The knobby digits didn't look quite right...

"Feck me sideways," Cas exclaimed. "It's a four-toed humbug!"

Twenty-Six

Angry shouts erupted from the assembled mortifexes.

"Quiet!" Justinian growled. He gave the humbug a shake. "What have you done with Magnus?"

"The ... the real one?" the humbug squeaked.

"Yes, the real one," Justinian snapped. Another vigorous shake set the humbug's teeth rattling.

"He is here," the humbug stammered. "Trapped in an iron cage deep in the mountain."

Justinian stared at the creature, his grip slackening in disbelief. Then he hurled the humbug aside. The little man crumpled to the stone floor in a heap.

"I should take your head right now—"

"Wait!" Gerda hobbled over, her puckered face set in grim lines. "What is your name?"

The humbug shrank back against the base of the throne, withering under her glare.

"Talon, good mistress." He smiled and bowed, though his eyes darted around the chamber seeking an exit.

"How did you manage this charade?" Gerda demanded.

"And how long has it been going on for?" someone shouted.

"I...I..." Talon stammered. His hands fluttered like pale moths in the sleeves of his overlarge robe.

"Go help her," Cas whispered to Felippa, nodding at Lo.

Both Orm and Skegg were too busy watching the drama unfold to notice Felippa slip over to the statue and pull down Lo's gag. Then she slid around the back, presumably to work on the rope around her wrists.

"I heard the name Talon in Dreamhaven," Cas called out.

The mortifexes turned to him, their expressions ranging from curious to hostile.

"He owned a tavern near the Laughing Gull," Cas said. "But he traded in illegal nightmares and the, er..."

"D.C.C.," Lo supplied helpfully, blowing a lock of hair from her face.

"Right," Cas said with a nod. "The D.C.C. kicked him out. He disappeared after that."

At the mention of the Dream Collectors' Collective, Talon's features twisted. He stood, face mottled red with rage just the way Magnus's had been.

"Those sanctimonious fools!" he spat. "They were jealous of my success, of the power I had gathered. They conspired to destroy my business, to cast me out and leave me with nothing!"

Talon's hands clenched into fists. "They thought they could break me." His voice rose to a fevered pitch. "But I found a new path to power, one they could never imagine!"

The humbug's resentful gaze swept over the mortifexes. "Well, I got them back, didn't I?" he crowed. "You did my bidding for years, collecting 'taxes' for Magnus." An unpleasant smile curled his lips. "Driving my enemies out of business, just as they did to me."

His manner changed abruptly, becoming fawning and obsequious once more. "But I never meant you any harm, my friends!" Talon simpered, pressing his hands together. "Just those who deserved it, those who wronged me!"

Justinian stalked forward, his eyes blazing like twin infernos. "Just those who deserved it?" he echoed, his voice dangerously soft.

Talon shrank back as the mortifex loomed over him.

"I knelt at your feet," Justinian snarled. "Obeyed your every whim!" His hands flexed, as if longing to wrap around Talon's scrawny neck. Justinian shook his head, disgust etched on his features. "No. You could not have done this alone."

He seized Talon by the front of his robes, hauling him up until they were nose to nose. "Who aided you?" Justinian demanded.

Talon's pallid face turned a sickly green.

"Speak up, you little shit!" Gerda snapped, hobbling closer.

Quick as a viper, Talon spat a jet of dark liquid. If Justinian's reflexes had been a hair slower, it would have hit his face and as bad he looked now, well... The marble smoked where it struck.

Talon spat another stream of venom. Cas ducked and it shot over his head, missing him by a hand's breadth. The sizzling poison struck a column behind him, melting the stone like butter left out in the sun.

Talon's form shimmered and blurred. A heartbeat later, a second Justinian stood before them, identical in every way. Talon twisted free, robes hoisted above his ankles as he ran down the red carpet.

"Stop him!" Justinian roared.

Orm lunged for Talon, but the humbug's form shifted

again. Now he was a copy of Orm, grinning wickedly. Orm's hands closed on empty air as Talon dodged away, weaving through the mortifexes crowded into the archways.

Cas tried to track the humbug's path, but it was impossible. He changed form every few seconds, one after another. The chamber dissolved into chaos, the fexes shouting and cursing, shoving at each other. Jets of venomous spittle flew through the air. Where the poison touched, it sizzled through undead flesh like acid.

Cas whirled, searching for Lo and his sister amidst the pandemonium.

"Don't move," a voice said in his ear.

Cas stiffened as a blade touched his back, but it sawed through the rope around his wrists. He turned to find Darius, wearing the glassy-eyed look of a drunk who just woke up in the gutter.

"Is ... is my daughter here?" he ventured.

"Aye." Cas spotted her crouched behind the statue. Lo's hands were free and she was cradling Lip in her arms, trying to shield them from the venom. "Over there."

Darius stared. "But she is so *old*..." He turned to Cas, stunned. "How long have we been here?"

"Eight years."

"Holy Father," Darius said hoarsely.

Nazafareen was looking at Lo, her brow pinched. Cas saw the instant the last shreds of Talon's illusion lifted. Her gaze sharpened. She started to run and so did Lo. They met in the midst of the chaos, wordlessly embracing. Darius strode over and crushed them both to his chest. He seemed to be weeping.

Cas looked down as small arms wound around his waist. Felippa smiled up at him. "They found each other," she said.

"Aye, I'm glad. But I'd say it's a good time to get out of here," Cas said as a glob of poison sailed over their heads.

Lo and her parents seemed to agree, for they cut the reunion short and everyone regrouped. A seething mass of angry mortifexes blocked the archways. Talon was still leading them on a merry chase.

"There!" Darius pointed to a narrow stone bridge leading to the neighboring tower. Cas felt vertigo just looking at it. But it was the best way out.

"Take my hand," he said to Lip. "I'm not losing you again."

She rolled her eyes but laced her fingers with his. The five of them veered for the bridge, hoping no one noticed. Cas spared a moment to wonder what had happened with Jaskin Cazal. More than an hour had passed, so either Nathan had betrayed them or both did.

Cas had expected it from the start, but he still felt hurt. Nathan had been...not so bad the last few days. He'd had a hundred opportunities to knife them in the back, but instead his necromancy had saved their lives more than once. Maybe Jaskin had done something to him—

Halfway across the vast hall, Cas heard the tinkle of breaking glass. He stumbled as colored smoke billowed up around them. Strong odors filled his nose — the sun on pine needles, murky swampwater, rain sluicing over stone. Moss and elderflower. Smoldering embers and rotting fruit. A metallic scent like iron and charred cinnamon that he somehow knew was the blood of a phoenix.

Shadowy shapes galloped, slithered, and loped through the smoke. A silver-maned centaur charged past, hooves striking sparks on the stone floor. Hands with long, sharp-nailed fingers burst from the stone at his feet, grasping. A beautiful woman in white walked toward him, smiling — then dropped to all fours and turned into a shaggy red-eyed wolf. It snarled and leaped for his throat, vanishing to mist in the split-second before it hit.

His bladder nearly let go at that one. What new devilry was this?

Ghostly laughter echoed from nowhere — raising the brief hope that Jaskin Cazal had come to their rescue after all. But it faded quickly, and a small green dragon swooped past, followed by its war galley-sized mother belching flame.

"Talon's smashing the dream vials!" Felippa's voice cut through the din. "Cover your ears, don't breathe the smoke!"

Cas pressed a sleeve over his nose and mouth. He gritted his teeth and forged ahead. Screeches and howls dogged their steps, but he dared not look back.

"Just a bit further," Lo's voice urged from somewhere off to the left. "Shite, did you see that? Like an owl..."

"With the body of a giant spider?" Cas managed. "Yes, yes, I did."

He smelled maidenhair ferns and untouched snow. Heard a woman's anguished sob, followed by the thunder of a thousand hooves crossing a grassy plain and the beating of great drums. On and on it went, a waking phantasm that veered from wonder to nightmare and back again in the span of seconds.

Then they passed beyond the worst of it, for the clamor and visions faded. Everyone was still together — Lo and her parents, him and Felippa, all in a tight little knot. They were seconds from the bridge when a figure stepped from the shadows.

Justinian. Because *of course*.

Cas's heart seized as Felippa yanked her hand free and darted forward. "Lip!" he hissed. "Are you mad? Get back here!"

She ignored him. Cas watched in horrified disbelief as his sister marched up to the monster who'd nearly taken her life. She had to crane her neck to look him in the eye.

"Just let us go," she said firmly. "We don't have what you want, and we're no use to you anyway."

Justinian stared down at her. To Cas's amazement, his scarred face softened a fraction.

"You may leave," he said to Felippa. "As you reminded me, I have taken enough from you." His gaze cut to Nazafareen. "But you cannot take the Breaker. She stays with us until I find the Grand Menotte. I need her to destroy it."

Darius stepped forward, murder on his face, but Nazafareen bulled him aside.

"I have no breaking power anymore, you idiot," she growled. "Kaethe took it back."

Justinian went still. "What do you mean, *took it back?*"

"Exactly what it sounds like. Do you think I would have been so easily entrapped if I still wielded negatory magic? I would have seen straight through the illusion that pitiful creature wove and torn it apart like cobwebs. You kidnapped the wrong person. I cannot help you!"

Shock slackened his face. Then, slowly, it twisted. "Do you know how long I have searched for the Grand Menotte?" he hissed. "Decades. Enduring the burning sun, the sickness of crossing rivers. Surrounded by you vile mortals. All for nothing!"

Justinian advanced on Nazafareen, his bulk making her look even smaller and very young. Cas's hand twitched for a weapon he didn't have.

"You were my only hope," Justinian snarled. "Without your power, it doesn't matter who has the talisman." His face contorted into a rictus of fury. "But if I cannot leave this place, none of you will! You will stay here until you die, and even then, I will not let you cross."

Nazafareen winced. "Perhaps I spoke in haste..."

A blur of movement caught Cas's eye. He turned. His staff spun end over end through the air.

"Catch, Quietus!"

He moved on instinct, the yellowed wood smacking into his palm. Nathan stood on the bridge, legs braced against the wind, dark hair whipping across his face.

Cas was wondering how in hell he'd gotten up there when Skegg strode forward, blade falling like a hammer. Nathan pivoted and the blow glanced off the stone, shaving a slice from the bridge. Then another fex seized him from behind. They grappled. Nathan tossed ash in the creature's face and it screamed, releasing him so abruptly that he skidded sideways and tumbled over the edge.

Justinian's shout sliced through the chaos. "Stop them!"

Nazafareen drew the sword from her shoulder baldric and charged. Justinian batted her blade aside and bore down, raining a flurry of heavy blows. Step by step, she gave ground, the chasm looming at her back.

Cas's gaze snapped back to the bridge. Nathan clung to the edge by one hand. Skegg stood over him, boot drawing back to kick him in the face.

Turmoil drained away, leaving crystal clarity. *Quietus*. It's who he was. Who he would always be. He was made for this fight, and it's time they knew it. He ran for the bridge, knocking aside anyone and anything that stepped into his path.

Skegg's bone-white blade met the staff in a clash of blue sparks. It was the color of protection, Cas grasped that now, and he was drawing it from the collective sorrow of the souls Jaskin Cazal had bound.

He pitied Skegg, but the man was already dead. Cas feinted left. Skegg took the bait. With a twist of his wrist, Cas hooked his legs and sent him tumbling into the ravine. The yellow-haired giant vanished into the mist without a sound.

Cas reached down and grasped Nathan's arm just as his trembling fingers lost their grip. He hauled him up onto the bridge.

"Where's Jaskin?" he asked, panting.

"Gone." Nathan's voice was tight. "He abandoned us the moment I freed him, the coward."

Cas tamped down his own ire. No time for that now. Darius was fighting three fexes at once, his sword darting as light and swift as a dragonfly, while Nazafareen engaged their fearsome leader. Cas was amazed they were still alive at all, but it was obvious they'd reached their limits — and more of Justinian's minions were running the length of the hall to join the fray.

Now or never. Cas found the still point within. His gaze fixed on Justinian's face. It was intent with concentration as he fought Nazafareen, but beneath the surface Cas sensed a deep well of rage.

With discipline born of Gui's tutelage, he set aside his own grudge and opened himself to the aura of sickly colors dancing around Justinian. Centuries of hatred and despair almost swept him away.

Be the reed in the current. Let it wash through you.

The black tide scoured his veins. His pulse thrummed, heat rising to his face. *Do NOT think about how much you fecking hate the bast...* Cas drew a deep breath. Tried again. *Not his fault, not his fault. Jaskin's fault. All Jaskin's fault.*

Calm came once more and the power swirling inside him flowed into the staff. Rune-marked ash warmed against his palm. It wasn't the blue protective magic he sought this time. No, he wanted something a bit *stronger*.

Crimson light exploded outward, engulfing the audience chamber like a dying sun. There was no sound, only a faint buzzing in his ears. He was dimly aware that the staff had grown cool again.

Cas blinked away the afterimage. Some of the fexes lay stunned. Others staggered, clutching their heads, eyes squeezed shut against the searing radiance.

The living were unharmed this time, thank Kaethe. Felippa peeked out from behind Lo, who wore that unhinged smile. Darius and Nazafareen lowered their swords, staring at Cas in amazement.

"It worked!" he exclaimed, turning to clap Nathan on the shoulder.

The necromancer was sprawled senseless on the stone bridge, out cold yet again.

"Sorry," Cas muttered.

He slung Nathan over his shoulder, grunting at the weight. Running footsteps approached. Darius gestured with his blade at the tower across the bridge.

"A stair on the far side leads down," he said.

Cas adjusted his grip on Nathan and followed. A glance to either side revealed a plummeting drop into gray nothingness. He stared straight ahead, trying not to imagine the long, long fall.

They were halfway across when Lo, who'd taken the rear, gave a shout. Cas risked a quick look over one shoulder. Justinian had recovered his wits and was charging after them, eyes like hellish coals. The other fexes were upright and shaking off the effects of the staff.

Cas shifted Nathan's dead weight and plunged across the bridge. The wind threatened to sweep them both into the abyss below. He leaned into it, fighting for each step. Nazafareen beckoned from the far side. Darius was carrying Lip on his shoulders.

"Don't look back," Lo urged from behind. "Or down."

Cas grunted. "Bel's balls, Nathan looks like a skinny bastard until you have to carry him!"

"It's all those iron charms," Lo said. "Or maybe his hair. Almost there!"

A moment later his boots hit the far side of the bridge. The others had already passed through an archway. Cas turned at the threshold, his staff leveled back the way they'd come.

Justinian was three-quarters of the way across. He must have learned something from the last time he faced this staff, when Gui had wielded it on the bank of the River Forkings, and would not be caught off-guard again. The red flare of Justinian's anger was hidden. Buried deep. Another direct assault was off the table.

Blood, frost, bile, and rot.

Rot.

The fourth humour of the dead.

Cas plucked at the swirling colors, focusing on the strands of green. Justinian's envy of the living, of their *freedom*. It was the poison that fueled his hatred.

"Cas, come on," Lo screamed. "Quit messing around!"

He backed through the archway, a flash of emerald light bursting from the staff. Stone convulsed. Justinian lost his footing, but quickly regained it. He gave Cas a cold smile ... that faltered at an ominous series of cracks. A moment later, the bridge collapsed in a roar of falling masonry, taking the mortifex with it.

Breathing hard, Cas lowered the staff. He met Nazafareen's wolfish yellow eyes in the sudden stillness. She nodded once, then turned to lead them into a tunnel. Cas knew the fexes would be regrouping, finding another way to follow. He hitched Nathan higher on his shoulder and hurried after her into the darkness.

TWENTY-SEVEN

The clop of hooves echoed in the courtyard below, punctuated by the impatient shouts of chamberlains and footmen. Enrigo lay staring at the stone ceiling, arms limp at his sides.

For a week now, the Alcazar had bustled with frenetic activity — nobles from the mountain provinces arriving in gilt carriages, servants rushing about with armfuls of linens and cutlery. All in preparation for Beatriu's wedding to Vazsoly Marcel at the temple of Kaethe and the grand fete in the Alcazar's ballroom after.

The memory surfaced for the hundredth time. Beatriu perched like a porcelain doll on her throne of ancient skulls, the handsome, *loathsome* Duc of Cavet at her side, as she informed Enrigo their betrothal was cancelled.

In front of the entire court.

Lucius had shot him a pitying glance. Of course, Enrigo had lost him, too. He wore Beatriu's colors now.

"Surely there are no hard feelings, Your Grace," Vazsoly had said, an amused smile on his lips. "We value your duchy's continued friendship. Please, I insist you remain for the ceremony."

Rubbing his nose in it, more like. Mother had agreed, of course. She never openly defied anyone. But Enrigo saw the quiet fury simmering in her eyes. He himself had simply stood there, cheeks aflame, glaring at Beatriu, who barely seemed to notice.

Deceived. Humiliated. And she wouldn't even let him slink home to lick his wounds. That it also happened to be his thirteenth birthday was the icing on the moldy rat-shit cake.

Enrigo swung his legs over the side of the bed and reached for his boots. The sooner this farce was done with, the better. Then he could finally escape this wretched place and the piercing ache in his chest whenever he thought of her.

He walked to the connecting door of the suite and knocked softly. "Mother?"

There was no reply. He unbarred it and pulled on the knob, the heavy oak door swinging silently on well-oiled hinges. Enrigo stepped through. Jak, ever a shadow at his heels, trotted after.

He needed to forgive Mother. She was all he had left now. Lucius, gone. Beatriu, lost to him forever. Even the young Quietus named Castelio whom Enrigo had always been friendly with had run off, accused of murdering one of the servants. He bit his lip. Surely Mother had only been trying to protect him, to secure his future. She deserved a chance to explain herself.

But her chamber stood empty, with only a faint trace of rosewater lingering in the air. Enrigo sank into a padded chair, shoulders slumped. Jak rested his head on Enrigo's knee with a soft whine.

What would it be like, returning to Clovis? Lucius had served their family for a thousand years, bound by ancient oaths. Now he was a weapon in the hands of their enemies, and it was Enrigo's fault. His naive trust in Beatriu's promises had cost them everything.

Cavet and Galatia would be united against his own duchy. Across the Boundary to the east was Nathan Ouvrard. Enemies on all sides.

Enrigo clenched his fists, fingernails carving half moons into his palms. How had it all gone so wrong? But deep down, he knew. His own stupidity had doomed them all.

A glint of glass caught his eye. There, in the corner — his mother's liquor cabinet, usually kept locked. But Enrigo knew her hiding places. He'd seen her slip the key into the blue porcelain vase on the windowsill.

He crossed the room and reached into the vase, fingers closing around the cold metal key. The lock clicked open easily. Enrigo surveyed the neat rows of crystal decanters and bottles.

One in particular drew his gaze. Thick green glass with no label, the top sealed with red wax. He lifted it from the shelf, turning it over in his hands. The liquid inside sloshed sluggishly, tinting the glass a murky amber.

On his mother's writing desk, an engraved letter opener gleamed. Enrigo snatched it up and worked the tip beneath the wax seal until it popped free. He was a man now, wasn't he? Thirteen, old enough to make his own choices.

Old enough to face his failures. He would attend the wedding and watch them gloat. Watch his future crumble to dust. But he wouldn't give them the satisfaction of seeing a hitn of emotion. He would be like Beatriu, cold and distant.

Enrigo tipped the bottle to his lips, inhaling the sweet, fruity scent. The only way he would make it through this day was to dull the pain. He squeezed his eyes shut and took a long, burning swallow.

A man's solution to a man's problems.

LUCIUS STOOD before the oval mirror, examining his reflection with a critical eye. The seamstress had outdone herself with his raiment for the Damiata's wedding. A severely cut doublet hugged the lean lines of his torso. A new cloak fell from his shoulders, clasped with Beatriu's heraldic device — a couchant lynx atop a treasure chest, proclaiming patience and cunning.

He allowed himself a sardonic smile. At least the Do Santillan colors complemented his snowy complexion. Silver and black, a fitting motif for a creature such as him, forever caught between the dark and the light.

Lucius ran a comb through his copper hair, more out of habit than necessity. His immortal body remained untouched by time's hand. No lines creased his brow, no silver threaded his temples. Only the weariness in his eyes hinted at the centuries he'd endured.

What did it matter, in the end? One master or another, it made no difference. Beatriu was merely the latest in a long line of petty tyrants to hold his leash. The iron cuff around his wrist, his constant companion, ensured he would never know true freedom.

His thoughts drifted to the Grand Menotte. Had Justinian and the others found a way to break its hold? To slip the yoke of servitude and chart a course across the Cold Sea to whatever waited beyond?

Lucius liked to believe they had. That his brothers and sisters had found some measure of peace. But he was still glad he hadn't joined them. Justinian was a twisted remnant of the man Lucius once called friend, a monster wearing a familiar face.

He might not own the clothes on his back, but at least his soul was intact.

Well, mostly.

He was turning to leave when a muffled scream came through the thick walls, followed by frantic barking. The Damiata hadn't yet ordered him to vacate his old quarters, allowing him to keep a watchful eye on the Redvaynes. Their suite was just down the hall.

He burst through the door, the scene before him etched in stark relief. Orlaith knelt on the carpet, hunched over Enrigo's body. The boy's lips were frozen in a grotesque smile, his eyes wide and vacant. Jak paced and whined, sensing something amiss.

Lucius's gaze fell on the bottle lying nearby. It had tipped to one side, leaving about a quarter of the contents intact. The rest seeped into the carpet, staining it a dark hue.

Lucius's first thought was that the boy had been so besotted with Beatriu that he took his own life rather than see her marry another. Yet where had he gotten the poison from?

Then Orlaith looked up, her eyes wide with guilt and horror, and he saw the truth. The bottle had been meant for Vazsoly or Beatriu, perhaps both. Her favorite trick, one she'd employed before with deadly results.

He thought of Esme, the serving girl in Aquitan who had drunk the tainted wine intended for Castelio. Orlaith had confided in him then, boasting of the lethal properties of dwale berries. She must have brought more of the deadly nightshade from Aquitan.

Now her own son lay dead at her feet.

"What have you done?" Lucius growled.

Orlaith crawled over and seized the hem of his cloak. "Bring him back," she pleaded hoarsely. "Bring back my son. It's not too late!"

Jak's barking reached a frenzied pitch. Lucius scooped up the terrier and carried him to the doorway, depositing him in the hall. It stood empty, the servants occupied with preparations for the wedding. The Redvaynes had been left to their own devices, forgotten in the midst of the festivities.

Lucius shut the door on the yapping dog and turned back to Orlaith.

"Do it!" she snarled through bared teeth. "You have the power. I command you!"

Lucius thought of the late Duc Robert, the stench of his infected wound and the sheer relief Lucius had felt when the man finally succumbed to it. Then, his young widow begging for Lucius to bring her husband back.

He had agreed. At the time, it had been just another way to manipulate her. The necromantic spell tethered Robert's soul to his lifeless body, a twisted mockery of existence even worse than Lucius's own.

Now, the thought filled him with revulsion. Enrigo had been better than either of his parents. Poor boy. He never stood a chance, did he?

"I will do no such thing," Lucius said, his voice a whip crack. "And need I remind you, I no longer serve the House of Redvayne. Your commands hold no sway over me."

Orlaith's fragile composure shattered. She wept — raw, heaving sobs that wracked her thin frame. He tried to step away but she skittered forward and grasped his cloak again, white fingers clutching the fabric.

"Yes, yes, of course you are right." Orlaith licked her lips. "I beg one last boon, Lord Bittencourt. If not for me, for Enrigo."

Lucius eyed her warily. "What is it?"

Her gaze darted to the door, wild and unhinged. "Don't tell the Damiata. Not yet. Let me mourn my son. Just a few minutes with him, that's all I ask."

She sank to her haunches and began to stroke Enrigo's hair, her trembling hand tenderly wiping the stain from his lips. Then she gathered the boy into her arms, cradling him against her breast, rocking back and forth.

"My poor, sweet boy," she murmured. "My darling son."

Lucius hesitated. Once the facts came to light, there could be no doubt that Orlaith had plotted an assassination. If she were very lucky, she might be exiled. But knowing Vazsoly Marcel, she would be tossed into the Alcazar's oubliette, a lightless pit where the condemned were left to rot.

"You have until after the ceremony," Lucius said tightly. "Then I must tell my new mistress what you've done." A pause. "And he must be stilled by the nuns before he rises again on his own."

Lucius turned on his heel and strode from the room, leaving Orlaith alone with her grief.

TWENTY-EIGHT

Morgen hurried along the fifth floor of the convent dormitory, white robe swishing at her feet. It was quieter than usual, with all the sisters already gathered in the temple of Kaethe for the Damiata's wedding.

Morgen's scalp itched; how she despised being forced to shave her head every third day! At least the nuns of Vellio did not coat themselves in human ashes like some of the more extreme sects. A waste of perfectly good remains, in her opinion.

Her palms were damp, and her mind kept jumping from one thing to another. She'd barely touched her breakfast. Not that she relished the tasteless gruel served in the dining hall, but she usually managed to get it down. Today, her stomach felt like she had swallowed a school of live minnows.

It was ridiculous, yet she couldn't deny the truth. She was *nervous*.

Not even when she'd walked alone into Vazsoly's camp during his bloody sacking of her homeland had Morgen felt so skittish. That day, she'd taken the first step toward her revenge, offering her services as a necromancer. The first task he'd set before her was to kill their father — not that Vazsoly had any idea who she really was. He thought she was just a heathen sorceress from the Western Isles.

After he became the Duc of Cavet, she had shared his bed, endured his temper tantrums, advised him on matters both large and small — all so she could learn everything about him, unearth his secret dreams and aspirations, and when the time came to draw her knife, she could place the blade with perfect precision.

Vazsoly had been scheming to wed Beatriu since the girl was named Damiata. Even before he lost his duchy, she'd been an integral part of his ambitions. Now she was indispensable. Without her army, he could never return to Prydwen.

Morgen could have portaled into his bedchamber and ended him in the same way she'd done to his father Andrzej Marcel, but she wanted the world to know what he had done. To destroy him at the very moment he believed himself untouchable. Vazsoly was a bully, and all bullies were cowards at heart—

Two novices popped out of the room just ahead, startling her. The girls bobbed their heads and hurried down the winding staircase, chattering excitedly about the Damiata and her handsome bridegroom.

Morgen drew a slow, calming breath. She had imagined his destruction so many times, planned what she would say and how he would die, it almost seemed like it had already happened.

"Nothing will go wrong," she muttered to herself. "I am ready."

Once she had collected the box containing the Grand

Menotte, she would join the guests in Kaethe's temple. It would be a memorable occasion indeed, though not the way everyone expected.

She reached for the latch of the chamber door. A rustle of movement behind was all the warning she had before pain exploded through her skull. Morgen crumpled. Strong hands dragged her inside the room.

Through a red haze, she made out a familiar pair of polished boots.

"Shut the door," Vazsoly told someone. His voice was muffled, as if underwater.

Morgen clawed herself up to sit, ears ringing, liquid warmth trickling down the side of her neck. Vazsoly stood in the corner with a knife against Jaelle's throat.

Morgen's gaze flicked to Dravka, whose eyes held both rage and terror, and the big straw-haired man standing over her. It was the same one who had watched them crossing the cloister a few days before. His fist was still clenched from clouting her.

Their meager belongings lay strewn across the chamber, bedding ripped apart, goose feathers drifting through the air.

"You faithless bitch," Vazsoly said with a smile that brought out his dimples. "How I've missed you."

Morgen blinked, trying to focus through the hot throbbing in her ear. "What do you want?"

"What the fuck do you think?" He pressed the knife harder against Jaelle's throat, drawing a thin line of blood.

She had a cut on one cheek and her eyes were glassy and distant, like she had gone to a place beyond fear. The hare in the jaws of the wolf. Yet the girl had refused to reveal the box's hiding place. She had more backbone than Morgen had given her credit for.

"Give me back what's mine," Vazsoly said slowly, "or I'll saw her fucking head off."

Power stirred, dark and seductive. She could reach out and seize his soul, tear it screaming from his body. But the knife at Jaelle's throat was a hair from opening her up. Morgen might not be fast enough.

"All right," she said, the words slurring. "You can have it."

"Did you open the box?" he asked eagerly.

Morgen managed a bitter laugh. "Would I be at your mercy now if I had?"

"Get her on her feet, Demares," Vazsoly said.

The big straw-haired man grabbed her by the arm and hauled her to standing. Morgen walked drunkenly to the cot, each step driving a shard of broken glass into her skull. She pushed it against the window and climbed up, steadying herself on the wall with one hand.

"I don't understand why you give a shit," Vazsoly remarked, brow furrowing as he regarded his sisters. "They're both useless." His voice turned almost tender. "I would have kept you as my mistress if you hadn't betrayed me, pet."

Morgen's fingers closed around the iron box concealed on the ledge.

One chance. When she handed him the box, he'd have to release Jaelle. Then she would—

Dravka made a strangled sound of warning. Too late. A line of fire blossomed along Morgen's ribs. She looked down at the knife wielded by Demares. The blade was so sharp, she barely felt it slide in. Her legs folded. She crumpled to the cot, then rolled to the floor, pressing a hand to her side. Blood welled between her fingers.

Vazsoly shoved Jaelle away and snatched the box from Morgen's weakening grip. Blue eyes glittered. "You're certain you can't open it?"

She shook her head. Her vision was going black at the edges, but she refused to faint. She was gathering her power when a hot, piercing pain spread through her chest, far worse than the first wound. Then it faded, and everything went numb.

Dravka flung herself across the room. She cradled Morgen in her arms, cursing Vazsoly with every vile oath she knew.

"Shall I dispose of them all, my lord?" Demares asked.

In the pause that followed, Morgen noticed the knife jutting from her breast. Seven times she had died — the first just moments after she was born. The manner of each was different, yet it was always the same in the end.

"No." Vazsoly's voice sounded far away. "I'll marry my sisters to some Galatian lords to cement the alliance."

Footsteps receded down the corridor.

"You fatherless cunt!" Dravka screamed after him. "I'll cut your wee prick off and—"

It was the last thing Morgen heard before Kaethe claimed her.

* * *

THE TEMPLE'S INTRICATELY PAINTED ceiling soared overhead, its buttresses rising to a central dome. Lucius stood to the left of the altar, face impassive. The chamber buzzed with Galatian nobles in opulent but subdued fabrics, dark red garnets and star sapphires glinting at their throats.

Columns ringed the circular space, each carved with rosettes and thorny vines. Embedded in the marble floor was a massive nine-pointed star — three triangles superimposed over each other to symbolize life, death, and rebirth. At its center stood Beatriu, looking tiny in a gown the color of Kaethe's black roses.

The abbess shot a reproving glare at Vazsoly as he strode up the aisle and took his place, several minutes late. No doubt he'd been preening in front of a mirror. Even Lucius had to admit he looked resplendent in a gold breastplate worked with silver, the light of a hundred candles burnishing his fair hair. The very image of a charming prince.

Did anyone else see past the gilded facade to the predator that lurked beneath? Vazsoly would use Beatriu's army to retake his lands. After that, who could say? Perhaps an unfortunate accident would befall the young queen, leaving Vazsoly to rule in her stead.

Well, she might be a murderer, but Lucius belonged to her now. He would make sure the bastard didn't lay a finger on her.

Vazsoly surveyed the assembled nobles, brow furrowed. He leaned over to mutter something to his guard captain standing at attention nearby. "...grave insult to stay in their chambers. I want them both punished after the ceremony. A day in the stocks will teach them respect."

Lucius' keen ears picked up every word. He was speaking of the Redvaynes. Lucius wondered if Beatriu ever felt anything for Enrigo. Would she be sorry to learn of his death?

The abbess stepped forward. "We are gathered here today in the house of blessed Kaethe to join this man and this woman in sacred union..."

As she droned on about duty and obedience, Lucius studied Vazsoly. The man seemed distracted. He was probably already plotting his next step. Lucius knew his type too well. Arrogant, ruthless, assured of his own immortal greatness. Men like that left a trail of corpses in their wake — until they became one themselves.

The abbess raised her voice. "If any here know cause why this union is not just and right, speak now or forever remain silent—"

A crash echoed through the temple as the doors burst open. Morgen Nadezhda stood at the entrance, her robe drenched scarlet from neck to hem. Lucius's nostrils flared at the scent of fresh blood. How was she still alive?

Onyx eyes locked onto Vazsoly Marcel. Her lips twisted in a jagged smile. "Hello again, pet," she said.

TWENTY-NINE

S hocked murmurs rippled through the wedding guests as Morgen strode into the temple, her bare feet leaving bloody smears on the marble floor.

Two novices slipped in behind her, the same ones Lucius had glimpsed a week before entering the convent. Up close, their resemblance to Vazsoly was unmistakable — his younger sisters.

Lucius tensed, moving closer to Beatriu, but Morgen seemed indifferent to the young Damiata. Her gaze was fixed on the man standing before the altar.

Lucius's boredom vanished. Things had just gotten interesting.

Vazsoly stared at his former lover with comical surprise, mouth agape. Almost as if...

As if he'd spilled her blood himself.

"What is the meaning of this intrusion?" the abbess demanded. She squinted across the chamber. "Sister Mara, is that you? What has happened, child?"

"I have come for my due, Mother Pedrosa," Morgen replied in a steely tone. She pointed a finger. "I have come for *him*."

Vazsoly's shock melted into hot rage. "Get her out of here!" he barked at his soldiers.

Six drew their swords and charged. Morgen regarded them with contempt. When they were nearly upon her, she raised one hand and clenched it into a fist. Shining ribbons erupted from the crowns of the soldiers' heads. They crumpled, dead before they hit the ground. Lucius knew this because he heard their hearts stop. Morgen slowly lowered her hand, arm rigid. The silver ribbons sank into a puddle of darkness and vanished.

Kaethe's tits, Lucius thought.

There was a moment of perfect silence. Vazsoly turned ashen, stepping back. Morgen skirted the bodies without glancing down, heading straight for him with murder in her eyes.

"No one is leaving this room." Her harsh, throaty voice sliced through the din. "You will bear witness first. Be assured, I am here for one man only. The rest of you won't be harmed unless you try to interfere."

The guests creeping toward the doors halted in their tracks.

Morgen stalked to the altar, her shaved skull gleaming in the candlelight. She stopped before Vazsoly Marcel.

"On your knees," she spat. "You will die like the coward you are."

Vazsoly's eyes darted to Beatriu. Lucius probed at her emotions but as usual, he sensed nothing.

"Do something!" Vazsoly snapped, jabbing his chin at Lucius. "Unleash your wolf!"

Beatriu ignored her betrothed. To Lucius's immense satisfaction, she turned to him instead, a question in her gray eyes. Lucius ascended the altar and leaned down to her ear. "Your Grace," he murmured. "That is the Duc's former consort."

If this revelation surprised Beatriu, he could not say.

"You know her?" the Damiata whispered back.

"Yes, and I advise you to hear her out before we take any action."

Beatriu held his gaze for a moment, then nodded. She turned back to Morgen. "We take it this man has wronged you," she said. "Tell us how."

Vazsoly sputtered. "You can't possibly entertain this lunatic's ravings!"

Beatriu stamped her foot. "Silence! Or my mortifex will burn you to ash where you stand."

Lucius gave Vazsoly a feral grin. The Duc went white with anger, but he clamped his mouth shut, glaring at Morgen with hands balled into fists at his sides.

"Thank you, my lady," Morgen said. "My past is a secret no longer, and I will gladly reveal the dark deeds committed by the Marcels to all assembled here."

Nobles and nuns alike leaned forward, riveted by this new spectacle.

"You may proceed," the Damiata said.

Morgen addressed Beatriu, but her words were pitched for all to hear. "My mother was Ingharad, necromancer to Duc Andrzej Marcel. She served him faithfully until the day he demanded more. Her power was not enough. He wanted her body and heart, as well. When Ingharad refused him, he drugged and raped her, and got her with child."

"Lies!" Vazsoly snarled.

Beatriu speared him with a look. "Let her speak, or you will be removed from my presence."

Vazsoly turned an ugly shade of puce, but he swallowed his protests.

"The old Duc kept my mother prisoner in one of the high towers," Morgen continued, as if there had been no interruption. "Without her tools and potions, she could not escape. He made sure that her food was drugged to keep her docile."

Murmurs swept the assembled nobles. Lucius felt revolted. He could easily imagine Andrzej Marcel doing such a thing. Like his son, the man had a reputation for ruthlessness.

"He planned to take the babe and forge it into a weapon to serve the ambitions of House Marcel. Once my mother realized this, she stopped eating and tied her bedclothes into a rope, which she descended and fled from the palace. But the Duc soon discovered her missing and set his dogs on her scent. She was heavy with child and could not get far."

Morgen paused, and the room fell quiet as everyone imagined a pregnant woman running from a pack of snarling hounds. The looks they gave Vazsoly turned decidedly hostile.

But the tale wasn't finished yet. "There is a gate hidden in the palace grounds that leads into the Dominion. She managed to reach it with the dogs on her very heels."

Lucius leaned in to Beatriu again. "I have seen this gate myself, Your Grace. She speaks true."

"Continue," Beatriu said.

"The strain and terror caused an early labor," Morgen said. "My mother gave birth to me in Kaethe's realm, on the bank of a river." Her voice held no inflection, as if she spoke of someone else. "I was born with the umbilical cord around my neck, blue and still. She wept bitterly, but a short while later I revived. That is when she realized that I was special."

Morgen lifted her chin. "My mother wandered in the Dominion, eventually finding her way home to the Western Isles. She hid there as Andrzej searched the realm for her. She raised me in the lore of necromancy, and on her deathbed, I swore to exact revenge on the Marcels."

She pointed a finger at Vazsoly, who flinched. "My half-brother commanded me to murder our father, which I did gladly. He did not know who I was at the time. Now it is his turn to pay."

"A pack of lies!" Vazsoly's voice shook. Sweat beaded his brow despite the cool air. "She is simply jealous because I cast her aside for you." His wild gaze sought out Beatriu. "Look at her! She is an abomination."

Morgen took a step forward, and Vazsoly stumbled back. "You are my bride," he snapped at Beatriu, his voice cracking. "You owe me obedience." His eyes snapped to Lucius, desperate. "Set your mortifex on her!"

Beatriu regarded him without expression. Even Lucius had no idea what she meant to do. The whole room held its breath, waiting.

"The nuns taught me that the thread of a man's life may be long or short," she said at last, "but it is for the Lady of Shadows to decide which."

The abbess nodded to herself. Vazsoly's shoulders slumped in relief.

"However," Beatriu continued, "my father Dom Alfonso taught me that while revenge is an act of mortal passion, vengeance is an act of immortal justice. Like the Lady's due, it may be long or short in coming. But when a person has been grievously abused, come it will."

The last sentence was spoken with heat. Lucius thought of the day she took his menotte and he asked her if she was guilty of killing her siblings. *Only one*, she'd said. *You may guess which*.

It was a clue. One of them had wronged her somehow.

Beatriu turned back to Morgen. "The elder Marcel was vile, but what has his son done to you?"

Now Vazsoly looked truly worried.

"He beat me if I displeased him in even the smallest of

ways. He burned and slaughtered entire villages in my home-land, the Western Isles." Morgen glanced at the two girls watching from the doors. "And he locked his sisters away for no other reason than that they are female and he deemed them worthless."

The elder — her name was Dravka, Lucius recalled — stepped forward, fire in her eyes. "It is all true, Your Grace. My brother is a beast. He left Morgen for dead. I saw him stab her."

"Shut up, you silly bitch!" Vazsoly erupted. "I'll cut you into pieces and feed you to my fucking..." He trailed off as he realized the entire chamber was staring at him.

All but Morgen and Beatriu. The little girl in black and the woman in bloody red had locked gazes. It seemed to Lucius that they shared a look of mutual understanding.

"You have our permission to do with him as you see fit," Beatriu said.

Vazsoly backed away from the altar, eyes bulging with disbelief. He'd convinced himself that his naive, malleable child bride would save him. But he had underestimated her, and now it would be his undoing.

Vazsoly broke and ran for the doors, his gold breastplate flashing. Morgen lifted a hand and blew a fine sift of ash from her palm. Black tentacles coiled around his torso, lifting him high into the air. There was a sound like wet cloth ripping. A fine red mist splattered the guests, who cried out in revulsion. The Duc of Cavet — or what remained of him — landed in a messy heap on the floor.

Lucius had never witnessed anything quite like it. Neither had the wedding guests. They shrank back as Morgen walked to the body. She let out a soft laugh. "He is gone," she muttered. "The last of the male heirs."

All heads turned at the sound of slow, mocking applause. A

man stepped from the shadows. A shock of dark hair swept back from a widow's peak, hanging to his narrow shoulders. His fingers were oddly long and tapered, like the pet monkey one of Lucius's old masters used to own.

"Nicely done!" he exclaimed. "I never liked the Marcels." He looked Morgen up and down, a smile on his thin lips. "You must be Sweet Morgen of the Isles."

She scowled. "Who are you?"

The man swept a deep bow. "Jaskin Cazal, the Duc of Vendagni."

Lucius stiffened. *Impossible.* Cazal had been dead for centuries, driven to suicide by his own dark creation.

Of course, Lucius was dead, too, yet here he stood. And the bloodline of Vendagni was steeped in necromancy. He studied the man, noting his antiquated garments and aura of power.

Jaskin turned to one of Vazsoly's surviving soldiers, a big flaxen-haired man who held a bundle wrapped in cloth. "I believe you have something that belongs to me."

The man's gaze flicked to his lord's mangled corpse. He swallowed hard, set the bundle on the floor, and backed away. Jaskin darted forward, but Morgen blocked his path.

"It's mine now, old man," she said. "I died twice for it."

"A pox on that," Jaskin replied, madness dancing in his eyes. "I made the thing, lambkin. 'Tis my own device on the lid."

Lucius realized with a jolt that the bundle must hold the Grand Menotte. He had no idea how it had ended up here, but he couldn't let anyone claim the talisman. Yet the last time he'd faced Morgen Nadezhda, she'd left him paralyzed on the ground, unable to twitch a finger. Engaging her directly seemed unwise.

Morgen raised her hands. Tentacles burst forth, blocking

the doors and coiling around Jaskin's legs. He gave a delighted chuckle.

"Kaethe has sent me a worthy adversary at last!" The old necromancer lifted a hand in response, flicking his own silvery dust into the air. Shadows boiled up from the floor, the guests started screaming, and all hells broke loose.

THIRTY

Darkness engulfed the temple of Kaethe. Lucius slid a protective arm around Beatriu's shoulders. "It would be wise to release my power now," he whispered in her ear.

There was just enough light coming through the barred embrasures to discern her nod. Lucius felt Beautriu's grip on their bond slacken. With a thought, he ignited the votive candles set into niches along the walls. Orange light flickered across a scene out of nightmare.

Jaskin Cazal and Morgen Nadezhda locked eyes across the round chamber; black tentacles erupted from their hands, colliding in midair with enough force to rain dust and chips of stone on the heads of the terrified wedding guests. In the darkest corners of the room, just beyond the edge of the light, liches materialized like shreds of midnight, only to be torn asunder by even more ghastly conjurings. Undulating curtains of blood blocked the doors.

Lucius crouched by the altar, Beatriu at his side. He eyed the iron box that sat midway between the two necromancers.

The Grand Menotte. If he could just sneak up while they were distracted...

Morgen ducked a whipping tentacle and sent a barrage of shadow daggers flying at Jaskin's face. He barely deflected them, staggering back. She managed to take several steps closer to the box before he unleashed a crablike monstrosity of jointed bone. It swiped a foreleg at her, then decayed into a puddle of black ichor. Morgen was not simply holding her own; she was gaining ground. Lucius needed to act fast.

"Stay close," he told Beatriu, never taking his eyes from the dueling necromancers. His mind raced, calculating, searching for his moment to lunge for the box. It had to be timed just right. Too soon and he'd be ripped apart. Too late and the menotte would be lost again.

Jaskin's lips twisted into a snarl. His voice took on a guttural, inhuman quality as he spat out words in the language of the dead. The temperature plummeted. Frost crept across the stone floor, coating everything in a slick, crystalline sheen.

Jaskin lunged for the box, his fingers closing around it. But as he straightened, his feet slid on the ice. The box fell with a heavy thud, lid springing open. Something glinted darkly within. Lucius felt the skin-crawling wrongness of cold iron.

A small shape darted out of the panicked crowd. It was Enrigo's terrier Jak, barking furiously as he skidded into the fray. Morgen tripped over the dog and crashed into Jaskin, their skulls colliding with an audible crack like a mummers' farce.

"The cursed Quickening!" Jaskin howled.

Some of the guests had shoved a table against the wall and were pleading for aid through the bars of the embrasures, but most milled around near the doors. They were trying to shove through a narrow gap. Shrieks and curses filled the air as the mob stampeded over the fallen.

A flailing body slammed into Lucius, sending him sprawling. Morgen and Jaskin grappled, hands locked around each other's throats. The dog darted between them, snarling and snapping. Lucius surged to his feet, scanning the mayhem for Beatriu. She was gone, lost in the rioting tide of bodies. He tore his gaze from the melee, searching for the Grand Menotte. It had rolled out of sight, but he could feel its malevolent presence, the dark power gathering like an incoming storm.

His eyes fell on the corpse sprawled before the altar. Vazsoly looked like he'd been... Lucius squinted. *Turned inside out?* Something along those lines, anyway. Now, crimson rivulets flowed along the grooves of the nine-pointed star carved into the temple's stone floor. The blood moved with unnatural swiftness, as if it had a will of its own. Where it touched the frost-rimed floor, wisps of steam curled upward.

Lucius backed away, his eyes locked on the star. Primal instinct screamed at him to flee, to put as much distance as possible between himself and whatever was about to happen.

Too late, too late. He whirled to run—

A jolt shot through him, freezing him in place. It originated from the petite menotte encircling his wrist. He felt something snap inside it, a sensation like a hair-thin filament parting. For an instant, he couldn't process what had occurred.

Then the iron cuff flared with heat, searing his skin. Lucius bit back a cry of pain. The cuff had never burned him like this before, not in a thousand years of enslavement. It was enchanted not to. Beatriu must have done something, must be using the power against him, but what—

Crystals of frost raced across the surface of the cuff around his wrist, rendering the engraved phoenix of House Redvayne in stark white. With a crisp pop, the cuff cracked down the center.

Somewhere deep inside him, a second thread snapped and recoiled. Thicker, this one, more substantial. Lucius stared dumbly at the broken halves of the cuff on the ground. Around him, the chaos in the temple continued — screaming and shoving, the awful sound of tentacles battering the door, dust sifting down from the dome overhead. Lucius registered none of it.

A thousand years.

A thousand years he had worn the petite menotte, bound to serve House Redvayne. Now it lay in pieces at his feet.

Fear held him immobile, as surely as the binding spell that had trapped him at Bel Mara. He wanted to test his power, to see if it was truly his own again, but terror locked his muscles. If he tried and failed... Hope was a shard of glass lodged in his chest.

A final thread snapped.

Fire surged through Lucius's veins. Flowing directly from the Nexus, not drawn through the siphon of the cuff. Purely *his*, in a way it hadn't been since he'd died on a scorched battlefield a thousand years before.

A wild, strangled laugh tore from Lucius's throat, but it died as quickly as it had come. The rivulets of blood were racing along the grooves, moments from joining each other and completing the huge nine-pointed star carved into the rock.

An icy darkness gathered at its center. It sucked the light from the temple, pulling the last of the warmth with it. The terror of the mortals around him was palpable, and he drew on it to fuel the explosion building in his core.

Lucius turned to face the lashing tentacles. Flames roared from his palms in a blistering torrent, racing from one to the next. The air filled with an acrid stench. He strode through the inferno, embers swirling around him. He slammed a boot heel into the doors. They exploded outward, ripping from their hinges and crashing to the flagstones.

More screaming erupted behind him as he entered the hall

and nearly ran into Orlaith. She shambled forward like a ghost, her pupils black and empty. She must have drunk what was left of the dwale-poisoned wine.

They regarded each other for a moment. Perhaps he should pity her, in the end, but felt nothing but a cold distaste. He wanted to tell her how he helped Castelio escape her clutches. How he'd lied to her all those years about her husband. Robert Redvayne was nothing but a mindless wraith, and Lucius had invented every word he claimed to translate from Tongues.

He wanted her to know every falsehood, every betrayal, to know how utterly he despised her.

But he said nothing.

Orlaith pressed against the wall with a glazed expression. Suddenly, it hit him.

He was free. *Truly free.*

People were jammed up in the doors, too many trying to force their way through at once. Inside the temple, the screams rose sharply in pitch. That roused Orlaith from her daze. With a snarl, she flung herself at the doors, trying to claw a path through the writhing bodies.

"My boy is in there," she shrieked. "My son!"

A wind rose, tearing the black veil from her head. The urge to run grew overwhelming. Lucius gave in, running down the corridor as if Kaethe's hounds were snapping at his heels.

THIRTY-ONE

Lo's boots skidded on the rain-slick steps, sending a shower of loose rock skittering into the abyss below. She just managed to catch herself on the wall, scraping her knuckles bloody. The crumbling staircase plunged down the side of the tower towards another dark tunnel, its mouth lit by flashes of lightning.

An hour or so had passed since Cas destroyed the bridge and sent their pursuers tumbling to the rocks below. Her father led them on a winding route over more precarious stone spans and through the twisting corridors of the citadel. It felt like they were going in circles, but Darius insisted that the way was heading downward.

The fog was so thick, Lo could scarcely make out the next step, but she thought her father was correct; the hulking silhouette of the main tower did seem to be above them now.

"Shelithoth," she whispered. "Please come."

He made her wait for a few long moments, but Thistle finally appeared at her feet, whiskers twitching.

"I expected you to summon me earlier," he hissed with ill humor.

"Oh, I'm sorry," she said with equal tartness. "I've been busy running for my life." She crouched down. "I presume this storm is your doing? Because to be honest, it's not helping."

His fur puffed. "Not mine." The cat's luminous gaze rested on Darius and Nazafareen, who picked their way down the stairs ahead. "You found them."

"And the enchantment is broken, too. It turned out to be a four-toed humbug who was casting it!"

A slow blink was the only sign of surprise.

"Tell me what happened to Lord Bag o'Bones," she said, resuming her cautious descent.

"Jaskin Cazal is not dead," Thistle hissed. "He was imprisoned in the mirror with one life remaining. Now he has gone after the Grand Menotte himself."

Lo digested this as a violent gust of wind buffeted them both sideways. "Oh, that's bad. I almost hope Justinian gets to it first."

"You told him about Morgen Nadezhda?"

"I had no choice. You know I can't lie. I said she took it from us, but I had no idea where she'd gone."

Despite his girth, Thistle leapt lightly over a missing step. "And he accepted that?"

She gave a small shudder. "Yes. But only after Magnus — I mean, the humbug called Talon — rifled through my memories. I could feel it. Like a cold finger poking around. Most unpleasant."

Lo glanced above them. The remains of the collapsed bridge were lost in the gloom and swirling mist. No sign of pursuit — for now.

Her father emerged from the shadows ahead, dark hair

plastered wetly to his forehead. "The passage becomes a tunnel up ahead, but it's out of the rain."

"I see it," Lo called back softly.

They followed Darius into the mountain's depths, footfalls echoing in the darkness. Cas walked ahead with his sister, a snoring Nathan slung over one shoulder.

"The necromancer showed courage," Thistle said. "After Jaskin fled, a longboat full of High Dead came upon us. Nathan turned them into moles. I nearly ate one until I remembered that it would revert to its original form."

Lo winced. "What would have happened if you had?"

"I cannot say." The cat's tail swished. "Although my stomach is larger than you might imagine. Much larger."

She pondered that for a moment. "How did Nathan get up to the bridge?"

Thistle gave a sort of cough that might have been embarrassment. "I didn't see. I was ... playing with the moles."

"The poor little blind things?" Lo clucked her tongue. "Well, probably serves them right—"

A hand fell upon her shoulder, causing Lo to flail awkwardly and bang her head on the low ceiling. But it was only her mother, who was taking up the rear.

"Quiet." Nazafareen raised her right arm, the stump hidden in her coat sleeve. "Something is following."

Blades rasped from the sheath as she and Darius took up positions on either side of the tunnel. A yellow flame appeared in the darkness behind. Had Justinian caught up to them? Falling a thousand paces to jagged rock would be little more than an inconvenience. Lo grumbled under her breath. There had to be a way to banish them onward. If she only had Jaskin Cazal's knowledge—

Two tall figures emerged, one carrying a stub of candle. Darius let out a happy shout. "Tijah! Achaemenes!"

The mortal warrior and her bonded daēva embraced their old friends, laughing. "Tired of playing pirates?" Tijah asked.

Nazafareen's smile soured. "I still cannot believe it." She glanced at Lo. "Eight years we lost."

"I know," Tijah said quietly. "I'm sorry. But you are free now. And it is just an eyeblink in the lifespan of all three of you." She grinned at Lo. "You will have centuries to make it up."

Lo's gaze slid to Cas. The words, she found, did not cheer her. Her parents had the bond. They would be together as long as her father lived, even though her mother was mortal. It was the same with Tijah and Achaemenes. But there were no more talismanic cuffs to link human and daēva; they had all been destroyed.

She shook off the dark thoughts. She was not like them, anyway. Who knew how long her final life would be?

"How did you find us?" Darius asked.

"We've been wandering this maze looking for a way up," Achaemenes said. "I heard you about twenty minutes ago, but it took as long to find a corridor that would cross your path."

"Have you seen any fexes?" Cas asked.

Tijah shook her head. "No, but we found something else. A man, locked in an iron cage."

Lo's eyes widened. "You found the real Magnus?"

Tijah stared. "What do you mean, *the real Magnus*?"

"The one sitting on the throne was an imposter," Felippa chimed in.

"A humbug named Talon," Lo explained. "He must have been impersonating Magnus for who knows how long. That's how he enchanted the whole citadel."

Tijah looked dubious. "Talon? As in, the shifty hustler who owned a tavern in Dreamhaven?" She shared a look with Achaemenes. "That's ... *unexpected*."

"No argument there," Lo said. "Felippa exposed him."

Cas's sister flushed. "I did have help," she said.

"We managed to get away in the chaos," Darius put in.

"But they'll be after us soon enough," Cas said. "We need to keep moving."

Achaemenes clapped a hand on his shoulder. "Then let us tarry no longer. I will take the necromancer."

Cas looked grateful for the reprieve. He handed over Nathan — who was finally showing signs of life — and they plunged back into the twisting, turning passages. The route led ever downward, past endless treasure chambers and rooms filled only with dust and mouse droppings.

At last they came to a tunnel Darius said would let them out at Imp's Claw Point, near where the ship was anchored. Lo squeezed Felippa's small hand.

"Almost there. We *are* going to make it."

The girl nodded wearily, lank hair falling across her face. She wore an oversized blue cloak that seemed to swallow her up. They walked for a long while more, following a switchback route that sloped steadily down. The tunnel dead-ended at a rough wall, but Darius touched a hidden lever and the stone gave way. A crack of gray light illuminated the tunnel.

"We'll go first," Darius said, looking to Nazafareen.

She reached over her shoulder and drew her blade, *Nemesis*.

Tijah's fingers flickered in the semi-darkness, a question in her eyes. It must be the hand-language she'd used with the daēva she was bonded to before Achaemenes. Lo's mother had spoken of it.

"This isn't the only back way out," Nazafareen whispered. "There are several. Let's hope our captors have chosen a different one to watch."

Lo and Felippa waited with Cas at the tunnel mouth while they went to investigate. She could hear the patter of rain outside, and the rhythmic roar of the surf. The storm had not abated. If anything, it was worse. But that would help cover their escape.

Nazafareen squeezed through the crevice and dropped to a crouch. Her gaze swept the shoreline, searching the thick curtains of mist and rain for any sign of movement. Darius and Tijah circled out of sight in opposite directions. After a tense moment, they returned and signaled the all clear.

Achaemenes went next, with Nathan draped over one broad shoulder like a sack of elegantly dressed barley. His eyes were blinking open, lips murmuring in a slurred protest. Thistle padded silently at Lo's heels as she exited the tunnel with Cas, who held Felippa's hand.

They grouped together, breath misting in the chill air. The large mortifex ship was anchored out in the bay, its decks silent. Lo pointed east, toward the faint silhouette of Imp's Claw Point. Their boat was anchored in the tiny cove beyond. So close now.

But she didn't dare hope, not yet. That only invited disaster. She glanced beside her at Cas. Rain darkened his chestnut hair, beading on his lashes.

"Single file," he said softly. "We stick next to the cliff—"

A screech ripped the air. His face tilted up as an enormous winged shape dropped out of the fog. Its clawed foot slammed into his chest, flinging him back a dozen paces. He crashed to the ground and lay unmoving, the staff tumbling from his limp fingers.

"Cas!" Felippa screamed. She sprinted to her brother's side, falling to her knees beside him. Lo raced after her. Let him be alive. Please, let him—

Dark shapes plummeted from the sky, resolving into mortifexes astride their winged mounts. They landed in a circle around the companions, white faces devoid of humanity.

Achaemenes slid Nathan from his shoulder and laid him gently on the sand. He drew his sword.

"We are brothers and sisters," he said. "Remember who you were. Don't do this!"

Orm stepped forward, his single eye blazing. "If we are brothers, why do you run from us?"

"Because you're dead, motherfucker," Tijah said. "I'm sorry, but it's true."

"That's not helping," Achaemenes said with a frown.

"They weren't going to let us go anyway," Tijah retorted, which was also probably true.

Thistle growled, a low rumble in his chest, as the fexes dismounted, cutting off any hope of escape. Without another word, the horde surged forward.

Darius and Nazafareen moved as one, their blades flashing. Beside them, Tijah and Achaemenes fell into a deadly dance. The four fought in a knot, back to back, but they were outnumbered twenty to one.

It would have ended very quickly indeed if Nathan had not come to his senses. He brandished something pale and shriveled — a thumb? a nose? — and shouted in Tongues. Even the fexes paused at the resonant note of command in his voice. Sand creatures rose up, formless but vaguely humanoid. They resembled his ash servants, with thick arms and legs.

The fexes' bonewood swords sliced right through them with no effect. The sand creatures, while otherwise harmless, created a sufficient distraction for the companions to rally.

Lo pushed Felippa behind her as Justinian broke from the throng. His empty eyes locked on her. "You can still be of use. Your blood will give us strength to pass through the Veil. I mean to hunt Morgen Nadezhda to the ends of the earth."

Rain lashed Lo's face as she backed away. "Hear me, Kaethe," she whispered fervently. "You gave me this gift, so you're kind of like my second mother, right? I'll gladly trade my life for a little help here. If it's my last, no problem. Just help me send these pissed-off spirits somewhere better!"

Silence, of course. Gods never answered when you needed them.

But the Fates...They must be laughing their bony asses off right now.

She leaned down to Felippa. "Run," she urged. "Hide yourself."

The girl looked stricken. "I won't leave you—"

"Please." Lo took her hands. "I must do this alone."

"Do what?"

Lo hesitated. If the Moirai were listening, she didn't want to give them ammunition to screw her over again.

"I can't lie," she told Felippa. "So I won't say have faith and everything will be fine. But there's nothing you can do to help right now, and if you stay, I'll be distracted worrying about you." She glanced at Justinian. To her surprise, he had not attacked, but rather stood watching them.

"Do as she says, little one," he commanded roughly. "Run!"

Felippa cast her an anguished look, then took off down the beach. None of the mortifexes bothered to chase her.

But from the waves came a haunting, ethereal melody. Sleek bodies broke the surface, liquid eyes gleaming. The dukka had come to join the feast.

Lo turned to face Justinian, the eerie song rising and falling from the surf. It was a lure, a trap, but it did not work on either of them. Perhaps it was because, as much as she despised him, they shared one thing in common. Part of his soul was caught in the Grand Menotte, and hers was divided in half.

She knew there was something missing. She could feel it. A

dull emptiness where her heart should be. Even seeing her parents again hadn't brought the joy she expected.

"I'll make it quick and painless," Justinian said, hunger in his voice now. "There's no point in fighting."

Lightning forked across the boiling clouds. Lo shivered, rubbing the scars along her arms. She knew what Jaskin Cazal's spell required — the blood of a Shadow Soul and a reaper. Her blood. Cas's blood.

Justinian lunged for her, fingers clutching at her sleeve, but she wrenched away. She sprinted across the sand to where Cas lay sprawled in a heap, blood running freely from his nose. An abbadax crouched over him like a vulture over some tasty morsel. Thistle leapt at the creature, raking his claws along its scaly leg. The abbadax screamed in pain and fury before launching itself skyward.

Lo fell to her knees, searching for something sharp. Justinian was coming, his rapid strides crunching in the sand. Then she spotted it — a glimmering blue feather, fallen from the abbadax wing. She snatched it up, its barbs keen as razors, and sliced it across her forearm. Crimson welled. She held the cut above the sand, letting her blood mingle with Cas's.

His eyelids fluttered open, then closed again. She clasped his hand and tried to set aside her own hate for the creatures who had done this. He'd invoked the staff's power through compassion. The mortifexes had been daēvas once, like her father's people. Twisted into nightmare things by Jaskin's evil magic.

"Shall I take him first, while you watch?" Justinian asked. He gave a hollow laugh. "We know each other, your friend and I. In fact, I first met him when he was just a boy." He touched a scar on his face, barely visible through the burns. "He gave me this."

"I'm sorry," Lo said.

Justinian's red eyes narrowed. "For what?"

"For what was done to you."

"I don't need your pity," he snarled.

His hands gripped her. Cold sank into her bones, a chill so deep she thought they would crack. Bit by bit, the raw flesh of his face began to knit together. Underneath the mask of a monster, Justinian had a noble countenance. His skin grew smooth, his lips fine and well-formed. And with every breath, Lo grew weaker.

She gathered her will and formed a picture in her mind. Not the dark portal with its howling wind but a sunlit green shore.

"Rosori solemar," she whispered. "Rosori pe rehiera."

I bid thee farewell. I bid thee go in peace.

She'd spoken the words before, but she had not meant them then. Now she did.

"What are you doing?" The rasp was gone from his voice. His eyes looked clear, the pupils tiny sparks.

"Setting you free," Lo said.

The dukkas' song abruptly cut off. They sensed it, the sudden charge in the air. With soft splashes, they fled into the depths.

Justinian's brow furrowed in puzzlement. He opened his mouth to reply when blinding white light exploded across the beach. A concussive force hurled her back. She struck the ground hard, ears ringing and skin tingling all over. It was like being kicked in the head by a mule. After a minute, she managed to open her eyes and look around. Wisps of smoke rose from her clothes.

Down the beach, she saw her parents with Tijah and Achaemenes, all four bloodied but on their feet. Justinian was gone. Where he had stood, she saw shards of glittering black glass. The rest of the mortifexes had vanished, as well.

Lo struggled to her knees. Had she sent them onward? Alone, operating solely on instinct? It seemed ... very, very lucky, which didn't make sense.

But perhaps no spell was required after all; just simple forgiveness. Beyond the light had been peace. She was certain of it.

"*Putain!* How did I get down here?"

Nathan craned his neck up at the citadel, hands casually tucked into his pockets like a man checking the thatch on his roof.

Then Felippa was flying back down the beach, hugging her brother, whose eyes fluttered open again.

Kaethe had heard Lo's prayer after all.

THIRTY-TWO

The storm passed and the skies cleared, dawn and dusk visible again on each side of the bay. Felippa helped Lo build a fire with driftwood. Then she snuggled next to Cas, who draped an arm around her shoulders. His nose was still swollen, but he seemed unable to stop smiling every time he glanced at Lo.

The two of them leaned toward each other in a way that made Felippa glad. It was good to see her brother so at ease with someone, especially after all they'd been through. And Lo — well, Felippa had taken a liking to the mysterious beau. There was a blunt honesty to her.

"I almost forgot." Felippa lifted the silver disk over her head and held it out. "This belongs to you."

Lo fingered the sun and moon engravings, then pressed it back into Felippa's hand. "I don't need it anymore. You keep it."

"Are you sure?" Felippa asked. "It's valuable. It saved me from Justinian. The silver burned him. And I think it helped me to see through Talon's illusions."

"It is a protective charm," Lo said, confirming her hunch. "But you earned the right to it."

"Thank you!" Felippa hung it around her neck again. It probably wouldn't make her grow, but it was still the best present she'd ever gotten.

Thistle, the peculiar talking cat who had appeared in Prydwen, lay curled up by the flames, striped tail wrapped over his nose. Next to the cat was the lanky man about her brother's age whom Cas had carried out of the fortress. He wore all black and had milky-pale skin. He was nursing a split lip and a cut above one dark eyebrow.

"I don't think we've been properly introduced," she said. "I'm Felippa."

His gaze was intent and curious, but not in a gawking way. "I am enchanted, demoiselle." He took her hand and kissed it, making her cheeks warm. "My name is Nathan Ouvrard."

Felippa stared. The flush drained away and she went cold all over. "Nathan..." She turned to Cas, who shrugged. "*The Duc of Vendagni?*"

Her time at the court of Vazsoly Marcel — not to mention Cas's treatment by Orlaith Redvayne — had given Felippa an abiding hatred of the nobility. Now she felt confused. She knew the houses of the Moon Courts practiced necromancy, which she had been taught was unspeakably evil. But Nathan Ouvrard had helped save her, and her brother obviously didn't mind him.

"There is no need for formality," Nathan said to her. "You may dispense with *Your Grace*." He paused. "Although milord would certainly be appropriate."

The crunch of boots on sand signaled the arrival of Tijah and Achaemenes, their faces streaked with chalky dust.

"No one's calling you that," Tijah said. "How about Sir Peter Pickled Penis?"

"Bit of a tongue-twister," Lo remarked. "Try saying it ten times fast."

"If we were in Vendagni," Nathan replied icily, "I would feed you to the Devouring Darkness."

"Remind me not to visit your castle again." Tijah dropped to her haunches next to the fire. "We searched all the tunnels. Magnus is gone, and his cage is empty."

"What about Talon?" Cas asked, poking the coals with a stick.

Tijah exchanged a wry look with Achaemenes. "We didn't see anyone else. I promise I'm me and he's him."

"The humbug is likely long gone," Nathan said. "If he can mimic anything, he could become a gull, like Bergmann's obnoxious pets."

"Or a moth," Felippa added. The thought of the grim, mercurial Talon as a fluttering insect made her giggle.

"Or a fish," Cas said, flashing her a grin.

Felippa laid her head on his shoulder. For the first time in a long while, surrounded by faces quickly becoming familiar, she felt safe.

Tijah peered down the beach, then rose to her feet, one hand casually resting on her sword. Nazafareen and Darius had returned, and with them a gaunt, hobbling figure. It was Gerda Kafsnjór. The ancient mortifex's white hair floated around her head like spun sugar.

"Well, look what the tide dragged in," she said, the flames in her eyes dancing as she regarded Felippa.

"And look what the dukka coughed up," Felippa retorted.

Gerda laughed, a sharp bark. "I could crush you with one hand. You'd fit in my pocket like a stray kitten."

"Better a cute little kitten than a ghastly old fossil."

"At least I'm not a miserable wisp," Gerda's head jutted forward. "What do you weigh? A sparrow's feather?"

"More than your last good idea, it seems," Felippa said.

"Ah, clever words from a child who looks like she's just escaped a dollhouse."

Felippa laughed aloud, as the others stared at them both. She was surprised to find that she was happy to see the crotchety old fex again.

"We found her skulking around the feasting hall," Darius said.

"I was not *skulking*," Gerda snapped. "I was looking for wine. But it's gone! The bottles are all empty." She squinted. "What have you done with my kin?"

"They went to the far shore, grandmother," Darius said. "I tried to tell you that."

"But how?" Confusion clouded her eyes. "They were bound here."

"My daughter broke the magic that held them captive. Just as you helped to expose Talon's imposture."

Gerda looked stunned, but covered it quickly. "Good riddance, then. Never much cared for any of them."

"What will you do now?" Felippa asked.

"I don't know." Her mouth turned down. "Stay here, I suppose."

"Can't you follow them?"

"Ships of the dead know better than to come near this isle, brat. I'm stuck." She shrugged. "Am I your prisoner?"

"Gods, no," Darius muttered with feeling.

"Then I bid you farewell."

With a curt nod, the old mortifex turned and shuffled back the way she came. Felippa watched her go, a swell of pity rising in her chest. To be alone for eternity... It seemed a cruel fate.

"Wait!" Felippa called out. She hurried up to Gerda. "If you *could* go to the far shore," she asked in a low voice, "would you want to?"

Gerda paused. For an unguarded moment, her expression softened. "What do you care?"

Felippa knew the old fex well enough to realize that any show of sympathy would be taken badly. "Oh, I don't give a bat's fuzzy arse either way. I just thought maybe someone was waiting for you on the other side."

Gerda was silent for a long moment. "My Albert," she said at last. "He died more than a century ago, though it doesn't seem so long." She touched the emeralds sewn along her sleeves and smiled wistfully. "He gave me these."

"Albert was your husband?"

Gerda nodded, the coals of her eyes dimming. "I think ... I said his name at the end."

She was talking about her own death now. Felippa had never asked about that. "So, you old harridan," she said, "would you rather moon about this place, where there isn't even a drop of wine, or go find your Albert?"

Brief longing crossed Gerda's face. "What if he's not there?" Her voice trembled. "What if what's waiting isn't ... what I hoped for? I... I haven't always been good."

So that was it. The reason she'd abandoned her passage and chosen to join Magnus.

"I'm sure your list of wicked deeds is as long as the hairs on your chin," Felippa said, "but you helped us when you had nothing to gain by it. Justinian wouldn't have listened to me, but he listened to you."

Gerda sucked her teeth, staring at the horizon.

"Justinian did plenty of bad things," she continued, "but I'll wager he made it to the other side. It's take a chance or sit around until you fade away into one of those nasty shadows. What are they called? Liches."

That seemed to decide her. Quickly, her body angled so no one else could see, Gerda squeezed Felippa's hand. Of course, she did it too hard, but Felippa felt sure she didn't mean to.

"I've made my peace," Gerda said loudly. "Had my little adventure. When the time comes to move on, I'm ready."

"Then it's our duty to help," Felippa told the others. "But she needs a vessel to cross to the far shore."

To her surprise, it was the pretty-but-scary woman fighter who spoke up first.

"How about Baba-hor's boat?" Tijah ventured. "Technically, it belongs to the dead anyway." She pointed to the larger mortifex ship anchored off the beach. "We can sail that one home."

Nathan sniffed. "How do we know she isn't Talon in disguise? Trying to escape the island?"

Gerda threw back her head and gave a harsh cackle that made Felippa wince. The old woman turned to Darius. "I never mentioned it before because your wits were too scrambled to grasp anything besides feasting and plundering, but I've known who you were from the moment we met. Your father is that preening idiot Victor Dessarian. I met him when my great-great-grandson, Culach—"

"Wait!" Lo shot to her feet, astonishment written across her face. "You are related to Culach?"

Gerda fixed Lo with a piercing stare. "Is that big blond lummox alive?"

"Very much so." Lo grinned. "I just saw him a few weeks ago."

Gerda grunted. "He was the last of the Kafsnjór line, and what did he do? Mucked everything up!"

"Well, he's not the last anymore. He and Mina are having a baby."

Nazafareen looked delighted. "Are they? We must visit them soon!"

Gerda sucked her teeth. "Let us hope the mewling infant has more sense than its father."

Nazafareen nodded to herself. "I can attest that she is Gerda Kafsnjór. Culach told me about her before he left Nocturne. He said she was as agreeable as a mule with a mouthful of wasps."

Gerda's snowy brows inched up her forehead. "He spoke of me?"

Darius cleared his throat. Nazafareen caught his eye and muttered under her breath.

"Oh yes," she said sweetly. "He doted on you!"

"That's a lie." Gerda smiled. "But you tell him... Tell him he's forgiven. And that he's a better man than his father ever was."

"We will relay the message," Lo said. "The last I saw him, he was headed back to Nocturne."

Gerda nodded briskly. Her face hardened into its usual dour lines. "Well, get the vessel ready. I don't have all day!"

Felippa covered a smile, tagging along as Lo sailed the small boat down the cove and dragged it into the shallows. She explained that they had nothing of value aboard, since all their earthly possessions had gone with her own vessel, the *Wind-Witch*.

"Which you lost in a riddle contest," Felippa said, delighted at the foolishness of it all.

"With the son of a giant eel," Lo agreed. "Don't forget that part."

Felippa grinned. "It's quite a story. You must let me write it down before you forget. I'm a scribe, you know."

"Cas mentioned." Lo grinned back. "I will tell you everything when we get out of here, but I doubt people would believe half of it."

Thistle leaped onto the foredeck and let out an eerie yowl. The wind stirred, ruffling the demon cat's fur.

Darius offered his hand, and Gerda stepped aboard. "Well, that's that then." She sniffed. "No need to stand about gawping."

"Goodbye, Gerda Kafsnjór!" Felippa called, waving. "I'm truly sorry we met!"

She pulled a face, then winked. "So am I, brat."

A fresh breeze filled the sails and the boat moved swiftly past Imp's Claw Point, its prow aimed at a point on the horizon between the rosy promise of dawn and the fading grandeur of dusk. Gerda stood at the wheel, silver hair streaming behind her. She did not look back.

"DID you have to eat *all* the hardtack?" Lo's stomach gave another indignant rumble. "Even a tentacle would be welcome right now."

Thistle waddled alongside, his stomach swaying. "I was hungry."

Her parents waited at the skiff that would carry everyone out to the larger brigantine. Above loomed the empty lair of the Cold Sea pirates, still sinister even with its undead masters gone. Nathan strode next to her, hands moving animatedly as he spoke.

"After Jaskin abandoned us, I knew it was up to me to save everyone. But the citadel seemed unreachable, and I had a boat-load of High Dead coming for me."

"Oooh, what did you do?" Tijah asked breathlessly, eyes wide.

"I am going to pretend that you are grateful," he admonished. "After dispensing with the mortifexes, I transformed my mother's knuckle bone into a rope ladder and set about climbing up to the bridge."

Nathan paused, clearly waiting for something.

"But I thought your transformations don't last," Cas said innocently.

"Thank you! *Someone* grasps the exquisite danger I placed myself in. The ladder reverted when I was two-thirds of the way up. I had to leap for a tiny ledge." He held his fingers an inch apart.

"What happened to your mother's knuckle bone?" Lo asked.

"Thankfully, my reflexes are excellent. I caught it with one hand before it could plummet into the mists and managed to make a second ladder to get me the rest of the way. Once there, I spotted Castelio's staff in the possession of a mortifex. The rest of you were in dire straits, about to be slaughtered like helpless little lambs."

"It wasn't that bad, was it?" Cas muttered.

"Yes," Lo said, "it was."

Nathan beamed. "I like you ever so much better this way. As I was saying, I overpowered the mortifex and liberated the staff…"

He cut off as a sleek dark head popped up just offshore. Then another, and another — dozens this time. They did not sing, merely stared with glistening, patient eyes.

"Dukka!" Darius shouted, backing out of the shallows. Achaemenes helped him pull the skiff farther up the shingle.

"Will they eat us if we're in a boat?" Cas asked.

"Not a larger vessel," Tijah said dolefully, "but that skiff is too low in the water, especially with eight people and a fat-ass cat aboard."

"What if we went two or three at a time?"

She shook her head. "No good. They'd swarm it. And once it capsizes..."

"So we're stuck here until they go away?" Lo asked.

"Well, we can't reach the damn pirate ship now," Tijah said.

"I knew we should have kept Baba-hor's dead people boat," Nathan muttered.

"Just turn them into something harmless," Cas suggested.

"How about adorable yellow ducklings?" Lo put it. "It'll only take a few minutes to row out there."

"I suppose I could... *Putain*!" He slapped his forehead with a groan. "My luggage was still aboard! That old crone took everything. Even my favorite cape. It had special pockets to hold the skulls of small mammals."

With a scowl, Nathan picked up a stone and skipped it into the surf. The dark heads submerged, then popped up again a few feet away. Needle teeth flashed in silent laughter.

"Ironically," Lo said, "it seems the rescue party is now trapped on this island. And there's no one coming to rescue *us*."

"I'd almost be glad to see those rusalki right now," Tijah said. "What's the food and water situation?"

Thistle slunk away, tail low.

"None and zero," Lo said.

"What about up there?" Tijah gazed at the citadel.

"The feast was my favorite part," Nazafareen said, walking up with a wry expression. "But it was all an elaborate farce."

"You didn't starve," Tijah pointed out.

"Because Talon somehow brought in real food," Felippa piped up. "It was just for Darius and Nazafareen, and then for me. Fish and potatoes every night."

"Where'd he get it from?" Lo wondered.

No one had an answer for that.

"I survived on mussels for a while," Felippa said. "They get washed into the tide pools. But don't touch the berries. They're poisonous." She touched the silver disk around her neck. "I'm pretty sure I would have died without this."

The rest of them surveyed the barren cliffs with dismay.

"Very well." Nathan sighed. "We shall draw lots for who gets eaten first."

"It's been five minutes," Lo said. "Isn't that a bit premature?"

He shrugged. "Better to face the inevitable."

The dukka vanished, submerging into the depths. Dark clouds mounded again on the horizon. A ferocious wind rose, whistling across the bay and whipping the water to a white froth.

"I no longer regret coming with you," Nathan said, "but the Quickening is very tiresome. Now we are to starve in the *rain*?"

"You don't have to blame Lo for everything," Cas snapped.

"I did not blame *her*. I blamed her *curse*. There is a difference."

"Not from where I'm standing."

Nathan's eyes narrowed. "I think we should eat *you* first—"

"Shut up, both of you," Tijah said. "What's that?"

Then Lo saw it — a small gray cat perched on the bow of the mortifex ship. At first she thought it was Thistle, that he'd somehow gotten past the dukka, but then she saw him streaking for the edge of the surf. The first cat hopped down and, pretty as you please, walked across the churning waves, tail upright in a friendly hook.

"Anuketmatma!" Nazafareen cried, wonder on her face.

"Who's that?" Cas looked befuddled.

Lo's eyes burned. She finally felt something, a tightness across her chest.

"She is one of the Five gods of this place," Lo replied, "but more than that, she is my dear friend's mother."

Anuketmatma leapt lightly over the last wavelets to the shore. Thistle rubbed against her and was greeted with a lick on the head.

"I think we've just been rescued after all," Tijah said with a grin.

THIRTY-THREE

It seemed that Anuketmatma had indeed heard her son calling for aid, but it took her a little while to return from the Marakai ships to the Cold Sea.

With the dukka gone, everyone piled into the skiff and Darius rowed them out to the brigantine. As they boarded, Lo spied brass fittings proclaiming it "Property of the D.C.C." Apparently, the vessel had served as a merchant ship for the Dream Collectors' Collective before it was stolen by Magnus. Or Talon. One of them, at least.

"Someone should tell Bergmann what happened," she said to Thistle. "Talon had a huge stockpile of stolen dreams. I imagine the other humbugs would like to get them back."

The cat eyed her solemnly. "Mother agrees. We have already spoken of it. She is calling a council of the Five to discuss the lawless situation in their realm and ensure it is remedied. I would like to remain with her for a while."

A knot cinched tight in Lo's stomach. "Not forever?"

He smiled faintly, as cats do. "Of course not. My place is with you."

She sank down, throwing her arms around him. "Don't you forget it."

Thistle suffered her embrace for a moment more. Then he prowled away, only pausing to thoroughly lick the spot where she'd kissed him.

Lo set about rigging the ship alongside her parents, who knew the vessel well. The *Reverie* was twice as long as the *Wind-Witch* and flew far more canvas, with a gaff sail, square topsails, and topgallant sails — twelve in total, all dyed a menacing black. Cas offered to help so she gave him orders, which he followed without too much trouble.

"I'll make a first mate out of you yet," she said, as the brigantine sped handily past Imp's Claw Point. "Ready to come about!"

They tacked around the northern tip of the isle into the Grayscar Passage and set a course for the Dominion.

"Well, we did it," Cas said, wrapping his arms around her waist.

"I've no idea how," she agreed, "but we failed at failing."

"I was going to say fecked up brilliantly, but yes." He eyed Nazafareen and Darius. "Your parents are intimidating, I must admit. How is it to have them back?"

She chewed her lip. "I thought I'd be over the moons, and I *am* happy, but it's more like..." She tried to think of a way to explain. "So there's this tiny stand near the Acropolis in Delphi that sells the absolute best kebabs. I always stop by when I'm there on business. We'll go together sometime. It's like that level of happy."

Cas gripped the wheel as the *Reverie* dipped into a trough between waves. "What's a kebab?"

"Roasted meat on a stick." She remembered his aversion to eating animals. "They do vegetable ones, too, don't worry."

Cas nodded slowly. "So seeing your parents after eight years is like eating a really good kebab?"

"I know there's something wrong with me. The whole soul division thing." She studied his face. "We haven't talked about it, but do you like the *me* that's here right now? Is it just horribly weird?"

"I like all of you," he said. "Every version." A pause. "Even the one with the..." He patted her back solemnly. "Well, the hump. And the lazy eye—ow!" He rubbed his bottom with an accusing look.

She formed her hand into a claw. "Oh, did a crab get you? Watch out, they'll all over the place."

Cas laughed and leaned in to nuzzle her neck, then saw her mother coming and hastily stepped back. "I'll go check the, ah, mizzenmast."

"There is no mizzenmast," Lo said. "But you can go roust Nathan. I think he's hiding in his cabin again."

Nazafareen took her hand. "You must fill us in on the last..." She trailed off with a frown. "How long have we been gone again?"

"Eight years," Lo said, her voice cool.

"You are angry." She sighed. "And you have every right to be, mouseling."

As a child, Lo would sob herself to sleep worrying that no one would call her that ever again. But the term of endearment no longer fit. She was twenty years old.

Lo stared out to sea. "It's not that you put yourselves in danger. It's that you never told me who you really were. I wasted years searching the wrong places. If you'd just confided in me, I would have known where to start. And I might have found you sooner."

Her mother's brow furrowed. "You're right. And I'm sorry. We should have told you the truth."

"So you were rounding up the restless dead for Kaethe." Lo paused as her father joined them. "I grasp that it's not a normal occupation, but I don't see why it had to be a secret."

"It's my fault," Darius said. "Your mother wanted to tell you, but I was afraid it would give you nightmares. You were so young."

They looked at her earnestly. Both had makeshift dressings wrapped around various appendages. They'd taken wounds in the fight, and no healing could be done until they were back in the world of the living. Lo sighed.

"Javid and Katsu took me in after you disappeared," she said. "I became a wind ship captain for their trading outfit, Falcon Couriers."

Darius frowned. "That sounds—"

"Dangerous?" Lo arched a brow.

"We're proud of you," Nazafareen said quickly. "Whatever life you chose, we would be proud."

Just ask.

"I do have a question for you," Lo said. "When you were pregnant with me, did you happen to... Oh, I don't know, cross the Veil? Perhaps make some kind of deal with Kaethe?"

Her parents swapped a shady look, which was all the answer she needed.

"Why do you ask, mouseling?" Nazafareen said.

"Don't you think she's a little old for that?" Darius muttered.

He was always the more perceptive one.

"Yes, she is a little old for that," Lo said. "Well, did you?"

"The bargain was mine," he admitted. "Its terms had nothing to do with you. Kaethe told me that explicitly."

Lo drew a deep breath. "I believe you. But she still marked me."

Her mother froze. "Marked you how?"

Lo took the wheel, adjusting their course. "Let's start with the first time I crashed my wind ship."

———

THEY TOOK the news better than she'd expected. Well, her father did. Her mother was pretty angry. Both of them wanted to see Kaethe straightaway, which was fine with Lo. She had her own questions, such as what would happen to her when she died for the last time. Seeing the old mortifex Gerda had only cemented her desire to know for sure that she wouldn't be damned in some way.

Exhaustion finally overtook her and she fell asleep on deck, rocked by the gentle sway of the ship. She woke to a dark shoreline ahead.

"We're nearing the border of the Dominion. You're going to see Kaethe, aren't you?"

She looked up at Cas, his hair tousled by the wind. He sat down next to her.

"I must," Lo replied, stretching cramped limbs. "She's the only one who knows what I am."

He sighed. "I would go with you in a heartbeat."

"But you have Felippa, and she must be brought home." Lo took his hands. "I'll find you in Prydwen after I see Kaethe. Perhaps we can visit my homeland together. Susa is a sunny little port town with very good wine. And Samarqand is even grander."

He brightened. "Aye, I'd like that."

"Dammit, Sleepy-Eyes, I'll miss you, even if it's only for a day or two." Lo pulled him into a hug, which turned into frantic kissing.

"You shouldn't have let me sleep on deck," she said, a bit breathless.

"I took pity on you. You were snoring like a hibernating bear."

"Was I really?"

"No," he admitted. "But you looked knackered."

"You snore," she said. "More like grunts, really. Have you ever heard a sow rooting for truffles?"

"Oh gods, that's the truth, isn't it?"

Lo looked around. They snuck behind a large sail on the forecastle deck. "More kissing," she said. "That's an order."

———

The border between the Cold Sea and the Dominion had neither walls nor signposts. Yet Lo felt it as she stepped ashore — a shiver running through her, as though a cold hand stroked her brow. They were no longer in the realm of the Five but in the demesne of the Drowned Woman.

Thistle and his mother Anuketmatma took possession of the *Reverie*, setting a course for Dreamhaven to inform Bergmann about the demise of Magnus the Merciless. The rogue humbug Talon still had to be hunted down, and the guild needed to know everything.

The rest of them walked into the shadowed woods, where a circle of nine stone gates stood in a clearing. Each shimmered with fey green light that flowed like running water. Waymarkers jutted from the earth, covered in tiny lettering.

"They are written in six languages, most of them very ancient," Nazafareen said. "Tijah, you know them better than I do."

Lo's mother was the child of a nomadic people called the Four-Legs Clan and could barely read her own native tongue.

Tijah nodded and pointed to a pair adjacent to each other.

"Left leads to the Ducal palace in Prydwen. Right opens into a pass through the Mountains of Nightmare."

"Ah," Nathan murmured with a happy sigh. "Home sweet home."

Cas looked down at Felippa. "Ready to see Da and Teo?" She gave a nervous nod. He turned to Nathan. "What about you?"

"I plan to hunt down Lord Bag o'Bones," he replied. "Jaskin is my responsibility and I won't let him run loose, not when he's capable of the worst mischief."

Tijah stared at him in mock disbelief. "Well, shit. I can't find a single thing wrong with that sentence."

"And you, *mercenaire*?" Nathan asked dryly.

She glanced at Achaemenes. "We're going to see the boss lady. Make our report and get back to business. I'm done with this hellhole."

"The Empire is not exactly paradise," Achaemenes pointed out.

"True," she conceded. "But at least the dead don't walk."

He cleared his throat. "Revenants?"

"Oh yeah, right." She shook her head. "Fucking revenants."

Nathan was following the conversation with interest. "What is a revenant?"

"Undead soldiers. About twelve feet tall, carrying broadswords." She smiled grimly. "Every time you kill a necromancer in our world, three of them come tearing out of the ground. Then you have to kill *them* too. It's a real bitch."

Nathan didn't seem offended. "Fascinating. I've never heard of such magic."

"Well, the Antimagi in the Empire are a lot worse than you are," she conceded.

"Antimagi," he echoed. "I like the sound of that."

"No, you don't." Tijah scowled. "They're flaming pieces of—"

"Perhaps you'd better go now," Lo said, sweeping Cas, Nathan, and Felippa into an incredibly awkward group hug.

"I think that's a good idea," Cas said, his cheek smooshed against hers. "Find me in Prydwen as soon as you can."

"Summon Thistle if you... Oh, dammit, you can't. He isn't coming with me. Never mind. I'm good at finding things." She smiled ruefully. "Just not keeping them."

They embraced again, just her and Cas, holding each other tight for a long moment.

"I still have your braid," he whispered. "In my pocket."

She grinned against his neck. "Deviant."

"Promise me something," he said.

She pulled back and gazed at his warm, handsome face. "Name it."

"Be polite to Kaethe. No backtalk, and no leaping into danger. You have to save one life for me."

His words made her throat tighten. "Like normal people?"

"That's a stretch." The corners of his eyes crinkled. "But we'll get you a new ship and see where it takes us."

"Then I promise not to sass the goddess of death." Lo released him and stepped back. "Be careful in Prydwen. I doubt all the fires have been put out yet."

"At least the Duc is gone," said Felippa. "It can't be worse than it was with him in charge."

Cas smiled down at her. "I can't dispute that."

"Might I have a hug?" Lo leaned down and Felippa gave her a fierce squeeze. "Take care of him," she said, winking at Cas. "Make him wash his ears."

"I will," Felippa whispered. "Come see us soon."

"Give my warmest regards to Vigo," Cas told Nathan.

The Duc of Vendagni gave a lazy-cat grin. "I will be sure to do so. And if you ever return to Castle Cazal, you may stay in the Ambrosia Suite. It is somewhat less haunted than the Blood Labyrinth."

Cas nodded at Lo's parents, along with Tijah and Achaemenes. Then he took Felippa's hand, staff gripped in the other, and the gate swallowed them both in a shimmer of emerald light.

"It is *adieu*." Nathan looked around and cleared his throat. "I despise sentiment, so I will depart now. Good luck with Kaethe."

In three long strides, black half-cape flapping behind, he was through the gate to Vendagni.

Lo stared at the portals for a moment, then turned resolutely towards the dark woods. *Get it over with. The sooner it's done, the sooner you can return to the world of the living.*

After so long at sea, the Dominion's pines seemed even gloomier, their branches knitting into a dense canopy that blocked out the sky. An oppressive atmosphere pressed down as they set out for Kaethe's abode, the air heavy with the scent of decaying leaves. Lo couldn't shake the feeling of being watched. Phantom eyes seemed to track her from the shadows. She glanced over her shoulder but saw nothing, not even a bird or squirrel. The place was empty of life, and yet...

"You feel it," her father said.

He spoke softly, but his voice still sounded too loud.

Lo rubbed her arms. "I hope I don't attract the dead. They like me a bit too much."

"It would certainly be better not to meet any," Darius agreed, "but with luck we can avoid them."

"Kaethe's realm is a strange place," Nazafareen added. "The veil between worlds is thin here."

Lo thought of her final death and what mysteries lay

beyond. Perhaps it was nerves, but she had a strong feeling that she would not like the answers Kaethe gave her.

She opened her mouth to ask more about the Drowned Woman when a sudden frenzy of barking shattered the quiet. Six enormous black mastiffs burst from the trees, bounding toward them. Lo stiffened, looking frantically for somewhere to hide, but Tijah laughed and strode forward to meet the pack.

"Don't worry," she said over her shoulder. "They're tame little puppy dogs. *Aren't you?* Oh, yes you are!"

The giant hounds milled around her, tails wagging furiously. She greeted each with an affectionate pat on the head. Nazafareen and Achaemenes joined her, but Darius hung back, eyeing the beasts warily.

"They treed me for hours once," he admitted. "It was a long time ago, before you were born, but I've never quite gotten used to them."

"I don't blame you," Lo said, also keeping her distance from the lolling red tongues and sharp teeth.

"They belong to Kaethe," Tijah called over, scratching one behind the ears. "They guide the dead to the boats and keep out anyone who doesn't belong."

Lo's fear ebbed. "Why are they here?"

"It's a good sign," she replied. "Kaethe must be expecting us."

With the hounds racing ahead, they set off once more, climbing a series of hills beneath the changeless white sky. Each summit gave a view of boreal forest stretching to the horizon. Lo saw the glint of rivers, and a lake nestled in a distant valley, but there were no buildings or other sign of life.

"How much farther?" she asked, turning to Darius.

He pointed ahead. "We're here."

Lo turned back. Between one moment and the next, a

tapered spire had appeared, rising above the treetops. She blinked. "That was *not* there a moment ago."

Darius glanced at Tijah. "You told me once that Kaethe's tower was never in the same place twice. And that it only appears if the Drowned Woman is willing to grant an audience."

Tijah smiled. "I remember. Like I said, a good sign."

As they drew closer, Lo noticed her mother frowning, her gaze fixed on the tower.

"What's wrong?" she asked.

Nazafareen hesitated, then shook her head. "I am still getting used to how like your grandmother you look. The spitting image." She gave a distracted smile. "Let us go inside, mouseling."

It was a poor excuse since she'd been looking at the tower and not at Lo. Well, she *had* been under an enchantment for eight years. It would make sense that she was still muddled.

And yet... Lo studied her mother's face, sensing there was something she wasn't saying. But Nazafareen's expression gave nothing away, and Lo decided not to push. She had enough to worry about without adding new mysteries to the list.

At the base of the tower, Lo craned her neck, trying to see the top. It was impossibly tall, its black surface absorbing the light around it. There were no visible windows or doors, and she wondered how they were meant to get inside.

She'd been here once before when she accidentally created a portal while fleeing from Morgen. The memory of watching the Duc's consort die slowly of a broken neck made her stomach twist. Of course, Morgen had come back and stolen the Grand Menotte, so it was hard to feel too sorry for her...

A concealed door opened on one side of the octagonal structure, startling Lo from her ruminations. Just beyond the threshold stood the bearded young man in purple robes whom she'd met briefly on her previous visit. He had a kind, guileless face and was obviously pleased to find them there.

He greeted Tijah and Achaemenes, then turned to Lo's parents, clasping their hands. "Darius, Nazafareen, it brings me such joy to see you again!" His mild gaze settled on Lo. "We were never properly introduced. I am Nabu-bal-idinna, Kaethe's companion. Welcome to her House."

Lo forced a smile. The last time she saw Kaethe, the goddess had demanded the Grand Menotte and she'd refused to hand it over. The encounter hadn't ended well. But Magnus and his mortifexes had gone to their final reward, the talisman that bound them rendered harmless. Surely Kaethe would see there was no threat anymore. Lo squared her shoulders and followed Nabu-bal-idinna inside.

"My lady awaits you all in the Chamber of Souls," he said.

They stood at a juncture of nine corridors radiating out like the spokes of a wheel. All were lined with identical doors, and none appeared to have an end. It defied logic, considering the tower's narrow width, but the place was as Lo remembered.

She followed Nabu-bal-idinna through a series of similar junctions; at last, he opened a door, revealing a cavernous room with a barrel-vaulted ceiling that stretched into shadows.

Hundreds of tiny white sparks floated above the floor... No, not a floor but a world in miniature. Ghostly mountains and forests and rivers, each rendered in meticulous detail.

"You are looking at a map of the Dominion," Darius whispered. "The brightest lights are gates and the souls streaming through them."

The sparks swirled and eddied like leaves in the wind. In some places, they gathered in glowing clouds; in others, only a few lonely motes drifted.

Lo sensed the goddess before she saw her; a sudden icy cramp in her left arm. A moment later, a figure emerged from the gloom. Water streamed from the corners of her stern mouth, pooling around her feet as she glided across the floor. Her hair twitched like a basket of snakes, and dark veins pulsed beneath her nearly translucent skin.

"Welcome back, half-child," Kaethe said. "I've been expecting you."

Lo ducked her head and swallowed hard. Kaethe's gaze slid past her to Darius and Nazafareen.

"It is well to see you returned safely," the goddess said. She turned to Tijah. "So you found them at last."

Tijah stepped forward. "My lady, we bring news from Glash's Tusk. Odd as it may seem, a four-toed humbug named Talon was impersonating the mortifex known as Magnus the Merciless."

"A humbug?" Kaethe accepted a cup from Nabu-bal-idinna, never taking her eyes off Tijah. "What a peculiar turn of events."

"When the fraud was exposed, Magnus's followers were furious," Achaemenes added. "They tried to stop us from leaving."

Darius glanced at Lo, pride in his voice. "But then my daughter used the power you gave her to send all the mortifexes to the far shore—"

Kaethe laughed, a sound like frost-rimed bells chiming on a winter morning.

"If I may, er, Lady," Lo said. "Why is that funny?"

The goddess sobered. "It isn't funny at all. More ironic. Do you know the difference?"

Lo decided she didn't much care for Kaethe. "I do," she said warily.

"Good. Because you did nothing of the sort." Kaethe gestured at the sparks drifting above the landscape. "Some fool put on the Grand Menotte and summoned the mortifexes through the Veil. I saw their souls flit past two days ago." A pause. "All one hundred of them."

An appalled silence greeted this statement.

"But I saw a white light," Lo protested.

Kaethe's eyes narrowed. "Hmmm. You were probably struck by lightning again."

"Dammit." Lo wanted to hit something. "I *knew* I smelled burning hair!"

Kaethe studied her for a long, uncomfortable moment. "In fact, I'm afraid you're down another life."

"So I died again for *nothing*?"

Kaethe gave a careless shrug. "It happens."

The puddle of water around the goddess was spreading outward. It reached Lo's boots, and she shuffled back before she slipped and broke her neck. *Be polite. No backtalk.*

Tijah and Achaemenes had their heads together, whispering. "Jaskin Cazal must have found the Grand Menotte," Tijah said grimly. "He abandoned us to go look for it."

"Or it's Morgen Nadezhda," Lo said. A bitter taste filled her mouth. "She's the one who had possession of it. All she needed to do is find a spell to open the box."

"It could be either of them," Kaethe said, "or someone else altogether. I do not know. My sight is dim in the living world."

Everyone turned to the door as Nabu-bal-idinna bustled in.

"Wine?" he inquired, coming around with a silver tray.

Lo and Tijah exchanged a glance, then downed their cups in one long swallow. The tart vintage did little to chase away the dread settling in Lo's stomach.

All this while, her mother had been standing in silence, amber eyes distant and thoughtful. Nabu-bal-idinna moved about, refilling everyone's cups. When he reached Nazafareen, she seemed to wake from her trance.

"It is so good to see you again," she said with a smile. "How

I have missed your rutibaya stew." A wink. "Nothing like the smell of fresh thyme!"

Nabu-bal-idinna smiled and stammered a thank-you.

"Remind me," Nazafareen continued, her tone oddly light under the circumstances. "Which king did you serve before coming to the Lady's tower?"

"Teispes," he replied.

"Of course. You were his alchemist."

He nodded, stroking his beard. "That's right."

"Did you turn base metal to gold?"

Lo wondered if her mother's wits were permanently addled. They had just learned that an undead army was under someone's command — and none of the likely culprits were mentally stable to begin with. Well, it wasn't her problem. Not anymore.

Nabu's brow furrowed. He smiled uncertainly. "I suppose so. It was a very long time ago. I have not thought about it in ages."

"Naturally." Nazafareen's gaze sharpened. "What was Teispes like? As a king, I mean. Was he good to his people, or did he abuse their trust?"

Her eyes flicked to Kaethe. Something passed between the two women, a current of understanding Lo didn't grasp.

Nabu-bal-idinna opened his mouth. Closed it. Tried again. "Er, I—"

"His memory is not what it once was," Kaethe cut in. "As he already told you." She dismissed him with a curt wave of her hand. "Leave us."

He left with an injured expression. When Kaethe turned back to them, her eyes were chips of black ice. Nazafareen's stare was equally frigid.

"I had hoped you would not remember," Kaethe said.

"Remember what?" Darius asked.

Nazafareen turned to him. She rubbed the stump of her right wrist. Lo knew the habit well. Her mother did it when she was anxious or unsure about something. "It's still foggy. I think I told you on the ship. Didn't I?"

"No." Fond exasperation colored his tone. "Tell me now."

Nazafareen pointed a finger at the door where Nabu-ba-idinna had disappeared. When she spoke, her voice was firm. "That man is the Sun God."

THIRTY-FOUR

Darius burst out laughing. "Nabu-bal-idinna?" he said. "The kind, humble servant we have known for more than twenty years?"

"Yes," Nazafareen insisted. "He is Bel. Or Apollo, if you prefer."

"Whatever his name is, can we get him back in here with more wine?" Tijah quipped.

When Kaethe did not join the amusement, her mirth slowly died.

Achaemenes wasn't smiling, either. "I assume you have good reason to make this charge," he said to Nazafareen.

She nodded. "The last time we were here, eight years ago, I was in the kitchen with Nabu as he prepared supper. He was chopping garlic with a large knife. I told him how I'd once used my sword *Nemesis* to slice a tomato when I camped with Darius. Then I made some jest about it being so sharp, I accidentally cut my hand off."

Knowing her mother, Lo felt certain all that was true.

"Nabu laughed so hard that the knife slipped and he

severed two of his own fingers." Nazafareen folded down her thumb and forefinger. "Just above the knuckles."

"Now *that's* irony," Lo interjected. When everyone stared at her, she cleared her throat. "Sorry, go on."

"Naturally, I was horrified," Nazafareen said. "But Nabu smiled as if it were nothing and tossed them in the bin with the garlic skins. Then a golden light surrounded his bloody hand, and new fingers appeared. Just like that. Quite a trick, even for a famous alchemist."

Kaethe said nothing, but her onyx eyes bored into Nazafareen.

"It was not magic. It was *power*. I knew then he must be a god like you," Nazafareen said. "But which? The Greeks have their pantheon, the Persians another. Yet only one god disappeared. Only one left the sun frozen in the sky after the Sundering."

"I hoped you had forgotten," Kaethe said flatly. Her thin slash of a mouth tightened.

"I did forget." Nazafareen met the goddess's angry gaze. "But now I remember. And I remember that you were standing in the doorway, Lady of Shadows, and you saw the same thing I did, and it was that very same day you sent us to hunt Magnus the Merciless."

Lo's mind reeled. *Kaethe* was behind it all?

"But she sent Tijah and Achaemenes to find you!" Lo said.

"A diversion," Nazafareen replied. "What she really wanted was the Grand Menotte."

Lo glanced at Kaethe. She remembered the goddess looming, hand outstretched. *Give me that box!*

"But why?" Lo asked. "What could she want with it?"

"Not to send the mortifexes to the far shore," her mother replied, "nor to wear it herself, but simply to ensure that Magnus never found it. She needed them to remain in the citadel as our jailers so we never escaped. The thing I don't understand is how Talon figured into it."

Kaethe lifted her chin, her expression cold and remote. "Magnus grew difficult, demanding. I had told him that you were a Breaker, to give him hope and ensure he wouldn't kill you, but I feared he would mistreat you. So I found a humbug to take his place." Her lips twisted. "Talon is a petty creature, I admit, but he was willing to do anything if it served his own vengeance. And he had strong powers of enchantment. It was kinder than a cell. Or a cage, like Magnus."

The last mystery was solved. "It was you who provided the real food for the feast," Nazafareen said.

Kaethe nodded. "I used the one called Gerda to smuggle it in."

Darius gazed at the goddess in furious disbelief. "We served you faithfully for years! Did whatever you required of us without complaint! We kept our end of the bargain, even though the price was high."

A flicker of regret passed over Kaethe's austere features. "I know. That is why I insisted you were treated well." She waved a dismissive hand. "Come, now. Was it truly so bad being sea wolves?" She shot Nazafareen a pointed look. "From what I heard, you rather enjoyed it."

Nazafareen scowled. "That's hardly the point."

"But we had a child," Darius cut in with barely contained rage. "Do you not grasp what we have lost? What she has lost? All those years!"

"Delilah was raised by dear friends of yours," Kaethe retorted. "Look how she's turned out. She's perfectly fine."

Lo raised a hand. "I have to disagree with that."

No one seemed to be listening.

So Kaethe had deliberately engineered her parents' kidnapping to hide the secret of Bel. She could imagine Cas's face when he found out. How she wished he were here with her now.

"And the real Nabu-bal-idinna?" Nazafareen said. "What have you done with him?"

Kaethe sniffed dismissively. "Nothing. He visited my tower once, but I let him leave. He must have died centuries ago. I never saw him again." She lifted her chin. "It seemed plausible to borrow his name. So you see, there is no real harm done to anyone. As long as Bel remains within these walls, he will not recall who he was. Which is for the best, believe me."

Nazafareen took a step forward, head lowered like a bull about to charge. "You enjoy playing with people's memories a bit too much," she snarled.

Her mother was clearly on the verge of doing something rash. The pair of them locked eyes.

"Perhaps I did overreact," Kaethe conceded after a long moment. "If you promise to keep his identity a secret, then I will not hold you here—"

A kerfuffle in the corridor cut off her words. Six of the giant hounds stalked into the chamber, herding a bedraggled figure between them. Lo was amazed to see Jaskin Cazal. She was so accustomed to viewing him in the mirror, it came as a shock to see him standing before her, perfectly solid and real — if rather the worse for wear.

His lace-trimmed frock coat hung in tatters, scratches marked his sallow face, and his raven hair was matted with leaves and twigs. Wide, dark eyes darted around the chamber.

One of the dogs padded up to Kaethe and licked her white hand. It whimpered and barked.

"They caught him creeping around in the woods," she said.

Tijah marched over and yanked up each sleeve. His wrists were bare. "Where's the Grand Menotte?" she demanded.

"Unhand me, wench," Jaskin said haughtily, yelping as Tijah rifled through his clothes.

She finally stepped back, lip curled in disgust. "The fucker doesn't have it."

Kaethe did not appear to move, but an instant later she was looming over Jaskin, dark veins pulsing under her skin. "Speak, necromancer! Where is it?"

Jaskin gave a mad hoot of laughter. "Round and round the rugged rock the ragged rascal ran!" he sang tunelessly.

A black-nailed hand gripped his dirty coat and lifted him off the ground. "Answer me or suffer the consequences."

Jaskin grinned. "The box, the box, sealed up with locks! Inside awaits a nasty shock!" He dissolved into incoherent muttering, punctuated by sobs.

Kaethe gazed into his face for a long moment, then released him with a sigh. "His mind is half gone." She snapped her fingers at the hounds. "Take him to the sixty-third garden and enclose him there."

One of the dogs gave a sharp bark.

"No, not the one with the carnivorous azaleas," Kaethe said with a touch of impatience. "That's the sixty-fourth. We are trying to soothe his mind, not break it further."

The beasts snapped at Jaskin's heels, nudging him from the chamber. Kaethe turned to the others, fixing Lo with a pointed stare.

"You caught me unprepared before, but I've fortified the wards. There won't be any unauthorized portals. Cazal can cause no trouble, and in time, we might get coherent answers from him."

In time? "I don't plan on staying long," Lo said. "Ah, my Lady. I promised a friend I would meet him."

"The Quietus?" Kaethe laughed. "I do like that one. We shall see."

"So we're your prisoners now?" Darius asked hotly.

"Not at all," the goddess replied. "I admit that I acted rashly. It was a poor repayment for your service. If you will all swear an oath to keep Nabu's true identity secret, I will let you go." Her gaze darkened. "I am certain you will keep your promise since every one of you will come to me, in the end, and you would not enjoy the reckoning if I am betrayed."

Lo could see that her parents were still furious, but the offer was the only way out of the Drowned Woman's tower. None but a fool would reject it.

"Very well," Nazafareen said. "We will swear."

"And we will," Achaemenes said, sharing a look with Tijah.

"Sure," Lo said. "Whatever you want. But I have some questions for you myself, Lady of Shadows, if you would grant me a private audience."

Kaethe did not seem surprised. "I will answer them tomorrow. But you have journeyed hard. Stay the night first. The usual guest quarters have been prepared."

Lo wondered if it was some new trap, but the thought faded as she covered a jaw-cracking yawn. It *had* been a very long day. She was eager for answers, but perhaps it would be better to face Kaethe again after she was rested.

The goddess glanced away, lost in thought. "Tomorrow I will explain why I did what I did. It is not as selfish as you think. Nabu-bal-idinna is a kind and generous man. But Bel?" Her gaze turned flinty. "He is more dangerous than you can imagine."

JASKIN CAZAL SAT against a persimmon tree, picking twigs from his hair. It was an idyllic spot. Broad, heart-shaped leaves fluttered in a gentle breeze, the branches above heavy with golden fruit that glowed in the dappled sunlight.

He drew a deep breath, briefly savoring the bittersweet scent of persimmons mixed with the rich, dark soil beneath. Wildflowers grew in abundance along a burbling brook, attracting swarms of butterflies, their delicate wings shimmering as they swooped from one bloom to the next.

"A pox on this gilded cage," he muttered. "And a pox on the Lady of Shadows!"

Again and again, he had tried to tear open a portal, but she had chained his magic. Of all the enemies to be caught by, Kaethe was surely the worst. At least she believed his pretense of lunacy. But he'd escaped one prison only to find himself in another.

Soft footfalls signaled a visitor. Jaskin tensed, thinking it was the virago with the curved sword come to question him, but it was Kaethe's bearded servant, carrying a steaming bowl that smelled strongly of thyme.

"Lord Cazal." His tone was kind as he set the bowl on one of the tree's great roots. "You must eat."

Jaskin glanced up, taking in the silly purple robes and cow-like brown eyes. "You show me courtesy, unlike your mistress."

The servant cast him a look of reproval. "Do not speak ill of her. Kaethe is wise and good."

"Then why does she immure me here?" Jaskin demanded.

The man looked uncertain. "I do not know. But you must have done something to deserve it."

Jaskin heaved a gusty sigh, affecting an air of remorse. "The greatest scholars are not always the wisest men. I made grave mistakes in my lifetimes." He smiled. "But you have me at a disadvantage. What is your name, good fellow?"

The servant glanced around nervously. "I am Nabu-bal-idinna. But I'm afraid I must leave you now. Kaethe's orders were very specific. I was only to bring you food. No conversation."

"Of course, of course." Jaskin waved a hand magnanimously as he turned to leave. "My thanks for the stew."

A small sally gate had appeared in the brick wall enclosing the garden. Nabu-bal-idinna reached into his robes and withdrew a heavy ring of keys. He was about to open it when Jaskin called out, "Did she mention how I made a talisman to command an army of dead daēvas?"

Nabu-bal-idinna paused and looked back, eyes wide. "Oh my. No, I don't believe so."

"It is a most dreadful device," Jaskin confided. "I tried to retrieve it, but someone else took possession of the talisman."

"You don't know who?" the alchemist asked, his bovine eyes growing even bigger.

Jaskin shook his head. "When I saw the mortifexes had been summoned, I fled for my life. They would love nothing more than to rend me limb from limb, you see."

"Truly?" Nabu-bal-idinna looked aghast.

Jaskin gazed around ruefully. "In my haste, I opened a portal to the Lady's realm. I did not mean to come here, but alas, no misfortune comes singly."

He took a spoonful of stew and was hit with a blast of thyme so overwhelming his throat closed. Nabu-bal-idinna was watching him anxiously. Jaskin managed to chew and swallow. He sighed with exaggerated bliss. "I haven't tasted anything this delicious in centuries! Thou art a gifted cook indeed. It was almost worth being captured just to sup at your table."

Nabu-bal-idinna flushed with pleasure.

"But enough about my woes," Jaskin said, forcing himself to tuck into the vile stew, which was also too salty. "I'm sure you lead a far more exciting life as consort to the Lady of Shadows."

Nabu drifted back to the persimmon tree, tucking the ring of keys into his robe. "My life here is not so thrilling as you might imagine," he confided. "Kaethe is perfection itself, beautiful and gracious." He chewed his lip. "But she does have her moods. And nothing ever changes, save for the occasional caller like yourself."

Jaskin nodded sympathetically. "Don't you ever wish to travel? Visit the world beyond this tower again?"

Nabu laced his hands together. "I think not," he said primly. "It has been so long since I ventured outside."

"The living world is perilous, I'll not gild the truth," Jaskin said, choking down another bite. "But Aveline, the land I hail from, brims with marvels."

He launched into the tale of how magic had transformed the barren darklands into the lush Nightwood. Of the swimming bears of the Frost Fens, the midnight bazaar in Loris, the Voidwalker's Gate, and the northern tribes of the Icemarch who would sing down the aurora.

Nabu listened raptly, a wistful look on his face. "It does sound wondrous."

"What if we embarked on an adventure, you and I?" The necromancer's eyes glittered. "Explored the far-flung reaches of the Moon Courts together?"

Nabu blinked, taken aback. "Oh no, Kaethe would never permit it."

"Must you always abide by her decrees?" Jaskin cocked a brow.

"I..." Nabu faltered. "Well, yes."

"Do you not deserve some *small* measure of freedom?" Jaskin pressed, holding his apelike fingers a hair's breadth apart. "A brief respite from the Lady's whims? Mayhap if you stole away for a while, she would learn to cherish you more."

That seemed to strike a nerve. Nabu-bal-iddina drew out

the ring of keys, twisting it in his hands. There were hundreds, no two alike in size or shape. It took all of Jaskin's considerable will not to lunge at him and tear them from his grasp. But he did not know which key unlocked the gate, and without Nabu's aid, he knew they would not make it past the hounds.

"I don't know…" Nabu whispered, though he seemed to be weakening.

"Absence makes the heart grow fonder," Jaskin remarked. "Would she truly begrudge you a *single day* in the living world? Once we are outside the walls, I can take us anywhere you like. Then we can just hop back when we wish to!"

Nabu gazed at the distant tower. Jaskin knew they were actually *inside* it somehow, but thinking too hard about that made his head ache.

"I would like to," he murmured, "but she has *such* a temper."

Jaskin leaned forward. "In that case, she need never discover you were gone at all."

"She would know," Nabu said, glancing around. "She knows *everything*."

The necromancer's whisper reeked of thyme. "Then allow me to make a suggestion…"

THIRTY-FIVE

L o woke in a feather bed piled with quilts. She lay there for a while with her eyes shut, enjoying the content, semi-drowsy state that comes after an excellent night's sleep.

Her guest chamber at Kaethe's House was much cozier than expected. It had a window, for one thing (how that worked she couldn't guess, since the outside of the tower appeared solid) through which she enjoyed a vista of distant mountains. There was a shelf of books — all by Nabu-bal-idinna — whose varied titles included *Journeys Behind the Veil*, *Poetic Odes to Kaethe*, and *The Alchemist's Kitchen*.

A table, chair, and wardrobe completed the furnishings of the bedroom. A smaller door led to the privy, whose stone bench opened to an infinite-looking darkness that made her scalp tingle. She did her business as quickly as possible, then padded to the washbasin and rinsed her teeth and face. A proper bath would have been nice, but that would require summoning Nabu-bal-iddina.

And demanding hot water from a god, even if he was the only servant around, felt a bit cheeky.

She did take a moment to inspect herself, though; Kaethe was right. She had new scars on her lower back, fresh pink ones, and chunks of her hair looked suspiciously frizzy. An indirect strike, perhaps, but still fatal.

It's why I didn't feel the pain. I was *dead*.

And the black glass she'd seen... yes, it could have been fused by the intense heat of the lightning striking sand.

She must have woken quickly this time since no one noticed. Lo bit her lip in frustration. The rules kept changing — if there were any rules to begin with.

She rooted through the wardrobe and found a clean linen tunic and wool trousers, plain but of good quality, which fit as if they had been made for her. Before going to sleep, her mother had told her about the bargain. Apparently, she had died and the only way for her to come back was to serve Kaethe for half of each year. At first, Lo's parents had left her with the Maenads. But they missed her too much, so they brought her along on their jaunts to the underworld.

Several of Lo's early childhood years had been spent here at the Lady's tower. When her mother pressed a little wooden horse into Lo's hand, one she'd been very fond of, a host of buried memories surfaced. Cardamom drifting from the kitchen as Nabu baked a treat; digging for treasure in Kaethe's many gardens and careening wild down her endless corridors.

She even recalled meeting another little girl named Mara, who was quite timid. Lo feared she'd been a bully, teasing her and bossing her around.

Anyway, she understood now why her parents had done what they did. As excuses went, theirs pretty damned good. She resolved to let go of her grudge at being deceived and decided the wisest course was to be grateful that she had them back.

She combed her singed, lopsided hair — the bilge pump incident — and regarded herself in the wardrobe's mirror. Kaethe had promised to answer her questions today. Lo tried to imitate Tijah's steely-eyed demeanor; the look of someone who knew a thing or two and wouldn't be put off.

But in truth, she was eager to be on her way to Prydwen. She missed Cas already and was dying to tell him everything.

She found Tijah in the kitchen with her parents and Achaemenes, all of them peering into cupboards. The stove was cold and there was no sign of...

"Where's Nabu?" Lo asked, poking around the pantry.

Achaemenes shrugged. "No one's seen him since yesterday."

"I was looking forward to an omelet, even heavy-handed as he is with the turmeric," Darius remarked.

"Found the eggs!" Lo said, holding up a cloth-covered basket.

Her mother pulled out a loaf of dark bread. "I suppose we'll have to fend for ourselves—"

A flood of water gushed into the kitchen, sloshing around the large butcher block table. Kaethe appeared in the doorway, her face livid with outrage.

"Jaskin Cazal and my husband have run off together!" she announced, gnashing her teeth. "That traitorous snake let them both out of the tower with his keys."

"Shit," Tijah said, stretching the word to at least three syllables. "How can you be sure Jaskin didn't coerce him?"

Kaethe brandished a piece of parchment. "Because Nabu left a note!"

"What does it say?" Lo ventured.

Kaethe recited the words without looking. Clearly, she had memorized it.

"O Most Noble and Beloved Mistress," she snarled. "I have gone away for a little while, as we are out of sheep's milk. I will return as soon as I have located some more. Your consort in eternity, Nabu-bal-Idinna."

"Well, okay, so he's coming back," Lo said. "Let's stay calm."

Kethe's eyes were wild. "There's plenty of sheep's milk. I already checked." She pressed a dramatic hand to her forehead. "He has deceived me!"

"Uh-oh," Tijah murmured as Lo's mother strode forward. She wore a look of satisfaction.

Much later, Lo would wonder what might have happened if Nazafareen had mastered her infamous temper. It was one of those small moments upon which the fulcrum of exceedingly large future events rested. The pebble that set off the landslide.

Nazafareen might have said, "Oh, that bastard!" Or, and here's a novel thought, she might have simply kept her mouth shut.

Her mother did no such thing. Instead, she laughed in Kaethe's face. "You can hardly blame him for leaving you. After the way you've treated him—"

Kaethe flung out a hand. A swirling hole opened in the middle of the kitchen. With a sweep of her arm, Kaethe hurled Darius and Nazafareen through it, followed seconds later by Tijah and Achaemenes. They vanished with startled cries, leaving Lo clutching an egg in each hand.

"Where are they?" she cried. "What have you done?"

Kaethe began to pace, sending little wavelets across the flagstones. "I sent them home to Nocturne. They'd only get in our way."

"*Our way?* What are you talking about?"

Kaethe's head swung around like one of her hounds catching a scent. "You will bring my husband back."

"Me?" Lo barked an incredulous laugh. "I just returned from one misadventure. Get him yourself!"

"I cannot leave this tower," the goddess admitted.

Lo set the eggs in the basket before she threw them at her. "Are you a *complete* idiot?"

"Watch it, girl," Kaethe snarled, her hair spiking like the roots of an ancient tree.

"If you want him back, why didn't you send *them*?" She stabbed a finger at the place where her parents had stood a minute ago. "They're your hunters! They know how to fight with swords! Oh, and they're not *cursed*. Don't you think they'd have better odds of success?"

Kaethe's face grew even more grim. "Your mother is a stubborn, proud woman. After what I did to her, she will never serve me again. If she will not, your father will not. And Tijah and Achaemenes wouldn't betray them." Lo didn't care for the way Kaethe was looking at her. "That leaves you."

"What if I refuse?"

"Go ahead." Her black eyes glittered. "I will not force you."

Lo sighed. "I sense a *but* coming."

With another sweep of her hand, the light dimmed and they were standing in the Chamber of Souls. Lo's gut wobbled at the abrupt transition — and Kaethe's next words did nothing to improve it.

"I have locked all the gates to my realm so no souls can pass," she said, gesturing to the miniature world laid out at their feet. A few motes of light drifted toward the shore of the Cold Sea, but the rest of the Dominion was dark.

Lo sagged. "You can do that?"

The Lady's voice was bleak. "It is already done."

As Jaskin Cazal might say, it was a nasty little tickle. If

Kaethe pulled up the drawbridge like a castle girding for siege, the dead would be trapped in the living world. Not just a few, like in Aveline. *All of them, everywhere.* And each time one of the risen killed someone, their numbers would swell, until they overran the whole world.

Not to mention the suffering of all those poor, confused souls who had nowhere to go and nothing to do but haunt the living.

Lo forced her fists to unclench. "Why don't you just let Bel have his fun? I'm sure he'll come back eventually."

"You don't understand," Kaethe retorted. "Now that he is outside these walls, he will gradually regain his memories."

"Good for him," Lo muttered.

"You do not know my husband, girl. Bel would have let his precious fire daēvas lay waste to every kingdom before raising a hand against them. Perhaps you are familiar with that episode?"

It was a thousand years ago, but Lo knew the history. "It led to the Sundering of the world into light and dark," Lo said. "That was the only way to stop them. The Vatras were exiled to the Kiln."

"Correct." Kaethe inclined her head. "And I broke my rule about interfering in the affairs of the living to aid the other daēva clans. But Bel would never have allowed it, so I enticed him to visit me." Her bloodless lips crimped in a tiny smile. "My powers are strong here. Stronger than he knew. After a night of riotous lovemaking—"

Lo held up a hand. "Please don't."

"I made him forget who he was," Kaethe continued without pause, "and convinced him he was an alchemist from the golden age of Samarqand who had stumbled across my tower."

"That *is* pretty smooth," Lo conceded.

"As Nabu, he is kind and gentle. But Bel is arrogant and cruel. His burning gaze will scorch your precious darklands. And I can promise you, he will do nothing to stop whoever has the Grand Menotte. In fact, he will take delight in the mortifexes' rampage." Kaethe's frank gaze was unsettling. "But if you bring him back, not only will I open the gates for the dead, but I will personally destroy the Grand Menotte."

"This is blackmail," Lo growled.

"Call it whatever you like," Kaethe arched a brow. "So what'll it be?"

LO RIFLED THROUGH THE PANTRY, shoving bread, cheese, dried beans and packets of spices into her pack. The sweet, salty aroma of shelled pistachios filled her nose as she tossed a handful into her mouth.

"Bel kept a well-stocked larder," she remarked to Kaethe, who lurked in the doorway watching her.

"Nabu-bal-idinna," Kaethe corrected. "Bel required an army of servants just to get out of bed in the morning."

"And yet you want him back." She popped another nut in her mouth. "You're lonely."

"I am *not* lonely."

"Yes, you are. I don't think you give a fig about the Grand Menotte, or living people, for that matter. You just want him back to break the tedium."

Kaethe's shadow reached for her, the candles on the kitchen table guttering in a chill draft. "You dare speak to me this way?"

"It's not my fault," Lo protested. "I can't lie, remember? So I get to say whatever I want with no consequences." She ate another handful of nuts, crunching noisily. "These are good.

But I must say, you and Bel seem so different. I can't picture you two together. It is true that Telasius set you up?"

A hard light entered Kaethe's eyes. "How do you know that name? Have you seen him?"

"I did. He's still running from you."

She gave a silvery tinkle of laughter. "I have not thought of him in an age, but let him skulk and hide. He is a fraud."

"I wouldn't say he's *skulking*," Lo replied. "In fact, he's still marrying people who are wildly unsuited for each other."

Kaethe's laughter died.

Lo tipped the last of the pistachios into her mouth. "Maybe you should consider—"

She cut off as something sharp slipped down the back of her throat, lodging in her windpipe. Somehow, an unshelled nut had gotten mixed in with the rest. A thin wheeze came out as she pantomimed frantically for help. Kaethe strode over and slapped her hard on the back. The pistachio flew through the air.

"The Quickening," she gasped. "Can't you ... turn it off?"

"It is not my doing," Kaethe said.

Lo rubbed her neck. "I thought you made me."

"Your parents *made* you. Shadow Souls occur spontaneously, although under very specific — and thankfully rare — circumstances. Passing through the Veil while a child is forming inside the womb is one such cause."

"I knew it," Lo muttered. "Is that what happened to Morgen, too? How many of us Shadow Souls are there?"

"As to your first question, yes. I knew her mother, Ingharad. You met Morgen when both of you were here at the same time. She was called Mara then."

Lo blinked. "That scaredy little thing was *Morgen*?"

Kaethe nodded.

"I had a dream about her!" Lo exclaimed. "We were playing

hide and seek in *your* tower. Running mad through the halls. At first it was fun, but then the game took a turn. I finally caught her, and she wedged herself against the door, but I was stronger and I forced it open. I told her I was going to eat her up or some such thing."

It was hard to reconcile the memory of the sobbing child with the confident, powerful woman she had met at the Ducal palace in Prydwen.

"Morgen — or Mara — just cried harder. I feel bad now. In the dream, she wore my face. I had a braid, because my mother always put it in a pigtail, but I remember Mara's hair was chin-length... Are you listening?"

Kaethe's eyes snapped open. "Sorry, I must have dozed off. Other people's dreams are so boring."

Lo folded her arms with a scowl.

"As to your second question," Kaethe continued, "I know of no other Shadow Souls besides you, her, and Jaskin Cazal."

Lo considered this. "Does the Quickening affect us all?"

"I believe so. It is a natural consequence of disrupting the Covenant."

Lo squinted. "What Covenant?"

"Not your concern," Kaethe said, her face severe again. "All you need to know is that your very existence is an offense to some of the other chthonic deities."

Lo buckled the pack. "Well, that's lovely."

Kaethe studied her. "Perhaps you are this way because you were born to a woman who was supposed to be dead."

"So you don't actually know," Lo said flatly.

"I just said that, didn't I?"

"I don't know. Did you?"

They stared at each other for a long moment.

"Okay," Lo said. "This isn't going anywhere." She reached for the pack.

"Wait!" Kaethe said, her face softening. "I have some parting gifts."

The Lady of Shadows held out a cloak of rich, warm fabric, dark blue on the outside and lined with silver cloth that gleamed like moonlight on water.

"This will conceal your presence from the risen and most living creatures, as well," Kaethe said. "If you are going to the Nightwood, you'll need it."

Lo took the cloak, feeling the whisper-soft material between her fingers before swirling it around her shoulders. It fell to her feet in elegant folds.

Kaethe then handed her a crossbow, the wood polished to a smooth, dark sheen, along with a quiver of silver-tipped quarrels. Last, she gave her a small wax-paper packet.

"These are special leaves," Kaethe said. "If Bel has regained his memories by the time you find him, he may not wish to return of his own volition."

Lo raised a brow. "You think?"

Kaethe ignored the sarcasm. "Brew a tea with these leaves and get him to drink it. For a brief period, he will forget again and believe he is Nabu-bal-idinna."

Lo opened the packet and stuck her nose in. She smelled a minty, peppery odor...

A cold, wet hand patting her cheek — none too gently — brought her back to her senses.

"Where'd you go?" Lo blinked. "What happened?"

"Did I tell you to sniff it?" Kaethe demanded. "Just the odor can wipe one's mind blank."

Lo stared down at the packet in her hand. *Right: the knockout tea.* "Sorry." She refolded the packet and tucked it in her bag next to the dried beans. "How am I supposed to make him drink it?"

"Improvise," Kaethe responded tartly. "But there's only

enough for a single cup, so don't waste it. Now, is there anything else you need for your journey?"

Lo fastened the cloak. What she really wanted was her parents back, dammit. She'd just found them again after all these years, only to lose them once more, hurled through a portal by this cunning woman who clearly couldn't be trusted.

"What if I bring the Quietus along?" she asked.

Kaethe gave her a nasty smile. "Castelio zah Nerides would be no good to you. None of my signs or symbols will repel the dead anymore. Nine-pointed stars? Ha! Kaethe's Tears? Useless. Iron? Good luck. Not until I get Bel back."

Lo swallowed her dismay and hefted the crossbow, testing its weight. It was surprisingly light.

"That is made from the horn of the fabled Minotaur," Kaethe said solemnly. "It contains traces of the beast's magic."

Lo stared at the crossbow, impressed. "Is it really?"

The goddess laughed. "No, it's just plain oak. Good craftsmanship, though."

Lo set the weapon aside with ill humor. "Tell me one thing, and be honest. What will happen to me when I die for the ninth time?"

Kaethe's eyes glinted. "Do you want the nice news or the less-nice news?"

Lo drew a sharp breath through her nose. "Good news first."

"The two halves of your soul will merge and you'll be whole again."

"That *is* good," she said warily. "How about the bad news? Do I end up in the lowest abyss turning sinners on spits or something?"

Kaethe regarded her with some amusement. "Not quite so bad. But like I said, you shouldn't even be standing here. For starters, you were born to a dead woman. Then she came to see me when she was pregnant with you. Which, in retrospect, wasn't a great idea."

"Just say it straight. What exactly happens to me?"

Kaethe sighed. "You won't be permitted to cross the Cold Sea. I'm afraid you're fated to linger forever in the Dominion."

"What?!"

"But if you remain at my House, your soul will not be corrupted."

"So I'll be your hostage," Lo muttered.

"I prefer the word *guest*. There are many rooms here. Books and other entertainments. Bel was perfectly content until that meddler Jaskin Cazal came along."

"Do I have to give you foot rubs, too?" Lo asked.

Kaethe's eyes narrowed to slits. "If you have a quibble with being a Shadow Soul, take it up with your mother. She is more to blame than I."

Lo grumbled under her breath. She did not want to think about the consequences of this revelation. Not now. One nasty little tickle at a time.

"How am I supposed to pick up Jaskin and Bel's trail?" she asked. "They could have taken a gate to anywhere."

"True, but Jaskin will stop at his stronghold in Vendagni, you can be certain of it."

"That makes sense," Lo admitted. "And I must warn Nathan."

Another blurred eyeblink and they were standing in the doorway of the tower. The pack was slung over one of Lo's shoulders, the crossbow over the other. She pinched the bridge of her nose, where a headache was forming. "Can you please stop doing that?"

Kaethe gave her a little push through the door. A pack of hounds trotted out of the pine woods, sniffing at Lo's boots.

"They will escort you back to the gate to Vendagni," the Lady said. "You can start the search there. Good luck!"

The door started to swing shut.

"And by the way," she added through the narrowing crack, "this is your last life, so don't screw it up!"

The door to the tower slammed with a resonant thud and vanished, leaving the obsidian surface unbroken once more. Lo considered shaking a fist, but what was the point?

Instead, she stalked off, her new cloak billowing behind as she followed the hounds into the gloaming.

Thirty-Six

Morgen stirred the pot of bubbling ash paste. Through the mullioned window, she could see Dravka stomping around in the shallows of the sandy beach, skirts tied up to her knees. The girl had never been allowed to bathe in the sea before and was having a grand time.

Inside the snug cottage on Juniper Isle, her younger sister Jaelle sprawled on a pile of cushions, nose buried in a thick tome on spellcraft. The child had been reading for hours, pausing only to ask the occasional question. Both girls had fair hair and crystalline blue eyes, but their resemblance was skin-deep. In temperament, they couldn't be more different.

Dravka, Morgen reflected, was a brawler with a good measure of native cleverness. Had she been born a man, she would be off conquering some foreign land — though she lacked her brother's taste for cruelty. Jaelle, on the other hand, had the intellect and patience of a true scholar. Much could be made of them both, Morgen felt certain.

She returned to the paste, crushing the last lumps with the pestle. Grave soil and bone dust — the staple ingredients of most necromantic spells — along with a single black lotus petal, six tears of a grieving widow, a pinch of adder's tongue from her herb garden, and a few fingernail clippings from a nine-day-old corpse. Her own recipe, guaranteed to obscure one's presence from the dead. Something told her they might need it in the days to come.

"Sisters!" Dravka burst in, dripping seawater on the rough plank floor. "Can we visit the cove with the tide pools again? I want to catch crabs for supper."

"You may go yourself. I have work to do." Morgen ladled the paste into a small clay jar. "And change out of those wet things before you catch a chill."

"But it's not cold!" She winced at Morgen's glare. "Yes, sister," she added meekly.

Morgen didn't wish to quench the fire in her, nor to break her spirit. But she could not afford to give the girl too long a lead.

"Go to the cove," she said, softening her tone with an effort. "Change when you return."

Dravka grinned. "Come with me," she said to Jaelle. "There's two buckets."

Jaelle looked up, the slanting light gilding her hair to a silver corona. "Not right now." A finger held her place in the book. "I'm in the middle of something."

Dravka rolled her eyes. "Fucking hells you're boring!" she declared cheerfully. "I bet the nuns would have loved you."

She strode out the door. Jaelle, accustomed to such uncouth statements, returned to her book. Morgen wiped her hands, surveying her tidy home. Bundles of dried herbs hung from the rafters. Bookshelves lined every wall, crammed with arcane tomes, and ladders led to even higher nooks piled with more cushions. Pots of poisonous plants crowded the sunny windowsills.

She'd brought the girls there by portal from the convent in Vellio when it became clear that they would all die if they remained in that room.

"This passage describes a ritual to compel a shade who died by murder to reveal the name of their killer," Jaelle said. "Is that something you can do?"

"There are many things I can do. That spell is one of the simpler ones, actually." Morgen found herself warming to the girl's keen interest.

Jaelle stroked the little terrier curled up at her feet. It had a black spot over one eye and looked to be barely a pup. Where the dog had come from, Morgen didn't know, but it ran toward them, barking hysterically, just as she opened the portal and Jaelle had scooped it up. The girls swore they'd care for the creature, so against her better judgment, Morgen was letting them keep him.

She focused on the second cast-iron pot bubbling over the cookfire, lifting the spoon to examine the consistency. Nearly ready.

An oval mirror above the stove reflected a pair of cold eyes wreathed in steam, her dark hair grown out to an inch-long stubble. The Grand Menotte was lost; she presumed Jaskin Cazal had it, though in the chaos she had not actually seen him put it on. The question now was whether she should hide here or try to stop him.

If that were even possible.

Her lips tightened as she doused the flame and waited for the paste to cool. At least Vazsoly was dead. She had accomplished that much. Yet the victory didn't taste as sweet as she'd expected.

It was due to her condition. She could not feel as others

did. Oh, she had hated Vazsoly, but even that was a frozen thing, brittle and lifeless. Now that he was gone, she wasn't sure what her purpose should be.

She had never regretted her gift, but for a fleeting moment, Morgen wished she were someone else. Someone *whole*. She knew her manner was distant and aloof, even forbidding, and made an effort to temper it for the sake of the girls. But she wondered what it would be like to experience joy, like Dravka whooping boisterously in the waves, or love or sorrow or any of the things other people felt.

Morgen stirred the decoction one last time, then dipped a pinky and began to paint her face with whorls and runes. Words of power in the language of Tongues — secret words her mother had passed down. For protection, for binding, for seeking.

Jaskin Cazal.

No, Morgen was not nearly done with him yet.

THIRTY-SEVEN

Cas pulled his scarf lower, shielding his eyes from the harsh sun as he walked along the canal's towpath. Boats drifted past of every description, from gaily painted gondolas to tiny coracles. Most rode low in the water, packed to the gunwales with refugees and their bundled belongings. He scanned each face, hoping to spot Da and Teo. Three days had passed since he'd arrived in Prydwen. Three fruitless days of searching while the city convulsed.

Wild rumors swirled through the streets. The Duc had gone off to recruit an army of giants from the Icemarch. No, he was in Galatia wedding the young Damiata. Or he'd faced the Red Rogue in single combat and they'd slain each other.

Cas did his best to sort fact from fiction. He knew the nuns of Kaethe had fled after a mob burned their convent — the charred building was plainly visible in the distance. Whatever had happened to Vazsoly Marcel, his margraves still held the hills beyond the city. The rebellion's leaders were trying to enforce order and reopen food markets, but criminals were taking advantage of the chaos to loot and intimidate, especially with the Sons of Bel gone, too.

Cas thumbed the scars on his palm, a nervous habit. He was starting to lose hope, but he couldn't let Felippa see that. She'd been through enough already. The first night they arrived, they'd been forced to sleep in a filthy alley. Then a kind woman had taken them in, letting them stay in the dress shop she'd turned into a refuge for lost children. While Cas searched the city for his father and brother, Felippa helped Mother Morrigal care for the orphans. Having a purpose seemed to steady her.

He turned down a side street, leaving the canal-front mansions of Rosnamore behind. Here, the buildings were more modest, though still luxurious compared to the stilt shacks of the Shambles. There had been fighting in the area not so long ago. He saw the remains of burned barricades and smelled the rusty tang of old blood. Ribs poked through the fur of a mongrel sniffing through a refuse pile. Cas kept walking, one hand near his knives.

After investigating four empty houses, and being thrown out by squatters in six others, Cas entered a narrow four-story building. The front door had been torn off its hinges, and shattered glass crunched under his feet as he crossed a black-and-white tiled foyer. Plaster dust filmed everything. Brighter gaps in the paint showed where paintings had hung before being looted.

Cas climbed the grand staircase, tracing his fingertips over the words gouged into the wall. *Death to the Cockatrice.* The Duc's heraldic device, now reviled. Would things get better, he wondered, or worse?

He tried each door along the upstairs hallway. The rooms were bare of furniture, stripped by scavengers. But behind the last door, two familiar figures were sitting at a table, oiling and cleaning a pile of mismatched armor.

"Da?" he called, heart lifting. "Teo?"

They raised their heads. Da shot to his feet.

"Cas? Blessed Bel, is it really you, lad?"

Then they were all embracing, laughing and weeping at once.

"The city's getting worse by the day," Da said. "But Teo and I knew you'd return. Figured we'd best wait. So you came from Aquitan?"

Cas had never told them what happened to Felippa — that she'd been sucked into a banishing and hurled to the land of the dead. With Da's poor health, it might have finished him. Cas had claimed he was merely taking her away for a bit, until the fighting died down.

"Er, not exactly." No point burdening Da with the whole truth now — or so he told himself. "But Felippa is well. She can spin the yarn herself when Teo fetches her. We're staying not far from here. At the house on Oxbow Street that takes in children."

Teo's eyes brightened. "Aye, I know the place. Mother Morrigal." He darted out the door.

Da smiled, the lines around his eyes crinkling. He looked more sober than Cas had seen in ages. "There's someone else here who'll be glad to know you've returned."

Cas eyed him in puzzlement, wondering if it could possibly be Lucius. "Who?"

Da winked. "You'll see."

Cas followed Da up the stairs to the top floor. Voices drifted out from one of the rooms, men and women quietly discussing food stores, patrols, how to quell the lawlessness that gripped the city. And there, standing among them, was Gui Harcourt.

He looked so much older than Cas remembered. His dark face was heavily lined, and he was thicker around the middle. The funny heart-shaped bald spot on the back of his head — which Cas had often teased him about — had grown past his ears, leaving a fringe of white hair.

Cas realized that the mental projection he'd seen in Dreamhaven, with the humberg Bergmann, was a younger, strapping version of Gui. The one who had saved him from the gallows and seemed invincible.

Only his clothes were the same: a dark green cloak, leather braces to hold his Quietus tools, and stout calf-high boots.

Gui must have sensed him looking for he turned, their gazes locking. Did Gui think he'd killed Esme? Had he been sent to execute Orlaith's warrant? Well, Cas wouldn't run again, not until he told his side of things — even if Gui did clap him in irons and drag him back to Aquitan.

They stepped onto one of the balconies overlooking the canal two streets away, Gui moving with a slight limp. Cas studied his mentor's face for any hint of accusation.

"I came looking for you soon as I heard about that bounty on your head," Gui said. "Murder? Not the man I know. Didn't believe it for an instant."

Relief crashed through him. "But what about Orlaith? Didn't she try to stop you?"

"Aye, if I'd told her," Gui replied dryly. "I waited 'til Her Grace left for Galatia before I slipped away. But your kin had moved to Prydwen. Seemed the obvious place to seek you out."

Cas leaned against the railing, gazing out at the sluggish waters of the canal. "There was so much I couldn't say when we met on the road. I knew the guards would be coming after me at any moment. And well, we'd barely seen each other in months."

Gui's gray-blue eyes were serious. "Then tell me now, lad."

He gathered his thoughts. "It all started when Orlaith sent me to Tjanjin to steal a wind ship."

Gui listened in silence. When Cas got to the part about Orlaith staging her son's abduction, and the ghoul chained in the wine cellar, Gui's jaw tightened. He drew out a pipe, packed it with tabak, and lit it with a coal from a tinderbox in his pocket.

"I've no proof," Cas admitted. "But it's the truth, I swear it."

Gui puffed a stream of smoke that curled up to the eaves of the house. "I believe you, lad," he said. "The way she handled Esme's death, blaming you straightaway after she favored you for all those years, made no sense. When I spoke to her, she refused to even consider that another could have done it. Made me suspicious." He shifted his weight, sounding a bit sheepish. "Could you fetch a chair? My leg pains me."

Cas hurried to bring one back. Gui sat heavily. "I remember when Duc Robert died. How lost her ladyship seemed, how she leaned on Lucius." He shook his head. "I could well imagine the mortifex corrupting her. But you say that's not so?"

"Aye. Lucius took advantage, but he's a better man than I thought. It's Orlaith who's rotten to the core." Cas couldn't keep the anger from his voice. "She poisoned the wine that killed Esme. It was meant for me, but she didn't care if Es drank it too."

Gui shook his head. "You should have told me everything before."

"I know." He met Gui's eyes. "There's more, since I'm confessing my darkest secrets. That vial of Kaethe's Tears you gave me all those years ago." He drew an unsteady breath. "It was my own carelessness that broke it."

To his surprise, Gui chuckled. "Lad, I've known that from

the start. Found the shattered vial swept into the corner of the barn. Hidden away. I knew it didn't break in the fight."

"I'm sorry," he managed. "I was frightened, and it made me stupid. I threw it to Teo and he dropped it, but the fault was mine. If I'd kept it safe, I might have saved Ma."

Gui was quiet for a moment. "Or maybe she was already gone. But I do know one thing. Your brother and sister are both alive because of you. It's time to move on, lad."

Cas managed a smile. "You're right." He glanced at the staff he'd propped against the balcony. "I finally figured *that* out, though it took some trial and error. Mostly the second."

Gui smiled back, some of the weariness lifting from his face. "You'll have to tell me about it on the road. But we'd best leave the city while we still can. I'll take you and your family east, across the Boundary. You'll be safer in Leonia. I know people there, good people, who can help you start over."

A two or three-week journey, at least. Cas's heart sank. He'd promised to wait for Lo. But the safety of his family came first. She'd understand.

Boots clattered up the stairs. A moment later, Teo burst in with Felippa. She was delighted to see Gui, even allowing him to sweep her up in his arms. Cas felt sure that if *he* tried such a thing, he'd get a stern lecture that she wasn't a child. But Gui was... Gui. A favorite uncle and fearsome protector rolled into one. They gathered their belongings while Lip chattered about their adventures.

"Magnus the *what*?" Teo demanded. He looked at Cas and swirled one finger at his temple. "Has she gone barmy?"

Felippa swatted him with a rolled-up blanket.

"It's true," Cas said, firmly shaking his head when Felippa glanced away. "Every word."

Teo stifled a laugh, but Da shot him a narrow-eyed look, which he tried to ignore. There'd be time later to pay for the trouble he'd landed his sister in. For now he agreed with Gui: a storm was brewing, and they needed to get out of Prydwen before it hit.

The streets were eerily quiet when they stepped out, like a collectively held breath. Watchful eyes tracked their progress from behind boarded-up windows. Gui set Felippa into the saddle of his black charger, walking it along by the reins. He tried to hide his limp, but within a few blocks, it grew more pronounced. Lip tried to make him ride the horse, Gui refused, and they were still arguing about it when the city gates came into view. A steady trickle of people was leaving, Cas noticed, and no one was coming in.

Teo recognized two of the men holding a barricade near the guardhouse. They stopped to get the latest news.

"You're wise to take the young 'un," one said, eyeing Felippa. "Our spies say an attack's coming. The margraves mean to take back the city. These gates'll be sealed tight at eleven bells and they won't open again, not for love or gold."

Cas exchanged a quick glance with Gui. They'd come damned close to being trapped. Three days he'd been searching. If it had taken him one more day to find his family — or even a few more hours — there'd be no way out of Prydwen except to swim.

Something struck him as wrong, *off* in a strange way, and then he realized what it was. He'd actually gotten lucky.

Because Lo wasn't here.

The thought immediately made him feel disloyal. He hoped she was faring well with Kaethe. Somehow, they'd find each other again, even if he had to search for the rest of his life.

"But we mean to defend this city," the man was saying. "We bought our freedom with blood and we ain't going back to the ways things were."

His companion's appraising gaze settled on Teo, whose

work in the Duc's stables had added muscle to his height. "Sure you won't stay? We could use another fighter at the walls."

"He sticks with us," Cas said quickly. "He's only sixteen and never been trained as a soldier."

Teo shot him an embarrassed look but didn't object. Perhaps he'd seen enough death to realize war wasn't like the stories.

The men nodded reluctantly and wished them all well. Cas hustled his family through the gates before anyone could change their mind. They joined a river of people, carts heaped with meager possessions, faces pinched with fear.

To Cas's surprise, a league or so outside the city, Gui left the road and brought them to a meadow shielded from the road, bright with clover under the hot sun. Two men waited, one older with salt-and-pepper hair, the other younger but with a strong resemblance. Farmers, by the look of their calloused hands and dung-caked boots.

After a few words were exchanged, coins passed from Gui's gloved hand to the men's palms. Three horses nickered and stamped in the far corner of the field, reins trailing. Nothing fancy, just dependable-looking geldings with shaggy manes and mud-speckled hides.

Felippa scrambled up behind Cas while Da and Teo used a stump to awkwardly mount their own horses. Gui swung up to his black charger with a wince. He seemed grateful not to be walking any further.

When they were back on the road, Gui drew alongside Cas. "Seemed wiser to arrange for horses outside the city," he said softly. "Too many desperate people willing to pull folk down from the saddle and steal their mount." His eyes turned to Felippa. "Especially small folk."

Cas glanced behind at the shrinking walls, imagining the scuffles in the market squares, the grim-faced men at the barricades, the gangs skulking in shadowed alleys. "Aye. You did well, thank you."

He hoped the extra speed would help them stay ahead of the chaos that spread like rot across the west.

Felippa's arms tightened around his waist. He could feel the bones of her ribs press against his back; she was still too thin. He covered her hands with one of his own, giving a reassuring squeeze, then kicked his horse into a steady canter. Teo and Da were already trotting ahead on the straight track, Gui keeping pace beside them. Cas focused on the road unspooling before him.

They rode hard, stopping only briefly to water the horses and refill their skins at a stream. Gradually, the knot between Cas's shoulders loosened. The leagues fell away and Prydwen shrank to a smudge behind them. Ahead lay Alessia, a new beginning for them all.

Then, as he passed beneath the branches of a willow, a cold shock rippled through him. He gasped, hands spasming on the reins.

"Cas?" Felippa's voice came from over his shoulder. "What's amiss?"

He twisted in the saddle. "Felt like we rode under a spout of snowmelt. You didn't feel it?"

She shook her head. Cas's gaze dropped to his hand — and his breath seized. The blue star tattoo was gone. Kaethe's mark, vanished.

Gui had already reined up, consternation on his face. So he'd felt it, too. Cas tapped his hand, holding it up. Gui yanked off his gloves. When he looked up, his eyes were grave.

Cas guided his horse closer, dropping his voice so Teo and Da couldn't hear. "What does it mean?"

Gui's jaw worked. "I don't know, lad." He scanned the open fields around them and the dark eaves of the distant forest. "We'll discuss it later. But I mean to put as many leagues behind us as I can first. Hie!"

He spurred his mount to a gallop. Cas followed, Felippa clinging tight as they flew down the road, Prydwen's shadow looming long at their backs.

LUCIUS REINED up to a stop at the crossroads. Refugees from the west straggled past, their faces drawn and haggard. He felt a moment's pity. There would be no safety for them in Vellio.

He gazed across the land he had watched grow from a trackless wilderness into the six duchies of Aveline. It was all falling apart; the fragile balance of power between the great houses had been shattered. The only question was what would rise next?

And whether he would remain to find out.

The sky was heavily overcast, sparing him the need for a hood. He kept glancing at the strip of alabaster skin at his wrist, even paler than the rest of him. How strange it was not to see the despised menotte. For a thousand years he had been a servant to mortals. Now the puppet's strings were cut. It was a heady feeling, this sudden freedom. Unnerving, too. There was no one to blame for his choices but himself.

The wind lifted his hair as he studied the rutted roads stretching into the hills. Half a day's ride and he would be at Midgate. He could leave this simulacrum of life behind, discover what waited on that distant shore. If he did not cross soon, he would become like Justinian. A creature of shadow.

He could feel the Cold Sea tugging at him. A new thread had been tied to his soul, invisible but strong as steel wire, and it took all his will to ignore it.

A swirl of white crystals blew down from the leaden sky. Lucius glanced at his horse's mane. It was dusted with snow. His frown deepened. *In Galatia?*

Someone had taken possession of the Grand Menotte. He could feel its power beating like a dark heart. Lucius touched the ruby-eyed lynx at his throat. The sigil of House do Santillan. He was about to cast it away, but instinct stayed his hand.

I might need it.

Lucius wheeled his horse to the west, away from salvation and toward Brennos Fearghal and his rag-tag army.

There was one last battle to fight before he could rest.

EPILOGUE

Orlaith stood at the arched windows of the council chamber, gazing out at the blanket of white covering the city's rooftops. It was the first snow-fall Vellio had seen in a thousand years. A blizzard that showed no sign of stopping.

The air inside the Alcazar was nearly as cold as it was outside. No matter how many layers of clothing she donned, Orlaith could not get warm. The chill was inside her.

Memories clawed to the surface. The horrors that had emerged from the floor at the temple of Kaethe. People pushing and shoving at the doors, limbs tangled, unable to escape. So much blood...

She stiffened her spine. If wielded properly, those same horrors could destroy her enemies. Yes, the dark could be forced to consume itself.

Something had cracked open inside her when Enrigo died. A fissure to a barren place where monsters roamed. But her son would be avenged. She would see to it that the Moon Courts paid dearly for what they had done. All the evil began with

Nathan Ouvrard and those wicked twins, Lady Caul and Lady Chaos. Enrigo would still be alive, and so would her husband Robert, if not for them.

Oralith's fingers twisted the iron cuff around her wrist, the frigid metal biting her skin. She startled as a hand tugged her sleeve. Beatriu peered up at her, delicate features grave.

"Are you certain Lucius is gone?" the girl asked.

Orlaith swallowed past the lump in her throat. "I cannot feel him at all. I think the oaths that bound him broke when..."

The words faltered as her gaze fell on the iron band encircling Beatriu's plump little arm, twice as large as Orlaith's own. The sigil of Vendagni, a left hand with flames dancing above the fingertips, was inscribed on the outside. And on the inside, a litany of names. One hundred undead demons, now compelled to carry out the child's every whim.

The Vanguard Knights of the Fourth Empire, Beatriu called them.

Knights, as if they cared anything of chivalry.

Orlaith clamped her jaw against a bout of hysterical laughter.

"It is a shame we lost Lucius," Beatriu said with a frown. "I'd grown fond of him."

Bitter hatred surged at the name. He had driven Enrigo to renounce her. Planted the wedge between them. He was as much to blame as the others.

"Must I wear this?" Orlaith muttered.

Empty of its magic, the petite menotte felt heavy as a manacle.

The child gazed at her. She had the eyes of a curious insect. "Yes, you must. It is a keepsake to remind you of the importance of loyalty."

In the chaos that followed the disastrous wedding, Enrigo had been just one more corpse for the nuns to dispose of. No one knew he had drunk poisoned wine meant for the Damiata and Vazsoly Marcel. Orlaith prayed the child never learned the truth.

"Do you think he will come after you," Beatriu said, "now that he is unbound? Will he seek vengeance for his years of servitude?"

A fresh chill ran along her skin. "I do not know, Your Grace."

"Your Majesty," Beatriu corrected crossly. "I am an empress now. How many times must I remind you?"

Orlaith sank into a deep curtsy, knees trembling. "My humble apologies, Your Majesty."

The day of the wedding was fragmented into bright shards of nightmare. First, the discovery of her poor son and Lucius's refusal to bring him back. Then a long stretch of gray blankness. When she came to her senses, she was cowering beneath an overturned table, hands pressed to her ears. It seemed like hours before the screaming stopped. Everything was very quiet then. Orlaith came out and saw Beatriu standing amidst a sea of mortifexes, fiery eyes turned toward their new mistress in rapt devotion.

Running was not an option. They'd already noticed her. So Orlaith had crawled to the Damiata on hands and knees, begging to serve. To live. Beatriu had regarded her with pitiless eyes. Then she laid a hand on Orlaith's head, in much the same way Enrigo used to with his pup Jak.

"You may rise, Lady Redvayne."

Orlaith did so, keeping her eyes fixed upon the Damiata's tiny pearl-encrusted slippers. Anywhere but at the abominations surrounding them.

"I have need of a highborn lady-in-waiting," Beatriu said, as if they conversed over tea. "Would you like that? You may write my letters and help me dress."

Orlaith had stammered something about gratitude and yes, of course, it would be an honor. She would have said anything not to be torn to shreds. That is when Beatriu gave her back the menotte that had once bound Lucius, and ordered her to put it on. How she had acquired the other one, Orlaith feared to ask.

The remainder of that day was another blur. She was not sure how much time had passed since. She slept at the foot of the girl's bed, combed her hair, and read aloud to her. The Galatian nobility was almost all dead, so there were no letters to write after all. Orlaith had expected Beatriu to quickly go mad from the strain of wearing the Grand Menotte, but the child remained eerily composed, her gray eyes clear and inscrutable.

"Bring us refreshments," Beatriu commanded. "The apricot wine, well watered, and some of those pink iced cakes."

Orlaith curtseyed and did her bidding. If she tried to run away, she would be caught. And what did she have to run to? Her only son was dead, and the person she'd trusted the most, the one she always turned to in times of need was gone, too.

Where are you, Lucius? Have you passed on, or are you out there somewhere, enjoying your freedom?

Anger made her clumsy and she nearly spilled wine on the eleven-year-old empress's gown. Orlaith's heart seized in terror, but thankfully Beatriu did not seem to notice.

She no longer wore the dark colors of her father's court. Beatriu favored white now, like the snow falling outside. Unlike Orlaith, she did not seem troubled by the cold.

"What are your plans, Your Majesty?" Orlaith asked. "Will we remain in Vellio?"

Beatriu took a dainty bite of cake. "No. I told you yesterday, don't you remember?"

"I... No, I am sorry, Your Majesty. I forget things sometimes, but I am sure it will pass."

It was the gray, clouding her thoughts, making her lose

track of time. Orlaith knew she was not entirely well, but if she confessed it, Beatriu might not want her anymore. And then...

"Of course. You are in mourning for poor Enrigo." She licked icing from her upper lip. "I mean to unite both east and west under a single banner. First, I will occupy Cavet. With Vazsoly dead and his realm in pieces, it is low-hanging fruit. Once they see what my knights can do, I doubt I shall meet with any resistance."

Beatriu plucked another cake from the tray, eyed it for a moment, then bit off the icing rosette and stuffed the whole thing into her mouth.

Orlaith gazed down at her folded hands, waiting for her mistress to chew and swallow.

"I shall build an army worthy of the old conquerors," Beatriu continued, sipping her apricot wine. "Once I am done with Cavet, we will sail from Conbelin to Pilli, and from thence we will march to the Boundary."

"Sail? I beg pardon, Your Majesty, but the dead cannot abide running water, not even your dauntless knights," Orlaith reminded her in a carefully diffident tone. "You know best, of course, but it might be wiser to wait for Prydwen to settle down first. You would take the city easily, I am sure, but holding it is another matter. I fear anarchy would resume the moment you depart, unless you leave a large force there to occupy it indefinitely."

Beatriu considered this. "Which would hinder my efforts to bring the eastern duchies into the fold," she said. "Perhaps you are right."

"So you mean to crush the Moon Courts, Your Majesty?" Orlaith asked eagerly. "Show them the full measure of your strength?"

Beatriu frowned. "If they kneel and swear fealty to me, as you have done, there will be no need for bloodshed." She lifted her pointy chin. "I am Kaethe's divine representative on earth. For those who worship the Lady of Shadows, my rule will be benevolent. A time of prosperity for all."

Orlaith wrung her skirts, the knuckles going white. "But Nyons and Vendagni have no honor! They are treacherous snakes—"

"So you have said many times," Beatriu interrupted coldly. "I weary of this argument. Now fetch my cloak."

Many times? Orlaith had no recollection of it.

"Yes, Your Majesty." She backed away, teeth grinding.

It was ridiculous that a mere slip of a girl should wield such power. She had no idea what she was doing. Now she claimed to be anointed by a god! She—

Orlaith's thoughts stilled as she came face to face with the one called Janus. Something about him frightened her even more than the others. Like a rabid dog pretending to be tame.

"Lady Redvayne." The flames in his eyes were tiny pinpricks, candles floating on a dark sea.

Orlaith dropped into a curtsy, averting her gaze. As Beatriu's lady-in-waiting, she outranked him, but that was a formality. He wielded far more influence than she did. Beatriu had named him captain of her Vanguard Knights.

He has been feeding well. Look at him. Cheeks flushed, lips red, his body warm from the blood of others. That is what keeps him in line.

She hurried past the mortifex without a word and fetched Beatriu's cloak — also pure white, save for a crimson nine-pointed star on the breast. When she returned, the two of them had their heads together, deep in conversation. They did not invite her to join them, so she stood for several minutes just inside the doorway, holding the cloak like a handmaid. One more humiliation.

Let them underestimate me. Robert used to say it is the unknown enemy one should fear the most.

At last, they rose from the oval council table. Orlaith fussed with the cloak, a smile nailed to her face as she settled it over Beatriu's shoulders. It was like dressing a little doll. A spoiled, unspeakably dangerous little doll.

Then Beatriu was skipping through the frigid corridors of the Alcazar, her rabid dog beside her and Orlaith three paces behind. Stone-faced soldiers threw open the doors to the main plaza, where the rest of her Vanguard Knights waited. They had uniforms now, white tabards bearing the sign of Kaethe. The hideous flying things they rode like horses were crouched along the wide brick wall enclosing the gardens. They made Orlaith think of carrion birds waiting for a fresh carcass.

Her breath hitched as Beatriu floated down the steps several paces above the ground. Janus watched her intently; Orlaith knew he must be using Air to keep her aloft.

Beyond the ranks of mortifexes, a crowd had gathered — or more likely been rounded up. Shaven-headed nuns at the front, regular folk in the middle, and Galatian soldiers at the rear, to ensure the others didn't try to bolt.

A hush fell over the assembly as Beatriu's gaze swept across them.

"People of Vellio!" she cried, her high voice ringing across the plaza. "I address you from the heart on this third anniversary of my father's passing. Some have claimed that the House of Do Santillan is cursed. My family is dead, and now my betrothed has joined them, along with many of our most exalted citizens."

The crowd shuffled their feet for warmth in the drifting snow, faces sullen.

"But after much reflection and prayer, I had a vision! This was all meant to be, for I am destined for greater things." Her face shone with conviction. "To unite the land that was Sundered! To serve the Lady of Shadows, for it is Her wrath we must fear! Kaethe sent this army to bring lasting peace and end the plague of risen that has long ravaged—"

"Queen of the Fexes!" a slurred voice mocked. A filthy, unshaven man staggered forward, weaving on his feet. Some in the crowd hissed for him to be silent, but he ignored them, pointing a finger at Beatriu. "Murderess!"

Janus simply looked at the man and his head burst into flames. The madwag or beggar or whoever he was stumbled about, flailing, mouth wide in a soundless scream. There was a commotion as the tightly packed crowd jostled to move back. Orlaith watched in amazement as the body was hurled, still trailing fire, over the red-tiled roof of the Alcazar like a missile launched from a trebuchet.

Then Janus bellowed, "All hail Queen Beatriu, Empress of Aveline!"

He had the voice of a general, loud, rough, and commanding. The dead knights roared in response. "All hail the Empress! Long may she reign!"

Janus's hand pressed down on Orlaith's shoulder, encouraging her to her knees.

"All hail the Empress!" she shouted lustily. "Long may she reign!"

The good folk of Vellio took up the chant. They weren't stupid.

We are all at her mercy. Orlaith brushed snow from her skirts, her gaze falling on the Grand Menotte around Beatriu's arm.

For now.

AFTERWORD

Dear Reader,

I hope you enjoyed *A Wicked Wind*! It was a nostalgic pleasure to write this one because the story brought back characters from my earlier series (The Fourth Element and Fourth Talisman) whom I'd missed a lot and always meant to catch up with again. So if you're curious about Tijah's backstory and the other "Empire" she refers to, you can start with *The Midnight Sea* (free to download everywhere). Darius and Nazafareen are in that one, too.

As for this current series, there will be one more book: the epic finale! You'll find a a first look at the cool cover on the next page. I'll be announcing the release date and preorder links in my monthly newsletter, which also includes sales and book news, so if you want to give that a whirl, you can sign up here: https://katrossbooks.com/newsletter/

Until then, be safe and happy reading!

Warmest, Kat

SHADOW SOUL

THE FOURTH EMPIRE
BOOK 4

COMING SPRING 2025

ABOUT THE AUTHOR

Kat Ross worked as a journalist at the United Nations for ten years before happily falling back into what she likes best: making stuff up. She loves myths, monsters, magic, and doomsday scenarios.

Join Kat's list, *The Sorcerous Pen*, and never miss a new release!

https://katrossbooks.com/newsletter/

Her ravens will also deliver a free ebook, along with early access to sales, giveaways, diabolical potions, and arcane lore.

www.katrossbooks.com
kat@katrossbooks.com

Also by Kat Ross